Shadowbound

Miriya Greer

First published by Miriya Greer 2023
Herndon, Virginia

This novel is entirely a work of fiction. The names, characters
and incidents portrayed in it are the work of the author's
imagination. Any resemblance to persons, living or
dead, events or localities, both real or fictitious,
is entirely coincidental.

First edition

Ebook: 979-8-9891065-0-9
Hardcover: 979-8-9891065-1-6
Paperback: 979-8-9891065-2-3
Library of Congress Control Number: 2023919564

Cover art by Elanor Greer

To my family,
Who have helped me find my passion
And pushed me to always perform my very best.

I

Asandra

Chapter 1

The air is alive with the strong buzz of magic as shouts ring out up and down the thin stretch of grassy land. The sky is blue, the twinkling stars just barely visible. A large wall of shimmering ice blocks much of the battle that can be heard on the other side. The wall itself is manned by a line of wizards in silver armor that radiates frosty mist, standing with their arms calmly raised.

"20 meters!" comes a shout, causing Amber to turn around. A young man in a purple t-shirt and shorts is addressing a small section of wizards who crackle with bright white electricity. They each raise an arm to the sky, and somewhere on the other side of the ice wall lightning strikes down upon the enemy, followed by screams in the near distance.

The Storm wizard who had shouted has no facial features, with only a generic nose and mouth to give him some form of realism. He turns to an Ice wizard who stands apart from the wall defenders, his arms folded as he watches the wall with a hard scowl.

"How long will the wall hold?" the Storm wizard calls.

The Ice wizard turns his head, his face also given the generic treatment. "If the pirates keep this up, not long."

A soft snicker sounds, drawing Amber's attention to her left to a faceless female wizard in a short red dress. Behind her is a line of Fire wizards throwing fireballs over the wall.

"They should burn before that ever happens," she comments.

And then, without warning, the scene pauses. The sounds abruptly silence themselves, and the wizards freeze in an instant. *The demonstration is over already?* Amber can't help but think.

Her teacher melts into existence before her very eyes, green robe just barely managing to stay above the floor, and stands next to the Storm wizard.

"Ice, Fire, and Storm," he says, waving to each of the three faceless wizards. "These three here were the Generals of their magic branches during the Great War. Though their names are lost to time, their legacy lives on. For your midterm project, you will each be assigned one of these branches of magic and given sixteen cycles to complete a presentation on what those types of wizards of the War Era did in battle and where the magic branch is now."

The scene finally fades away, bringing Amber and the rest of her first term peers back to the reality of the Life Hall. The stone walls are covered with all sorts of plantlife sticking out of every crack that they can, with green banners hanging from the ceiling, each stitched with the symbol of Life magic. Her teacher stands up at the front of the Hall behind a lectern, an Illusion wizard standing silently next to him. The Illusion wizard's bright yellow outfit clashes with the soft greens of the room, making it hard for Amber to ignore his presence.

She shifts her weight and looks around the room instead. Her legs long for a rest, to be able to sit down and sink into her desk as she tries not to fall asleep so early in the cycle. Yet, for the demonstration, the desks and chairs have all been pushed to the very edges of the room, forcing her and the rest of her class to stand.

She watches her teacher step down from the lectern and approach a small table. On the table are three different small stacks of books, red, blue, and purple respectively. Her teacher picks up these books and turns to the rest of the class.

"Please form a line to receive your assignment," he tells them. "I will give each of you a random magic branch."

Amber blinks as a murmur rises from her peers behind her. *Random* magic branch? She was under the assumption that they'd be allowed to pick their secondary branch!

There goes my plans for Fire magic, she thinks glumly as she steps up to the slowly-forming line in front of her teacher. She watches him pull books at random from the pile he is holding and hands them to the next in line.

She reaches the front of the line fairly quickly, and her teacher pulls out a bright blue book and hands it to her. Amber takes it daintily and stares down at the cover. The Ice magic symbol takes center-stage on the smooth surface, painted in white to contrast the blue. Slowly, she steps away from her teacher and stands off to the side of the room.

Ice magic. She didn't really know much about Ice magic. She had studied for Fire and a little bit of Storm as a second option, but Ice? She narrows her eyes at the book cover. She'd have to know what Ice does if she wants to become a Healer in the future, right?

She opens the book and stares down at the front page.

Ice, a History

It is written in flowing black script in the center of the page. No author is given, though she can only assume that the Ice teacher, current or old, has composed this volume. It doesn't matter.

Flipping through, it's only about 70 pages long, though it's packed with small lettering arranged into large, wordy paragraphs. Scavenging for information is going to be painful. She can almost see it now: many late nights by Firelight, laying in bed or sitting at her desk, combing through this little book with ink and quill, and getting little to no sleep at all. Her free time would be consumed by this book, hardly stopping for lunch and dinner and relaxation as she devotes more and more time to skimming the endless paragraphs a hundred times over to prepare the perfect presentation…

Why does it have to be Ice?

***

Any book ever written can be found in the Library of Asandra. Out of all the islands, the Library is the only one of its kind. Though it looks somewhat average-sized on the outside, inside it never runs out of space and seemingly never runs out of copies. Quiet study areas of round tables and chairs are scattered across the expansive first floor, while students can overlook the maze of shelves from the balcony of the second.

Amber twirls a part of her long pink hair around her fingers, the blue book from class closed on the table in front of her. Her silver eyes stray elsewhere, not wishing to linger on the cover for long. She doesn't even want to think about it.

The cycle is slowly turning to night. The sky outside is turning shades of orange and yellow, the stars beginning to sharpen into view. Students return to their dorms as families begin to sit down for dinner. Small balls of Firelights burn in their little iceglass jars in windows, winking merrily to those who pass them by.

The Library is quiet, aside from the occasional loud exclamation or laugh off in the distance, just barely managing to overpower the nullifying effect of the numerous large bookshelves.

Amber doesn't come to the Library often, but this cycle is different. This cycle she finally signed up for the tutoring program, and is waiting for her tutor to show up.

Third and fourth term students are allowed to be "tutors" to first and second terms, and it's all voluntary. Amber definitely feels, though, like the tutors have their work cut out for them with all of the students who are probably asking for help with their midterm projects.

"Excuse me?" chimes a voice, dampened by the books. Amber spins around in her seat to face the newcomer. A girl who appears a few years older than her walks up to Amber's table with a smile. Her puffy sleeved dark blue t-shirt melds with her icy blue-white skirt and gray corset. Underneath her skirt, she wears white knee-high socks and bright blue heels. Her hair is also blue, a snowflake clip keeping back part of her bands, and so are her eyes, with her snowy skin tying all of her colors together. The air around her seems to glitter in a way Amber has never seen around an Ice wizard before, a mesmerizing sight to behold.

"You're Amber, right?" the Ice wizard asks, snapping Amber out of her spell. She nods silently, her voice wilting as her anxiety spikes. The Ice wizard smiles and takes a seat at the table across from her, readjusting her sapphire-embedded choker with a single finger.

"My name is Kimberly," she says. "I'm a fourth term." She pauses, as if waiting for Amber to speak. "I like your hair."

Amber blushes. "Thanks…"

Kimberly folds her hands on the table and glances down at the book in front of Amber. "So… you have been assigned Ice magic for your midterm project."

"Yeah," Amber nods, quickly placing her hands over the book's cover. "I… I skimmed through it already, just to see what it was going to be like, and I could hardly understand any of it."

"May I see?"

Amber slides the book across the table to Kimberly. She spins it around on the table top with her hand and flicks through the pages. A small sigh escapes her lips, almost as if she's disappointed.

"I can hardly read this as well," Kimberly finally says, closing the book. "They never do a good job with these sorts of midterm project texts." A distant smile slowly creeps across her face. "I remember my first and second terms, I had this exact same problem as well. But, of course, it *is* doable from the book alone."

"But there's just so *much*!" Amber moans. Her body hunches forward, deflating at the thought of the incredible mountain of work ahead of her.

"Don't worry," Kimberly chuckles, "I'm here to help you for a reason. Now, how about we begin?"

Chapter 2

Amber trudges down the midcycle-clogged street, Ice book in hand. This is the cycle that she will be finalizing the details of her script before presentations are due to begin. The thought of the impending presentation is enough to send her stomach fluttering nervously.

She bumps into students as she weaves her way through the crowd, not bothering to apologize. There are too many beings she'd have to mutter it to, beings she'd probably never see again.

Lunchtime. Many wizards are heading to the Straightway, the longest street on Asandra. There are tons of cafes and restaurants there, where many students and families eat regularly. Not only that, but there are many other shops along the Straightway as well. Clothing, aids, and enchantment stores. Keystone dealers and estate scouts. Any sort of business one may need, it'll be along the Straightway.

And, apparently, Kimberly runs a successful ice cream shop there.

She glances upwards every now and then, at the colors and beings around her, before dipping down again. It's mostly wizards like her, with their colorful robes bunched into small social clusters as they traverse the street, but mixed into the chaos are Feni students as well. The fuzzy ears atop their heads are perked up high as they listen in to all the conversations around them, with some of them showing off their bushy tails. Lining the street are even more Feni, though these ones are refugees draped in faded rags with dirty skin, kneeling on rough rugs and cradling cups, muttering pleas for iron coins.

Amber quickly passes them by.

This isn't the first time she's been to Kimberly's place. Amber would get invited over almost every midcycle for project work, and earn a little extra pay for when Kimberly called on her to be a sort of personal Healer. She lives with her boyfriend, Jake, who's a third term Fire wizard with a wonderful sense of humor and who usually gets sick once every other cycle, which is quite a lot for a typical wizard but he tries not to let that keep him down.

Eventually, the tight street widens, allowing the flow of beings to spread out more freely, and she looks up. The Straightway is just a long, wide street that practically stretches from end to end of Asandra. From where she stands, the street is seemingly endless, just a mass of ever-moving color and the sensation of every magic branch pressing against her skin. Hot and cold air dance and swirl in their invisible pockets. Her clothes crackle with static electricity. The dourness of Death fights against the enthusiastic energy of Life. And on top of it all, Illusionboards float high above the crowds, shimmering with different brightly-colored advertisements everywhere she looks.

Amber takes a deep breath and steps into the much larger crowd, keeping her head down and walking quickly. It's much easier to dodge other wizards here, with the street being so wide, allowing her to make quick progress. When she looks up again, she can just manage to see a large sign not too far from her that reads *The Magic Cone*, Kimberly's shop and home.

She steps up to the large front window, her eyes first

drawn to her reflection. Her dark green robe hangs over her dress and brown corset, with her mint-trimmed leather boots stretching over her knees. She reaches up to the transparent scarf that wraps around her shoulders and neck and readjusts its position, then higher to the small laurel of twigs and leaves that hangs on her ears and circles around the back of her head, holding her long pink hair in check.

As she gets closer to the window, she sees the long line of customers that stretches from the front counter all the way outside, spilling into the street. She can somewhat see Jake walking around behind the counter, his bright red hair making him stand out as he works.

Slowly, she approaches the window, trying to make it clear to others that she is only looking, not wanting to buy or cutting the line. There's Jake in his bright red t-shirt, short reddish-brown jacket, and yellow sash holding his glittering gold shoulder plates in place, smiling at customers as he takes orders and shuffles around for cones. Some being must have wanted theirs toasted, as the cone he grips in his bronze fingers slowly turns a rich shade of crisp gold.

He hands it off to Kimberly, who stands ready with a metal scoop. She reaches into the display cabinet and produces a large white ball of ice cream. She shoves the scoop on top of the cone and hands it back to Jake, who turns to the person at the front of the line and hands it off. The customer places a couple of iron coins onto the counter and walks away, and the line shuffles forward ever so slightly.

As Jake takes the next order, Kimberly looks out at the beings collected inside her shop, sitting and eating at small tables. And at the window. The two wizards lock eyes, and Amber musters a small smile and wave. Kimberly smiles for a brief moment in return, then frowns with worry and looks behind her, where an open door reveals the back of the shop where all her ice cream is made and stored, as well as where the staircase is located that leads to her living space above.

She turns back to Amber and holds up a finger. *One moment*.

Amber stares on in confusion. What's going on? Normally Kimberly would have waved her in without a second thought.

Kimberly turns to Jake and says something to him. He pauses his work briefly and looks to the window. He gives Amber a little wave and grin, trying to not appear too concerned, yet scowls back at Kimberly all the same. There's a bit of discussion between the two as Jake reaches for another cone and hands it to her. Work doesn't stop for no being.

After fulfilling the next order, Kimberly turns and hangs in the open doorway. Probably checking the room, but Amber isn't completely sure.

No, wait… there's movement. Amber's eyes widen as she watches two more wizards step out from the back room with confused looks on their faces.

Blaze and Ethan, the two most well known wizards attending the Asandra School of Magic.

Ethan, a Death wizard, dresses more old-fashioned than most. A plain purple t-shirt hides underneath a short black cowl that covers his shoulders and a long black robe that stretches down to his ankles, its edges held close to his body with the light gray stretch of cloth tied around his waist acting as a belt. The hems of his robe and cowl are stitched with silver runes, though from this distance Amber can't make out what they are. His eyes are as dark as night, a rather large scar decorating his left eye, his stare able to pierce into one's very soul. From any distance, he appears rather menacing without even needing to do anything, and the dark aura that seems to follow him wherever he goes makes many wizards keep out of his way.

Name aside, Blaze is actually a Life wizard. On the surface, with his dark green shirt and short hooded jacket, cloth silver belt, skinny brown pants, tinted goggles held together with small vines, light brown hair with soft green tips, and semi-tanned skin, he would appear rather friendly, like many Life wizards are. But instead of going down the path of a Healer or Botanist, he turned down the path of the Naturist, the path of Life magic that has hardly been explored since the end of the Great War. It's very close to the path of the Botanist, who mostly work in agriculture, except that Naturists weaponize nature rather than simply helping it to grow healthy and strong.

And if those two are in the back of Kimberly's shop, it can only mean that they're employed here.

Amber half-turns away from the window, not wanting either of the wizards to take notice of her staring. She's only heard rumors, but the rumors were all she needed to hear. They're strong, *scarily* strong. Blaze likes to use his magic to intimidate and grandstand to other Life wizards, and Ethan… Well, he's not really used his magic much outside of the Death Hall, but he's been pegged as a real Death prodigy, able to fluidly summon and use spirits of Fire, Ice, and Storm decent to his advantage. He's been offered the chance to skip terms multiple times, and even graduate early, all of which he's turned down. Rumor has it that he's just trying to show off to his lesser-skilled peers while he's still young.

She's never seen them every other time she's been to visit. Maybe luck just isn't on her side this cycle. She can always come back later. Blaze and Ethan are both third terms, just like Jake, meaning that they have their class right after lunchtime. They'd be gone shortly, and then she'd have Kimberly all to herself for a good while.

There's a small shimmer that appears in the corner of Amber's eye, right up against the store window, causing her to look back. There's some writing in snow stuck to the iceglass this time.

Sorry, come back after lunch. I owe you a cone.

Amber grins and looks up at the counter. Kimberly has a

13

finger pointed in her direction, though is trying to not have it be too noticeable. Blaze and Ethan have disappeared, possibly already having returned to whatever they had been doing before in the back of the shop. Jake is still taking orders at the front counter. Kimberly gives Amber a small smile in return as soon as she sees that the first term read her message, and lowers her finger. With it, the snow instantly evaporates. Amber gives her a small nod before walking away.

She clutches her textbook tighter, her stomach becoming ticklish and light, as she makes her way over to a nearby bench and sits down, staring at the cobblestone underneath her feet. The noise of conversation surrounds her, the air of magic dense and buzzing, making her skin start to crawl. For as long as she remembers, she's been sensitive to the magical atmosphere around her. Too much makes her feel uncomfortable, like it's pressing against her body and trying to crush her. Too little makes her feel like something is missing, a void in the environment around her. She wonders if Kimberly, or any other being for that matter, ever feels the same way she does.

She lets out a sigh and opens her textbook. There's some loose paper wedged between the front cover and first page, covered with small writing. It's her presentation script that she's been writing the last couple of cycles. Well, with Kimberly's help, of course. It's one and a half pages long, and kind of short when she practiced speaking it to herself in her dorm room. But she's still nervous. This is a big part of her grade for the midterm, after all.

Might as well review while she waits.

***

When next Amber looks up, the line in front of Kimberly's shop is completely gone, and the noise of the Straightway has died down significantly. Looking around, she sees that the crowd

14

is starting to thin, with many young wizards surging back in the direction of ASM. Third term classes will start soon.

"See you later, Kim!" comes a call Amber picks out from the sea of dying conversation. She turns back to Kimberly's shop and sees the three third terms leaving. Jake, the one that called, is waving to Kimberly, standing behind the counter. She's waving back with a smile. Then Jake runs after Blaze and Ethan, who are already walking briskly away.

Amber stands from the bench and crosses the street, eyeing the three wizards as they mingle with the rest of the leaving beings. Then she slips inside the store.

The cold hits her first, a sudden difference from the rather temperate afternoon outside. The crisp smell of snow, ice, and sugary ice cream stirs around her. The smell makes her hungry, particularly because she didn't eat any lunch yet. Kimberly smiles from the counter, a small flurry of snow sparkling around her.

"Sorry about that," she says. "It was busy and I couldn't get rid of them. Can you flip the sign?"

"That's fine," Amber replies. She turns and flips a small hanging sign from "Open" to "Closed" and walks up to the counter. "I didn't know those two worked for you."

"Blaze and Ethan?" Kimberly asks as she lifts a section of the counter, inviting Amber back. Amber nods.

The two girls walk into the back of the shop. Large ice boxes are set up around the edges of the room, where all the extra ice cream is kept. A large, tub-like sink that has both dirty and clean ice cream tubs stacked on either side of it stands against the far right wall. And towards the back of the room, sandwiched between two countertops, are two large mixing bowls that Kimberly uses to make her sweet cold treats, with the counter drawers full of all her ingredients.

They turn into a small doorway off to the side, the stairwell, and walk upstairs into the front hall of Kimberly's home.

"I didn't want to scare you away," Kimberly admits, leading the way into the living room. Amber trudges across the red rug and stands opposite Kimberly, who takes a seat on her dark blue sofa with a weak grin. The room opens up into the dining room further along, which is also connected to a small kitchen area. Amber has only been in the kitchen twice, and it's a little cramped to say the least. "I know what sort of reputation they have."

"Thanks, I guess," Amber shrugs. Truth be told, if she *did* know that those two were employed at Kimberly's shop, she probably would have had second thoughts about working with Kimberly. "Are you... *friends* with them?"

Kimberly looks down at the floor and starts fiddling with her skirt. "Yes. For three years now." But it doesn't sound like she likes to admit that fact aloud.

"Why?"

"Well..." Kimberly lets out a small sigh, "they were different wizards back in first term. *Very* different wizards. Now..." she pauses, then shakes her head and looks up at Amber again, "advertising our friendship is... sort of bad for business."

"But-" Amber stops herself, her eyes darting away from her tutor. She still can't believe that Kimberly is friends with the two most fearsome wizards at ASM. And she kept this from her for almost sixteen cycles.

"Okay, okay," Kimberly interrupts Amber's thoughts, "how about I hear your presentation now?"

"Uh..." Amber's stomach flutters uneasily. To be put on the spot so suddenly! She fingers her textbook and takes out her small script from the pages, placing them on top of the cover and lets out a deep breath to try and calm her nerves. Why is she nervous? It's just one being! Granted, this is the being that has helped her make her speech in the first place...

Amber starts to read, "Ice magic is one of the three

secondary magics, created from Life and Illusion.

"Ice magic's purpose is to protect and to last. The Ice General understood this role perfectly during the Great War, training the Cryomancers in his care in bravery and coolheadedness in the midst of chaos. He was also the being that introduced the concept of spells such as Ice Dome, by teaching the Cryomancers to form their defensive ice walls with curved tops to shield the wizards maintaining the wall from incoming projectiles.

"While the principles of Ice magic have remained somewhat the same, the job of a Cryomancer has changed over the millennia. Ice wizards now work as ice-makers for preserving food and drinks, waterworkers to supply the islands with fresh water for drinking, farming, and cooking, and as protectors for the miners of Gardall in unstable shafts. However, the strength and durability of Ice spells are still tested and celebrated among Ice wizards, not straying too far from their roots that rest in a bygone Era." Amber looks up from her paper and smiles weakly at Kimberly. She grins back at her.

"That sounded really good!" she claps. "Can I see those papers now?"

"Uh, sure…" Amber timidly hands over her script to her friend. Kimberly's smile fades as she studies the small written words, constantly looking between papers and filling the silent room with their loud rustling.

"It'll do," Kimberly finally hums, putting the papers onto the low table between the two and smiling back up at Amber.

"'It'll *do*'?" Amber echoes.

"It's fine," Kimberly corrects. "As far as information goes you pretty much nailed it. You got this!" Amber nods once with a thankful smile. That's all she needed to hear, though it won't make giving the presentation on the actual cycle any easier.

Even with most of her nerves at ease, her stomach aches uncomfortably as it begs for food. Right, she hasn't eaten any lunch yet.

"Thank you for all your help, Kim," Amber says. "I'll let you get back to running the shop. I need to go get some lunch anyway."

"You didn't eat yet?"

"I was a little too nervous to remember," Amber chuckles halfheartedly.

Kimberly stands from the sofa. "I can make you some lunch if you'd like."

"Thanks, Kim, but you really don't have to-"

"Then why don't I rephrase that." Kimberly steps behind Amber and puts her hands on the first term's shoulders, smiling all the way. "Have a seat on the sofa and I'll go get you some food."

"You don't mind?" Amber asks.

"Nope," Kimberly nods. She pats Amber twice before heading off towards the dining room. "Just sit and relax! I won't be too long."

With a reluctant sigh, Amber walks around the low table and sits on the sofa, grabbing her script and placing it in her lap to read. She scans the words silently, wishing now that she had a quill with her to make small edits. Every time she stares at it, there's something that she sees that she feels the urge to fix. And Kimberly even advised to look at her wording again. But should she really? How much more can she edit in order to make this script the best script ever? And what if she messes it up in the end?

She lets out a sigh and shamefully shoves it back into her textbook, hiding it from her view. She sets the blue book onto the table and sits back, sinking into the cushion.

Kimberly comes back a little later with a small sandwich on a plate, and a cut jamba fruit and spoon. She hands the plate to Amber with a smile. "It's kava beef. And I… I probably should have asked if you liked jamba."

"That's fine," Amber assures her, accepting the plate. "I don't eat enough fruit to be completely honest." Kimberly lets out a small laugh.

Amber starts with the jamba fruit, which has a red-orange patterned exterior peel and inner edible white parts. It's wide and flat, and almost resembles a small drum of sorts. She digs into it with the spoon, making it squirt its sweet juice. The bite is both sweet, cool, and tangy on her tongue. She sucks it up greedily and goes for another spoonful.

Kimberly leaves and returns rather quickly with her own plate of jamba fruit and sandwich, and plops down next to Amber. Snow swirls in the air around them, shimmering in the light of the room.

It's almost easy to forget that Kimberly is actually a Blessed wizard herself, gifted a small fragment of power from the first Cryomancer of Astria. And whenever she sits next to Kimberly like this... Amber can't help but feel like she doesn't belong in her sphere.

Even among her own peers, Amber isn't very strong in her own right. She's always in the shadow of other aspiring Healers in her own class that simply learn the healing spells better and faster than she does, with Blaze being naturally gifted in some of the most powerful and notoriously difficult-to-learn Life spells that can possibly be learned at ASM. So Amber even being friends with a Blessed wizard, a being who's gone above and beyond with their ambitions to be granted such amazing power, feels almost *wrong* somehow.

She doesn't even realize that she's gradually stopped eating her food.

"Is something wrong?" Kimberly asks, shaking Amber from her spell.

Amber blinks, then musters a weak smile and raises her spoon again. "No, I'm fine. Just... thinking."

"About your project?"

"…Yeah."

Kimberly elbows her lightly. "Well then eat up! You're not doing yourself any sort of favor starving yourself half to death."

***

Kimberly flips the shop sign back to "Open" as the two wrap up their time together. The crowd of the Straightway outside has greatly thinned from when Amber first came in.

"What are you going to do now?" Kimberly asks her as she steps back up to the front counter.

Amber shrugs, hugging her textbook a little tighter. "I… don't know."

She has two options. Option one is to return to her dorm and study, even though there is nothing much to study at the moment. She'd probably drive herself crazy obsessing over her script. Option two is to go to the infirmary, where she's employed as an intern Healer. Because she's an intern and still in school, her work times are much more flexible than that of other Healers. Usually, she works during second term classes and then spends the rest of the cycle studying, though she can always work longer if she wants to. It's a good way to get her mind off of her presentation for a while longer, except…

"Can I stay here?" she asks quietly.

Kimberly frowns in confusion. "Stay here?"

"I don't want to go to my dorm… or the infirmary."

"Oh. Are you interned there?"

Amber just nods in response.

"Do you not like it there?" Kimberly presses.

"It's not that…" Amber trails off. The infirmary *is* a nice place to work. The Healers are well compensated and the interns are treated nicely. Besides, there's always a need for new Healers, so the infirmary does everything in its power to get interns to seek full employment.

Kimberly folds her arms and heaves a reluctant sigh. "You can stay so long as you tell me what's going on."

Amber nods, placing her textbook on a shelf under the counter to get it out of her hands.

"It's… a lot," she eventually replies. "I can only work one quarter of the cycle, so I'm struggling to save for my second term. Plus there's a lot of favoritism and gossip… I hardly do much healing at all. Aside from Jake, of course! But he doesn't count."

Kimberly offers the young Healer a sympathetic smile. "I'm sorry, Amber."

Amber shakes her head, mustering a thin smile. "Don't-"

Before she can even begin to say the rest of her sentence, she's interrupted by the chime of the store's front door opening. Kimberly spins around in surprise as well. It's a Feni mother with a little boy, both with soft purple hair and tails. Their clean clothes and neat hair makes it clear that they weren't like the many Feni beggars on the street.

"Ah, hello there!" Kimberly greets the two, quickly rushing back behind the counter. She gives Amber a light push on her arm, whispering. "You can scoop." Amber nods and shuffles over to the side as Kimberly turns back to the customers with a wide smile. "What can I do for you both?"

"One orabo cone and one jamba cone please," the mother replies simply.

"One moment!" Kimberly nods. She reaches for a stack of ice cream cones stored under the register and hands two to Amber.

Okay… Amber breathes to herself as she takes the cones, turning to the tubs of ice cream before her. There's a little cone holder in front of her, and a red-handled scoop sitting in a small bucket of water to its right. She can see the tub labels, but the wording is upside down.

She places the two cones into the holder and plucks the

scoop from the water bucket, shaking it dry as best she can. She leans forward and scoops up a sizable chunk of brilliant white ice cream, the jamba flavor, and plops it onto one of the cones. The orabo flavor rests two tubs to the right of the jamba one, a bright orange-yellow with little white chunks. As she scoops up the ice cream and moves to place it in the cone, the sweet smell of the cold treat hits her nose. Even though she just ate, it's enough to make her mouth water all the same.

She places the scoop onto the second cone, sets the scoop back into its water bucket, and hands the ready ice cream cones over to Kimberly as she finishes processing payment for the order. The ring of iron coins falling into the tray of the register is soft yet sharp all the same as they tumble from Kimberly's hand. She pushes the tray closed, then turns to take the cones from Amber's hands.

"Thank you for coming!" she says to the mother. "Enjoy the rest of the cycle!"

Amber also smiles at the pair, though her stare is on the little Feni boy. He looks back at her with wide, sparkling eyes. As his mother motions that it's time to go, Amber gives him a little wave. The boy smiles back at her for a moment and waves with his tail as he walks away with his mother, swishing from side to side rather happily. Then the two step back through the front door, and are gone.

"Do you get those sorts of beings all the time?" Amber asks, watching the mother and son disappear down the Straightway through the shop windows.

"*Most* of the time," Kimberly corrects her. "There's always those pushy characters, you know?"

"I know..." Amber lets out a small sigh. It still must be nice to work here.

"You did a pretty good job scooping, though," Kimberly comments, leaning against the counter.

Amber blinks once, surprised. "I did?"

22

Kimberly nods back. "Yeah, you did. Have you done scooping before?"

"I… don't think so?" Amber replies unsurely, furrowing her brow. As far as she knows, *this* was her first time scooping ice cream in her life…

"You know," Kimberly continues with a light chuckle, "if the infirmary is too much for you, I could always hire you as a designated scooper."

Amber can't help but giggle in response. "Well, I'd have to see…"

"You can intern next *cy-cle*," Kimberly sings with a smile. "I'll even pay you."

"Well…" Amber hums thoughtfully. It's an offer almost too good to pass up. It'll get her out of the infirmary *and* doing something with her free time. Plus, she can help Jake if he ever falls ill during the midcycle. "I'll have to ask the infirmary about it, but I think I can."

Kimberly claps her hands. "Jake will be happy to hear that. It gets a little boring with just the four of us here all the time."

In the distance, a loud, melodic chime rings down the street, warning the shopkeepers that the third term classes have just finished. Kimberly lets out a small sigh.

"Time for me to go," she says.

"I can walk with you," Amber offers, withdrawing her Ice textbook from the shelf under the counter. "The infirmary is in the same direction, anyway."

Kimberly smiles. "I'd like that."

She lifts the counter up and waves Amber through the small space first, following close behind her and closing it gently behind them. As they pass through the front door of the store, Kimberly flips the sign to "Closed".

"Jake will flip it back," Kimberly says as they go. Amber nods, hugging her textbook close to her chest.

23

The two girls walk down the half-empty street, taking in the afternoon light.

"It's such a nice cycle," Kimberly says, taking in a deep breath of air.

"It is," Amber agrees simply. As they walk, they pass a few beggars, who look up at them wearily and reach for their small cups that they keep their coins in. Kimberly gives one a pitiful frown and tosses him a coin. It rattles inside the empty cup, and the Feni smiles in thanks.

"I wish I could give one to all of them," Kimberly says as they walk away, keeping her gaze forward to ignore the other pleading faces around them, "but then I'd be broke myself."

Amber just nods wordlessly. She'd also give a coin if she could spare one. After all, these Feni struggle to even get food most cycles.

It's not their fault. Over half of their population was displaced a few decades ago. They used to live on Korodon, a rural island which was in charge of agriculture. Amber has heard countless stories of the beautiful orchids of fruit trees and tall stalks of grains and vegetables that covered the once-green land. And now no being is allowed to travel to the island at all, or risk never leaving the island alive ever again.

It's uncomfortable silence the rest of their walk.

Eventually, the road opens up to a wide green space. It's a ring of two-story buildings around a small lake area and patch of vibrant green grass. The lake itself is rather shallow, having been hand-dug and costly to keep full, but it reflects the stars in the sky effortlessly, making its surface glitter. The Library stands tall opposite the main walking path the two are currently on, its red bricks glowing in the light of the cycle. Close to the Library stands a lone willow tree, its long leaves waving over the lake's surface in the soft magical breeze.

If they keep walking straight ahead, they'd arrive at the ASM grounds. But there is another path that leads off to the left, towards a low building of gleaming white stone. The infirmary.

"Thanks for walking me," Kimberly says.

"No problem," Amber nods. "I'll let you know if I can make it to the 'scoop internship'."

Kimberly can't help but laugh. "Sounds good to me."

The two wave each other goodbye and head off down their differing paths.

Amber walks quietly towards the infirmary, commotion rising behind her as the third terms are finally released from their Halls and have met up with their friends.

Despite everything she dislikes about the infirmary, it's kind of nice to not be working all the time like some of the other interns, allowing her to rest in the break room and snack on the little cookies and drinks that are always provided for the workers. And when she does eventually work, she mostly deals with minor injuries and mild illnesses.

Not counting the times where she visited Kimberly's place to heal Jake. That was more of a favor rather than actual work. But she always feels like her healing magic is getting stronger the more she works. As the saying goes, practice makes perfect.

In fact, it's probably thanks to Jake that Amber has gotten better at treating some of the more uncommon illnesses - a lot of first-time Healers struggle with them, and especially interns - since he gets sick so often. It's never severe enough to keep him from class, just to make him feel miserable for the better part of the cycle, but Amber always heals him before then anyway.

She steps into the infirmary's waiting room, which is large and filled with dark blue chairs. It's lit by bright white lights above, the bulbs buzzing quietly from their fixtures. The facility has its own private generator in the basement and employs their own Storm wizards to keep it running, meaning that if anything were to happen to the rest of Asandra's power, the infirmary will still be able to operate normally.

There are few beings in the waiting room, all of them

25

spaced out from one another and rather quiet. There are two children present as well, though they are sitting next to different adults and silently playing with their own toys.

Amber walks right up to the front desk, a long wooden structure towards the back corner of the room. There is a single wizard sitting behind it looking over paperwork. As Amber approaches, however, she pauses her work and raises her head to greet the Healer.

"Amber!" the wizard chimes merrily. "Are you here for a second shift?"

"No, Clare," Amber replies with a weary grin. "I just want to speak with Azna for a spell. Do you know where he is? If he's free?"

Clare looks down at her papers once again and starts shuffling through them. She's a third term Enchanter and rather important to the infirmary. Because of her receptionist position, she is given express permission to take her classes in the evening. Otherwise, she's pretty much aware of everything that goes on inside the infirmary walls.

Clare finally unearths the paper she was looking for. "He should be free right now for a little while, then he has an appointment to oversee. Why?"

"I've been offered an internship for a new job," Amber answers with a small smile. "If it goes well, I'll probably be hired."

"*Oh*, where is it?" Clare hums with interest.

"Mm, I'd rather not…" Amber trials off, shaking her head. "So… he's in his office?"

Clare lets out a defeated sigh. "Should be."

"Thanks, Clare."

Amber walks off down the halls of the infirmary, navigating the twisting and turning halls with ease. She learned the layout of the place fairly quickly. One has to if they hope to work here full-time in the future. For some it takes a week, others it takes longer. Amber didn't really start memorizing the hallways until her third month. But now she knows them almost like the back of her hand.

Eventually, she leaves the general medical rooms behind and enters the small office space towards the back of the large building. It looks no different from the other hallways, except that each door doesn't just have numbers on them, but names as well. The most important and skilled Healers get their own office spaces. Every other being gets the break room.

She stops at the end, a single doorway with an iron plaque that reads "Azna Izola, Head Healer". A Feni that is thousands of years old, who has dedicated his life to this infirmary. The other Healers and interns always joke about what might happen to the infirmary when he finally decides to Fade. But the old Life wizard never appears like he is ready to pass on into the White Beyond just yet. In fact, for a many-thousand-year-old Feni, he still looks quite young.

For all the accomplishments he has made in his long lifetime, he's still a little intimidating. He's not only head of the infirmary, but he's a part of the Council of Asandra as well, the collective that governs the entire island. And he takes both his Healer and Council jobs *very* seriously.

Amber takes a breath, knocks on the door, and waits for a tense moment.

"Come in!" comes a faint call.

Amber opens the door and steps into the office, closing it gently behind her. The room is a soft green color, lined with potted plants and a rather large filing cabinet that fills the entire back wall. Close to the back there is a large desk with a set of "In/Out" trays and a chair. And in the chair sits Azna, the old Feni himself. The only sign of his old age is his hair, which is a shimmering silver-gray, so old that he can't even change its color to hide it anymore. Otherwise, he wears a long white robe with a green shirt underneath, the simple yet standard uniform of an important infirmary Healer. He stares at Amber with his piercing green eyes and mild scowl on his face. He holds a quill in one hand, making it clear that he had been writing something before Amber showed up.

"Sorry to disturb you," Amber says sheepishly.

Azna nods back at her. "Your name…?"

"Amber."

"One of the interns, correct?"

"Yes."

"What seems to be the issue?" the Feni asks.

"Uh, well…" Amber clutches her textbook harder. There's no need for nervousness here. If she were to undergo a job change or be offered an internship away from the infirmary, she's doing the right thing. But his stare… "I was offered a different internship. So… I'd like to skip my infirmary duties to give this new job a try. Just for the next cycle at least. Unless I get hired, of course."

Azna raises an eyebrow. "What *exactly* is this job opportunity?"

"Working at an ice cream shop," Amber answers almost instantly.

"And who's the owner?"

Amber stares for a moment. She knows that he wants to know so that he can call on her if anything were to arise. Every Healer has to do it if they're planning on skipping their usual shift, even interns. But considering how many Healers there are at the infirmary already, Amber highly doubts that she'd be needed for much of anything.

"Kimberly Starshield," she says.

"One of the Blessed, I see," the head Healer finally lets out a long sigh. "Yes, you can be excused from your duties next cycle. But I want to hear your decision when you make one to see if we must process any paperwork. And always remember that you can return here if you are unsatisfied with that ice cream shop… job."

"I know," Amber nods furiously. "Thank you."

"And if you ever come in for a shift, you will still get paid for it, of course."

"Yes, sir."

"Anything else you want to discuss?"

"No, that's everything. Thank you. Sorry for interrupting your work."

Azna nods once, then wordlessly returns to his paperwork. Amber quickly turns away from his desk and leaves the room.

Her body is shuddering from the nervousness she had been forcefully keeping in check on her way back to the waiting room. Talking to Azna is always nerve-racking. While he encourages Healers to talk with him, his intense seriousness is an aura that always gets on her nerves. But at least she won't have to talk with him again. If she winds up getting hired, maybe she can just send him a letter next time.

Chapter 3

The next cycle, Amber shows up at Kimberly's shop not too long after her class ends, her little Ice textbook held tightly in her hands. She's both nervous yet eager at the same time. Over the last fifteen cycles, the two have gotten really close. And now Amber's going to be *working* for her.

But then there'll also be Blaze and Ethan she's going to have to deal with…

Kimberly will protect me, Amber thinks, trying to keep herself cheerful as she walks through the door. The little bell chimes as she enters, causing Kimberly to perk up from behind the counter.

"You're here!" she says with a wide grin.

"I am," Amber chuckles nervously, approaching the counter.

Jake comes out of the back room as soon as she is let behind the counter. "Kim-Star told me that you might be joining us this cycle."

"This just means no getting sick, okay?" Amber chides. Jake rolls his eyes back at her.

"I might as well introduce you to the other two," Kimberly steps in. "Jake, watch the counter for a bit?"

"Sure thing, boss," Jake replies playfully. Kimberly grins

back at him, though it appears a little weak. Amber lets Kimberly grab her arm and lightly guide her into the back room.

Blaze and Ethan are huddled at the far back of the room, whatever conversation they had been having put on pause as Kimberly and Amber enter. Blaze is quick to shoot Amber a silent, uninviting sideways glare, making her stomach churn uncomfortably. Ethan simply regards her with little emotion.

"Blaze, Ethan," Kimberly says, "this is Amber. She'll be working here for this cycle trying the job out. Maybe I'll hire her if she wants to work here full-time. Please treat her well."

Blaze narrows his eyes and fully turns his body to face the two girls.

"We've been doing fine with just the four of us already," he says firmly.

"Having an extra hand around won't hurt," Kimberly defends.

Blaze rolls his eyes and replies sarcastically, "You're the boss."

Kimberly then turns to Amber with a sad expression. "I'm sorry, Amber, but since this is your first time working here, I want you to stay in the back for now."

Amber blinks in surprise. Panic begins to build in her chest. "W-Why?"

"It can get a little stressful handling customers," Kimberly replies, "but you can help out front when third term classes are in session. There's not many customers then, so it's an ideal time for a being like you to practice customer interaction."

"But you're leaving me here with…" Amber trails off nervously, scared that the other two were listening in, which they probably are.

"I know, I know," Kimberly sighs. "Just… don't get in their way, and everything should be fine. Now, I need to go help Jake."

Kimberly turns away from Amber and exits the back room,

and that was that.

Amber stares out the open doorway, the back of her neck icy cold from the staring from the other two wizards present. She doesn't want to turn around, but she knows that she can't stay fixed in one spot forever, especially in front of the doorway.

She takes a glance over her shoulder. The two wizards have their eyes on her, both dreadfully silent. They're most likely sizing her up, though she can only guess what's going through their heads right now.

She turns her body to face them once again, mustering all her courage to draw a thin smile across her lips.

"Hello," she says politely, breaking the silence.

Ethan nods back at her in response, something she wasn't expecting. But Blaze, as per her expectations, sneers at her and looks away.

"Is there… something we should be doing?" she asks.

"*No*," Blaze replies rather forcefully, as if it were an obvious fact she should know already. The word makes Amber's stomach flutter uncomfortably. "And if you *ever* get hired, which I *doubt*, you'll spend your cycles back here with your head in the ice boxes for the rest of your employment."

"*Chill*," Ethan growls beside him.

"Who's the one that decided to let a first term intern for the cycle?" Blaze retorts angrily.

"Kimberly can do what she wants."

"Kimberly deserves better beings."

The statement stabs at Amber's heart.

Blaze shoves his hands into his pockets and turns away from Ethan. "I'm going out front." As he walks towards the door, his arm hits Amber hard, pushing her out of his way. He doesn't even falter.

Amber doesn't watch him leave, instead letting her gaze drop to the floor as she clutches her textbook close to her chest.

"Hey," the sound draws her attention. Ethan is giving her a

small sympathetic look. Even so, he tilts his head downward as soon as her eyes land on him, hiding half of his face from her under his hat. "Don't let him get under your skin. He just has some unreasonably high expectations."

"Thanks," she mutters quietly, unsure if she should truly be thankful or somewhat skeptical. For all she knows, Ethan hates her just as much as his friend does.

"I… don't believe we've met before," Ethan eventually hums, trying to spark some sort of friendly conversation.

"We haven't," Amber replies stiffly.

"How long have you known Kim-Star?"

Amber hugs her textbook tighter. "Only a couple of cycles. She's my tutor."

The third term's gaze lands on her blue book in her grasp. "Ice magic."

"Yeah. You?"

"I ended up with Fire this term," Ethan says halfheartedly. "Jake hasn't been much help though. Are you close with him, too?"

"Kim calls me over whenever he gets sick, so I guess we're on friendly terms."

Ethan shrugs. "I wouldn't know. I've hardly seen the two since the midterm projects were assigned. But at least I'm done with mine now, so I can get back to work…" he trails off for a moment, then rolls his eyes. "And by 'work', I mean 'standing around back here all cycle and talk with Blaze'."

"You don't work at the counter at all?"

"Sometimes we do. We take turns. But working the counter keeps some beings away, if you know what I mean. It's easier if we stay back here and watch over the extra ice cream. Besides," he turns his head to glance at the unwashed ice cream tubs, "there's always something to clean."

Amber can't help but smile, her tight grip on her textbook relaxing. Who knew that Ethan can hold a *regular* conversation?

33

"Why are *you* here?" he asks.

"Me?" Amber echoes. "I'm… looking for a better job."

Ethan frowns back at her in confusion. "You're a Healer, right? The infirmary should be the best place for you."

Amber licks her lips, letting her gaze stray away from the third term. "It's… mostly the social environment I don't like."

The two continue to stand in silence, unsure what to say or do next. Amber's hands slowly grow tired of holding the textbook, her palms beginning to burn uncomfortably.

Wordlessly, she walks over to the counter and sets the book down. She's got loads of time to practice her presentation for next cycle. Sixteen cycles isn't even that long in the first place, and now her time is almost up. She'll be much happier when she finally does her presentation, because then it'll all be over for the time being and she'll be able to worry about other important issues.

Like how she's going to pay for her second term.

A hand lands on her shoulder. "Are you alright?"

Amber inhales slowly and nods, her mind numb.

"You're as pale as a spirit," Ethan says.

"I am?" she breathes back. She feels fine, if not a little weak in the stomach. She's been trying not to think too much about paying for her second term, but now that she's nearly half way through with her first term it's been slowly gnawing on her mind. She's hardly earned much from her internship at the infirmary just because of class, and now she's well behind where she should be with her tuition savings. And it's not like she can ask her parents for help because-

She places a hand on her forehead as she leans on the counter with her other arm, steadying herself. Her head throbs painfully in some sort of protest.

"Do you need to sit down?" Ethan asks beside her. "I can get you some water."

"Yes… water," Amber echoes with an airy breath.

Ethan cautiously steps away from her as she remains hunched over her textbook, her head spinning. She hears water run for a brief moment, then a small cup is slid in front of her across the counter. She takes it weakly and sips on the cold, refreshing liquid.

"Thank you," she mutters under her breath.

"The *last* thing I want to happen this cycle is for you to pass out and have Kim blaming me for it," Ethan simply replies with crossed arms. Amber nods back at him and returns to her cup of water. She doesn't want him to get in trouble if she were to pass out, either.

"How about you sit down for a spell until you're feeling better," he strongly suggests.

"Maybe…"

Ethan disappears again for a brief moment, and soon she hears the scraping of chair legs across tiled floor. She looks up to see Ethan fiddling with a small wooden stool in the far corner of the room, shifting it into whatever position he wants it to be in. Once he's satisfied with the stool, he helps to guide Amber over to it, keeping a hand on her shoulder at all times to help keep her upright.

She plops down on top of the stool heavily and gives Ethan a thin smile. "Thank you."

"Just take it easy," he only replies.

***

Amber sits in the corner for stars-know-how-long, waiting for her dizziness to pass. Ethan paces around the room idly, his expression distant as he quietly thinks to himself. Occasionally, he has to trade out an ice cream tub with Kimberly, which he carelessly throws over by the sink before returning to his quiet pacing.

She hates to admit that Blaze is somewhat right. If she's

35

not working the counter, the job is kind of boring.

"How's your project coming along?" Ethan asks, breaking the long silence between them. He pauses his pacing momentarily to stare at Amber's bright blue textbook.

"It's mostly finished," Amber replies softly, cradling her water cup in her hands. "Kim said that it'll do for now, but... I don't know."

"Can I take a look at it?"

"Sure..." Amber mumbles. Ethan picks up the textbook and opens it, promptly withdrawing Amber's script sandwiched between the front cover and the title page. He turns the pieces of paper over in his hands, inspecting it quietly. Then he begins reading.

Amber can't bring herself to look at him as he scans her writing, wondering if he can even read it in the first place. She'll probably stress herself out again if she *did* watch, and then she'd simply not be able to work at all.

"Hm," Ethan eventually hums aloud. Amber looks up again to see him placing the papers back into the textbook.

"Do you like it?" she asks, her stomach churning nervously.

Ethan turns his head to look at her, his lips partly open as he thinks of something to say to her. Amber tightens her grip on her cup to try and calm her nerves, though so far it's not working.

"It's..." he starts, though he ends up frowning to himself as he continues to think. "It's not bad."

But it's not good? Amber wonders, looking down at her cup in defeat.

"Have you only read what's in this textbook?" Ethan asks her, tapping the cover.

"Yes..." Amber admits quietly.

"You should probably read *The Last Monarch of Korodon*. It talks about the Ice General and his role in the War much better than the ASM textbooks do... if you're ever curious."

36

Amber looks up at Ethan once more, her eyebrows arched high. "I've not heard of that one before."

"It's an old book," the Spiritist chuckles halfheartedly, "but it's a good read. You'd probably have to ask for help finding it, though."

Amber nods. "Thanks."

"Feeling any better?"

"I do."

"Nerves?"

Amber shakes her head. "More than that." Ethan just nods back at her and doesn't press for details.

Amber stands and sets her cup aside. Her gaze strays to a piece of paper she didn't notice before, neatly rolled up and bound by a small silver string sitting on the back counter where Ethan and Blaze had been standing when she first arrived.

"What's that?" she asks, pointing to the roll of paper.

Ethan heaves a heavy sigh. "It's a side project me and Blaze are working on."

"What is it?"

"A map."

"A map?" Amber echoes curiously.

Ethan steps up to the back counter and takes the roll of paper in his hands, staring down at it with a vacant gaze. "We... just like making maps."

"What's it a map of?" Amber presses.

"Korodon," Ethan replies simply.

Amber can't help but frown. There are already maps of Korodon in the Library, though they're most likely a little out of date. Why would they be drawing their own map of an island that no being is allowed to go to in the first place?

Before she can even begin to ask questions, heavy footsteps ring behind her, and she and Ethan turn around. Blaze comes storming into the back room with his dark scowl pointed directly at Amber.

"Kimberly kicked you out?" Ethan asks him lightly.

"Yes," he replies curtly. "Did you tell her about *that*?" He jabs a finger at the map in Ethan's hands.

"I just told her what it was, not what it was for," Ethan replies simply.

The Naturist shoots the Healer a dangerous glare, which causes her stomach to drop nervously.

"If you tell *any being* what we're going to talk about, it will not end well for you," he threatens. Amber just stares back into his cold eyes blankly, unsure what to say or do. What's going on?

"Kim won't let her run the front?" Ethan wonders aloud.

"She's too new," Blaze growls back.

"Can't we save this for another time?"

"This is the only privacy we've got at this point, Eth, with or without *her*."

Ethan frowns and shakes his head. "She'll be getting involved then-"

"She's already involved *now*," Blaze growls back. He runs a hand through his hair and looks up at the ceiling above him. "She became involved the moment you told her what that map was."

Amber draws a shaky breath, her gaze darting over to Ethan. He ignores her, his expression dark and unreadable, eyes hidden under the brim of his hat. What are these two talking about? What are they going to do with that map? She doesn't want to assume the worst, but...

Blaze grips her shoulders firmly, drawing her attention back to his intense stare. "*Swear* that you'll keep this a secret. Even from Kimberly and Jake."

Amber nods back at him reflexively. "I-I swear I won't tell."

Apparently satisfied, Blaze lets her go with a small shove, then turns to anxiously pace around the room, still clearly losing his mind, hands gripping his hair in frustration.

"W-What's going on?" Amber stutters quietly to Ethan. He only holds up a finger back to her as he watches Blaze intensely.

"Okay…" Blaze finally breathes. He stops pacing and looks over at the open door that leads out to the front of the shop, probably to make sure neither Kimberly or Jake are listening in, then steps back up to the back counter, rubbing his hands anxiously. "Tell her, Eth."

"We're going to Korodon," Ethan states bluntly in a low voice.

Amber stares back at Ethan with wide eyes. What did he just say?

"Roll it out," Blaze orders, gesturing to the map in Ethan's hands. The Spiritist quietly unties the silver string and rolls the paper out on the counter in front of the three wizards, smoothing it out for Amber to clearly see.

It's a map of Korodon all right, a rough oval ring filled with different lines for roads and labeled circles for towns. If Amber didn't know what she was looking at, she would have probably figured that the roads were simply a poorly drawn wheel.

"Why are you telling me all of this?" Amber asks quietly, staring down at the map before her.

"Wrong place, wrong time," Blaze replies simply. "We were going to talk about this whether you were here or not."

"Couldn't we have discussed this elsewhere, Blaze?" Ethan asks again.

The Naturist shakes his head. "I've had some of the teachers appear outside my dorm without warning recently, and any being can overhear us at the willow tree. This is the last place we can speak freely."

Ethan folds his arms and scowls at his friend. "Why am I hearing about all of this now, then?"

"Because then we'd not raise their suspicion too much," Blaze replies, frustration in his voice, "but they've not gone away since they started patrolling the hall."

39

"Why are you going to Korodon?" Amber can't help but ask, turning to Blaze this time. "It's illegal."

Blaze quickly turns away from her to look down at the map. "Because the Council isn't doing anything about it."

A tense silence descends on the three wizards. Amber's head is spinning with all this information just because she decided to become Kimberly's intern. Information that she *really* should report to the proper authorities.

"If you're thinking about snitching," Blaze hisses in her ear, causing her body to tense, "I'll make sure to drag you down with us."

"Stop scaring her like that," Ethan sighs on her right.

"I'm *not* going to let her ruin our plan," Blaze retorts on her left. "We've come this far already, haven't we?"

"This is all a bit much for her."

"I'm aware."

"Does this mean that we're bringing her with us?"

"What? No!" Blaze snorts. "What'll she be? Fodder?"

"She's a Healer," Ethan replies simply.

"I can heal, too," Blaze points out.

"Not as well as an *actual* Healer can."

"I'm not that good at *that* sort of healing, actually..." Amber can't help but mutter aloud. It's not like she *wants* to actually join them on their self-imposed and highly illegal mission, but it's also true. She's better at curing illnesses and small cuts. She'd be no use in any sort of combat situation. "Not like the rest of my class."

"See? She's just useless."

Ethan's eyes widen in an instant, rage igniting within them. He steps forward, pushing Amber aside so that he can get up in Blaze's face.

"Take that back," the Spiritist growls.

"What is there to take back?" Blaze scoffs. "I'm right, aren't I? She just confirmed-"

"I don't care *what* she said," Ethan replies sharply. "She is *not* useless."

"Stars, Ethan, what's gotten into you?"

Amber stands quietly off to the side, wondering the exact same thing. Ethan's not known her long, and yet now he's suddenly upset as if they've been close friends the entire time.

"Take it back and apologize," Ethan repeats in a dangerous tone.

Blaze simply folds his arms and scowls back at him. "Or *what*?"

"What on Astria is going on back here?" a new voice chimes in. The three wizards pause and turn to Kimberly, who regards them with a furrowed brow of concern and confusion, though her gaze is fixed to Blaze and Ethan in particular.

"Kim!" Blaze exclaims in surprise. "We were just-"

"*He*," Ethan interrupts, giving Blaze a sideways glare, "called Amber 'useless'."

Kimberly stiffens as she turns her attention to a very quiet Amber. "Did he?"

Amber's heart pounds in her chest as she clasps her hands together in front of her. She's scared, she really is. If she spills what Blaze and Ethan are planning… Well, Blaze already promised to bring her down with them. But if she just says "yes" without giving context, then Blaze will still be upset with her either way, except that Ethan won't get in trouble.

Slowly, she nods.

The temperature of the back room drops dramatically, sending chills down Amber's spine as she quickly hugs herself to stay warm. Her tutor glowers at Blaze as the air around her shimmers with small snow flurries, her hands balling into fists.

"Get out," she demands, jabbing a single finger at the door.

Blaze blinks once, shocked. "Kim-"

"*I SAID OUT!*" Kimberly roars over him. "I *will not* tolerate

41

you insulting my intern on her first cycle."

Blaze's expression slowly morphs from bewilderment to fury, and his gaze shifts to Amber in an instant. He says nothing, for if he does then he would be ousting his illegal travel plans to the one wizard who can and *will* report him to the Council authorities in a heartbeat.

"Fine then," he growls.

With that, the Naturist storms out of the back room, leaving behind a very tense atmosphere.

Kimberly is the one to break the silence by letting out a frustrated sigh, placing her hands on her hips.

"Think he'll be back next cycle?" she asks Ethan.

The Spiritist shakes his head. "I have a feeling he won't."

"Remind him to send a letter if he decides to quit."

"I will."

"Amber," Kimberly turns back to her student, giving her a sympathetic look, "I'm sorry things ended up happening this way. I hope you'll still consider applying for a full-time position."

"Uh…" Amber mutters, glancing over to Ethan. He looks back at her expectantly, his gaze practically warning her to stay silent. "I… I'll still need to think about it."

"You can always come back next cycle if you want," Kimberly suggests. "If Blaze doesn't show, then maybe it'll be better for you?"

"Maybe," Amber shrugs back.

"Kim?" Jake calls from the front. "Everything alright back there?"

"Yes," Kimberly calls back with an airy sigh. She turns back to Amber briefly and says, "Just… think about it." Amber nods back, not trusting herself to speak any further as Ethan's cold gaze bores into the back of her neck. Kimberly smiles for a mere moment, then quickly rushes back out to the front of the store.

The moment she's out of earshot, Ethan lets out a sigh of

relief. "Thanks for not… saying anything."

"I feel bad…" Amber admits softly.

"She'd never understand," Ethan replies. He turns to the map of Korodon and quickly rolls it up once more. Once he finishes retying the string, the roll of paper melts away into a plume of black smoke.

"Why did you stand up for me like that?" Amber asks him.

Ethan stands completely still, his body facing away from her. She can't see his face, but she doubts she'd be able to read any of his expressions anyway. The buzz of conversing beings leaks through the back room doorway as their numbers inside the small ice cream shop grow.

"It's time for the lunch rush," Ethan comments flatly, dodging her question.

"But why-"

Ethan walks away from her and over to the large ice boxes, trying to appear busy. He's not going to answer, even if she presses him.

She looks over her shoulder at the pile of dirty ice cream tubs next to the large wash bin of a sink and lets her shoulders sag in defeat. Might as well do the job she came here to do in the first place.

***

Blaze strides briskly down the Straightway, his sharp glare parting the lunch rush crowd before him. To them, he's the golden wizard with an attitude, willing to bully students below his term and any who he deems to be inferior. While he's never wanted to be seen as such a bad guy, it's helped to keep beings out of his business thus far. It's how he and Ethan have been able to plan so much of their Korodon mission in secrecy.

He's angry, and he's not hesitant to let the beings around him know that. He's angry about Amber. He's angry about

43

Kimberly. His job at Kimberly's shop has been jeopardized as well, and he's angry about that, too.

Everything had been going so well. Then *Amber* decided to appear, and now she's in on it, too.

He doesn't know what she and Ethan talked about while he was working the front counter, but he can't help but feel like Amber's more than just the innocent facade she shows. She got Ethan wrapped around her finger so fast.

And now the teachers are patrolling his dorm hall. His safe spaces are becoming fewer and fewer. Their private plan has been intruded upon. *Everything* is falling apart.

He just needs to keep it all together just a little longer. Once the midterm projects are done, he and Ethan will leave.

But he can't get the thought out of his mind that Amber could possibly be a Council authority in disguise, trying to size them up and stop their plan before they have a chance to act on it. They didn't give her many of the intricate details to their plan, so she should have no idea how long they've been plotting for, assuming that Ethan hasn't been completely compromised yet. All she knows is that they're planning to break the law, and it might be happening very, *very* soon.

He arrives at the lake area and approaches the willow tree. It's where he met Ethan for the first time and the two became friends. It's been their meeting spot ever since, where they hang out to study and relax in between classes and work.

It's peaceful, where he's surrounded by nature, however sparse it may be. The willow keeps out the glare of the cycle's light and the distant sounds of the bustling city of Asandra.

He parts the hanging leaves of the willow tree and sits up against its sturdy trunk, getting comfortable. With each breath, he allows his anger to drain away and welcomes in the stillness of nature for the time being. The tree is a place of serenity, not frustration, and he intends to keep it that way. He'll worry over his troubles when he leaves.

He runs his hands through the soft grass, feeling each and every blade under his fingertips. He smells the fresh air of magic, full of energy that seeps into everything and every being around it. He hears the sway of the willow's leaves in the invisible breeze, brushing lightly against each other. All other noise, from the beings beyond the ring of willow leaves, drains away, fading into nothingness.

Nature at its finest.

***

"Blaze?"

The sound of his name cuts through the stillness. Slowly, Blaze opens his eyes again, which now feel heavy and tired, to see Ethan standing over him.

"When did you get here?" he mutters tiredly.

Ethan scowls. "Lunch is over. You're going to be late to class."

"Give me a break," Blaze sighs, slowly getting to his feet. He leans on the tree trunk for support, his body still half-asleep. He must have fallen asleep again. It always seems to happen.

The two step through the curtain of willow leaves once more, and are greeted by the sight of third term students heading to class, all smiling and laughing as they go.

"Ethan," Blaze starts. He takes a breath to continue his thought, but the air catches in his chest. He has no idea how he's going to start outlining all his worries and issues to his friend before they reach his Hall.

He feels Ethan's quiet stare rest on the side of his hanging head, waiting for him to continue speaking.

He lets out a heavy huff. "I'm… concerned," he continues slowly. "About the plan."

Ethan snorts in amusement at his statement. "That's new."

45

Blaze shoots him an irate scowl. "I'm being serious. What if we're caught before we can act?"

Ethan shrugs. "Then I guess it's over."

"And Amber. What if she's working for the authorities?"

"She's not," Ethan replies, his tone flatlining in an instant. "She just became an unfortunate accomplice-"

"You don't know that," Blaze states. "She could be playing us."

"It's not your place to accuse her of doing or being *anything*," Ethan says darkly.

"Why are you defending her like this, Eth?" Blaze asks him. "You hardly know her."

Ethan stares straight ahead, not paying Blaze any attention whatsoever. His gaze is distant, lost within whatever world he has inside his head. He's used to his friend spacing out every once in a while, but it's only seemed to get worse the last couple of cycles. It almost feels like Ethan isn't even there anymore.

"Okay, *maybe* I was a bit of a jerk to her," Blaze reluctantly admits as the two enter the crowd of third terms, which brings Ethan's vacant stare back to reality, "but it doesn't help me feel less… *worried* that she's going to mess it all up."

"She won't," Ethan assures him. "She doesn't have that kind of power."

Blaze nods to himself. He's got a point. Probably.

They reach the split in the path where it spreads out to the left and right in a wide circle around a large, central brick building. On the outside of the circular path are the magic Halls, each one constructed with their own character - the Ice Hall is literally sculpted out of blue ice, the Fire Hall is perpetually on fire, and the Storm Hall is mostly made of metal, acting as a lightning rod to keep other non-Storm students safe during class time, to name a few of each of the Hall's unique characteristics - different colored banners and magic symbols proudly hanging outside of each one. While the two of them are both heading in the same direction for a little longer, Blaze's Hall is the very first building directly to their left.

"Gonna go back to the shop after class?" Blaze asks.

Ethan shrugs. "Possibly. You quitting?"

"I… think so."

"Don't forget to send her a letter."

"I won't, don't worry."

Chapter 4

"Are you *sure* you're doing okay?"

"Yes, Kim, I am."

Jake can't help but linger near the back room doorway when he should be sweeping the floor instead. Amber's seemed a little shaken ever since Blaze got kicked out of the store during the lunch rush. She's a really nice first term, and he can't help but feel bad for her.

"Do you think you'll be back next cycle to give it another go?" Kimberly asks hopefully.

"Maybe," Amber replies softly. "I don't know yet."

"Well, we'd like to have you back again, Amber. You know that, right?"

There's a pause as Amber moves her head in reply, which he can't see.

"And if you decide not to come back, let me know and I can give you your pay whenever you come by again."

"Okay."

"Want me to walk you to the dorms?" Ethan offers. He stayed late just to make sure Amber was doing alright as well, which Jake thought was nice of him to do. He's not as massive of a jerk like Blaze is, though he does have his moments on occasion.

"Sure…" Amber's quiet voice replies sheepishly.

Jake quickly turns to trying to appear busy with his sweeping as the other three exit the back room and into the front of the store.

"Take care, you two," Kimberly says to the Healer and Medium as they make their way to the front door. Amber smiles back at her weakly, her blue textbook hugged close to her chest, as Ethan lingers by her side. He's certainly taken a liking to her pretty fast.

"Bye, Jake," Amber says to him.

"Have a good evening," he replies with his best grin of encouragement. "And good luck with your presentation next cycle!" Amber lets out a small halfhearted chuckle, though she appears to become even more anxious with his reminder.

"You too," she replies quickly. With that, Amber and Ethan step out of the store and disappear down the Straightway, the light of the cycle dimming as it comes to a close.

Once they're out of sight, Jake leans forward on his broom with a small frown. A pit of nervousness sinks in his gut as he asks, "What about Blaze?"

"He's not coming back," Kimberly answers flatly.

Jake looks at his girlfriend with mild shock plastered on his face. "Oh."

"He's going to send a letter of resignation next cycle, from what Ethan told me," she continues with a small huff. "Can't say I'm sad to see him go. There's always a place out there that will certainly hire him and his ego."

Jake nods alone quietly. With Blaze gone, business is sure to boom even more once word spreads. After all, he's kept a lot of customers away by simply being employed, even if he mostly worked out of sight.

Yet, at the same time, it's a little hard to accept. Blaze has been working here since Kimberly opened shop last year. Same with Ethan. Same with himself. With Blaze suddenly gone like *that*, without so much as any prior warning or good bye… He can only shake his head sadly. At the end of the cycle, Blaze is still his friend.

"How's the sweeping coming along?" Kimberly asks, clearly wanting to take her mind off of Blaze as fast as possible.

"Nearly done," Jake lies through his teeth as he smiles back at her.

She smirks at him suspiciously. "You know I love you, Jake."

"I love you too?" he replies cautiously.

"How much is left?" she presses.

"Just this corner, boss," he answers quickly, gesturing to the corner behind him. He actually has half of the store left to sweep, though it doesn't look that way.

"I'm going to start making dinner," Kimberly announces, turning to leave. "If you *really* are that close to done, I expect you to be upstairs to help cook."

"Ah, mhm! I'll be right up!"

Kimberly pauses in the back room doorway and gives him a knowing smile. "Take your time, Jake. I don't want to have a dirty floor when we open for business."

"Yes, boss!" Jake replies with a salute. Kimberly can't help but laugh as she disappears into the back room to make her way upstairs. Once she's out of sight, he turns back to his broom and continues his cleaning.

His feelings towards Blaze are mixed. Both Jake and Kimberly know that he's actually a very nice wizard when he wants to be, but he simply chooses to be mean to every being around him for whatever reason. Jake's never asked, nor does he care to ask. Maybe Blaze just has trust issues and can only be nice around beings he truly cares for.

And Jake likes Ethan a lot, he really does. He's amazed that Blaze's attitude hasn't affected Ethan at all. Or maybe it has and he does a good job keeping it in check. He *is* very distant, though, and it seems like the others have noticed, too. His work is kept very light, because he completely shuts down the moment he disappears into himself.

Issues aside, the two make a good pair, but Jake's enthusiasm to hang out with them has drastically dwindled in the last year. It's just not the same anymore…

"Hey, Jake!" Blaze announced as he and Ethan entered the shop.

Jake looked up from the counter, giving it one final wipe down before business was supposed to start. "Hey, guys."

For whatever reason, Blaze was all smiles this cycle. Ethan, however, remained as stoic as ever, following in his close friend's shadow.

As the two let themselves behind the counter, Blaze gave Jake a hearty pat on his shoulder as he passed. "Keep up the good work, man."

"Thanks…?" Jake replied cautiously, staring after the Naturist. His brow knitted together in confusion as he turned to Ethan, who lingered by the back room's doorway. "What's up with him?"

"He got a good grade," Ethan replied, a slight grin managing to briefly flash across his lips.

"Ah."

"It wasn't just a good grade," Blaze said, reappearing in the doorway, leaning up against it with one arm and a smug smile. "It was the best *grade in my class. Dunno why. That test was super easy."*

"Not every being is as gifted as you are," Jake hummed with a slight eye roll.

Blaze just laughed at his statement. "They're just not trying hard enough. Believe me, if they put in the time and effort to practice, they'd ace it just like I did."

"Mhm…" Jake turned back to the counter, his earlier task left half-finished. "Can you two bring out the fresh tubs?"

"Sure thing," Blaze chimed. Ethan reluctantly huffed through his nose.

"Jake's got a point, you know," the Spiritist said as the two head off to get to work, their voices in the back room just barely audible. The heavy creak and subsequent 'thump' of the lid of one of the large ice chests opening muffled Blaze's voice momentarily.

"…not hard, though."

"It was a combat test, was it not?"

"Sure it was! We have those just like every other class."

"Do you not see why you'd have an inherent advantage for such a test?"

There was a break in the conversation as ice cubes rustled about, the tubs of ice cream finally being retrieved.

"Hmph," Blaze only huffed in reply.

"You're still in the lowest five for your healing tests," Ethan continued to point out.

"C'mon, Eth," the Naturist moaned, "you don't have to remind me."

"You can't ignore it, either."

"If we weren't friends, I'd kick you."

"I'd like to see you try."

"Hey, hurry it up!" Jake had to interrupt.

"Yeah, we're coming," Blaze replied. The two emerged from the back room, each with a singular tub of ice cream in their hands. They approached the ice cream display and began switching out the old tubs for the new ones.

"This'd go so much faster if I could just use my vines…" Blaze muttered aloud.

"Kim wishes we had more freedom like that, too," Jake agreed, "but it's the law."

"We're wizards! It's our right to use our magic however we

52

want! Kim owns the place; she should be able to dictate how much magic we get to use in her establishment."

Jake just shrugged. He aired his opinions about this before, that being he hated the current system as well, but trudging back across this old ground only made him feel weary inside. He said his piece many times over. What else is there to talk about?

"Magic use in business establishments is limited for a reason, you know," Ethan said.

"Yeah, you made that point already, thanks," Blaze grumbled back at him. The Spiritist just stared at his friend for a long moment wordlessly, then turned and wandered back into the back room, empty tub swinging in his hand. The Naturist shook his head and followed after him.

The memory fades as Jake finishes his sweeping. He'll miss those kinds of cycles, where they all just stand around and talk like regular friends instead of co-workers. Not being able to spend as much time with them outside of the shop like they used to do in their first term seemed like such a detriment in the past, but now almost feels like a minor blessing in disguise.

Jake happily stores away the broom and pan in the back room, then walks up the small flight of stairs to the second floor.

The building has three floors in total. The first floor is used for the ice cream shop, with the second and third floors used as living space. The second floor has a bathroom, the kitchen, dining room, and living room. The third floor is Kimberly's bedroom, a small study, a second bathroom, and a storage space for boxes and other things. Jake actually sleeps on the sofa right now, which he doesn't mind all that much. The two aren't at "sleeping in the same bed" just yet.

A sweet smell wafts from the kitchen, making his mouth water hungrily. He strides across the living room and into the dining room. The two rooms are connected, with the only indication that they are separate areas being the change from carpet to hardwood flooring. Though the table can seat six beings, four of the chairs don't see much use.

He peeks into the kitchen, connected to the dining room by a small doorway, and watches Kimberly shift in front of the stove, open flame burning a dull blue. Steam emanates from the black pot over the flame as Kimberly takes slices of potatoes and plops them into it.

"Smells delicious," he comments longingly.

Kimberly casts him a glance with a soft smile. "It'll taste even better than it smells."

"I know."

"Do you mind setting the table?"

"Not at all, boss."

Jake steps into the kitchen and assembles the plates, cups, and utensils for them to dine with. Then he takes his things and sets up two places at the dinner table across from each other and takes a seat, waiting patiently for his meal.

As he waits, however, he decides that now is the perfect time to bring out his sword.

In a gust of flames, the ruby blade appears in his hands, with an ebony hilt wrapped in worn leather and complete with a little silver decal of the symbol of Fire. He's had this sword for as long as he can remember, and he loves it all the same. He is among one of the few wizards at ASM that requires an aid for magic usage. He doesn't mind it most of the time, but there are cycles where he wishes to be "normal" like the majority of his class.

But where he lacks in the magic department he sure makes up for it with his swordsmanship. Wielding a blade had never been very hard, and he's only gotten more skilled over the years. Now he just needs to find a way to incorporate his magic into his preferred fighting style and he can be considered a rather formidable foe… if he ever gets into a fight.

And holding it now, he can feel his magic stir inside of him. It courses through his veins with its fiery warmth, empowering him with its might. The blade is light, almost as if holding air itself, yet hums with energy all the same. It is his focal point, a conduit. Without it, he wouldn't even be able to conjure even the smallest of flames. But he can still toast stuff without it, at least.

Kimberly finally steps out of the kitchen, pot in her hands, as he twirls his sword in the air around him. Steam rises from the top of the pot as mist radiates from Kimberly's hands, her fingers and possibly palms covered in a thin layer of white ice.

"Dinner is ready," she grins. "Time to put your sword away."

"But what if I want to cut my dinner?" Jake whines.

"No aids at the table," Kimberly chides. Jake holds up his hands in surrender, and his sword disappears in a swirl of fire.

Kimberly places the pot between the two of them and sits down in her seat. She reaches for the ladle, which rests inside the pot, and spoons out some of the food. Boiled vegetables and meat cubes.

Jake scoops a large helping for himself and plops it onto his plate. Skinned potatoes, carrots, and chunks of what he thinks to be kava beef. They have a lot of beef.

"Kava?" he asks.

"Yep," Kimberly chuckles. "What else would it be?"

Jake keeps back a small, disappointed frown. He likes pretty much anything put in front of him. But meat… It's always left a foul taste in his mouth, so to speak. To the extent that sometimes it upsets his stomach, or makes him feel queasy. He's never mentioned it, not even to Kimberly. In order to really feel like he's eating well he snacks on at least two whole pieces of fruit a cycle, but normally he consumes three or four.

"You know what we need?" Jake says.

"What?" Kimberly asks.

"Kava-flavored ice cream."

Kimberly rolls her eyes.

"Or maybe potato. Do you think beings would like potato ice cream?"

"*Jake…*"

"It's not *that* bad of an idea, is it?"

"If I had an iron coin for every dumb ice cream idea you've proposed," Kimberly says, "I'd have enough to close shop and live comfortably for a *long* time."

"I've not made *that* many proposals, have I?"

"I wish I was keeping track somewhere so I could tell you."

Jake just laughs and takes another bite of food. He bites down on a chunk of beef, making it squelch and spit its meat juice back at him in protest. It hits the back of his throat and burns it, and he raises a fist to his mouth to try and keep himself from coughing.

"Are you okay?" Kimberly asks, leaning forward in concern. Jake grins suspiciously and quickly finishes his bite.

"No, I'm *dying*!" he exaggerates, leaning to one side in his seat and tilting his head to look up at the ceiling. He uses his free hand to hold onto the table to keep himself from falling. "*Oh*, the pain!"

"Cut it out, Jake," Kimberly sighs, leaning back in her seat.

"I'm sorry," Jake continues, sliding forward to lay on his side on his chair, "I… I can't bear it anymore. I'm going to die, Kim…"

"No, you're not. Sit up."

Jake does as he's told and is met with her loving smile, which he can't help but reciprocate with a wide grin of his own.

Chapter 5

Ethan walks alone down the street, heading towards Kimberly's shop. The homeless rise from their slumbers with his footsteps, which create sharp tapping sounds as he strikes the stones. Normally he'd have Blaze to keep him company in the early light, but now he is his own company.

The sky is starting to brighten with light, the cycle bringing forth another morning. And yet… It could be his imagination, but everything seems darker. The light, the beings, the buildings.

The shadows.

There's a sense of foreboding in the air. He can feel it. It's been growing the last couple of cycles, making him uneasy. The shadows grow long, warping around his feet as he walks along the quiet street. But they don't feel as safe as they once were. He can't describe the feeling beyond the fact that there is now something living in the dark spaces of the city of Asandra. Something dangerous.

Ethan? a voice chimes in his head. It's that of a girl, young and light, full of wonder and innocence. He stops dead in his tracks. *Where are we going?*

It takes him a moment to realize he's not walking anymore, and he twists his face into a sneer. He hates it when that happens.

He starts walking again, quicker this time. He wants to make it to Kimberly's shop before it happens again. It *will* happen again. He can't stop it. He fiddles with his gauntlets nervously under the hanging folds of his cape, making sure they're still there.

He pauses in front of Kimberly's shop and stares through the windows. The lights are on inside, everything ready for customers to begin arriving, yet he doesn't see Kimberly nor Jake behind the counter. But the sign is flipped over to "Open", so one of the two *must* be awake.

He invites himself in, listening to the little bell on the door chime merrily as he enters.

What is this place?

His body freezes once more as he stands in the doorway, the voice buzzing in his head.

It's so big! it continues in breathless awe. The arm that holds open the door begins to shake, its strength quickly draining. Still, he can't shake himself out of his spell. The longer he stands there, frozen in the doorway, he helplessly watches the shop begin to melt, its welcoming blues and whites turning to dark purples and blacks.

"Ethan," a relieved sigh snaps his world back to attention, and he stands a little straighter to appear casual. Kimberly stands in the back room doorway with a weary smile across her lips. She either didn't take note of his trance-like state or doesn't care to ask about his mindless standing. "It's just you."

"Where's Jake?" Ethan asks, finally stepping into the store. The bell rings once more as it fully closes behind him.

"Jake's sick again," she informs him as he lets himself behind the counter.

"Are you going to call Amber?" Ethan inquires. She did mention last cycle that she's been helping to keep Jake healthy, even if she did also say later that she wasn't a good Healer. She could have been lying, and he wouldn't put it past her to do so.

"She has class first thing," Kimberly replies, "but she'll be here once it's over. She won't be very long."

"Have you found out *why* he gets so sick all the time yet?"

"No. Frankly, we've given up trying. He's a regular wizard, like me and you. The Healers told us as much, anyway."

Ethan has to suppress a scoff at her second statement. Yet it's only fair for her to say such a thing. He doesn't blame her.

"I'm going to need you to run the front until Jake is feeling better," Kimberly informs him.

"Will do," Ethan nods. Kimberly half-smiles and rushes away, heading back to Jake's side.

Ethan looks around the vacant shop and heaves a heavy sigh, wondering how long he'll be standing here for, all alone with his thoughts.

It's so big, the voice speaks again, *and empty. Why are we here, Ethan?*

Somehow, he manages to curl his fingers into fists, and he stares down at the counter quietly. He *hates* being alone with his thoughts.

***

A bell rings in the distance, deep and rich. It echoes through the air and seeps through the windows of the storefront. First term classes are over.

Ethan lets out a sigh and fiddles with the edges of his cape. Amber should be coming now. It's been… a while, since Ethan's been on his own for this long. Just standing around.

Waiting.

Ethan!

The sharp, angry page makes his body tense up, and he stands a little straighter, alert.

He's alone. He can't let his guard down until Jake is feeling better.

The cycle drags on, but eventually Amber makes an appearance, walking with a wide smile and head held high. Her presence seems to make the light around her brighten as she strides towards the front door. The little blue textbook is absent from her grasp, already returned to her teacher.

She throws the door open, her silver eyes sparkling with delight. "Hi, Ethan!"

"You're awfully happy," Ethan comments as she approaches the counter. He flips up the little movable section to let her through.

"My presentation went better than I expected," she replies.

Ethan can't hold back a small smile anymore, and he lets it pull at his mouth. "So you listened to my pep talk the other evening, then."

She nods back at him. "After everything that happened, I kind of needed it. Thank you. I should thank Kim-Star as well…" Her cheerful mood falters ever so slightly. "Where… Where is she? And Jake?"

"Upstairs," Ethan replies simply. "Jake's sick again."

"Oh…" Amber frowns with mild concern. "I should probably go check on him then…" She hurries off quickly, urgency now in her step. He stares after her as she disappears into the back room.

Stay right there, the voice chimes, *I'll be right back.*

And then, suddenly, Kimberly steps through the doorway, a spry Jake following close behind her. She smiles at Ethan, though it thins ever so slightly as she notes his blank stare back at her.

"Thank you, Ethan," Kimberly says, shaking him from his spell. "We'll take it from here."

Ethan blinks back at her. "No worries," he nods casually. He quickly takes his leave from the front of the shop and moves to the back room. Amber is standing next to the back counter, her expression now slightly troubled.

"Everything okay?" he can't help but ask, approaching her.

"Is Blaze coming back?" she inquires quietly, looking up with a dim gaze.

Ethan shakes his head. "No, he's not coming back."

"What about your plan?" she says.

He snorts back at her. "What plan?"

"Your-"

"I know what you're talking about," he cuts in quickly. He folds his arms and scowls down at the countertop quietly. He likes Blaze, he really does. He's been one of the few beings he's ever known that he can truly call a good friend. "I think I'm going to back out."

Amber blinks at him. "*What*? But... after all *that*..."

"I... had a change of heart," he replies. He doesn't want to see Blaze get hurt, which will certainly happen if they follow through on their plan. He doesn't think he'd be able to handle that kind of guilt.

"It's not that I don't want to get in trouble with the Council," he clarifies quickly. "It's that... I'm just worried for him. That... he's in way over his head. This was all his idea to begin with. I just... I enabled him. I shouldn't have."

He'll probably end up like the last wizard if he ever steps foot onto Korodon.

Hold him, the voice demands, older and smoother than it had been before. Ethan places his hands on the counter to stabilize himself. His eyes twitch, refusing to fully blink, as his entire body trembles, reliving the moment.

"Ethan?" Amber places a hand on his shoulder, and the trembling stops. He takes a moment to catch his breath, his chest constricting. "Are you okay?"

Her touch is light and warm, even through his cape and

robe. It's a sensation he's not felt in… a long time.

"I'm fine now," he breathes quietly. He reaches up and pats her hand with his own. "Thank you."

***

Blaze opens the door to his dorm and smiles when he sees Ethan.

"Hey there," he greets his friend. "Want to come in and talk?"

Ethan shakes his head reluctantly. He's been dreading this all cycle long, and now that the evening has come, he can't hold back on it anymore.

"I don't want to do it anymore," he states clearly, letting the sentence roll off his tongue.

Blaze frowns at him in confusion. "Do… *what*?"

"Leave at first light," Ethan replies. Alarm flashes across his friend's face, indicating that he knows what Ethan's talking about. "I… I can't anymore."

"I thought we were friends, Eth," Blaze says, anger beginning to manifest in his voice. "We spent *years* planning this! And you want to just throw it all away *now*?"

"It's too dangerous," Ethan snaps back firmly. "I don't want you to get hurt."

"I don't want *you* to get hurt, either," Blaze echoes irritably, "but you're not going to get very far with anything if you can't deal with a couple of scrapes and bruises along the way."

"I don't want you to *die*, Blaze!" Ethan hisses through his teeth. "I just don't want you to die."

Blaze grits his teeth and glowers accusingly back at Ethan. "Which was why we were going *together*, right?"

Ethan takes a deep breath. "If you want to know who tipped off the teachers, it was me." Another bout of panic flares in his friend's rage-filled eyes. "If you try and leave at first light, you'll be arrested."

"Ethan…" Blaze breathes in disbelief.

"I care about you, Blaze," Ethan adds calmly. "You're more important to me than I can possibly try and explain to you right now. And if anything happened to you… I'd never forgive myself."

Blaze just sneers back at him, "If you really *did* care about me that much then you'd not be backing out of our plan right now."

"It was never *our* plan to begin with," Ethan says. "It was *yours*. It has always been yours."

"Good night," Blaze states suddenly, then promptly slams his door closed in Ethan's face.

Do you even care about me? the young voice accuses. Ethan squeezes his eyes shut and focuses on his breathing to try and combat the paralysis trying to settle back into his limbs. He *does* care, to the point where he refuses to have his close friend leave by any means necessary.

He turns away from Blaze's door and strides down the hallways to his own dorm room. They stay at opposite ends of the same hallway, which had been convenient for them both in the past. Now it just makes his stomach churn nervously at the thought he may come knocking later in the evening to-

Ethan shakes his head to rid himself of the thought. Even if Blaze is upset with him, he'd never come and cause him harm. That's not Blaze. That's not his friend.

Quietly, he enters his dorm room and closes the door softly behind him, letting out a small sigh of relief to be within its safe walls.

He takes his hat off and tosses it onto his desk. Then his cape, which he lays on top of his bed. He stares at the fabric, tracing the large symbol with a delicate finger. It's a four-pointed star with an additional four rays of "light" emanating from it. The symbol for Light, stitched into the fabric by thin white thread.

With Blaze's plan no longer an option, he has one avenue left for justice. It's an avenue that's been long and tough, with little progress made to it in the last couple of years. But he must keep trying to push forward.

He must convince the Council to go to battle for the first time since the Great War.

Chapter 6

Blaze paces his room long after nightfall, unable to sleep. Ethan's words bother him greatly. The Ethan he talked to at his door wasn't the same Ethan he knew. Maybe he was right about Amber, and that she was working against them the entire time. Maybe she talked his friend down from the plan while they were at Kimberly's shop that cycle. Maybe she had been talking with him for a while now, and convinced him to tip off the teachers in the first place.

After all their planning, to give up so soon…

His fists tremble as he clenches them tighter. It *has* to all be Amber's doing, it *has* to be.

Now he's all alone, with nothing left to do except to either take action now or give up on the plan himself.

The Council refuses to act. Either they simply refuse to take the matter seriously or are turning a blind eye in hopes that it will simply go away. But *he* sees that the time for waiting is over. Action needs to be taken now, or else whatever is afflicting Korodon *will* spread, and it will spread quickly.

He lets out a frustrated sigh and sits down at his desk, which is covered in sheets of drawings and writings and a single empty pot of dirt. Staring down at the papers, he raises a hand

and points it at his pot. The earth shifts as a small vine sprouts, slowly stretching over to his fingers. As soon as he can reach it, he runs his fingers down the vine's length, feeling the soothing chill down his own back as he pets the little green worm.

Ethan was the one who was drawing a new map of Korodon, which he'll now need to do without. He has other drawings here that he can probably use instead, as the island hasn't changed much in the last couple of centuries.

Korodon is a relatively small island. One could theoretically walk from Ica, the capitol where the Archway is located, to the old royal castle in a single cycle. He'll probably need a couple of cycles to even get there in the first place now, since he'll be traveling alone. He expects many fights while he's there, at least. That means that he'd have to skip class. His first absence will surely raise the alarm immediately, especially since the teachers are aware of his plan.

I can always die there, too.

His hand pauses mid-air as the intrusive thought stabs at his mind. He *could* die and never return to Asandra. He could fail in his mission. He'd be alone, with no hope of rescue and no being to watch his back.

He shakes his head. He can't dwell on the thought of death for long. If he dies, he dies. At least he'd die trying to save Astria. At least he'd set an example. Maybe he'd inspire more to attempt to complete his mission. Maybe he'd get the Council to snap out of it and actually try to find a solution.

He lowers his hand from the vine, which quickly retreats back into its pot, and reaches instead for a small box that rests on top of a book and stares at it. It's red, and just small enough to fit in his palm. Two of the sides are rough red strips, severely scratched with white lines from years of usage. A small tray slides out to reveal a compartment within, which holds a single wooden stick with a red tip. The graphic on the box is faded, yet he can still make out part of a yellow semi-circle.

66

It's called a matchbox. He doesn't even know where he got it. The stick inside always magically replenishes after a time once it has been used. All he has to do is strike it on the side of the box, and it'll produce a small, temporary flame. It's also his favorite fidget.

He has to leave tonight if he intends to make it to Korodon uncontested by the authorities. Exhaustion weighs heavy on his body, but he stands and brushes it off as best he can. He can see about setting up a small camp on Korodon to get rest later. He just needs to get there first.

Matchbox in hand, he turns to look at his bed and nightstand. The small white candle burns bright, the flame flickering as it sways gently back and forth, as if waving to him. Inviting him over. The red sheets of his bed are enticing, so he stares at them as little as possible.

He stumbles over to his nightstand and sets the matchbox down in front of the candle. Leaning against the nightstand, he stares at the little flame a moment longer. His room is quiet and peaceful. The hallway outside his door is silent. It's just him and the candle…

He turns away from the flame for a mere moment to inspect his room once more, and the light suddenly goes out, plunging him into darkness.

Any form of exhaustion he had been feeling before is replaced instantly with alarm, his heart jumping in his chest. He didn't blow out the flame, and it *never* goes out on its own accord.

His hand shoots for the matchbox, fumbling with the tray with panic-filled fingers. He manages to slide out the tray and retrieves the single match from within. Holding the stick tightly between his fingers, he strikes it against one of the rough sides of the box. He can hear the red tip fizzle and flare as a new flame is born in the dark.

He can see the flame, but it doesn't illuminate his hand

nor the room. A lightless fire that he can see.

A lightless fire…

He blows out the little flame and drops the match on the floor. The flame did *nothing*.

He spins around to face the rest of his room, squinting to try and make out his desk and chair, or the door on his right, or the window on his left. Normally there's starlight that makes the night bright, but it's like the stars have suddenly been extinguished along with his candle light. He can't see *anything*, not even his own body.

His chest tightens in panic as he touches the surface of his bed for reassurance that it's still there. Like a switch, the world became dark. Yet he knows he didn't suddenly go blind. That much is for sure. Blindness doesn't work that way. Or, at least he *thinks* it doesn't…

He is left standing in the dark in silence, with only his breathing and thoughts to keep himself company. He doesn't know what's going on. He can't sense the little pot of dirt on his desk. Usually he can, but not this time. It's almost as if he had suddenly been transported from his room to a world of black.

He takes a few deep breaths, allowing the noise to fill his ears. He's still alive. He's still breathing, and his heart beats like a drum in his chest to not forget that it hasn't stopped yet.

"Hello?" he calls into the dark. His voice sounds muffled, like he just yelled into his pillow. Silence roars back into his ears, an unnerving static.

Though not long after his call, a violet glow appears. No, two glows, right in front of him, hovering just slightly above his eye level. A lump jumps into his throat. They're not just violet glows. They're violet *eyes*.

His bed suddenly falls away. The hand he had on its surface grasps at the air, trying desperately to find an anchor to reality. His heart starts to pound in his ears. His body shakes with adrenaline.

How different it feels, to be thrust into a dangerous situation rather than envisioning one. He thought he'd be more confident, yet here he feels anything but that. He's alone in the dark with the violet eyes in his dorm room. He doesn't even know if he's still in his own room at this point.

And every part of his body screams at him to move. To do *something*! Yet he remains rooted in place. Frozen. He doesn't know *what* to do.

The eyes move, growing in size as whatever it is approaches him its features become clear the closer it gets, melting from the void. It's a knight in black armor, blacker than the darkness around them, who radiates a powerful aura of sickening dread. Its eyes are hidden in shadow, behind a helmet that covers its face entirely. He can't even see a nose or a mouth underneath it. Just the eyes. A stream of smoke waves from the top of its helmet. A sort of tassel, probably. The same mist rises from its armored shoulders. A long cape billows behind it.

The being is about a head and a half taller than Blaze is. Its eyes are trained on Blaze, piercing his soul. If he could shake, he would. But he can't. The eyes have him paralyzed. It almost feels like he can't move unless he is told to.

The two stare at each other in silence.

Blaze's heart skips a beat as the mysterious being reaches out to him, its fingers outstretched. He wants to close his eyes but he doesn't. More like he can't. He hasn't even blinked once since laying eyes upon the knight. His body refuses to obey him.

The fingers touch his forehead. The tips are deathly cold, sending shiver after shiver down his spine. Yet they don't rest on his skin, but instead it feels like they go deeper, to the point where they touch something *underneath* his skin. He can feel it, too. Some sort of solid surface just underneath. Warmth blooms from the touch, though his skin still feels cold at the same time.

The difference allows him to feel whatever the knight is

69

touching. He can feel a head, a face, and hair. As the sensation travels farther, a neck, a chest and arms and legs. An entire secondary form, just under his own skin.

His own limbs grow heavy. His nerves tingle, falling asleep before fading away into thin air altogether. Yet he can still feel the second form within him, pulsating with magic. It doesn't move in the slightest. It's hard to tell exactly *what* it is. All he knows is that it's there and he can't move.

With its other hand, the knight plunges it into Blaze's chest, causing a secondary ripple of feeling across his skin. The last he feels of his normal body. With a sharp yank, he feels the second form rip from his own, the essence being drawn from him. It creates a second body, a second *him*, colored in shades of black and gray. He watches the knight grab the second version of him with both hands, and the two melt back into the darkness.

Blaze is then returned to his room, darkness lifting, the candle still burning with its soft glow, illuminating his bed to his left and his desk across the room from him

His mind grows sluggish, his consciousness floating in the air. He can't feel his body anymore, yet he still stands. He doesn't even know if he still *has* a body at this point.

The room shifts. Slightly, at first, before being completely turned around. There is no pain when he eventually comes to a stop, his vision now sideways and parallel with the floor. And he lays on the floor of his dorm room, conscious of his surroundings yet unable to do or feel anything. Whatever the black knight did to him, it stole his essence. It's the only way he can really describe it. The essence that made him able to walk and talk and *live*.

The last thing he sees is Ethan bursting into his dorm room and crouching down in front of him. After a silent moment, he runs his hand over his eyes, and Blaze sees no more.

Chapter 7

Kimberly looks up from her aimless staring at the counter and smiles as yet another customer enters the shop. It's a young Feni boy in a Healer outfit, his face full of concern. Something tells her that he isn't here to buy an ice cream.

"Hello there," she greets him. "Can I get you anything?"

The boy shakes his head. "I'm not buying, thank you. Azna sent me to collect you and Jake."

"What for?" Kimberly inquires.

"I don't know," the boy admits. "Azna seemed to be very anxious, but he didn't tell me anything. Ethan is also waiting for you."

Ethan? What's Ethan doing at the infirmary so early in the cycle?

"Jake!" Kimberly calls. "Come out here!"

Jake appears in seconds, rushing through the back room doorway with a look of confusion and mild concern. "What's up, boss?"

"We're going to the infirmary," Kimberly tells him.

"Wait, why?" Jake asks, frowning even deeper.

"We're going to find out."

"You don't *know*?"

"Jake, from the sound of it, it's serious," Kimberly replies. "Ethan is there already. I don't know if Blaze is involved or not, but…"

Jake is silent, yet nods all the same. He closes the ice cream container lids, to prevent them from melting. Kimberly flips the front sign to "Closed".

They follow the Healer from the shop to the infirmary, tension growing in the air. No being speaks a word as they travel briskly. Kimberly can only speculate as to what has happened, and why her and Jake's presences were personally requested. And Ethan…

The Healer helps them navigate down the long winding hallways of the infirmary. The place is quiet. Not many Healers roam the halls.

Eventually, the Healer waves to a single door. "In here."

"Thank you," Kimberly says. The Feni smiles slightly, then hurries away.

Kimberly looks at Jake. Jake stares back at her. They're both worried, that much Kimberly understands. She doesn't want to go into the room. She doesn't exactly want to know what's on the other side.

"We shouldn't keep them waiting," Jake speaks.

"Sure…" Kimberly nods. She turns and opens the door quickly before she gives herself the chance to turn away and walk right back to the store.

The room is relatively bare, with a single bed and a few chairs. Ethan and Azna are already there, standing in front of the bed, obscuring most of it from view. They appear to have been locked in an intense discussion, though all conversation stops once Kimberly and Jake step in.

"You're here," Ethan comments, surprise in his voice. He probably wasn't expecting them so soon.

"We'll finish this discussion later, then," Azna hums. He turns his attention to the newcomers. "No doubt you two want to know why you're here."

"Please," Kimberly nods.

Azna and Ethan look at one another for a moment, then step aside, revealing the bed. Jake inhales sharply at the sigh. Kimberly places a fist on her chest.

Blaze lays in the bed, under the sheets. His eyes are closed, his skin deathly white. His favorite goggles rest on a small tray next to him.

In a daze, Kimberly approaches the bed and touches his cheek. His skin is cold as ice. No breath seems to escape his lips. He doesn't move at all.

"Is he…" Kimberly chokes, not wanting to finish her sentence. It's not been *that* long since she last saw him, even if they parted ways on such a sour note. Are they only here to watch Ethan perform the Fading ritual?

"No, he's not dead," Ethan says. Jake exhales thankfully. Relief washes over Kimberly as well. If Ethan says he's not dead, then he's not dead.

"Then why does he look… dead?" Kimberly asks.

"I…" Ethan pauses. He glances at Azna momentarily, as if looking to him for permission to speak. Azna nods back at him. He clears his throat and continues, "I found him this way in his dorm room at first light, and brought him straight here. Not even Azna knew what was wrong with him at first. But…" he takes a shaky breath, "his Shadow is missing."

"His… *what*?"

"It's the theory of Life," Azna replies. "To put simply, there are two aspects to all living beings: A Shadow and a spirit. The Shadow is in command of physical appearance and animation, as well as magical power. The spirit breathes life into the Shadow in the form of one's personality."

"The Shadow can be ripped from one's own body," Ethan adds, "but not just any wizard can do it. Only those who practice Shadow magic are capable of such a feat."

73

Kimberly folds her arms. "And you know this because...?"

"When any magical being decides to pass on, it destroys the Shadow and releases the spirit," Ethan replies, "so we have to study a bit of Shadow in order to understand the mechanics of death, and Death magic as a whole."

"So there's a Shadow wizard running around then?" Jake asks slowly.

"Theoretically, yes," Azna nods. "It's still hard to say since Shadow magic isn't taught by any being anywhere in Astria."

"So why are we here?" Kimberly inquires.

"To inform you of the situation," Azna tells her, "as well as to give you both some advice."

Ethan clears his throat. "Blaze is powerful. We all know that. Whoever did this probably wanted his Shadow for their own gain. I know you two already live together. So just... watch each other's backs."

"You think that whoever did this is going to strike again?" Jake gasps.

"I'm quite sure of it," Ethan nods. "Kimberly is the next likeliest target."

A pit of dread sinks in Kimberly's stomach at the news. Jake puts a reassuring hand on her shoulder.

"We'll be careful," he assures the head Healer and their friend.

"And one more thing," Ethan says. "Please don't tell Amber about this."

"Why?" Kimberly mutters.

"The less she knows, the better," Ethan replies simply.

***

"Hi, Kim!" Amber says cheerily as she arrives for work. Kimberly looks up from the counter again and musters a grin.

"How was class?" Kimberly asks as she lets her behind

the counter.

"Boring," Amber sighs. "Some being had to give their presentation this cycle because they got sick. Then we just read from the textbook."

"Lucky," Kimberly chuckles. "There's always work to do every cycle for me."

"Aw," Amber moans with a light smile, then gestures to the back room doorway. "Well, I'm gonna go back now if you need me."

"Amber…"

Amber pauses, one hand on the doorway. She looks at Kimberly, her eyes wide and full of curiosity.

Kimberly takes a breath. She doesn't know what to say. Or, rather, she *can't* say what she wants to say. She wants to tell Amber about Blaze. She wants to express her worries and fears and hopes and possible plans for protection with her. She wants some outside comfort, to know that everything will be alright.

Knowing that there's some being out there, stealing these Shadows for their own gain, and that she's the next potential target… it doesn't sit well in her mind. It makes her paranoid, constantly watched in secret when she knows she *probably* isn't. Where did Blaze's Shadow go? Will she end up there, too?

"Nothing," she says at last. "Sorry."

Amber nods slowly and disappears.

Kimberly turns to the counter again and starts drawing circles on its surface with her finger. She leaves behind a frosty line wherever her finger strays. The cycle has been slow so far. Thank the stars for her sake.

Jake is upstairs. Ethan stayed behind at the infirmary to talk with Azna further. Blaze is… well, she saw Blaze's current condition. And Kimberly is all alone at the counter, waiting for the next customer to appear.

She wants to talk with Amber. She *really* wants to.

"Hey, Kim?" Amber chimes, poking her head out of the

doorway. Kimberly straightens and turns to look at her. Her expression is one of casual concern. "Are you sure you're okay?"

Kimberly tries to fake another smile. "Yeah. Why?"

"You seem distracted," Amber replies simply.

"Ah…" escapes Kimberly's mouth, then she shakes her head. "Amber, I don't really want to talk about it."

"Okay," she hums. "But if you want to later, I'll listen."

***

"Bye!" Amber waves. The three of them wave back at her as she exits the store, the little chime ringing merrily behind her. In silence, they watch her walk out of sight down the emptying street.

Ethan lets out a heavy sigh and turns to Kimberly. "Are you sure you'll be okay?" he asks.

"I think so," Kimberly replies. Yet her stomach is aflutter with worry and doubt. She looks to Jake for comfort, who stares back at her with a concerned expression, although he tries to force a smile to reassure her.

"Let's try and have a normal night, 'kay boss?" he proposes.

"Sure," Kimberly nods back.

"Well, then," Ethan says, flipping up the counter to let himself out, "I'm going back to my dorm. Stay safe. I'll try and come early next cycle so we can discuss further steps."

"Have a good evening, Ethan," Jake calls after him. Ethan pauses at the front door for a spell, one hand on the handle. He half-turns to look back at the pair and gives them each a small smile. Then he opens the door and, with the flutter of his cape, he's gone too.

Kimberly leans forward on the counter and hangs her head. It's just the two of them now.

Jake places a hand on her shoulder. "Everything will be

alright, Kim-Star."

Kimberly musters a sad grin and replies, "That's what I like to believe." She shifts and straightens, smoothing out her skirt to distract herself. "Well, I might as well go get dinner ready."

"I can cook tonight, if you want," Jake offers.

"Oh. Thank you, Jake."

"Just relax on the sofa and read a book or something," he says, giving her a pat on her shoulder. He turns away and disappears into the back room, saying over his shoulder, "It's been a long cycle. You deserve some downtime."

Kimberly rolls her eyes and follows after him. She makes her way up the stairs, listening to her loud footsteps underneath stomp against the wood. How many times has she walked up and down these stairs? How many more times will she get to do so?

She drifts into the living room and sits down on the sofa with a sigh, relaxing into the cushions. The bulb above her flickers weakly, indicating the shift change at the electric plant as the night shift clocks in. Soon, the power will stabilize again.

The space in front of the low table is empty, with just a small bright orange rug to decorate the dark wooden floor. The wall is bare, however. She's always wanted to hang some art there, so there'd be something to look at. But, for now, her magic will suffice for entertainment.

She waves a hand in the direction of the wall, flakes of snow starting to swirl around her fingers up to her wrist. A flurry of small white dots appear, swirling in the center of the orange rug. They spin in a column, quickly condensing as she slowly curls her fingers inward, bringing the flakes together. She closes her hand quickly and points with her index finger, making a small circular motion in the air. The snow follows her gesture, the column becoming a large, lumpy ball. She drops the finger, letting it hang limp, and the snow finally settles.

77

She does this again two more times, making each ball smaller than the last and stacking them. Kind of like scooping ice cream, just making each portion a little different. In the end, she has three balls of snow stacked atop one another, largest on the bottom and smallest on the top. She lowers her hand and touches the sofa, just under the cushion she is sitting on. She feels the cold burst of ice spread from her fingertips, spreading across the bottom of the sofa. She wills the ice forward, and watches a thin line streak across the floor, under the table, and around the stacked snow. Little smooth ice buttons poke through the first two balls, running straight upwards, cutting them in half. Two long sticks of ice grow out of the sides of the second snowball, shining in the light of the room. The last ball has ice buttons that form a face, two eyes and a wide smile.

Kimberly smiles proudly as she stares at her handiwork. The construct sparkles as she shifts on the sofa to lay down on her back. Its blank stare continues on as she looks up at the ceiling, resting her hands on her stomach. She props her head up on the armrest. The angle is uncomfortable, to say the least, but she can still relax.

"Mr. Snow Man is watching over me," Kimberly calls. There comes a distant laugh in response.

"Am I still obsolete?" Jake asks.

"Yes," Kimberly replies with a smile. "Mr. Snow Man does a better job at protecting me than you do."

"I'm hurt," Jake chuckles. His voice is closer now. From the sound of it, he came out of the kitchen and into the dining room. Something rattles loudly, followed by mute thumps. He's probably setting the table.

"Hey, he caught me when I fell down the stairs," Kimberly says. "You just stood there and laughed."

"Yeah, well, I'm protecting your appetite right now," Jake replies. "Dinner is almost ready."

"That was quick."

"There was some fruit that was starting to go bad, so I fried them up."

"What about meat?"

"We can skip on the meat for *one* evening."

Kimberly rolls her eyes at the ceiling. With a grunt, she turns over and falls gracefully off the sofa and onto the floor. Mr. Snow Man stares blankly at her with his wide ice-button smile.

"Thanks," she mutters under her breath as she stands. She brushes her skirt and strides gracefully into the dining room with a half-smile. Jake stands next to her chair with a proud grin.

He shifts as she nears, grabbing the chair back with both hands and sliding it out from under the table. Kimberly lets out an amused huff. She stands in the space between the chair and the table, brushes her skirt again, and moves to sit down. Jake slides the chair forward underneath her, with a gentle shove to fully push her up to the table.

"Thank you," she says as he walks around the table to take his own seat.

"Just relax and eat," he says, gesturing to the steaming fruit slices between them. Kimberly takes her fork and stabs at one slice, plopping it onto her own plate. Though as she looks up to take another, she sees Jake's face contort into a frown.

"Are you alright?" she asks.

Jake looks back at her, his gaze snapping back to reality. He lets out a sigh, not bothering to hide his concern.

"I don't want you to be concerned with…" he takes a shaky breath, "what Ethan and Azna said this cycle."

Kimberly lowers her fork. "Jake, of *course* I'm worried about that. How could I not be?"

He scowls down at his plate, fork in hand. His grip is so strong that it turns his tan knuckles white. "I never thought there would be something that could take Blaze down so *easily*…" He looks back up again, something new glowing in his eyes. Angry flames that burn with determination. "I want you to be safe, Kim-

Star."

"I know, Jake," she hums. She leans forward and places a hand on one of his. Almost instantly, the fire in his eyes dulls to flickering embers, not entirely ready to be snuffed out just yet. "But there are some things that…" She trails off and licks her lips. She doesn't exactly want to finish her sentence. And yet, deep down inside of her, she knows she needs to say it. "There are some things that you can't take on yourself."

The two stare at each other in silence. Jake breathes heavily, his chest puffing in and out. For such a scrawny build, he is pretty strong for a third term Fire wizard, even with his aid. But he can get a little ahead of himself sometimes.

Kimberly lets her hand slide off his and settles back into her seat. She looks down at her plate, trying to ignore Jake's intense stare. "Let's just enjoy dinner."

It's eerie silence after that.

Chapter 8

Kimberly tugs at her nightgown, its light blue color on the verge of white. She lets out a sigh and looks at her bed. Her crystal ball glows a soft blue-purple on her nightstand, the same color as the mist that swirls lazily inside it.

"Hey," the word makes Kimberly spin around. Jake stands in her bedroom doorway, a small iceglass jar cupped in his hands. In it glows a little Firelight, just a small but somewhat bright spark of fire. His sword hangs loosely at his side through a little loop on his pants, glowing just as softly as the little Firelight. His face is only half-lit by the spark, hiding much of his expression from her.

"What's the plan?" he asks.

Kimberly inhales deeply. Her thoughts turn to Blaze, laying alone in the infirmary, surrounded by the best Healers in Asandra - no, in *Astria* - without a cure. He lays half dead in that bed. There's a chance that she'll be joining him.

She doesn't know where he had been attacked exactly, but it was most likely in his dorm room. Either there or the willow tree. Where else would he be than those places? Yet it only means that nowhere is really safe.

"What do you think?" she asks in return.

"We should probably stay together," Jake replies almost instantly.

Kimberly just smiles softly back at him. "Of course you'd say that."

Jake shifts on his feet uncomfortably. "What do you propose?"

"You can keep watch in the hall."

Again, her boyfriend shifts uncomfortably, but this time he remains silent. He turns away from her and, with one hand, pushes her door closed.

"Good night," he finally calls from the other side. She hears him tromp off down the hallway, possibly to go get a chair.

Kimberly drops her smile and turns back to her bed, promptly jumping in her skin as she is greeted by an unexpected sight.

A black knight. It's the only way she can describe the figure. It stands perfectly still, two violet eyes shining from under its helmet. A blast of ice cold air rushes from the figure as soon as she lays eyes on the knight, and her body tenses. She sucks in a breath and holds it. She doesn't know why.

The figure slowly approaches her without a word. Its footsteps make no sound, as if it were made of nothing but air. Kimberly hears her heart rapidly thump in her chest, making her ear pound. She wants to call out to Jake or scream or do *anything* of warning to any being nearby. And yet her lips refuse to part. Her throat closes up just at the thought of making noise.

The knight stops just one step away from her and looks down at her. As if it were reveling in her frozen distress.

You will do, it hisses.

Kimberly's eyes widen. *T-That voice-!*

It reaches for her, and her vision goes black.

***

Jake sets down the chair he managed to wrestle up the stairs to one side of the hallway, just outside Kimberly's bedroom. The door is still closed, the room beyond dark and silent. Maybe Kimberly has already gone to bed.

His stomach churns as he walks back down to get his Firelight jar. This probably isn't a good idea, just having him wait outside her bedroom. He can't protect her from the hallway. Yet he understands if she's uncomfortable with his presence still. He could have slept on the floor. Just so that nothing happened on his watch.

He scoops up the little jar from the sofa and stares into it. He feels his sword begin to heat against his hip, and a small spark of Firelight fills the center of the sealed space. With that, he heads back to the stairs.

One at a time, steps creaking under his weight, he returns to the third floor of the building. It's silent. *Too* silent. It makes his skin crawl anxiously.

He gets to his chair and stands in front of Kimberly's bedroom door. He stares at it long and hard, contemplating, the jar in his hands growing warm.

He should check on her. Just once, before he inevitably passes out himself.

He steps forward and puts a hand on the doorknob. The other balances the jar. Slowly, quietly, he turns the knob and pulls the door open. If she's sleeping, he rather not wake her. If she isn't, he's going to get an earful.

He's fully prepared for either of those outcomes. But not for the one he witnesses.

The Firelight casts the room in both heavy shadows and soft orange light, allowing him to just barely see most of the interior.

The light dances across an outstretched arm, fingers half-curled, half-opened. Body twisted on the floor, bent in a sort of crescent. Legs splayed to the left.

83

The light shines off Kimberly's eyes. They stare at him, large and lifeless. Her mouth is partially parted. Her hair is spread wildly around her.

Jake inhales, frozen to the spot. It seems almost surreal, like she wasn't actually there on the floor before him.

In a daze, he steps forward, boots stomping heavy across the floor. The jar in his hands burns his palms, yet he ignores it.

He sets the jar down next to her outstretched hand and reaches for her face. The light makes her skin look as warm and lively as ever, and yet his fingers brush up against cold skin. Even colder than she normally is, for an Ice wizard.

She's real. It... It's real.

***

Ethan was already up in a sweat by the time one of Azna's Healers knocked on his dorm's door. He didn't even bother to dress properly. He just grabbed his cape and left.

He hurries down the dark, empty streets in the middle of the night, cape fluttering behind him as he follows the Healer through the dark shadows of Asandra. His head feels cold because of the absence of his hat. A mild discomfort that will soon be forgotten, he knows.

He's dressed in only his long gray pants, a plain shirt, and his gauntlets. He even forgot his shoes until the last moment, yet he didn't turn around to get them. The pathway stones are cold and rough beneath his feet. He wonders how the infirmary floor will feel.

Clare stands from her seat behind the counter as soon as Ethan walks in, concern in her eyes.

"Don't you ever sleep?" he asks as a slight jest.

"I just got here myself," she replies. She gestures for him to follow, and together they make their way through the rather empty infirmary.

Healers are still around, yet few and far between. And of course there are Storm wizards underneath them, keeping the power running.

Clare finally opens a door and steps inside. Azna is there, and so is Jake. A new bed has been added.

Kimberly lays next to Blaze, her skin pale and her eyes closed. Her hair is messy, splayed every which way over the pillow.

Jake sits in a chair next to her, his head buried in the sheets beside her. Azna stands opposite the beds with arms folded, staring onward.

"He said he took his eyes off her for a spell and found her on the floor," the head Healer says without looking at Ethan.

Ethan remains silent, staring. The strike was indeed quick. But even if Jake had been present, nothing would have changed.

"You can leave us, Clare," Azna instructs. The receptionist nods wordlessly and promptly leaves the room.

"So he's been that way since arriving?" Ethan asks.

"Pretty much," Azna replies. Finally, he turns his head to the Death wizard. "Would you like to converse in my office?"

"Jake won't be going anywhere anytime soon."

The pair walk down the empty hallways in silence. Neither wants to speak for fear of being overheard. Even with the halls empty, there is no telling which room is in use or not.

Until, eventually, they reach Azna's office. Finally, alone.

The Healer takes a seat at his desk, leaving Ethan standing. He doesn't mind.

"Two of ASM's best wizards are now out of commission," Azna states. "No doubt beings will begin to take notice that something is going on. Blaze's absence is strange as it is, but Kimberly is a very public figure."

"Will the Council act, then?"

"We are left with little choice now," Azna leans forward in his chair, staring intently at Ethan now. "What do you think she's

85

trying to do?"

Ethan shifts his weight and lets out a hum, his mind already running through every strategic possibility he can think of. "She's backed herself into a corner, that's for sure. Since her takeover of Korodon, the other islands are on alert. And she can't exactly go after Mirage, either, without facing losses. The Feni aren't exactly magic experts like wizards, nor battle experts like the Serperas. No doubt she's trying to make a move."

"What sort of move?"

"I predict that she's after another island."

Azna leans back again, his gaze distant. "After all this time..."

"She finally realized that subtlety is no longer an option no doubt."

"And do you think you'll be able to stop another Tearing?"

Ethan stands rigid at the question.

"You've been having dreams, have you not?" Azna inquires.

"I have, but..." he licks his lips dryly, "I didn't have one until last cycle. When Blaze..." He trails off and shakes his head.

"How long was the gap?"

"Seven cycles."

Azna's expression grows as troubled as Ethan feels. Never has there been a gap in his dreams before.

"And how about your... paralysis?"

Ethan balls his hands into angry fists by his sides. "It's been getting worse."

Azna presses his fingertips together and leans back in his chair, his gaze distant as he thinks.

This is certainly a troubling situation. Ethan knows he can't help keep Jake safe by himself anymore, not in his current state. Nor is he willing to reveal everything to his last remaining friend so soon after the loss of Kimberly. Jake wouldn't take the information well, and would probably become reckless the

86

moment he hears the whole truth.

So you can look like… any being?

His chest constricts tightly as those dreadful words echo in his ears. His body grows icy cold as he trembles, trying to make himself move as his senses slowly dull. He can *see* his trembling, but can't feel it anymore. He almost expects to fall over at this rate.

A warm touch appears on his left shoulder, shattering his cold spell. He finds himself breathing heavily, staring down at his shivering pale hands.

Looking up ever so slightly finds Azna no longer sitting behind his desk.

"I hate to see you like this, Ethan," the old Feni speaks beside him.

"What's going to happen now?" he can only ask back.

"The Council is meeting in three cycles to discuss our next steps for reclaiming Korodon," Azna replies, his hand slipping from Ethan's shoulder. Ethan rubs the spot slowly, trying to keep in the heat. "I would like you to finally make an appearance."

Ethan looks up at the head Healer, his eyes wide with surprise. "Already?"

"She has made her move," Azna replies, gesturing in the general direction of his office door. "It's finally time to make ours."

Slowly, Ethan nods in agreement. Azna is not wrong, but he is *extremely* late. Though it's not his fault that the other Council members have been hesitant to take action due to the fact that not much harm has come out of Korodon since the travel ban. But with Blaze and Kimberly now out of commission, hopefully this will open their eyes to the true danger that they have let fester unchallenged for years now.

Ethan turns his eyes away from Azna. "I should go check on Jake."

Azna nods back. "Make sure he doesn't stay much

longer."

"Of course."

Ethan leaves the office room and briskly returns the way the two of them had come only moments prior.

His mind begins to race once more, theories swirling. Blaze and Kimberly were obvious targets. Blaze is not only a strong Life wizard, but was also looking to launch his own assault on Korodon. And Kimberly is a Blessed Ice wizard who has been somewhat close with Blaze for a few years now. *And* they're both wizards that Ethan can consider to be his friends as well. With that logic alone...

He shakes his head. He hates to think that Jake will most likely be next if the pattern continues like this. He has much to offer in way of both magical and practical strength, on top of being Ethan's last friend with his Shadow still in his body.

Ethan enters the room where his friends rest and stands near the doorway, silently taking in the room. Jake remains bent in his chair over Kimberly's bed, now holding one of her cold hands that lay on top of the sheets and staring at her face. Wordlessly, he walks up to the Fire wizard and stands next to him.

"It won't do you good sitting here all cycle," he says. Jake shifts in his chair, yet remains silent. Ethan puts a hand on his shoulder. "Come on, Jake. What about the shop?"

"She ran the shop," he mutters in response. "It won't be the same."

"I'll help."

"There will be questions..."

"You don't have to answer them if you don't want to."

Jake doesn't speak.

"Stop beating yourself up, Jake," Ethan adds. "There was nothing you could have done anyway."

"There's always something I could have done," Jake replies sadly. "I could have stayed with her." He lets out a casual yawn and continues to run his thumb over the back of her hand.

"Have you slept?" Ethan asks.

"No."

"You should rest."

"I don't know if I'll be able to at this point."

"It's better to try. I'll even walk you home. But you can't stay here."

"I know…" Jake mutters.

He stays at the bedside for a moment longer, then gives her a light kiss on her forehead and stands. His eyes are downcast. He doesn't even look up at Ethan, just trudges over to the door and pauses, waiting. Ethan approaches and pats his friend's shoulder with halfhearted encouragement. With that, they leave the room for yet another cycle.

Chapter 9

Amber stands in front of Kimberly's shop quietly, staring at the handwritten sign posted on the door.

Temporarily closed until further notice.

She doesn't understand why Kimberly would suddenly close up for stars-only-know-how-long. Beings pass by behind her, also eyeing the small sign with disappointment. Many were probably hoping for a nice cool treat, not a "Closed" sign.

"Well, there's something," comes a comment, making Amber jump. Ethan is standing next to her, also staring at the sign.

She lets out a thankful sigh and places a hand on her chest. "You're so quiet." She looks back at the dark shop. "Do you know what happened at all?"

"No," he replies flatly.

Amber laces her fingers together nervously. "I hope Kim is okay... And Jake."

Ethan nods. "Me too."

The two fall silent for a brief moment.

"What now?" Amber asks.

Ethan clears his throat and slowly turns to her. "I was wondering… if you'd like to help me."

"With… what?" Amber replies.

"Jake asked if he could have me get him some protection runes for the shop, and I've got my own business at the Enchanters Association as well, but I don't think I'd be able to carry everything by myself."

"Sure…" Amber nods reluctantly. She wants to help Kimberly and Jake out, even with the shop closed, but since it's Ethan asking her for help she can't help but feel backed into a corner.

The two make their way across the Straightway, Amber following Ethan closely. She's never been to the Enchanters Association before, which makes the prospect of finally seeing their building exciting to her.

And yet she can't ignore the fact that she's with Ethan of all beings. The same wizard who's been by her side since her first cycle interning at Kimberly's shop, who's been plotting to break the law and travel to Korodon. She doesn't know if he's trying to keep her close to make sure she doesn't say anything, or if he's simply trying now to be friendly with her after backing out of his friend's illegal plan.

And speaking of whom, she's not seen Blaze in quite a while now…

"Where's Blaze?" she asks quietly.

The moment she utters the name of his best friend, Ethan's shoulders appear to tense, rising ever so slightly.

"Busy," he replies.

"Has he… left?" she can't help but inquire.

"No," Ethan answers with a heavy sigh. "I… talked him out of it."

Amber can't help but mouth an "Oh" and look down at the ground beneath her. A wave of relief washes over her. At least the plot is mostly harmless to talk about now, though she still shouldn't go around discussing it in public, even if it never went through. It makes staying silent a lot easier for her now, since that pressure is no longer there.

They turn a corner and start down a narrow residential path. House doors line either side of them. Amber can just barely remain walking at Ethan's side without bumping into him.

"What do you need at the Association?" Amber inquires.

"I need some ink and see about getting my cape restitched," he replies. He grabs at the edge of his cape and pulls it around for Amber to see. A large white Light symbol is stitched right in the middle of the gray-purple fabric. "Some of the string is starting to wear away and the enchantment itself needs to be renewed."

"Why do you have... *that*, anyway?" Amber asks, referencing his enchanted cape. She didn't even notice the symbol until now. The string is so thin that it's hard to spot from far away or at a first glance. But now she's been told about it, the silver thread shines brightly against the long black fabric that hangs on his back.

"It's a rather old cape. I want to take good care of it," he replies simply, half-dodging the question.

"But why the symbol of Light specifically?"

Ethan is silent for a long time, gaze distant, contemplating his answer.

"For safety," he finally says.

Amber frowns back in confusion. She's never heard of the symbol of Light being used for safety. If anything, it's simply used to provide brief flashes of light. "But Asandra is about as safe as you can get though."

"You never know."

They emerge from the small street and into an open square, the center of which is occupied by a large red brick building that towers over the surrounding houses. Sparkles fill the air, magical in creation as they shine with all the colors in the universe. The air smells strangely sweet and inviting, beckoning her to come closer.

The Enchanters Association. It takes her breath away.

Many beings enter and exit the big front doors, some holding small square pieces of paper or pots of various sizes, their rims stained with ink of all colors. Some flaunt bright robes with glittering strings full of magical enchantments, or pieces of jewelry with many small runic engravings.

The two walk through the front doors and into the main room. It has a cavernous ceiling, covered in lavish paintings of many different types of runic, all overlapping and interlacing with one another. Protection runes are etched into the walls, glowing with magical power. Many gather around small tables, yet the most cluster in the center of the room, where a circular counter is located. A couple Enchanters are trying to facilitate the group of beings that hound them, and are somehow succeeding in keeping the hoard at bay.

Ethan pushes his way through the crowd, Amber following in his footsteps close behind, not wanting to become lost in the busy space.

"Belle!" Ethan calls, waving a hand above the crowd. But being stuck behind him currently, Amber can't see who he's waving to.

Once they are at the front of the crowd, up against the counter, Amber finally gets a view of Belle. A young woman with a vibrant orange robe adorned with silver runes, expertly sewn together to create a beautifully flowing design that mesmerizes her, and bright auburn hair. This must be Belle.

"Ethan!" she greets him with a wide grin, "How have you been?"

"Getting by for the most part," Ethan replies. He turns and gestures to Amber. "This is Amber. She's a coworker from Kim's place."

"Lovely to meet you," Belle says to Amber, extending a

93

hand. Amber takes it tentatively and shakes it. "My name is Belle, one of the senior Enchanters here at the Association."

"We're old friends," Ethan adds, turning back to Belle. "I need some wall ink, individual protection runes, and my cape restitched."

"Already?" Belle sighs, almost playfully. "I stitched it not that long ago-"

Ethan leans slightly over the counter, and Amber can just barely see his expression turn dark. "It's serious this time."

Belle's mood shifts ever so slightly at his words, her mouth pressing into a thin line.

"Right..." she nods once. Ethan reaches up to unclasp his cape from around his neck and rolls it up around his arm. He places the piece of fabric on the counter, which Belle slides down out of sight on the other side. With the cape out of the way, she smiles again. "And what kind of protection runes would you like?"

"Depends on how fast you can make them."

"How soon do you need them?"

"Now, preferably."

Belle lets out a thoughtful hum, the noise lost in the drone of the crowd around them.

"Well," she says, "the basic enchantment won't take long. However..." She reaches down for something under the counter and withdraws three squares of white paper, each painted with one rune. The same rune. "I have these three regular enchantments ready to go!"

Ethan looks at each of the papers carefully, shifting them around in front of them. Almost as if he were comparing them, to make sure they were indeed all the same.

"An advanced enchantment takes a quarter cycle," Belle continues, though it sounds more like a reminder. "How many do you need?"

"Six or seven," Ethan replies absently, still looking over

the tree papers already before him. Amber never thought he would be *this* interested in runes. Then again, she didn't really know much about him in the first place. He's very mysterious for sure.

She looks at Belle curiously, wondering how the two even *met*, let alone became friends.

"These three will do," Ethan finally says, looking up from the counter. "Basics should do the rest."

Belle nods. "Is this for you…?"

"No. Another friend."

"Ah."

"The wall ink is for me, though."

"I had a feeling," the Enchanter chuckles. Amber blinks. Why on Astria would *Ethan* need wall ink?

"How're your gauntlets doing?" Belle inquires as she shuffles around items unseen.

Ethan raises his arms to gently twist each of his gauntlets once. "They're still holding strong."

"If you keep doing that, they're bound to fall apart," Belle warns casually as she bends down to pick up Ethan's cape, which she gingerly cradles in her hands. "This should be done by the end of the second term classes this cycle. Please wait here while I get the other items that you've requested."

"Thank you, Belle," Ethan says with a smile.

Belle walks away from them, disappearing into the crowd. Ethan lets out a sigh and leans on the counter. Amber steps closer to him, trying to clear space for other beings behind her.

"Why do you need wall ink?" she asks him.

"A project," he replies without hesitation.

"And… about Belle."

Ethan turns his head ever so slightly and gives her a side eye. "What about her?"

Amber hesitates. Though he sounds relaxed, his posture is a little intimidating. So is the look he is giving her.

95

"How do you two know each other?"

Ethan is silent for a long time, his gaze flickering in and out of focus. Eventually, however, his eyes drop back to the countertop.

"She helped me with something important back in first term," he replies. "She's been my go-to for enchanting and stitching ever since." He doesn't elaborate further, which Amber doesn't bother to press. That's not her job.

The two stand there, waiting for Belle to return. Amber looks around the crowded room, at all the colors and races present.

It's rare to see a Shask on Asandra, or anywhere else in Astria aside from their home island of Kendon, and yet Amber is surprised to spot at least four or five of them in the bustling crowd. Their mostly-mechanized bodies are easy to spot, though some flesh and fur still remain in small patches. Due to their strange physical makeup, they don't often wear clothes, exposing all of their pistons, wires, frameworks, joints, and other nicknacks they have built into them. But also due to their unique appearance, the Shasks require special infrastructure to be in place for them to even function long-term, of which the other islands don't have. For what reason a Shask engineer would be at the Enchanters Association, it must be important to their work.

Nearby, Amber also manages to catch a glimpse of a Yafiir as they lift a beautiful silver hatchet etched with flowing runic symbols that seem to softly glow with magic. Their short stature makes them hard to find in large crowds, as a regular adult stands about as high as a wizard's shoulder. Covered head-to-toe in a thick layer of warm fur and sharp claws that extend beyond regular shoes and gloves, the Yafiir are known for their mighty strength despite their slender builds, making them the perfect loggers and miners to work in the harsh, snowy environment of Gardall.

"Here you go!" Belle says suddenly, causing Amber to

jump as she turns around. Belle places a pot on the counter, of which she was carrying with both hands. It's about as big as Amber's head, and its rim is stained with black ink. From between her fingers fall four more pieces of paper, each with the basic protection rune on one side. No wonder Ethan needed extra hands. That pot looks to be a hassle enough.

"Thank you," he says, reaching for the papers. "Amber, can you handle the pot?"

Amber eyes the pot cautiously. Can she? She's never handled a pot like this before. And what if she ends up dropping it? Will it shatter or break her toes? She's a far cry away from healing bones.

She's only vaguely aware of Ethan sprinkling some iron coins onto the counter in front of Belle. She quickly counts them up, yet slides four back to him.

"Cape is free," she says, her tone firmer than before. Ethan scoops up the coins with a weary grin and a nod.

"Let's go," he says, turning around to walk back through the thick crowd around them. Amber takes a deep breath and wraps her arms around the ink pot. Belle smiles at her, watching silently. Amber can't help but awkwardly smile back as she hefts the pot off the counter. It sways in her hands as the ink rocks back and forth with her movements. Could they not enchant the pot to make it lighter?

"Bye," she breathes, unsure if Belle heard her, as she quickly hurries after Ethan as fast as possible. It takes all her willpower to remain firmly latched to the pot as beings bump into her left and right.

Finally, somehow, she reaches open air with the pot still in her grasp. And yet her arms are already starting to ache from the heavy load. One more breath, she forces her legs to walk after a quickly distancing Ethan ahead of her. It's strange seeing him without his cape, with only the flutter of his robe to indicate where he was, which wasn't much to go off of in the first place.

"Wait up!" Amber calls after him, shuffling as fast as she possibly can without wearing her arms out faster or causing the pot to slip.

And yet he doesn't slow down, nor does he even seem to acknowledge her cry in the first place. He just keeps walking briskly along with purpose. She rolls her eyes at the back of his head.

She makes it to the street which they originally came down and pauses at its entrance. She is just far enough away from the crowd to catch her breath in peace. She sets the heavy pot down onto the ground and looks up at the sky as she breathes. Catching up with Ethan now is almost impossible when comparing his pace to hers. And yet she has his ink pot. Surely he'll come looking for *that* later. She closes her eyes momentarily, letting her arms hang at her side. No need to rush…

***

One thought propels Ethan forward. The little slips of paper he clutches tightly in his hand are the reason. He needs to give these to Jake as soon as possible.

He pops out of the little residential street and takes a precious moment to look behind him. He can't see Amber anywhere close behind. He can't help but feel slightly bad for her through his mild relief. At least he can deal with Jake in private.

He starts walking again, his speed only rising with each footfall. He still needs that ink for himself.

Enchantments first.

He weaves in and out of the beings before him artfully, his steps light on the stone road. No being pays him much attention, however, and they continue to mill about on their own accord. He only stops when he reaches The Magic Cone.

The sign is still in the door, yet he can see Jake inside,

98

wiping off the front counter with a rag. His gaze, however, appears distant. He's clearly not giving the action much thought.

Ethan knocks on the door forcefully. Jake looks up, at first startled before relaxing once he sees that it's just Ethan at the door and not some crazy being trying to forcefully obtain a cone.

Jake walks over to the door - it's more like a reluctant trudge - and opens it wide for Ethan and waves him in. Once Ethan is inside, Jake shuts the door behind him and locks it.

"How are you doing?" Ethan asks. Jake shrugs silently and drifts back over to the counter, picking up the rag and beginning his mindless scrubbing once again. Now that he's closer, Ethan can see that Jake is only pretending to clean the counter. His thoughts and priorities are definitely in some other realm of existence.

Ethan walks up to the counter, saying, "I know it's probably hard for you to not have Kim-Star here."

"It is," Jake sighs.

Ethan licks his lips and slides the seven pieces of paper onto the counter in front of him. This causes Jake to perk up a bit.

"For you."

Jake reaches out to the papers and touches them lightly, not saying a word. He just stares in surprise, awe, and disbelief. He probably didn't expect such a thing from Ethan. Especially not now.

"It's to help protect the house in the future," Ethan explains. "It'll repel most invaders after dark, but if anything powerful manages to break through… you'll know. It'll warn you."

"Do you think I might be next?" Jake asks blankly.

Ethan shrugs. "At this rate, almost any wizard is up for grabs. But as for you, it's more about how you use your magic rather than your strength."

"My style?"

Ethan nods.

Jake summons his sword in a swirl of fire and stares at it, holding the blade over the enchantment papers on the counter before him. Ethan can't help but grow slightly nervous about Jake possibly lighting the little paper squares on fire.

Jake is one of the few wizards with an aid, and probably the only aid-assisted wizard with a sword rather than a wand or staff. Without his sword, he can't do much magic outside of basic beginner spells. But his sword and bladesmanship paired with his magic makes him quite a formidable foe.

These protection runes won't completely work, but will give him some leverage in a fight. But if and when Jake ever becomes a Shadow, he'll be incredibly dangerous if let loose at full power.

"I have to go now," Ethan says. He *does* wish he could stay with his friend to console him, yet it's too risky. "Put them up as soon as possible."

Jake nods. "Thanks, Eth."

Ethan tips his hat with a slight grin. Jake can't help but mirror his mouth.

***

"Ethan!" Amber's voice rings out as he begins to make his way away from The Magic Cone.

He's quick to pick her out from the crowd, thanks to her bright pink hair. She shuffles down the Straightway, ink pot cradled in her hands. Her petite figure sways back and forth, making him almost worried that the poor Healer is going to drop it. He paid good coin for that ink!

She stumbles to a halt in front of him, stooping into a low squat to put the pot safely on the ground between them. Her brow glistens with the sweat of hard work and honest effort.

He grins. He doesn't know why.

"I had… a feeling… you'd be… here…" she pants heavily.

She straightens once the pot is out of her grasp, running a hand through her hair. "Why didn't you… wait for me?"

"I wanted to drop off those enchantments as soon as possible," he replies, still smiling. He has to concentrate to keep himself from chuckling as he speaks.

With Amber catching her breath, Ethan picks up the ink pot and rests it on one of his shoulders, his arm bent up and around to grip the rim at the top. His other hand rests on the front of the pot to keep it steady and balanced. The pot isn't *that* heavy to him. Maybe Amber just doesn't carry a lot of heavy things.

Amber's eyes widen with surprise with how easily Ethan handles the pot before her.

"Thanks for the help," he says, starting off again. He needs to get this back to his dorm before his arm begins to hurt. "Have a good cycle."

He feels Amber's quiet gaze follow him down the street a fair way before he is swallowed up by the buildings around him, disappearing from her view.

Chapter 10

Jake smooths the last square of paper onto the wall and steps back to admire his handiwork. The paper sticks to the wall easily, the ink of the rune starting to transfer off of the little white square and onto the paint. The other papers are also stuck up around the building. He put the three regular enchantments in Kimberly's room - for the future, of course - the living room, right over the sofa, and on the wall behind the register in the shop downstairs. The other four he spread throughout the house, such as in the dining room, bathroom, and the last two in the stairwells.

He lets out a heavy sigh and shakes his head. Night is fast approaching. Ethan delivered these enchantments just in time. He just wishes he wasn't spending the night alone.

His thoughts turn to Kimberly. How could they not? She had seemed so… *unconcerned* last night. It's been bothering him. Did she just accept her fate? Is that why she appeared so resigned? Why she had him go downstairs to get a chair? Did she want to spare him from… *something*?

He turns away from the wall and makes his way towards the kitchen, stomach starting to ache. Might as well cook some food while he waits for the enchantments to set in.

He pulls out some fruit from the small cooler box they have. It's full of odds and ends, with little dividers to separate the different foods. Kimberly usually restocks the ice every seven cycles or so…

The fruit is kept in the far left corner, and next to it are some vegetables and below them is the meat pile. Leftovers reserve whatever space is left on the right.

He's running low on fruit.

He rolls little bright orange "balls" in his hand as he drifts over to where the bowls are kept. Orabo is probably his favorite fruit to eat. It's also the easiest to prepare, if one knows how to do it right.

He gets down a bowl and sets to work peeling off the outer skin of the little orabo fruits. They grow in small bunches and it's possible to fit a fair few in the palm of one's hand. The outer peel gives the fruit its name, since it looks like a glowing orange orb. The skin itself is easy to peel. Of course, it has to be. When an orabo starts to rot, the peel splits and falls off, leaving the inside to decay and release its seeds. The inside of the orabo is red, and the seeds are easy to spot, being pretty much as close to white as can be. They can be eaten, but he's tried a few before and they didn't taste too great.

He throws the peels away and retrieves some blueberries, two peaches, and a single Light Tear.

The teardrop-shaped Light Tear isn't exactly flavorful, but its juices are extremely sweet, albeit a little acidic, and used to make all sorts of treats. He likes to juice them and use them for cooking, as it makes everything taste a little more rich and sweeter, especially other fruits.

Summoning his sword quickly, he takes out a pan and lights a burner with his finger, then sets the blade aside and starts on juicing the Light Tear, slicing it in half and squeezing the sliced fruit as hard as he can into the warming pan.

The clear liquid hisses as it hits the warming blackish-gray

103

metal. He throws away what remains of the Tear and sets to work quickly rinsing and cutting up the peaches and orabos before tossing the wedges into the pan. He listens to the fruit sizzle and pop, the Tear juice beginning to bubble beneath them.

He takes a quick glance back at the cooler. He should probably have something else to eat. Kimberly would have told him-

He almost wants to smash something. *Kimberly isn't* here *right now!*

He turns back to the pan, grabbing a pair of tongs and turning each wedge over and over in the pan, making sure they're cooked all the way through on all sides.

Finally, he deems his dinner ready, and he takes the pan off the burner. He sets it aside, reaches for his sword once again, and wills the flame to put itself out. The flame complies.

He takes the pan and gets out a plate, then uses the tongs to take out the wedges and places them on the plate, and tops them with the blueberries. Some of the Tear juice pools along the surface of the plate, now a crisp golden brown color. And he takes this plate, a fork, and his sword to the dinner table and sits down with a heavy sigh.

He throws his sword onto the table top and starts to eat. The fruit is sweet and juicy with a little crunch to it, thanks to his expert cooking. He should have made more for later, probably. But with Kimberly gone, he didn't think to make extra.

He looks up from his meal momentarily and looks around. The house is quiet and still, aside from him and his eating. Very lonely.

***

After eating and cleaning up his meal, Jake wanders around and peels off the enchantment papers from the walls, where the blueish-black ink glows gently before fading into the wall itself, finally set into place. Hopefully these enchantments will do their job and protect him and the shop and house, and also wake him if an intruder ever appears. After all, such an alarm is standard to include in all general protection runes.

And then he sits on the sofa and stares at the opposite wall aimlessly. He doesn't exactly feel tired, at least not right now, yet he can still feel his eyes drooping in preparation for rest. He doesn't even know if he *can* sleep. Not after last night.

He taps the hilt of his sword, feeling his magic come and go. The brief moments of empowerment and moments of emptiness are clear and distinguishable from one another. He doesn't understand why he's like this. He doesn't want to *be* like this. What if he finds himself in a fight where he can't use his sword? He'd be completely defenseless. The last thing he wants at this point is to be…

Jake jumps to his feet in an instant, a jolt of energy surging through him. His heart pounds in his chest, and his eyes and limbs now suddenly ache. Did he just pass out?!

He grabs for his sword and lets it hang loosely at his side. He takes a quick glance at the protection rune above the sofa, which is glowing an alarming bright blue.

It woke him up. Something's wrong.

His grip tightens on his hilt as he slowly looks around the house, first eyeing the dining room. Nothing *seems* out of place. But he knows that something bad is present. It permeates the air, chilling him to his bones.

He turns to the hallway and pauses. Though the house is dark, he can't even see the hallway walls. The darkness isn't natural, clearly. He raises his sword protectively and waits to see if anything happens.

So he prepared you.

The statement echoes from the darkness, catching Jake off guard. Almost like a loud whisper, but the voice itself…

"*Ethan*?!" Jake breathes.

105

The darkness shifts, and two violet eyes appear. The stare sends chills down Jake's spine. A moment later, the figure the eyes belong to steps through the doorway. Some sort of black knight, radiating dark mist from its shoulders and helmet. A long, needle-like sword hangs from its right hand.

No, the knight replies, still sounding very much like his friend. It raises its sword and points it back at Jake. *He will be the last.*

Jake grips his own weapon hard, almost to the point where it turns his knuckles white. How could this being *not* be Ethan, yet sound like him at the same time? His magic turns his blood hot all the same. Whoever this is, he is going to reveal who they truly are, one way or another!

The knight moves first, springing forward with alarming speed. Jake just barely raises his sword in time to block the attack, the strike of metal-on-metal ringing loud throughout the room. He comes almost face-to-face with the violet eyes, which are narrow and intense, almost pulsing with an intimidating aura. With a grunt, Jake pushes the knight backwards, flames curling around his ruby blade. He extends his right arm outwards, palm up and pointed at the knight, and a blast of fire shoots forward. The knight side-steps the horizontal column with ease and rushes forward again. Jake blocks it again with his sword, then steps and turns to the left, angling his blade downwards and causing the knight's blade to slide unexpectedly, making the knight stumble off-balance. Jake continues his leftward spin, separating his blade from his opponents, bringing it swinging around his body and striking at the knight's backside. Fire flashes from his sword as it connects with the dark armor, and the knight lets out a hiss of what he assumes to be pain.

And then it disappears.

In a blink, the knight is gone. Almost like it never existed in the first place. Jake's sword drops, surprising him and making him stumble a step. He almost trips over his own feet because of his position - his left foot was outstretched behind his right and twisted at an awkward angle - but manages to catch himself. The darkness in the hallway still remains.

A cold spot grows on the back of his neck, and he turns. The knight is back, sword raised high and ready to strike. Jake manages to quickly step out of the way, slamming his right hand into the knight's side as he goes, flames erupting around his fingers. His flaming hand meets deathly cold... metal? Whatever the case, there is another flare of fire as the strike connects, and the knight hisses and disappears once again. Jake takes a step backwards and looks around the room quickly. A teleporting knight that sounds like Ethan. Shouldn't even be possible. Is this a dream? It has to be a dream!

He turns around and spots the knight again, though this time it looks like the knight just appeared. Jake takes the opportunity to roar and slash across the knight's front. The violet eyes widen in surprise, yet it doesn't disappear this time, which Jake was expecting to happen. Instead, it goes for a thrust of its own.

Jake doesn't have time to block, so instead he springs out of the way. The needle-like blade just barely misses him, instead slicing through the fabric of his shirt and grazing the left side of his torso with ease. Though a light graze, the cut erupts into searing pain. Jake grits his teeth and readies himself again, sword raised at the knight. The knight turns to face him, and he sees the spot where he struck, a deformed and misty line created by his blade. No blood, no skin, no torn armor. It's almost like the knight's body *is* its armor.

Quickly, he slaps his free hand on his cut to cauterize it, just as a precaution against bleeding. It burns for a moment before subsiding to a dull, albeit still somewhat painful, throb. The knight appears to stall for a moment as it stares at him.

Interesting, it hums aloud.

"Who *are* you?" Jake rasps.

A mere servant.

The knight rushes Jake again. Jake keeps to its left, just narrowly missing its swipe, and strikes back with his own blade ablaze. He just barely manages to clip the knight's side as he puts some distance between himself and the knight. Right hand out, fire column. It slams into the knight's left shoulder as it turns to face him. Its shoulder immediately turns into a formless mass of black mist. Is it just him, or does it appear that one of the knight's eyes twitches, almost as if it were irritated?

This needs to end.

Sword flaming, Jake slashes at the air in front of him, sending a wave of fire at the knight. As it readies itself to defend, Jake surges forward. The knight cuts down the fire strike with ease, then turns its attention to Jake.

Both hands grip his hilt tightly, ready to decapitate this mysterious teleporting knight. He's far too close for the knight to defend. If he strikes true, then this should end the scuffle. Even if he possibly kills Ethan, this can't go on any longer. Not in *his* house.

And then a sudden chill ripples across his body, a sharp yank in his gut, and he finds himself flying backwards. His eyes widen in surprise at the sudden force, lifting him off his feet and sending him through the air. The knight didn't even move. Didn't even *flinch*. It used some sort of magic, for sure. But what…?

The last thing he sees is the knight rushing forward once again, this time far faster than before, to the point where it's almost a blur. Before the knight could reach him, however, Jake is swallowed by darkness. He feels something icy cold wrap around his arms and legs, tearing his sword out of his hand with such force that it would have possibly pulled his fingers right off if he didn't let go of his own volition.

Something stabs at his chest, cold yet powerful, and a numbing chill runs through his body before losing consciousness.

108

Chapter 11

"Hey, Amber."

The statement causes Amber to look away from her cup of water. A group of three Healers approach her, not beings she knows. Maybe a second term and two third terms.

"What?" she asks hesitantly.

"You've not seen Kimberly or Jake recently, have you?" one of the Healers asks her.

Amber shakes her head sadly. This isn't the first time she's been asked, and she knows it won't be the last. She doesn't know how, exactly, but word somehow got out that she had started working at Kimberly's shop until… *recently*. She only came back to the infirmary because she needs some sort of pay. "No, sorry."

Another opens their mouth to speak, saying, "Not even…" they hesitate for a moment, fear igniting in their eyes, "*Blaze*?"

"No," Amber replies quietly, raising her cup to her lips to keep herself from talking further.

"Oh, alright. Thanks."

The small group walks away, whispering among themselves.

Amber blows a small, thankful breath of air from her nose

and takes another sip of water. She's heard rumors begin floating around during class. Blaze hadn't been attending classes since midterms. Some think he's skipping class. Others think he snuck out to Korodon. In fact, the Korodon theory has been pretty popular. Where else is a wizard supposed to go without being seen by another being for so long?

But Ethan told her that he convinced Blaze not to leave in the first place, and she hates to think that he lied to her about it. Maybe he left anyway. Or maybe he was caught and such information isn't yet public. Or something *else* might have happened to him…

She shakes her head as her thoughts begin to run wild. It's actually Kimberly and Jake she's more worried about, and who every being has been asking about. The Magic Cone being closed for one cycle caused a small stir, but for *two* cycles? *And*, apparently, Kimberly didn't show up for class last cycle. Amber hasn't even seen Jake, which makes her almost sick to her stomach with concern. He falls ill easily, after all, and she's pretty much the only Healer who can help him. What if he got unwell to the point where he can't call for help?

She bites her lip and takes yet another sip of water to try and wash away her nerves.

To top it all off, from what she's overheard, Ethan's been pretty quiet about everything when he's asked about their absences, which isn't helping some of the… *other* rumors going around. More obscure ones, but some believe them…

Murderer.

Kidnapper.

Ritualist.

But Amber knows that Kimberly and Jake aren't dead. She just has that feeling. And Ethan… Well, aside from almost going to Korodon illegally, he's never struck her as the type to commit *those* crimes against wizards he's close with.

Or maybe that's what he wants others to think…

110

She shakes her head defiantly. All he's ever been is nice around her!

Amber quickly finishes her drink and places the cup on a metal tray, where it will later go to the infirmary's kitchen to be cleaned. With that taken care of, she makes her way towards the doorway leading out of the break room. Her entire journey is followed by the curious eyes of those who are essentially her peers, creating uncomfortable cold spots on the back of her neck. She bows her head, wishing that she could just disappear. She was never any being special until now. She doesn't like all this attention.

She pushes the door open and stands in the hallway, listening to the door swing closed once again behind her. Healers bustle around, entering and exiting rooms, escorting beings, carrying trays or papers and quills, or just casually chatting to one another as they go on their breaks. Even so, during the busy midcycle, there are still some eyes that turn her way, and paces slow and whispers erupt. She just stands there, staring back at them hopelessly.

Maybe coming back to the infirmary was a bad idea.

She looks around for a spell, just to make sure there isn't any Healer she could probably offer her help to at the moment, and stops as something catches her attention. Or, rather, some *beings*.

She can't exactly believe her eyes. Azna, for one, out of his office and walking down the hall so... *casually*. Not brisk pace, no clipboard in hand, no troop of Healers at his beck and call for whatever he may need. And walking right next to him, the being he seems so intensely locked in discussion with, is *Ethan*!

The Spiritist is speaking, a frown on his face, although Amber can't hear what he might be saying over the din of constant conversation. Azna, too, seems slightly agitated, his brow creased and his mouth pressed into a firm line.

Ethan's gaze darts away from Azna for a moment, quite

possibly sensing her staring, and at once his mouth closes as his eyes widen in surprise. He probably wasn't expecting to see Amber at the infirmary.

Before he can say anything else, she gives him a hard glare and turns away, starting off down the hall at a brisk pace away from the two beings. The last thing she wants is some being starting a rumor about *them*.

She can hear it now:

"Hey, apparently Amber and Ethan were talking in the infirmary this cycle!"

"They're not dating, are they?"

"Maybe they're partners in crime!"

"Amber? She wouldn't- I mean, is she even capable*?"*

"Hey, you never-"

She squeezes her eyes shut and shakes her head to try and rid herself of the voices. Her eyes begin to sting of their own accord, tears beginning to well up. She forces them back down and lowers her head further.

Maybe she should just go back to her dorm. And hide. Forever.

A hand clamps down on her shoulder, yanking her to a halt. "Amber-"

Amber turns around forcefully, batting away Ethan's hand.

"Leave me alone!" she tells him, trying to keep herself from yelling. Her chest wells with emotion, constricting her heart. A lump forms at the base of her throat, a ball that threatens to surface as she continues to speak, "I don't want to be seen with you! *Ever*!"

"Amber, calm down-"

"Don't you know what will happen?" she asks him. Tears water her eyes. Some even manage to slip down her face, no matter how hard she tries to keep them all in. Slowly, step by step, she backs away from the Death wizard. "Rumors, Ethan, *rumors*! I'm not important so *go away*!"

112

Ethan takes a step forward, one hand half-reaching out to her. "Amber, you *need* to calm down. You're only causing a scene-"

"We were looking for you."

Amber turns her attention to Azna, who is now standing just behind Ethan. His expression is serious, not an ounce of remorse for Amber's state displayed in his body language at all. His tone, however, is calm and unconcerned, the air around him shimmering with small green sparkles.

The storm of emotion inside her slows as she stares at the head Healer and sniffs. "Y-You were?"

Azna simply nods and half turns to leave. He outstretches a hand in her direction, an invite to walk with him. "Come. Let us talk elsewhere."

Wordlessly, she nods, not really seeing any other way out of the encounter. If Azna wants to see her, he's going to see her.

She keeps her eyes off of Ethan as she passes him, and the three start off the same way Ethan and Azna had just come from. Though, unlike when she was all alone, no being stops and stares at them, nor whispers in their presence. It's almost like she doesn't exist to them anymore. Just another Healer doing their job.

The thought soothes her nerves ever so slightly.

She lets out a deep sigh and wipes her face dry. Much of her earlier anxiety leaves with her breath, though some still remains.

"What upset you?" Azna calmly asks beside her.

Amber pauses for a moment, wondering if her answer will sound a little stupid. Maybe to Azna it will sound stupid.

"Rumors," she admits without looking at the Feni. "I've been asked so many times about Kim-Star and Jake and even Blaze. And... And I've heard what some beings think of Ethan. I just... don't want to be associated with him."

"No doubt rumors would have started about you, one way

113

or another," Azna hums, "but I understand. Hearing dark rumors about yourself would not be pleasing."

Azna stops in front of a doorway and opens it. He enters first, ears drooping low so that they avoid scraping the frame. Amber takes a step forward before Ethan quickly cuts in front of her, his cape billowing behind him. Since he showed her the stitching last cycle, she can make out the symbol of Light as clear as the stars against the dark fabric.

Amber stands in the hallway a moment longer, staring at the doorway. She can see a single leg of what she presumes to be a bed on the other side, before Ethan steps back into view with a somewhat concerned expression.

"Come on," he urges.

Amber takes a deep breath and steps into the room herself. Though she doesn't make it far before she freezes for the second time that cycle.

Ethan quickly moves to close the door behind her as Amber stares at the three beds. Jake, Kimberly, and Blaze all lay there. Their skins are deathly pale. It doesn't even appear that they're breathing.

"No..." escapes her mouth. The sight is almost surreal. This... This *can't* be!

"They're not dead," Ethan says, walking past her to stand with Azna near the beds.

Tears spring to Amber's eyes again. "T-They've been here... t-the entire time?"

"Jake was brought in last night," Azna replies. "Otherwise, yes, they have." Amber can't help but start to hyperventilate. Azna finally gives her a sympathetic stare. "I imagine this is a lot for you to take in." Amber nods, not trusting herself to speak. If she did, her voice would probably come out as a wail.

Instead, she squeezes her eyes shut, her mind reeling. This couldn't be right. This *can't* be right! Kimberly and Jake were alive... two cycles ago. She went to work, she *saw*

114

Kimberly with her own two eyes! And Jake… she helped him run the front when Kimberly went to class. They passed the cones back and forth! S-She handled the toasted cones, the ones he-

This… This all has to be a joke. This isn't real. This wasn't actually happening. Right? *Right*?!

An arm wraps around her shoulders comfortingly. "If you need to cry…" Ethan mutters.

Amber pushes him away and turns her back to him, staring at the floor with her arms tightly folded across her chest. Again, she wipes her face dry and takes a moment to collect herself.

"Why?" she finally asks. She turns around to finally face Ethan and Azna, trying to ignore the beds present. Azna remains as stoic as ever. Ethan appears sorrowful, probably from seeing her in… whatever state she's currently in.

"Understand that we never wanted it to come down to this," Azna says, gesturing to the beds. Amber continues to stare at the Healer, however. "Though if we remained silent, we may very well have been putting you in more danger than if we revealed all of this to you."

"…Really?"

Azna nods slowly.

"What… happened to them?" she asks, this time looking at Ethan.

Ethan casts a long glance at the beds as he replies, "They have been… hollowed out, in a sense. Their bodies can't function anymore. At least, not for the time being."

"How?"

"Dark magic."

Amber licks her lips nervously. "So… I can end up like them, then?" She steals a glance at the beds, her eyes landing on Kimberly for a moment. A strong sadness washes over her, and she quickly looks away again.

"There is a chance," Azna replies.

115

Ethan nods along. "At first, we thought that Blaze was targeted because he was powerful. Then because of their social status when we found Kim. But, in both assumptions, Jake doesn't exactly fit."

"The only thread we have right now that ties these three together is that they all know Ethan," Azna continues calmly. "So although we have no idea *why* these three have been targeted, we can still establish a pattern. You're the only other being that has spent significant time with Ethan recently, so it means that you may be the next target."

Amber's stomach drops at the news, and she can feel her blood run cold. Her being next to get "hollowed out" like Kimberly and Jake?

"You shouldn't be too worried. Arrangements have been made for you to stay the night with me," Ethan says simply, his hands fiddling with his gauntlets.

Amber simply scowls back at him. "Why would I want to spend the night with *you*?"

"It'll be safer for you this way," he replies, "believe me. It's only for tonight, until we can find some other way to keep you relatively safe." He reaches into one of his robe pockets and withdraws a small piece of folded paper. He holds it out to Amber expectantly. "This is my dorm number. You should find it easily." Amber takes it without a word and slips it into her own pocket.

"I'm sorry this is how you had to find out," he adds, though he makes no move towards her like last time. "Let's hope for a quiet night, yeah? And… maybe I'll tell you more."

"Can I go now?" Amber simply asks, looking to Azna for direction. The Feni stares back at her for a silent moment, seemingly lost in thought. Then he nods once. That's all she needs.

Ethan musters a slightly wider grin, as if trying to act like everything was suddenly alright. "See you later."

"Sure," Amber mutters quietly. Frankly, she doesn't know

if she *wants* to see him later.

Chapter 12

A loud knock on his door sounds just as he finishes drawing a rune on his wall, the fifth one he's done so far. Ethan jumps off his chair, throws the ink brush he had been using into the ink pot by his desk, and rolls down his sleeves as he approaches the door. He takes a quick glance over at his wardrobe as he goes, checking on his hanging cape and hat. Still there.

He opens the door wide and musters a smile, already knowing who it is. Amber stands on the other side of the door holding her green Life textbook in her hands.

"Come on in," Ethan says, motioning for her to enter. Amber's mouth twitches, briefly flickering to a grin of her own before falling away once again. Her half-dead expression lights up with shock and awe when she sees the state of his dorm, however.

Ethan looks up with her, grinning proudly this time at his handiwork. The walls of his dorm are covered from floor to ceiling with all sorts of runes of different sizes and complexity, painted entirely in black ink. His bed sheets are stitched with protective enchantments, creating a very lovely golden trim. Even his desk and chair are covered with runes, which he carved with a knife he had borrowed… a long time ago.

"I thought wall ink wasn't allowed…" Amber can only breathe.

"It's not," Ethan chuckles, "but I managed to obtain an exception. Well, *many* exceptions, but it's not like any other being will be using this dorm room aside from me."

Amber turns to him in an instant. "What do you mean?"

"Let's just say this place is like my home."

Amber frowns briefly at the answer, then looks around the room again as if searching for something she lost.

"Where will I sleep?" she asks.

"Here," Ethan snaps his fingers, and a mattress appears in a cloud of black smoke at the foot of his bed, already covered with sheets and everything. Azna prepared it for him, actually. He simply transported it from the infirmary to his own room. After all, he couldn't have possibly prepared it all by himself with the magic he currently has at his disposal. "I was waiting for you to arrive before bringing it out."

Amber throws her book down and sits on the mattress. She presses down with her hands to test the springiness, which causes her to bounce ever so slightly. After a moment, apparently satisfied, she lays down on her stomach and opens her textbook, legs kicking in the air behind her.

Ethan stares at her for a moment. She's not asked why he's got so many enchantments all over his dorm yet. Maybe she'll ask later. Or not ask at all. He doesn't exactly know. A place like his dorm isn't something one sees every cycle, of course. Then again, Amber's been through a lot already. Maybe she's simply accepted the craziness by now.

He lets out a sigh and turns to his own tasks at hand. He walks back over to where his chair is, still pushed up against the wall next to his dorm's window, and picks it up. He can finish painting later.

Careful not to hit Amber with it, he moves it back over to

his desk and sets it down again. Then he sits down and kicks his feet up onto his desk and leans backwards, lifting the front of the chair off the floor.

"Is this why you needed the wall ink?" Amber asks from the floor.

"Yeah. What about it?"

She turns a page, the paper fluttering gently with the motion. "Why?"

Ethan looks up at the inked walls. "I'm a cautious wizard."

Amber glances up from her book briefly to shoot him a questionable look. "Looks more like 'crazy wizard' to me."

"I guess I can see that, too."

"Does this mean you're also an Enchanter?"

Ethan purses his lips. "Well… not exactly. It's complicated."

"How so?"

He pauses for a moment, wondering what he should tell her. That he's been relying on them for the past three terms? That he can't use magic properly? That he's had plenty of time to learn enchanting anyway? He knows a handful of runes well, though they're not exactly useful in the Death Hall.

He decides to shake his head. "I rather not go into detail about that."

Amber lets out a low hum and flips another page. "And how well do you know Azna?"

"Well…"

His favorite color is turquoise. His favorite treat is vanilla cake with red wine. He doesn't have many interests that extend beyond the walls of the infirmary, where he's worked all his life. And he has admitted that he would sleep in the infirmary, too, if given the option. He had a younger sister, who Faded a long time ago, and his parents were well-respected farmers on Korodon in his younger years. He used to have a vast social group, but they all have since Faded as well. He almost feels

120

bad for Azna, but if the old Feni is content with his work then who is he to judge?

"...enough."

The two fall silent after that.

Ethan is grateful for a break in the questions. He doesn't want to give her many details, and with some questions that can be hard to avoid. There's a lot he can't tell her, or he'd only put her more at risk. Her fate has been sealed already, anyway...

Amber continues to study, her silver eyes appearing dim, drained of energy. Her pink hair hangs over her shoulders loosely, and her dark green robe covers her like a blanket. He never thought that a being such as her would end up in this mess. *His* mess.

Things have been happening too fast for him to fully process. Maybe that's the plan. To throw him off balance. At least he'll have his chance to appeal to the Council at first light. *Hopefully* these three Tearings are enough to spur them to take action, though it's sad that his friends had to be harmed like this for them to finally take his warnings seriously in the first place.

In a blink, Amber becomes a different girl, one with black hair, dressed in a dark gray shirt and skirt. The runes on the walls disappear, and the room is now lit with dim candlelight. This calm, quiet atmosphere allows his shoulders to sag and his mouth to curve into a soft smile.

What chapter are you on? he asks, though he doesn't actually say it aloud.

Seven, is the reply, the girl also not moving her mouth in the slightest. *How to use a spirit's magic.*

Sounds interesting, he replies with a light hum.

He stands from his chair and stretches, and the room devolves once again into his rune-painted room, Amber still reading quietly to herself.

"Would you like some space to change?" he asks.

Amber's mouth curves into a thin smile. "Tired already?"

121

"It's been a long cycle."

The first term nods. "It has." She closes her textbook and slides off her mattress to stand. "Sure, I guess."

"I'll wait in the hall then."

And Ethan does just that.

He looks up and down the hallway, watching for other students. There are a few, probably returning from work. They all look pretty tired, dragging their feet behind them as they make their way to their dorms. No being really pays Ethan much mind as he posts himself next to his door.

After a moment, the door opens a crack, and Amber asks, "Do you want a turn now?"

Ethan rolls his eyes. "I'll just sleep like this."

"You can come back in, then."

He steps inside his dorm again and finds Amber now dressed in star-covered pants and a dark green, long sleeved nightshirt. She gets comfortable on the mattress again and cracks open her textbook.

"What chapter are you on?" Ethan asks her.

"Five."

"Anything interesting?"

"Not really."

"What's it about?"

"Growing stuff. Grass and flowers, small things," she lets out a small sigh. "But I'm going to be a Healer. When will I ever need to grow plants?"

"It's good to know if that time ever comes," Ethan tells her.

"Well, I'll be bad at it," she huffs. She looks up from her book momentarily to stare at him. "What about you?"

"What?" he points to himself. "What am *I* going to be?"

"Yeah."

"A Medium, of course. What else *can* I be?"

Being a Medium is fun, actually. Grim, in a sense, but fun. The spirits always have interesting tales to tell. And, of course, it's nice to give families some sense of closure…

Distant whispers begin to rise in the back of his head, and he feels the stiffness beginning to grow in his limbs.

"Good night, Amber," he says stiffly.

"Night."

As he climbs into his own bed, he hears Amber snap her textbook shut and shift around on her mattress. Her head pops up for a moment as she goes to lay on her pillow. He settles under his sheets and stares at the ceiling above him. Though on the surface it looks blank, there is one last rune, only visible through its black aura. A single circle, complete with a small inner curve in what he can only say is the lower right section.

The symbol of Shadow.

Quietly, he exhales through his nose. What is he going to do with Amber? She can't stay in his room forever, and he *doubts* he'll be allowed to mark up her dorm with the same enchantments he's got. But Amber can't exactly be alone. So long as there are other beings around, *she* can't make any moves. And yet Amber probably can't handle such socializing in the first place.

Still staring, he feels the urge to reach for the symbol above him. If he were alone, maybe he would have.

He turns on his side and closes his eyes, gut twisting in knots. *I'm sorry…*

Chapter 13

Amber wakes early the next cycle, finding herself staring at Ethan's carved-up desk. The sight makes her frown. Right, she stayed with him last night.

She sits up and rubs her eyes, wiping away any crust that may have formed. The morning light from outside shines through the dorm window, filling it with a soft orange glow. Never has she woken so early feeling well rested. She can't help but wonder if there's an enchantment for getting a good night sleep somewhere on one of the walls.

Ethan shifts in his own bed, drawing her attention. Slowly, he rises as well, stretching his arms high in the air above him with a soft groan. Then his black eyes land on her.

"You're awake," he comments.

"So are you," she replies.

Ethan turns to the window momentarily, then scowls. A troubled scowl, she guesses.

"Is something wrong?" she asks.

"…No," he answers simply. He turns away from the window and musters a small smile. "How did you sleep?"

"Better than I do in my own bed," she huffs. She kicks off her covers and stands. The floor is cold under her bare feet, and yet her brilliant mind told her to put her shoes by the door last night. She lets out a reluctant sigh and carefully tip toes over to them.

"With any luck, you won't have to sleep here again," Ethan says behind her as he, too, slides out of bed. As she turns back to face him, she sees him idly fiddling with his gauntlets once again.

"That'd be nice," she nods.

"How soon is your class?"

"Probably soon enough. Can I change?"

"Sure. Sorry."

Ethan quietly slips out into the hallway, closing the door behind him.

Amber quickly works her magic. She takes a small step forward, one foot in front of the other, and dramatically extends her arms. In a puff of golden glitter, her robe appears. Then she places her hands on her chest, layering them one on top of the other, shifts her weight on her front foot, and swings her arms down and outwards. Her corset appears over her shirt, and her pants lose the star pattern and darken a couple shades. She feels her laurel brush against her ears as it, too, reappears on her head.

"I'm done!" she calls.

She hears Ethan step back into the room as she turns to pick up her textbook from under her pillow. She doesn't exactly know just *how* early she woke up. Usually it's a little brighter out, but then again she doesn't always pay attention. Normally, by the time she arrives at her Hall, class is just starting. Might as well go as soon as possible, just to check.

"Goodbye," she says, turning to leave.

"Where are you going?" Ethan asks in surprise.

"Class. Where else?"

She catches Ethan's eyes widening in surprise. Then he rushes over to his wardrobe, saying, "If you give me a moment, I

125

can walk with you-"

"I can walk myself, thanks," Amber cuts in. Yet she waits by the door, watching him grab his hat and cape. He takes a moment to briefly fiddle with his gauntlets before smoothing out his robe and giving her a weak grin.

"I rather you not be alone. Not just yet."

Amber just turns back to the door, placing a hand on the knob. "I'm just a first term Healer. I think I'll be fine."

The two of them step out into the hallway, Ethan closing the door behind them. Amber starts off without him, though she can hear his footsteps somewhere behind her.

"That's exactly why I don't want you by yourself," he says. "You can't defend yourself, can you?"

"I'm not a threat, am I?"

"Well, no-"

Amber stops mid-step and turns around to face him. Ethan pauses his own stride abruptly to prevent him from running into her.

"You know what happened to the others," she states quietly, holding back the lump forming in her throat. Ethan stares at her silently, his expression morphing into a mild sadness, eyes falling to the floor. That's all she needs.

"I don't want you anywhere near me."

That draws his attention very quickly back to her.

"What?" he breathes.

"You heard me. You..." she shakes her head and takes a step away from him. "I don't care if you're my only protection. I-" She stops herself as the lump jumps up, and she turns away from him again, hugging her textbook close to her chest. She swallows and manages to mutter, "Maybe this would all be better if we never met."

Aside from Kimberly and Jake, Ethan has been nice to her. But with everything going on now, with Kimberly and Jake in the infirmary all "hollowed out", this all proves that there's a lot

126

she doesn't know about him. Stuff he doesn't want to say. Stuff that's probably better left unsaid, for her own sake. And, who knows? Maybe, if they never met in the first place, none of this would have ever come to pass…

She starts walking again. This time, however, she doesn't hear Ethan following after her. Maybe it's for the best.

She reaches the end of the hallway, where the stairs are, and descends slowly. She doesn't check to see if Ethan is still standing where she left him. She just wants to get to class at this point. Yes, once class starts, she can try and put this all behind her. She can just go back to her dorm and study, call off her shift for the cycle. Azna would understand.

She doesn't stop until she is standing outside of the dorm building. The crisp air fills her lungs, and she pauses to take a breath and enjoy the morning. There's pretty much no being walking around. Not yet, anyway. First term class will be starting soon, after all.

As for class, she needs to see just *how* early she woke up.

She makes her way to the pathway that joins all the Halls, encircling the dorm rooms. Since she came out of the boy's side, she has to walk to essentially the other side of campus to get to her Hall.

She casts a quick glance at the Archway, one of two on the island of Asandra. It's as the name suggests, a big stone archway standing large and tall on a dias overlooking the Void, the empty space between islands that teems with magic. It's covered in carved-out white runes, meaning "space", "distance", and "travel", to name a few. It's how beings get from one island to the other. The second Archway is located in a more central location, used for public transportation. It's also the original Archway. The one here at ASM is but a replica, and only students can use it. How the school managed to accomplish *that* little feature Amber is unsure of, but it's nice having a private

127

Archway to and from campus. Simply convenient.

She passes the Death and Illusion Halls. The Death Hall sits on a patch of cold flat dirt, its black dyed stones etched with all sorts of spiritual symbols she doesn't understand as a heavy sorrow hangs in the air. The Illusion Hall, however, brightly shimmers as she stares at it, seeming to flicker in and out of reality. Each is decorated with banners of black and yellow respectively, proudly displaying their magic symbols like badges of honor. The lights beyond the windows, however, are out. Not a terribly good sign.

She stops and turns to face the doorway to her own Hall, one overgrown with vines, ivy, and an assortment of colorful flowers. The banners with Life symbols sway in some invisible breeze. And yet, peering through the front windows, there is no sign of light or movement within. Is she *that* early?

She steps up and tries the door. It doesn't budge at all. Locked.

She lets out a sad sigh. *Just my luck…*

A cold spot dances on the back of her neck, making it itch. She raises a hand to rub at it as she turns to see who may or may not be staring at her at such a time.

Her breath catches in her throat as she is met with two glowing violet dots, a pair of eyes peering at her from the dark shadow of the dorm room building. Her body freezes, rooting her to the ground. She can only watch helplessly as the eyes move, a figure emerging from the darkness. Some sort of black knight, something out of a story book. It takes slow steps, seemingly in no rush to approach her, not once letting its gaze stray away from hers.

She knows she's in some sort of danger now. This knight clearly isn't approaching her with good intent. And yet her body doesn't respond to the commands she is desperately trying to send, to run away and hide or get help. Panic jumps in her throat, but she can't even scream, either.

The knight doesn't even make it across the pathway when there comes a yell, "Spirit of Fire!"

The knight pauses its advance to look at where the yell came from, and is greeted by a large flaming fireball to its helmet. The force sends the knight flying backwards, away from where Amber stands. Whatever spell had been placed upon her releases its grip, and she lets out a heavy exhale and takes a look at who just yelled.

Ethan stands not too far away, his arms surrounded in a bright red hue, most definitely currently channeling the spirit of a powerful Fire wizard. She knew that Death wizards could do that, call on the power of the spirits to grant them different skills and magical abilities, but this is the first she's *ever* seen it happen. His eyes are narrowed, something dangerous overtaking his gaze. They snap to Amber in an instant, and he yells, "Archway, *now!*"

"W-Why?" Amber only stammers back. Surprise and fear grip at her mind tightly, once again shutting down most of her motor skills, leaving her immoble.

"Just go!" Ethan retorts, turning his attention back to the knight. She casts them a glance. The knight stirs from the ground, one hand propping itself up as the other rests on the side of their helmet. Though the front of its helm is now a collection of mist, its violet eyes are still visible, narrow slits of anger directed right at Ethan.

"*Move*, Amber!"

Ethan's voice briefly shakes Amber from her state of shock. Instinctively, she takes a single step away from the knight still on the ground.

Her body takes over for her mind. She turns and sprints in Ethan's direction, heading in the direction of the ASM Archway. Her textbook remains chained to her fear-gripped hand.

Out of the corner of her eye, she sees Ethan slowly running up beside her. Electricity arcs from where the fire once was, bright and powerful.

"Keep going," he tells her once he notices her staring. "That won't hold it for long."

"What-?" Amber starts, glancing behind them. A large curved wall of ice arcs high into the air, spanning from the dorms to the Life Hall. That wasn't there before!

She turns back to the path ahead, Ethan now just a few steps in front of her. The Archway is in full view as well, quickly growing larger as they fast approach.

"Thank you," Ethan mutters quietly. Almost as instantly as his mouth closed, the lightning that surrounds him dies out, and his pace just barely slows. Frantically, he begins to search his pockets.

"Ethan?!" Amber says.

"*What*?" he snaps back, still looking for... whatever he was looking for.

"What in the stars is going on? Who *was* that?!"

"Tell you later!" he then pulls something from his pocket with a thankful grin. Whatever he has, she can't make out, but she has a good guess as to what it is. "There you are!" Ethan turns to her, though still running, and grabs hold of her arm.

"Keystone?" she asks simply.

"Yes!"

Because of his cape, Amber has to run awkwardly to one side as to not get a face full of fabric or trip on it. Her legs are starting to burn, not used to all the physical exercise. She just needs to get up the steps-

However, just as they reach the small steps that lead up to the Archway itself, Amber feels a chill run down the back of her neck, and she freezes in her tracks. It's not like she wanted to stop. More like... like she had been told to stop. Ethan tugs on her arm on one end and pauses himself, turning around to look at her. At first, anger flares in his eyes, only to quickly be replaced with shock.

On the other end, something tugs at her hair, pulling her head backwards. The angle is such that it makes her neck ache painfully, as an icy burning sensation travels from the back of her head to the front of her face and down to her collar bone. She can't help but let out a scream at this point. It feels as if her body is being ripped in two!

"*Illuminae!*"

A bright white flash fills her vision. Whatever grips her hair lets go, and her head snaps forward. The burning sensation travels back up the way it had just came, ending at the back of her head. After that…

II

Mirage

Chapter 14

Amber's body becomes heavy, falling forward into Ethan's arms. The knight reels backwards a good distance, its entire body erupting into mist. Ethan pauses to stare at it. He can still see violet rays shining from the helmet, and the weight of hopelessness sinks inside him.

Ethan turns away from the reeling knight and to the Archway. The rip is open, revealing a tall orange-yellow dune beyond, with hot air blasting in his face.

Amber firmly in his grasp, he drags the both of them through the rip, still clutching the Keystone tightly in his hand. Only once his feet hit warm sand is when he stops, breathing heavily from the weight he just carried. He looks up at the Archway, this one tilted and sand-worn, and sees the rip snap shut, Asandra now a world away.

He lets out a sigh of relief and lets his legs collapse underneath him. He kneels in the warm sand, cape heavy on his shoulders and hat casting his face in long shadows. Never did he think that he'd need to use his cape. And yet he just did, saving Amber.

He won't be forgetting the sight anytime soon. Her eyes bulging in surprise, the knight just behind her, pulling the

Shadow from her body by the hair. It must have been incredibly painful for her. A pain she didn't deserve experiencing.

He looks at the young wizard. She lies where he left her, just in front of the Archway. She's breathing, but unconscious.

Legs still aching, Ethan crawls over to her and places a hand on her forehead. Her skin is warm to the touch, burning as if she were sick. No doubt her Shadow got damaged. Tearing a Shadow from the head is always a bad idea.

She won't be waking any time soon.

He decides to lay down next to her, just to catch his breath, and stares up at the sky above him, placing his hat and hands over his stomach. Stars twinkle in all their majesty, shining right back down on him. Though with the rising sun, they're starting to fade from view.

The Keystone in his hand grows cold, reminding him of its presence. It's a soft creme color adorned with two interlocking circles, meaning "balance" or "eternity". It brought the two of them to the desert island of Astria.

Mirage.

He's missed this island. The stars here are so vivid at night, as the desert has no other light around for as far as the eye can see. Just thinking about laying in the warm sand and stargazing the night away makes him feel slightly better inside. Though he's never actually explored Mirage in its entirety, nor has any sense of where any possible landmarks are in relation to the Archway. Needless to say, he'd only wind up lost if he were to simply wander in a random direction.

He sits up finally and gets to his feet, taking in his immediate surroundings. They're encompassed by high dunes on all sides, pretty much hiding the Archway from view.

It's either sandy shoes or bare feet, he thinks glumly. Readjusting his hat on his head, he attempts to climb up the nearest dune. The sand holds up surprisingly well, only giving way once or twice and causing him to stumble and slide. His

136

shoes are completely filled with sand by the time he reaches the top, however. The grains rub between his toes uncomfortably, trapped there by his shoes. Maybe he should have taken them off.

It's sand as far as the eye can see. The sun is just barely above the horizon, causing a bit of glare just off to his right. He has to raise a hand to keep himself from looking directly at it, not used to the presence of such a source of intense light. The sight makes his hopes fall. He doesn't want to turn around and go to another island. Not now. Then the chances of being found again will rise. Compared to Mirage, the other islands are small in comparison. It'd take too long to scour the sands of Mirage in one cycle, aside from, say, the dense forest of Gardall or the maze-like halls of gears and pipes of Kendon.

But Amber…

He turns to look back down at the Archway. Amber continues to lay still, just a green-and-pink figure on the ground. They're going to need some shelter soon, with the Mirage sun on the rise.

Though there is one idea he has to try.

He closes his eyes and presses his palms together, close to his chest, to pray.

"Spirits of the White Beyond, grant me your power, so that I may use it justly and to save the life of…" he hesitates a moment, "my friend, Amber. Thus, I call upon the aid of a spirit of Fire…"

He remains still, waiting for any sort of reaction. He didn't exactly need to pray, and yet he did it out of respect. It's the very first thing any Death wizard learns above all else. And it's especially important to pay his respects now, since he and Amber aren't in any sort of immediate danger.

Suddenly, a surge of magic rushes through his body, hot and blazing. Slowly, he opens his eyes to find flames spinning around his arms. The energy of Fire magic is eagerness and determination, filling him with a sense of honor and dignity.

Thank you, he mouths. He raises one of his arms to the sky, palm facing upwards and fingers spread. The flames around his arm collect in his palm in a single ball of fire. It takes just a mild mental nod towards the fireball to send it flying from his hand and into the air. He tilts his hat back with the same hand as he watches it travel high above him, slowly turning into a little red star. Eventually, once it runs out of energy, the ball bursts into smaller, glittering spheres of flame which linger for a long moment before winking out of existence. There isn't any noise, yet the bright flare should be enough to draw attention. It isn't every cycle such a sight appears deep in the desert, no doubt.

The Fire magic drains from his body, the spirit retreating back into the White Beyond, its job complete. It leaves Ethan with cold emptiness within, his own magic feeling thin and weak, as usual.

He rubs his hands together and turns away from the sandy view. It will take any being a good long while to reach the Archway, no doubt. Right now, he's got Amber to keep an eye on.

***

The wind batters his face and whips through his light brown hair, and he welcomes it. The day hasn't become hot yet, for the sun is just starting to rise, but it is not too cold, either. The dunes streak past him as he travels, weaving around the hills with ease. The freedom he has right now is fleeting. Why not enjoy it to the fullest?

Lukri spreads his arms wide and smiles up at the sky, remaining perfectly balanced on his sandboard as he does so. It's silver with green decal, and just big enough to fit both his feet on comfortably. It glides just above the sand with ease, kicking up a cloud behind him.

138

His gray shirt and white sash rustles against his skin, blowing cool air up his back. Since he's sandboarding, he had to put on some shorts before leaving, but left his sandals behind. It's not that he doesn't enjoy his legs, but that using his tail would cause all sorts of balance and steering issues.

When he turns away from his skyward grin, he spots something rise into the air over the dunes. A bright red light that flares and bursts, spawning smaller lights that slowly wink out and die. His eyes widen with surprise and curiosity. Who else would be out this deep into the desert at a time like this?

The flare is small and seems pretty far away from where he currently is. Though he's sure that if he travels in the direction the flare came from, sooner or later he will stumble upon the source.

It could be dangerous, nags at the back of Lukri's mind as he points himself in the direction of the flare. It *could* be dangerous. Especially since the Archway is somewhere around him. He doesn't know who would be able to get to Mirage in the first place, but such a feat is not completely impossible to accomplish.

Not for wizards.

He tries not to give the flare much thought as he travels, still enjoying his time out on the sands. Mostly.

He turns his head for a moment to stare at the dunes he passes. He extends a hand and lets his fingers skim the sides of the dunes, leaving behind little streaks as he goes. The sand doesn't sting his fingertips. On the contrary, it feels kind of nice.

Time melts away until he finally reaches a ring of tall dunes, taller than the usual ones around him. So far, he's not seen anyone. Maybe he might see something if he climbs up there?

He twists his board to the side and leans backwards, killing the board's momentum and kicking up a small cloud that attempts to batter his face, which he combats by simply turning away from it. With the board now stationary, he steps off, planting his feet firmly in the warm sand. He wiggles his toes playfully with a faint grin, then turns to pick up his board. It weighs almost nothing in his hands, and with just a small ounce of mental effort it crumbles away into sand itself. He'll summon it later when it's time to zoom off again.

Lukri scrambles up the large dune on his hands and feet, a skill any Serperas knows when it comes to traversing the sands on foot. It's easier to scale the dunes with a tail, yet these ones are angled to where using his tail would be more of a hindrance rather than help. Best case scenario, it'd simply make him slip and fall back down. Worst case scenario, he could bring the dune down on top of himself.

When he reaches the top of the dune, he pauses. Below, in what is essentially a hole of sorts, is the Archway itself, with two figures crouched beside it. A girl, with bright pink hair and green-shaded clothes, her eyes closed and her breathing even. And a boy, dressed all in black with a wide hat and long cape that is splayed out behind him. He sits at the girl's side, seemingly watching over her as she sleeps.

"Ah…!" escapes Lukri's mouth, and it takes a moment for him to register that it was *him* that spoke. It's been a good long while since he's heard his own voice.

The single word is enough to draw the boy's attention, and he looks up at where Lukri perches. Soulless eyes as black as night pierce his own green ones, sending a chill down his spine. Cautiously, he starts to shuffle back down the dune.

"Wait!" the boy cries, causing Lukri to freeze. He watches the boy stand and start to approach the dune quickly, urgency in his step. Lukri feels his heart start to pound in his chest in a panic. As a safety measure, he dips his hand into the dune and pulls out a long jade sword. Though light in his hand - all sand-made objects are pretty much weightless - it's still a very sharp and formidable weapon.

140

"S-Stop!" he commands, springing up straight and pointing his sword down at the mysterious boy. He stalls at the base of the dune and stares up at Lukri, yet remains silent. He appears rather unconcerned about Lukri's weapon. "W-Who…?" He grits his teeth, trying to find the right words to say.

"It's okay," the boy speaks slowly, holding his hands up in a gesture of surrender. "I just need some help. I'm not going to hurt you."

Lukri takes a moment to get his breathing under control.

"Name," he demands at last.

"Ethan," the boy points at himself, then to the girl, "Amber."

"Why is… ah-mm-brr…" Lukri pauses, cringing at his terrible pronunciation.

"She's injured," Ethan says, paying no heed to his terrible speaking. Well, not for long, as he then raises an eyebrow and asks, "Do you not… *speak*?"

"I…" Lukri shakes his head. "Serperas… not speak. M-Much."

It's true. Serperas normally talk with their body heat. They can regulate their temperatures to form pictures out of hot and cold spots, while also being able to see heat around them. So no, Serperas do not speak much. Sometimes, but rarely, and normally when there isn't a clear picture for a certain word, or for clarification.

"Well… uh…"

"*Lukri.*"

"…is there anywhere we can stay? Shelter?"

Lukri doesn't know how to reply. There is shelter, far from here. If they need a Healer, his home is pretty far for them to walk. If they just need a place to shield themselves from the sun, the Old Ruins are closer, but not by much.

"Injured… Want Healer?"

"Ah…" Ethan takes a quick glance at Amber, "possibly."

"Are you… wizards?" Lukri asks quietly.

Ethan doesn't respond, yet appears crestfallen. A nervous pit forms in Lukri's stomach.

He shouldn't be helping wizards. He shouldn't even be *talking* to wizards!

"Please," Ethan says at last. "Just for a cycle or two."

Lukri tilts his head in confusion. "A… sie-k-el?"

"Uh, you know, when the sun goes up and down?" Ethan does a little circle motion with a finger. "That's a cycle."

"Oh! A day."

"You call it a 'day' here?"

Lukri nods with a small grin. If they're looking for a day or two of rest, then maybe there's a Serperas he knows who could house them.

Or he could just leave the two here. It's the Archway, after all. They can probably go somewhere else. They don't need to stay on Mirage.

And yet, if they could seek shelter elsewhere, then why *haven't* they left Mirage yet? Why take the time to send a signal and *wait*?

"Can you… go?" he asks.

"What, go to another island?" Ethan echoes. "Not exactly, no."

"Oh…"

"So can you help us?"

Lukri furrows his brow and stares at the wizard long and hard. He doesn't want to say no. He really doesn't. If they have nowhere else to go and he just leaves the two here, with one of them being *injured* no less, then they most certainly wouldn't last long. But if he says yes, then he'd have to bring them home and somehow keep them a secret from the rest of his people. And if they're ever discovered… He doesn't want to think about that.

"Yes."

Ethan grins up at him thankfully. Then he turns and

strides back to Amber, crouching down next to her. Feeling the need to check on her as well, Lukri slides down the other side of the dune and slowly approaches the pair.

"Asleep?" he asks.

"Seems like it," Ethan replies. With a grunt, he digs his arms under her and lifts her up, her serene face skyward. It's amazing how the sunlight doesn't wake her. He turns to the dunes around them with a troubled look. "How in the stars am I supposed to climb those…?"

"I can push," Lukri offers.

The wizard nods. "Then let's give it a try."

Lukri drops his sword, and it disappears into sand once again. He hates to be disarmed, and yet so far there's been no hostility from the wizard. He seems to be more focused on getting care for Amber. How noble.

He's going to need both hands for this.

Ethan starts up the dune, Lukri following close behind him, his arms outstretched and waiting if he ever slips. And he does, a couple times, but it isn't anything too bad. Carrying a second person up the side of a dune must be hard. But with Lukri's help in catching him, the three make it up to the crest in no time at all.

"Now… where are we going?" Ethan asks. Lukri simply points to where the sun is rising in response. From where they are, the village can't be seen, but it's over there. Somewhere.

"Far," he mutters. Lukri slides down the dune again, planting his feet firmly in the sand below. He turns to look back up at Ethan, who stares down with mild worry.

Lukri doesn't exactly know how to describe how best to slide down the dune, so he tries to demonstrate for him. Legs apart, one in front of the other. Bent knees, of course, and a slight lean backwards. With Amber in his hands, Ethan should have a little more trouble trying to balance out the backwards lean, especially since he can't balance himself with his arms

143

anyway. And still, the wizard appears unsure.

"Healer or no?" Lukri asks.

Ethan appears to let out a small, reluctant sigh and shakes his head. Then he takes a cautious step forward and begins to slowly shimmy his way down. It's some sort of half-slide, half-step, yet it appears to be working fairly well for him. Not as good as Lukri's slide, but it's not his place to judge right now.

As Ethan gets his barings at the bottom of the dune, Lukri bends down and digs his hands into the sand and focuses. He feels cold metal form in his palms, and slowly he lifts up his sandboard. Tossing it aside, he does the action again, drawing up a second board for Ethan to ride on. He puts the second board in front of the wizard and gestures to it before hopping onto his own.

"Easy," Lukri assures the wizard calmly once he notices Ethan's uneasy staring. Slowly, the wizard places a foot on the front of the board, then quickly places his second on the back. The board dips ever so slightly, yet remains just barely above the sands.

Though… maybe he'll need a bit of a push.

"How do I use this thing?" Ethan mutters aloud, though probably to himself all the same, as he looks down at the board beneath him.

Lukri clears his throat rather loudly, drawing the wizard's attention. "Look."

A lot of sandboarding relies on the back foot, mainly the heel. To start momentum, Lukri places his weight on his back foot, pushing the board down to touch the surface of the sand. As soon as the metal touches the ground, it bounces back up again, lurching him slowly forward. He shifts his back foot, angling his heel to the left and slightly leans into it, sharply turning the board around to face Ethan. He slowly glides past the wizard and points down to his back foot.

"Heel steers."

He glides around and passes him again on the other side, this time pointing to his front foot.

"Balance."

Ethan nods along, seeming to understand the instructions being given. And then he gives it a try, bouncing off his back foot. The board jumps into the air, and Ethan makes a very audible inhalation of surprise. However, he seems to keep his balance on the board and his grip on Amber at the same time. The board bobs a little bit before smoothly gliding forward. Lukri half-grins and performs another bounce of his own, renewing his own board's momentum.

He tries to go slowly, not gliding too high on the dunes to pick up speed or getting too far ahead to where Ethan loses sight of him for more than a brief moment. Which is hard, because he's eager to get back home. Sooner or later, some being is going to notice that he's gone. And when that happens, he's going to get in *massive* trouble.

"How much farther?" Ethan calls.

"Far," Lukri replies, finding it hard to keep himself from sounding anxious.

"Are you in a hurry?"

"Yes."

"How come?"

"Not..." Lukri pauses to think, spelling out the sentence to himself before attempting to speak again, "I-I am not allowed to... to sandboard much."

Ethan remains silent behind him. Lukri turns to check and make sure that the wizard is still following. He is, though with a somber gaze towards Lukri himself. Lukri presses his mouth into a firm line and turns away again.

No, he doesn't need to know.

***

145

Eventually, the three leave behind the dunes and streak over a relatively flat plane of sand. Ethan spots a town just ahead, a collection of low buildings only a floor or two high and made of some sort of sandy brick. He can see figures milling about between the buildings as well, and a few other Serperas gliding around the outside of town on the same silver board Lukri gave to him.

"Not supposed to go to the dunes," Lukri throws over his shoulder. "Stay… *here*." The Serperas gestures to the large flat expanse around them with both his hands, spinning them in large circles with palms pointed down at the ground. It certainly sounds like he's starting to warm up to speaking. So long as they can understand one another, Ethan doesn't mind the broken sentences too much.

"And that," Lukri points at the sky. Ethan follows, though what the Serperas is showing him is fairly noticeable. Clouds in the distance. Dark, shadowy clouds. "Been there for… some time. Not harmful but…mist-er-ee-us? Yes, mysterious."

Ethan holds Amber closer to him, readjusting his grip. His arms are starting to tire from supporting her weight for so long. He's seen those clouds before. Maybe they're not as safe on Mirage as he first thought…

He follows Lukri closely as he steers towards the outer buildings of the town. Eventually, he stops, turning his board sideways and leaning backwards to slow his momentum. Ethan opts for what he thinks is probably a better method of slowing down. He slips off his back foot and digs it into the sand, which does indeed bring him to an abrupt halt. However, the force causes him to stumble, and he begins to fall forward.

He feels a being, possibly Lukri, quickly lift Amber from his arms as he tumbles to the sand. The grains batter his face and dig into his skin, making it burn. His eyes and mouth are close, and yet he can feel the sand seemingly come alive and try to

146

worm its way through his defenses. He pushes himself up quickly and sputters, wiping the sand off his face the best he can. Thankfully, much of the sand doesn't stick to his skin.

"Okay?" Lukri asks. Ethan looks up at the Serperas with a small grin. Lukri stares back in concern, Amber hanging in his arms.

"Yeah, I'm fine," he replies simply. The response causes Lukri to smile along with him.

"Come," he urges. He turns and steps into a small alleyway, leaving behind the sandboards. As Ethan stands, he notices the boards slowly begin to dissolve into sand. It may be because of what sort of magic Lukri used to make them. His sword did seem to magically disappear without him noticing earlier, too.

He follows Lukri down the alleyway, keeping his guard up. There's little reason for the Serperas to turn against him and Amber. He seems like a very compassionate being from the start, if not a little timid. But almost anything can happen at this point. He has to be ready for anything.

"Wizards… not liked here," Lukri says quietly.

Ethan nods, though the Serperas can't see the motion. "Okay."

"But wizards are… easy to spot."

"Oh…?"

"Serperas… talk with bodies," Lukri briefly laughs at his own sentence. "Ah… heat? Yes, body heat. We can see heat."

"You can communicate through watching each other's body heat?" Ethan clarifies.

"Yes, sorry. Words and mouth…" Lukri gives a small shrug.

"You'll learn," Ethan replies.

"Maybe."

The Serperas stops outside a wood-like door tied together with some sort of vine-looking rope and turns to Ethan. "Take?"

147

Ethan nods and reaches out for Amber again. Once she is back in his grasp, Lukri knocks on the door.

Almost instantly, the door flies open. In the doorway is a rather elderly Serperas, with silver-white hair, bright orange eyes, and a dark brown tail swishing behind her. Her upper torso is clothed in nothing but a single dusty shirt full of holes and tears at every opening. Underneath is a cleaner, whiter shirt, though that also seems to be slowly deteriorating.

His eyes dart to Lukri's outfit in an instant. The boy's gray shirt appears to be some sort of wrap, held together by a white sash and belt, with nearly non-existent sleeves and a bright yellow hem that glitters like gold. What a stark difference of dress…

"Anasi!" Lukri says happily, though that's about as friendly as the conversation seems to get. Anasi scowls down at Lukri, who stares back at her with a very pleading expression. Both their eyes flicker left, right, up, and down, seemingly reading what Ethan presumes to be each other's body heat.

"But-" Lukri speaks, panic in his voice, drawing Ethan's attention back to the two Serperas. Anasi is shaking her head, her eyes closed. Lukri bites his bottom lip, his expression downhearted. Then he turns away, the conversation appearing done and over with.

No!

"Please!" Ethan tries, drawing Anasi's attention to him. "Just for a… a day or two. O-Or until my friend wakes up. Yes, we can leave when she wakes up if you want. Just let us stay!"

Anasi's face crinkles and shifts from a frown into something that appears to be mild confusion and, quite possibly, sympathy. She probably wasn't expecting Ethan to plead with her. If he could have, he'd probably have gotten down on his knees and begged. He might as well do that now. It'd get Amber out of his arms for a little bit.

Eventually, Anasi lets out a reluctant sigh. "Fine. Come."

148

She moves out of the doorway and gestures for them to enter.

Ethan steps in first and finds himself in a small room with just a single table and one chair, made out of thin gray logs and planks of wood and held together with the same vine-like rope that has also been used on the front door. A small pit of ash and small twigs sits to one of the far sides of the room, with a small red clay pot set just next to it. A small staircase at the back leads upwards to a second floor, quite possibly where Anasi sleeps at night. The temperature inside the little house is the same as outside, for the windows are just holes in the wall rather than actual windows. And it doesn't help that Ethan is currently dressed in mostly black clothing. Amber's body must also be starting to overheat because of her robe's long sleeves and pants. Wizard attire isn't exactly for hot weather.

"Up," Anasi hisses behind him. "Bed for her."

"Thank you," Ethan nods to her. He makes his way across the room, careful not to bump Amber into the table as he passes it, nor have his own foot kick the pot next to the fire pit. He makes his way up the stairs, needing to let Amber sag in his arms to make sure she fits comfortably in the small stairwell. The stairs themselves have many of their rough edges smoothed over, possibly from years and years of Serperas slithering up and down them with their tails. Though it's hard for him to watch his step with Amber blocking most of his downward view.

He reaches the second floor and scans the room. It's much like the room below, with a small gray wood table and bed, and four "windows", one square hole in the middle of each wall. The bed itself is covered in nothing but a single ragged sheet, the same dusty off-white color as Anasi's top shirt and just as ragged. There's no padding underneath the sheet or even a pillow to rest one's head on.

Reluctantly, Ethan sets Amber on top of the sheet and fumbles with the clasp of his cape. The clasp clicks, and he brings the long piece of black fabric around and wraps it loosely around his arm. Once this is done, he slips it off his arm and lifts Amber's head to place it under her as a sort of make-shift pillow. She'll awaken stiff, sore, and even hot and sweaty, but at least she's got something for her head.

"Everything okay?"

Ethan turns to see Lukri standing in the stairwell, not quite at the top yet with only his upper body in full view.

Ethan musters a thankful grin for the young Serperas. "Yes, thank you."

Lukri smiles back. "Take care!"

And with that, he is gone.

Chapter 15

Something cold and sweet trickles down Amber's throat, bringing life back to her lips and mouth. Slowly, as she licks at the substance, the sensation blossoms outwards in a rush. It fills her arms and legs with energy, swirls around her beating heart, and brings life back to her face.

She opens her eyes to two strange beings staring down at her. One, the older one with the bright orange eyes, is holding their hand over her face, though reels her hand back once Amber shows signs of life. Another is a boy with a black-ish scar over his left eye. He seems strangely familiar…

"Amber!" he says, his face lighting up with relief. He leans forward, just in front of the old woman, as if to get a better look at her.

With a groan, Amber sits up. Her limbs protest the movement, the cool and revitalizing sensation fading into a warm and sticky stiffness. Her head pounds painfully. She grits her teeth and inhales sharply, lungs burning.

"Hey, take it easy," the boy says, placing a hand on her back to support her.

Amber takes a moment to collect herself through all the pain, then turns to the boy and asks simply, "Do I know you?"

The boy seems taken aback by the question, his eyes widening in what she believes is either shock, surprise, or both.

"Come on Amber, you don't recognize me?" the boy asks. Amber shakes her head slightly. "Ethan? Ethan Nightshade?" Again, she shakes her head. "We attend the same school."

"Which one?" she asks.

"The Asandra School of Magic. ASM?"

"I-I don't think I know that place."

Ethan scowls in frustration and turns away from her, first grabbing something behind her before standing and walking towards the middle of the bare room. He seems to fiddle with whatever he had just retrieved for a moment before shaking his head.

Amber turns to the woman, and almost immediately notices her brown tail. "Ah... and you are?"

"*Anasi*," the woman replies, partially drawing out the "s" in her name. Anasi reaches into a small brown pouch that rests in one of her hands and withdraws a small blue pebble. She holds it out to Amber. "Bite."

Amber takes the pebble and pops it in her mouth. It's tasteless, just a little rock rolling around on her tongue. She follows Anasi's instruction and bites it. The pebble is easily crushed between her teeth, and from it explodes cold water. Caught off guard, Amber holds a fist to her mouth to prevent herself from spewing. Then she swallows and lets out a gasp for air.

"Water pellet," Anasi says as she ties a small string around the top of the pouch. She turns and slithers past Ethan, still standing with his back turned to Amber, tail swishing as she goes. Then she turns and slowly descends to a lower level, out of sight.

Finally, Ethan turns back around, and Amber sees a mass of black cloth balled in his hands. This time he wears a worried expression.

"What *do* you remember?" he asks her.

Amber shrugs and shakes her head. "A flash. Everything before that is… hazy at best."

"Seriously?"

She nods. "What happened to me?"

Ethan presses his lips closed, his eyes glazing over. It seems like whatever he's thinking of blocked out her question.

"Ethan," his name brings his focus back to her, and his expression softens with a slight exhale through his nose, "what *happened* to me?"

Ethan lets out a small sigh and hangs his head. "An attack. We were trying to escape, but you got grabbed… You were knocked out, so I carried you all the way here."

"Who-"

"Not important," he snaps abruptly.

"But Ethan!"

Ethan shoots her an angry glare. Amber takes a hesitant breath as his stare bores into her.

"I think I deserve an explanation," she says.

Ethan continues to stare for a long moment, and Amber almost feels like taking back what she just said. And yet, before she can speak again, Ethan hangs his head and lets out a sad sigh.

"I guess you're right," he mutters. He unfurls the fabric in his hands and swishes it around to his back, clicking a silver clasp in place just under his neck. He had been holding a large, billowy cape. He grabs the edges of his cape and draws them close to his body, almost as if he were to wrap himself up inside it. When he looks up, there is barely a flicker of life in his eyes as he gives her a solemn and tired look.

"I had this friend a long time ago. She was a brilliant Spiritist, but didn't grow up at the best time. Her parents didn't support her, she had no friends, and was ostracized in school. When I met her, her mind wasn't in the best place. She had my

153

sibling do some pretty bad things over the last couple...
thousand years."

"How old *are* you then?" Amber breathes.

"Me specifically? Only a thousand and eight-hundred,
roughly. Otherwise... a lot older than that. I can't even give an
estimate at that point.

"Anyway, this former friend of mine decided to have my...
sibling pull a pretty ridiculous stunt recently. Uh... this would be
better if you were familiar with the theory of Life and Death,
but..." he shakes his head before continuing, "How a living being
is made is with a Shadow, spirit, and Husk. The Shadow is like
your magic personified. It's other things as well, like how you're
able to move and have unique physical features. The spirit is
your personality. And the Husk is... this," he simply gestures to
himself. "Your hair color and eye color and your physique. It's
like a house for your Shadow and spirit to live in.

"Without your spirit, you become an emotionless puppet.
Without your Husk, you die. And without your Shadow, your body
cannot function. So my sibling was forced to 'steal' some beings'
Shadows. It was trying to go after yours as well, but I stopped it.
Sadly, I stopped it a little too late. Your Shadow suffered some
damage to the head. No doubt that's why you've lost your
memories."

"But if you didn't step in, then we wouldn't even be
talking?" Amber asks.

"Pretty much," Ethan nods. He raises a hand and rubs the
back of his head, his eyes straying to the floor. "Look, I'm sorry
about all this, but-"

"I-It's okay," Amber steps in, mustering an encouraging
smile. "Everything will come back to me eventually, right?"

"...I guess so," Ethan eventually mutters.

In an effort to get her mind off of her missing memories,
Amber stands from the bed and brushes off her robe, then wipes
her brow with her sleeve. It sure is *hot*.

154

"Where are we?" she asks, looking out the nearest window at all the low buildings around them.

"Mirage, the desert island," Ethan replies simply. "I was led to this house by a Serperas called Lukri. If we ever run into him again, I'll be sure to point him out so you can thank him. He was a big help."

"I'm sure he was," Amber chuckles. Lukri is a very nice name.

"And Anasi helped to heal you."

"Oh!"

Just then, Anasi's head pops into view from the stairwell, her expression a half-smile. "Food?" Her sudden voice makes Ethan visibly jump and turn around in surprise.

"Yes please!" Amber replies.

"I guess some food wouldn't hurt," Ethan breathes.

Amber first, the two slowly walk down the narrow steps to the ground floor. A single clay bowl sits in the center of a table in the middle of the room, full of a variety of fruit Amber has never seen before. Despite her current memory issues, nothing seems familiar to her. Anasi sits on her tail next to the table, already munching on a purple-skinned fruit.

"Fruit?" Ethan asks from behind, not trying to sound too disrespectful but definitely a little irate at the sight. "That's *it*?"

Anasi frowns at him. "All we grow, *wizard*."

"Ethan! Thank her for the food!" Amber chides. Ethan clenches his jaw for a moment, then lets out a sigh.

"Sorry. Thank you."

The two approach the table and take a fruit from the bowl each. Amber finds herself staring down at one that is red and somewhat round, with a little brown stem poking out the top.

"Apple," Anasi says to her simply, then turns to Ethan, who is inspecting a red, yellow, and brown striped fruit. "*Jamba amar.*"

"This is jamba?" Ethan mutters in surprise. "It's got the

155

same shape… How do I open it?"

Anasi holds her hand out, and Ethan hands her the fruit without hesitation. The Serperas clutches the fruit tightly in both her hands and sharply slams it against the edge of the table.

Crack!

The fruit splits open with ease, some juice squirting out and staining the wood with dark gray droplets. Inside, the fruit is a pale red-brown color. She casually hands the two halves back to Ethan.

"Thank you," he says, sounding a little shaken. He stares down at the halves for a moment, then tries taking a bite out of the fruit. Almost immediately, his body jerks backwards, and his arms extend the fruit away from his face. "Ack! Blegh!"

"Bitter jamba," Anasi chuckles.

"*Now* you say it," Ethan grumbles.

"Maybe you shouldn't be so rude," Amber teases lightly. She bites into her apple, which is crunchy yet very sweet and full of flavor. The juice is cool and refreshing, especially so in such a hot climate. "This apple isn't so bad!"

"We grow many fruits," Anasi says to her. "All we have here."

"Is it because of the environment?" Amber asks. The elderly Serperas nods slowly.

"No wonder," Ethan hums aloud.

***

"Those clouds," Ethan says to Anasi, partly leaning on the table. "What do you know about them?"

The Serperas swishes her tail, and her expression turns into a frown of thought. In her hands, she holds a half-woven basket of sorts, which she had retrieved from somewhere outside not too long ago. The material is some sort of flat and dull yellow plant part, maybe a leaf, like aged paper. Amber is

156

back upstairs resting. He hopes that some sleep will do her head some amount of good. The sooner she gets her memories back, the better.

"Been there…" Anasi pauses and lets out a low hum, "a few days? Came from nowhere. Blocks out morning sun."

"And nothing's happened at all since?"

Anasi shakes her head. "Not here. Palace. Bad things. *Dark* things."

Ethan lets out a deep breath and bows his head. So it's as he feared.

"You know?" Anasi asks.

"I'm afraid I do," he replies quietly. He shakes his head. "I can't say much, though. You're already at risk from your own people if we are ever discovered here. I rather not add to your danger." He lifts his head again and forces a thankful grin. "Thank you, by the way. Whenever you want us to, we will leave."

Anasi lets out an amused huff and smiles back, flashing her long fangs at him. "Not the first Lukri asked me to take risks. Not the last, either."

There's a moment of pause between them.

"Do all Serperas sound… like you?" Ethan asks hesitantly.

Anasi nods, her gaze dark and distant. "Spoken is dying."

With a sigh, the Serperas sets aside her weaving, having hardly worked on it at all. Her tail lowers her body as it spirals outwards, creating a loose coil around her. The brownness of the tail slowly fades as the tail grows shorter and splits in two. Pretty soon, she's sitting with crossed legs, the skin tan and withered with age. She places her hands on the ground and pats it, possibly inviting Ethan to join her. Slowly, he plops himself on the stone ground in front of her and folds his hands in his lap.

"Once," Anasi recounts slowly, picking her words carefully, "it was common. Aside from our bodies, it was how we conversed. With family. With friends. With others. Then after the

War… we closed the island to outsiders. It became an art, a test of smarts.

But it quickly faded into… *irrelevance*. There are other reasons as well, but the big one is that we do not need it anymore.

"Magic is similar. With the War went our best shamans. They taught the young ones magic. But now, that is lost. Magic is… not used much here. When we do, it can be wild. We have ways to control it, but even then it is… *unrefined*."

"The wizards left you all this way?"

Anasi nods. "They offered no help. We were left with only our spring. This place," she gestures with one hand at the room around them, "is not old."

"Excuse me?"

"The ancestors became upset, and the old spring ran dry. It was big, enough for twice the people we have now. We were forced to move, and our numbers have been shrinking since."

Ethan's eyes widen. So the Serperas are having water problems? Normally, such a thing is an easy fix. And yet…

Anasi said it herself. They are unskilled with magic and can't control it. Even if they had any Ice users among their people, which they surely have none of due to the fact that they are having this water shortage, they'd probably not be able to use the magic as effectively as a proper Ice wizard from Asandra can. Maybe it'd even end up doing the Serperas harm.

"Spoken also dries the body faster," Anasi adds with a weary grin.

"You don't need to keep talking if you don't want to. My apologies," Ethan stands and brushes his robe. Anasi's legs morph back into her tail, and she, too, rises from the ground. She slides over to a small ledge poking out of the wall, where the water pellet bag sits.

"Stay as you need," she says, popping a pellet into her mouth. He hears the *crunch* and watches her swallow and replace the bag. "But I have only so much to give. Restrictions. To keep Serperas happy and healthy."

Ethan nods. "I understand."

***

"You were down there a while," Amber comments as Ethan rises from the stairwell.

The wizard chuckles weakly. "Yes, well, me and Anasi had some things to discuss. How long have you been awake?"

"Not long," Amber replies with a small yawn. "What were you talking about?"

"Just Mirage for the most part," Ethan takes a seat on the ground beside her bed and leans up against the wall, his gaze distant. "There's shadow on the horizon."

"What?"

"You can see it from here," he points to the window across from him, "the clouds. *My friend* got here before us. I don't know why…"

"What's her name?"

Ethan shifts uncomfortably. He is silent for a long time, staring blankly at the wall opposite him and ignoring her gaze.

"Riona," he whispers, as if it were spoken louder she would magically appear before him.

"Have I-"

"She's not been seen in many thousands of years," Ethan cuts her off quickly. "No, it's no being you know."

Amber is still, simply staring at him more intensely. He sure seems to hold a lot of resentment towards this Riona person.

Ethan shakes his head. "I don't know why she's got an interest in Mirage, but she's been causing some problems here. Granted, the Serperas have their own issues already. They don't deserve… whatever she's doing to them."

"What *is* she doing?"

"I don't know!" he exclaims loudly. His eyes snap to her, anger blazing. "I stopped knowing a long time ago. Do you know how *frustrating* that is? Not knowing anything? You should, since you're the one who doesn't *know* anything anymore!" He stands and walks over to the window, arms folded.

"I-I was just asking…" Amber mutters quietly. Her body shakes with nervousness and shame. She didn't mean to anger him. She just wants some answers for once in her life.

Then again, he probably wants some, too.

The two are silent for a long time. The air between them is full of tension. Ethan stares out of the window at the rest of town. Amber opts to remain in bed. She reaches for his cape - he gave it to her earlier to use as a pillow - and hugs it close to her chest. She squeezes with all her might, channeling her feelings into it. She doesn't dare speak. What if he shouts at her again? What if he…

She inhales sharply at her own thoughts.

What if he ends up *hitting* her?

Ethan lets out a deep sigh that causes her body to stiffen.

"I shouldn't have said that," he says. "Sorry."

Amber takes a deep breath. Should she respond? Is he expecting her to respond?

She looks down at the bed and doesn't speak.

"How are your memories doing?"

Again, she takes a deep breath, hesitant to answer. Sleeping did help, as he thought it would. Some have started to return to her, scattered and hazy but frighteningly vivid all the same. But what little she is able to remember she doesn't want to think about.

"Amber?"

His voice is quiet now. Her blood runs cold as she senses his stare lay upon her.

"T-They're coming back… slowly," she forces.

"What's the first thing that comes to your mind?"

The memory surges forward. A boy - Blaze - towers over her, even though he isn't looking at her. And he raises a hand and gestures towards her, saying bitterly, "See? She's just useless!"

She just squeezes her eyes shut and shakes her head.

After a quiet moment, she feels an arm wrap around her shoulders. Ethan doesn't speak, instead just holding her. With a sniff, she rests her head on his shoulder, tears beginning to stream down her face. She doesn't want to cry. Not now. Not here. Not like this.

"I'm sorry," he mutters.

It doesn't really make her feel any better, but-

"It's Blaze, isn't it?"

Amber lifts her head and attempts to wipe her face dry. Still, a couple tears fall. She looks at Ethan, her brow tightly knitted.

"How did you-"

Ethan shrugs. "I just assumed that you led a very average life until... *that*." Amber nods her head back at him, mostly out of instinct.

"Nothing else?"

She shakes her head. "Maybe if I sleep a little more..."

Ethan half-grins. "Resting always helps. Especially for Life wizards." He turns to glance out the window once again. "Well, it's still about midcycle, but it's not like we can go anywhere anytime soon anyway."

"Why?"

"Wizards aren't welcome here. I imagine we'll be punished if we're ever caught, along with Anasi and maybe even Lukri."

"Oh..."

"Don't worry, we should be fine for at least a little while." He rubs his hands together and hums to himself. "How about a game?"

161

As soon as "game" is spoken, Amber perks up a bit. At least it'll get her mind off of...

She smiles. "What sort of game?"

"With or without your memories, you've probably never heard of this one," Ethan says. He holds out a hand in front of him, and in a puff of black smoke two little boxes appear in his palm, one on top the other. "It's called Snap. Normally it's played in a larger group, but we can do it by ourselves. Here, take a look." He hands her one of the boxes.

Amber takes it and finds one end already open, full with... something. She tilts the box, and out slides numerous gray rectangles with colorful images.

"These are playing cards," Ethan continues, sliding out his own cards into his other hand. "Each one has a different amount of images, either circles or diamonds, and they're either white or black to represent Light and Shadow. There are fifteen numbers and four pictures, being officer, commander, knight, and champion." He turns over the cards one by one and places them on the bed. The officer is a person holding a bow, a quiver at their hip and dressed in plain clothing. The commander dons armor and spear, standing at attention. The knight...

A sharp pain ignites in Amber's head, and she winces.

"Is something wrong?" Ethan asks her.

"The knight," she mutters, eyeing the card. The knight wears white armor from head to toe, a long gold tassel swishing from the helmet. They have their hands folded over the hilt of a longsword, the tip resting level with their feet. "It looks... familiar."

"It probably should," Ethan sighs. "That's who attacked us earlier. See?" He hunts for another card and slides it over the white knight. This one wears the same armor, with the same sword and golden tassel, and yet the white armor is now as black as night.

Amber looks away from it and holds her head in her

hands. It throbs painfully. She can feel her heartbeat in her ears, making them ache and pop.

Pain. Pain is the first thing that comes to mind. Something yanking on her hair, pulling her head backwards. A burning sensation around the base of her neck, so hot it feels deathly cold. And that flash of light...

She hears Ethan shuffling cards around, and she forces herself to look up. The knights are gone.

"This is the champion," he says simply, sliding the last picture card forward. It's similar to the knight, except that the armor is twice as big and fancy. The helmet makes the head look small compared to the rest of the body. They hold a sword and shield close to their chest, a flowing cape billowing behind them.

"The rules are simple. Each player places a card out in front of them. If one card has a higher value than the other, then the 'winner' places their card at the bottom of their stack, and the 'loser' puts theirs in their discard pile. The one who still has cards to play wins overall. And if the cards are the same value, each player draws again until one gets a higher value. Color doesn't matter," he holds out a hand to her. "Give me your cards."

Reluctantly, Amber hands her stack over to him. Ethan starts quickly thumbing through them. "We won't play with the knight for right now."

She nods. "Thank you."

He finally withdraws two cards and sets them aside, careful not to show them to Amber. She knows what they are already. Then he puts her deck back together and returns them. "Go on and shuffle them."

She takes them and pauses for a moment, looking at him and wondering what a "shuffle" is. He gives her no attention and focuses on his own deck, taking a couple of cards from the bottom and wiggling them back into the stack.

That's probably what he meant.

Amber slowly "shuffles" her deck as well, mimicking his

actions as best she can. Though the wiggling part is hard at times, with cards often ending up getting stuck on one another and making her life a little more difficult. However, she doesn't want to force them to slide together and possibly ruin them. She doesn't even know where he got them from.

After a while, she deems her deck thoroughly shuffled, and she scoots back on the bed to give the two of them a little more room to play. Ethan places his deck in front of him, picture-side down, and looks at her expectantly. She does the same.

"Just take the top card and place it in front of you, like this," Ethan slides the top card off his stack and places it picture-up in front of it. He smiles weakly. "Ah, one of Shadow. Well then."

Amber chuckles and reveals her top card. "That's a… five of Shadow."

Ethan shrugs. "Well, you win this one. You can take your card and put it at the bottom of your stack," he shows off the winning action with his own card, though quickly removes it and sets it aside, picture-up. "But I lost, so I have to discard mine. And then we go again."

Amber takes her card and places it at the bottom of her stack, just as she was shown. "Simple enough."

They go again. Ethan draws a six of Light, and Amber a four of Shadow.

"Is this game not popular?" Amber asks.

"It's old," Ethan replies simply.

Five of Light and three of Light.

"How old?"

"All the way back to the Great War."

Three of Shadow and five of Light.

"Was the War two thousand years ago?"

Ethan pauses for a moment, card hovering in the air, and laughs. "No, of course not!" He places an officer of Light. Amber stares dejectedly at her one of Shadow.

"When did it happen?" she asks.

"Long time ago. No being knows exactly how long. Not even me."

"So how did you learn this game?"

"My... My Father taught me."

Thirteen of Shadow and ten of Shadow.

"You have family?"

"In a sense. It's complicated."

"How so?"

Seven of Light and officer of Light.

"Well, I'm more like a half-sibling. But I'm directly related to one who is also... directly related to the rest of the family."

"How does that work?"

Ethan scowls down at his cards, thinking.

Fourteen of Light and fourteen of Light.

"Ah, here we go," he muses. He draws another card and places it atop his fourteen. It's a six of Shadow. Amber does the same and reveals a one of Light.

"Tough luck," Ethan chuckles, placing his two cards under his stack.

Amber lets out a small hum and moves her own cards to her discard pile. "You didn't answer my question."

"Do I have to?"

"I'd like it if you did."

"Ah, how do I even begin?"

Nine of Shadow and ten of Light.

"Well, my sibling is a Shadow."

Amber pauses and looks up at him. "What?"

Ethan looks back at her, his expression dead serious. "My sibling is a Shadow."

"What does that even *mean*?"

Ethan lets out a sigh. "There are two types of Shadows..."

Eleven of Light and three of Shadow.

"One is just a regular Shadow, like yours. The other is

165

called a Fragment Shadow. Fragment Shadows, or just Fragments…"

Commander of Shadow and eleven of Shadow.

"…are created by the Spirit *of* Shadow. There is a Spirit of Light as well. The two of them created the universe, the beings, and the magic we practice…"

Three of Light and two of Shadow.

"As for me, I belong to a Fragment, therefore making me a half-sibling to the others."

"There's more than one Fragment Shadow?"

"Many more."

Thirteen of Light and thirteen of Shadow.

"So you're just a Husk, then?"

Amber places her card down, an officer of Shadow, and looks up at Ethan. His body is visibly tense, his eyes frozen on the cards between them. Slowly, he looks up at her, and his empty yet surprised stare sends a chill down her spine. Did she say something wrong?

After a long silence, Ethan lets out a heavy sigh and wordlessly places his card down in front of him. Four of Light. It takes Amber a moment to register that she has the higher card.

"Yes, I'm just a Husk," he finally admits, sliding his cards into his discard pile. He almost sounds ashamed to admit such a fact aloud.

"So… how are you able to… you know… *move*?" she asks. No wonder she found his eyes so lifeless and unnerving. That's because he's just an essenceless body masquerading as a living being.

Ethan shakes his head reluctantly in response. "It's a long story."

Two of Light and eight of Light.

"Can you give the short version?"

"That's kind of impossible."

"How come?"

"It involves Riona. A lot."

Nine of Light and six of Shadow. Amber stares at her dwindling stack of cards for a moment. Ethan sure is good at this game.

"You wouldn't understand without the full context," Ethan continues, moving to draw another card.

"Can you tell me anyway?"

"Maybe some other time."

Five of Shadow and twelve of Light.

"I miss it though."

"Miss who?"

"Shadow."

"*What*?"

"That's its name. Shadow," Ethan chuckles. "Creative, I know, but it insisted."

Four of Shadow and four of Light.

"It's been a while since I've seen it," he muses aloud.

Eight of Shadow and two of Light.

He exhales slowly as he moves his cards around. "Well, I've *seen* it, but not…" he shakes his head and amends with, "Shadow isn't who it once was. I want to see the old Shadow again."

"You two were close?"

Ethan lets out an amused chuckle. "Of course we were."

Ten of Light and champion of Light.

"I guess that's the simplest way to put my existence," he comments. "Shadow was lonely, so it made me."

"That's… kind of sad."

"It is."

Fifteen of Light and twelve of Shadow.

"We played Snap a lot, actually."

"Really?"

Ethan smiles. "It went a lot faster than this."

"Who won most of the time?"

"It was about half and half."

Seven of Shadow and seven of Shadow.

Fifteen of Shadow and nine of Light.

Amber slides the two cards into her discard pile with a sigh. "No wonder you're so good."

He rolls his eyes with a slight smile. "I think I'm just lucky."

She lets out a skeptical huff. "Sure you are."

Twelve of Light and six of Light.

"And what about the War?"

"What do you mean?"

"What *was* it?"

"Ah…"

Officer of Shadow and commander of Light.

"It was about the wizards and Guardians of old, to put simply."

"'Guardians'?"

"Once Astria was covered in a vast ocean…"

Two of Shadow and seven of Light.

"…which turned into what we know now as the Void. The Guardians made ships to travel across this ocean, and weapons of all sorts. But the one thing they didn't know was magic…"

Eight of Light and eight of Shadow.

One of Light and fourteen of Shadow.

"…which is where wizards come in. The first wizards were blessed with one of seven magics, although only six of them have been passed on through the generations after the War's end." He pauses for a moment, closing his eyes to recall something important. "There's a popular saying… 'From Light there is Life, from Shadow there is Death, with time but only an Illusion. Our history is preserved in Ice. Our dignity burns as bright as a Fire. And our strength is greater than that of a single Storm.'"

"That's a little long, isn't it?" Amber comments with a slight smile.

168

"It used to be much longer back then," Ethan chuckles. "While the use of magic has grown mundane in recent times, when it was first bestowed it was indeed a blessing to all of Astria. But in the years leading up to the War, it was twisted into a curse."

Champion of Light and thirteen of Light.

"What happened?"

"The Guardians got scared. The Spirit of Light instilled fear and paranoia into them, saying that the wizards would usurp their powerful grip over Astria. So, in retaliation, they started to kill the wizards. In secret, of course. They knew there would be outrage if they were ever found out. And the Spirit's so-called 'champion'," he holds up his champion of Light card, "was the worst out of all of them."

"But the wizards found out in the end?"

Ten of Shadow and commander of Shadow.

"Oh, they were furious," Ethan nods, "or so I was told."

"You weren't there?"

"I was… *Shadow* was made after the War ended."

"Oh."

Commander of Light and nine of Shadow.

"The wizards wanted vengeance. Simple as that. And that's how the War started."

"So… this is a Guardian game?"

"Yes."

Eleven of Shadow and champion of Shadow.

"Do other wizards know how to play?"

"Maybe at one point, but the resources that we have are better spent on other things instead of playing cards."

"Where did you get these cards from then?"

Twelve of Shadow and fifteen of Light.

"I created them."

"You made them… *yourself*?"

"Creation is a principle of Shadow magic, yes. But I can't

do it much."

Fourteen of Shadow and eleven of Light.

"But you can still make cards."

"It's pretty much *all* I can do. Anything I create needs a constant flow of magic to sustain it. Without Shadow, there's very little I can do."

"Because the Shadow is the essence of magic."

Ethan laughs brightly. "Yes, it is."

Champion of Shadow and fifteen of Shadow.

"I believe we're back to the cards we have used before."

Amber blinks. "You can tell?"

"Of course I can."

She looks down at her small stack, compared to Ethan's. "I think you won…"

"Not until one of us runs out," he replies with a sly smirk. He puts forward his next card. Amber, with a sigh, does the same.

Six of Light and five of Shadow.

Amber rolls her eyes.

Five of Light and five of Light.

Officer of Light and officer of Light.

The two are moving faster now.

Thirteen of Shadow and ten of Light.

Fourteen of Light and thirteen of Shadow.

Six of Shadow and officer of Shadow.

Snap, snap, snap goes the cards as they slam them down.

Eleven of Light and eight of light.

Commander of Shadow and twelve of Light.

Three of Light and champion of Light.

Nine of Light and commander of Light.

Four of Shadow and seven of Light.

Amber's stare grows intense. The only thing she is aware of are the cards before her, watching the numbers. She barely

170

even registers her hand movements.

Eight Shadow and eight Shadow.

Fifteen Light and fourteen Shadow.

Seven Shadow and commander Shadow.

Fifteen Shadow and champion Shadow.

Twelve Light and fifteen Light.

She's gotten rid of a few of Ethan's leftover cards. *Maybe I can still win this!*

Champion Light, officer Shadow.

Commander Light, champion Light.

Fourteen Shadow, commander Light.

Six Light, commander Shadow.

Five Light, champion Shadow.

Officer Light, fifteen Light.

Thirteen Shadow, champion Light.

Fourteen, commander.

Eleven, commander.

Commander, champion.

Eight, champion.

Fifteen, commander.

Champion, commander.

Champion of Shadow and champion of Shadow.

Amber pauses, her breathing heavy. She glances up at Ethan, who is also taking deep breaths. The two stare at each other in silence, not one of them moving. They're both down to their last three cards. They both have two champions.

"What if we're left with only champions?" Amber asks.

"Then it's a tie," Ethan replies.

Officer and champion.

Ethan lets out a low growl as he slides his officer into his discard pile.

Champion and commander.

Amber sighs, and her shoulders relax. She didn't even notice how tense she had gotten. Ethan runs a hand through his

171

hair and stares down at the cards, also releasing a blow of air.

"That was a decent first game," he says, finally looking up with a grin. "Well done."

"Thank you," she chuckles. "I guess I got lucky."

"You did make a good comeback at the end there."

"I thought I was going to lose."

"It may have turned out that way, but it didn't."

Amber moves to start shuffling her deck. "Want to go again?"

Ethan shrugs. "Sure."

Chapter 16

Lukri stares up at the second floor of the house. He can hear something snapping up there. It's sharp and quick and rhythmic. *What in the sands…?*

Anasi opens the door finally, its slight creaking catching his attention.

Good morning, Lukri, Anasi grins.

He smiles back. *Hi, Anasi! Thanks again for looking after those wizards for me.*

Are you here to see them?

Yep! Is the girl awake?

She has been for a while now. She roused yesterday, not long after you left.

Lukri looks back up again. *What's going on up there?*

He would have liked to continue staring, but then he wouldn't see Anasi's reply. He turns back to the elderly Serperas to find that she hasn't started her reply yet. She was probably waiting on him.

I don't know, but it sounds like they're having fun, Anasi says at last. She shifts out of the doorway and waves him inside.

He passes the dining table and fire pit quickly, heading directly to the stairs. He thought it'd be best to check on the two wizards before he went out sandboarding.

He pops his head up to find the two half-sitting on the bed, waving around flat white objects. They slam them down on the wood, each time producing that *snap* he heard from outside. Both are focused on the objects, sliding them around before slamming down more. Are they playing a game?

He doesn't want to interrupt them, so he watches quietly from the stairwell, resting his chin on the floor as he stares.

Eventually, Amber throws her hands up with a triumphant, "Yes! I win!" Ah, so it *is* a game!

Ethan just smiles along and claps. "Good job."

Amber bends over, probably collecting her white things. Ethan starts to do the same, but pauses and looks over at the stairs.

"Lukri!" he exclaims in surprise. Amber pauses and follows Ethan's gaze. The moment she lays eyes on Lukri, she jumps in surprise.

Lukri smiles. "Hello!" He places his hands on the floor and uses them to lift himself up out of the stairwell. "How are you?"

"We've been fine," Ethan replies, gesturing to Amber. "She's been recovering."

Amber nods. "Ethan told me you helped us get here the other cycle. Thank you!"

Lukri just chuckles and rubs the back of his head, unsure how to properly reply. She stares back at him with bright silvery eyes, the likes of which he's never seen before. Then again, he's never seen wizards until yesterday.

"I will sandboard now," he tells them. "Want to come?"

Amber tilts her head. "Sandboard?"

"It's pretty fun," Ethan tells her. "It's how we got here last cycle. Want to give it a try?"

Amber nods. "It'll be good to stretch our legs. Besides," she claps, and a burst of golden sparkles shimmer into existence, "I've not actually seen Mirage yet!"

174

"Then come!" Lukri beams, turning back to the stairwell. He doesn't even bother going around and walking down the steps like a normal Serperas. Instead, he crouches down and half-jumps down to the steps below. He turns to check if the other wizards are following.

"I'll clean up the cards," Ethan is saying to Amber. "Go on ahead."

"If you insist," she replies. She stands from the bed and strides over to the stairwell, the bottom of her robe fluttering behind her.

"Not hot?" Lukri asks.

"A little," Amber replies with a thin grin. As she speaks, she starts to roll up her sleeves. "But last night was really cold."

"Yes," Lukri nods, staring down the stairs, "the desert not hot at night. Cold helps Serperas sleep better."

Anasi is eating a piece of fruit at the table when he reaches the bottom. He gives her a smile.

I'm taking them sandboarding, he informs her.

Anasi arches an eyebrow and takes another bite out of her food. *Are you sure?*

Yes, Anasi. I'll be careful with them.

And what if you're seen with them, hm?

Anasi-

What will happen when your mother finds out?

Anasi-

Lukri, the suddenness of his name makes him pause. Something surges up from within him, making his gut churn and his chest flutter. Her colors are bright, normally meaning urgency or seriousness or shouting-

He shakes his head. *Snap out of it! It's Anasi, not mom. Anasi doesn't shout at you.*

You know I'm only trying to look out for you, Anasi says gently, probably only because she saw the alarm on his face. *You are a free spirit. She doesn't see that. But we both want you to be safe in our own rights.*

Lukri nods slowly. *I know…*

Anasi grins at him this time. *Now, go have fun little prince.*

Lukri nods again, his spirits only slightly lifted. *Thanks.*

"Lukri?" Amber asks behind him. "Is everything alright?"

Lukri turns to her and forces a wide grin. "Yes! Just talking." Amber just smiles along with him and nods. He's glad she doesn't question the matter further.

Ethan comes down the stairs finally, cape around his neck and hat firmly on his head, and nods to Anasi. "Morning." Anasi smiles and nods back at the wizard, the tip of her tail waving idly in the air.

Lukri claps, satisfied that everyone who is joining him on his excursion today is now present, and turns around again, striding to the door. He can hear the other two following along behind him, their footsteps loud and sharp on the sandstone floor.

They step outside, and Lukri takes a deep breath. The day is just starting, the sun just barely over the sands. He can't see it, for those dark clouds are in the way, but he's been awake at this time more than enough to know where it is already.

He gestures for the other two to follow him and starts off down the narrow alleyway that leads out to the sand plane. This time, he doesn't bother to check and make sure if the other two are following at all, rushing ahead eagerly. The sooner they are on the sands, the longer they'll have to explore.

Actually, he wants to take them over to the Old Ruins. He's only been a couple times himself, but he always finds them interesting to explore. They're not too far from the town, either.

He stops just at the edge of the buildings and stares out at the sand plane for a moment, breathing heavily. No matter how many times he looks at it, the vastness still entrances him. Throughout most of his day, he stares at them from afar, wishing he could spend all his free time gliding across them. Free time

176

he doesn't have.

He shakes his head and bends down. They're going to need boards.

He digs his hands into the sand and slowly exhales, focusing. The moment he feels the board's cold metal in his palms, he slowly rises the board up. The last few grains drip from the metal, and he grins in satisfaction.

Two more times. The others need one, too.

The second one emerges from the sands, though as Lukri stands to admire his handiwork the blood rushes to his head, and his vision blacks out for a moment. He takes a shaky step backwards, only for someone to catch him.

"You alright?" It's Ethan. They caught up to him finally.

"Y-Yes," Lukri forces, casting the board aside. No, he's not fine. Making two sandboards is an effort enough without his wand. He had tried hard just to be able to make *one* without passing out.

One more, he urges himself, feeling the hot and cold spots dance across his body chaotically. *One more…*

He kneels down and digs his hands in again. The sand was warm against his skin the first time, but now it seems to burn. He narrows his eyes and focuses, exhaling slowly once again. It feels like his insides are being sucked out of him, his stomach dropping as if he were airborne.

The metal brushes his fingers, and he lifts.

It's *heavy*.

He *feels* someone say something, for his ears vibrate with their words, but he's suddenly lost all capability to hear. Black spots dance across his vision, and he barely makes out a second person - Amber, he can see her green robe - bend down next to him and also grab onto the sandboard. With her help, the board pops up, and Lukri tumbles backwards and lands on his butt.

He squeezes his eyes shut for a moment and takes a

series of deep breaths, collecting himself.

"...you okay?" Ethan's voice fades in. Lukri opens his eyes for a moment and sees the two wizards bent down in front of him.

Lukri nods lazily, his neck feeling weak. "I..."

Amber reaches out with a hand and places it on his arm. Her touch is cold against his, making his skin tingle uncomfortably. A burst of golden sparkles rise from her fingers.

A cold yet calming energy flows from her touch, spreading up his arm to the rest of his body. Her silvery eyes are wide yet glazed, clearly concentrating.

The energy reaches from toes to fingers to head. It pulses, starting from his arm and rippling outwards. His breathing, first frantic from the sudden change in his body temperature, slows down significantly. His arms begin to tremble, becoming weak and heavy. His eyes close as his body relaxes, getting ready for rest.

And then the sensation drains away as Amber removes her hand. He blinks a couple times and turns back to the two wizards.

"He's okay," Amber says, mainly to Ethan. "He just needed some magic."

Lukri stares at her in confusion. Did she *give* him some of her magic? Is that what the coldness was?

She grins softly back at him. "How do you feel?"

"Better," he breathes. He pushes himself off his arms so that he's leaning forward, folding his legs underneath him. Amber puts a hand on his arm and helps to steady him as he stands. He gives her a weak smile. "Thank you." He puts a foot forward in the direction of the sandboards. "Come on."

He steps on one and bounces off, turning to check on the other two. Ethan is helping Amber with hers, teaching her as Lukri taught him yesterday. The sight makes him smile.

With the two wizards comfortably on their boards, they

start off, Lukri leading the way. With it being so early in the morning, very few Serperas are awake, and pretty much no one riding just yet. The perfect time to sneak off.

They leave the plane behind, weaving in and out of the dunes. Lukri spreads his arms wide and tilts his head back to face the sky. He feels his board rise and fall underneath him, letting the dunes take over for him.

"You were right, Eth," Amber shouts somewhere behind him, "this *is* fun! Haha!"

"So, are we just out for a ride?" Ethan asks loudly.

Lukri glances behind him with a smile. "Old Ruins!"

Ethan scowls in confusion. "What?"

"You will see!"

The group continue on in silence after that. Lukri is just happy to have the company. He's not really met many people. He's hardly allowed to run around on his own, let alone sandboard. It's unfortunate he can only explore during the early morning.

Besides, the two wizards have been nothing but nice to him. *Maybe mom was wrong about them.*

Finally, they ride over a dune, and Lukri points. "There!"

Ahead, hidden between the dunes, are a collection of sand-covered buildings. The place is bigger than his town, *much* bigger, with the old palace standing over the buildings, as if waiting for its previous inhabitants to return.

He hears Amber gasp behind him. "Wow..."

"Amazing," Ethan agrees.

The three ride up to the main street and stop. The street is wide and covered with small stone squares, many already half-buried in sand. Woven coverings are still, some with holes in them. Rugs are also covered in sand, their color faded and the fabric scratched.

Lukri's town has somewhat of the same set-up. The main street, where a lot of trade and distribution happens, cuts the town in half. In the center of town, which he can also see in the distance, is a water basin, where the pellets are kept. However, his always remains fully stocked. Here, it is only full of fine yellow-orange grains.

"Old Ruins," he says, waving a hand out over the desolate stalls, abandoned buildings, and run-down palace.

They walk down the street slowly. Lukri keeps an eye on the wizards, who stare at their surroundings in awe.

"This place is *huge*!" Amber marvels.

"And you can see the palace here," Ethan nods. "Why can't we see it at the other town?"

"Palace… kind of far," Lukri admits. "Was better that way?"

"You're in a desert," Amber points out.

Lukri just shrugs. "I didn't build it."

Honestly, he doesn't exactly know why the palace is so far from town. It was built there generations ago, long before his mother was even born. But no one complained about it, so there it stayed.

"Why did you leave this place behind?" Ethan inquires.

"Palace," Lukri gestures to the palace, "protects spring. Spring dried up. We were forced to move. Other spring… is far away, so we rebuilt.

"Royals in charge of protecting spring. Good fighters, good rulers. People have right to overthrow if royals are… *unfair*, too. Guards only meant to slow intruders. Royals are last to fall. At least, that is how they are seen." Lukri lets out a huff. "Stories are told of many royals. Some felled in battle. Some fending off entire armies. Some masters of the sands…" he trails off. Will he ever get to be like his ancestors?

"Is something wrong?" Amber asks.

Lukri forces a smile and shakes his head. "Good. Want to see inside?"

Amber's eyes sparkle with eagerness. "I'm sure it's

180

massive in there! Have you been inside?"

Lukri shakes his head again, though his excitement rises with hers. "Nope! Let's go!"

He and Amber break into a sprint, laughing the entire way. They weave around the empty water basin and streak past the empty buildings.

Suddenly, Ethan appears, running up next to them. Something bright flashes from his arms in long, jagged strings. He has a determined grin on his face, eyes on the palace gates ahead of them. His cape flutters behind him as he goes, almost looking like it's waving at them.

Slowly, he pulls ahead, leaving Lukri and Amber in his dust.

"No fair!" Amber calls after him.

"Nothing's fair!" he replies over his shoulder. Though it's said in a playful tone, the glimpse Lukri gets of his face tells another story. It's dead straight, the grin from earlier wiped clean off. He gets a sinking feeling that there's more to that statement than Ethan's letting on.

"Between us," Lukri breathes to her.

She smiles back at him. "Agreed."

The two continue, both exchanging first and second. Lukri feels exhilarated with the experience, alongside his growing tiredness. He's never been in a race before. Maybe against himself, but those races are no fun. Is this what it's like to compete with someone else?

The two reach the gate, made of large black iron bars, and collapse to the floor. Ethan waits for them to catch their breaths, casually leaning against the gate with his arms folded. He looks on like he is somehow in charge of watching after them.

"Who... won?" Lukri asks between breaths.

Ethan shrugs. "You two were pretty neck and neck."

"Tie?" Amber suggests.

Lukri nods along. "Sure." Even if they *both* won, he still

181

had fun.

The two pick themselves up and brush themselves off, then the three turn to the gate.

"It's closed," Amber mutters downheartedly.

"Why I not been inside," Lukri admits sheepishly.

Ethan rubs his hands together. "Shouldn't be much of a problem. Spirit of Ice!"

The temperature around them drops, almost making Lukri shiver. Mist rolls from Ethan's arms this time. He seems completely fine with it, unlike Amber, who hugs her arms close to her chest and seems to shake.

He raises his arms high, then slams his hands down on the ground. Something blue-white spreads from his fingers, shooting across the ground and stopping just briefly under the gate. Then there's a burst, and two glittering pillars shoot up from the places where the... *whatever-it-is* stopped. The pillars take the gate up with it and hold it in place high in the air.

"W-Wha...?" Lukri gasps.

Ethan turns to him, his lips pursed. He points to the pillars and asks, "Never seen ice before?"

Lukri shakes his head.

"It's like solid water."

"OH!" Imagine what his people could do if they had *ice*!

"Well? After you," Ethan steps aside and waves the other two onward. Amber giggles and starts forward, walking between the ice pillars without issue.

Lukri approaches one of the pillars and pauses. He can feel the coldness radiating from it, akin only to the chill of the night air. Slowly, he reaches out to touch it. Only for a moment, for he just as quickly reels away from it. The ice is so cold that it burned his fingers! He shoves his hand into his mouth and lets out a relieved sigh.

"Yeah, it's cold alright," Ethan says next to him, staring up at his handiwork.

"Do all wizards have ice?" he asks.

Ethan smiles and shakes his head. "No, not every wizard. But there are a lot that do."

"You?"

"I'm a Death wizard. I can talk to the dead and use their magic for a short time. Amber," he points at the distant girl ahead of them, "is a Life wizard. Her job is healing others and growing plants."

"Ah, we have... *Life wizards* too," Lukri replies, removing his hand from his mouth. "They do same as her."

"I figured," Ethan hums. "Now come on, let's not spend our time standing around all... *day*." Ethan walks through the pillars as well, hands slipping into his pockets. Lukri runs after him. He pretty much forgot that he doesn't have much time with them out here already.

Beyond the gate is the garden. Well, it *was* the garden. Now it's just sand and small patches of dead dirt. The gray stone pathway remains mostly intact, however. Even after all this time, the cut squares are still even.

Amber waits for them at the large front door. The other palace hardly has a door of the same size, or a garden as large as what this once was.

"You two took your time," she comments.

"*Some being* was admiring the ice," Ethan replies, jabbing a thumb at Lukri.

"Hey!" Lukri exclaims in irritation.

"That's okay," Amber chuckles. She turns to the door, one hand resting on the aged wood. With seemingly little effort, she pushes one half of the door open and peers inside. A quick moment later, she lets out a surprised gasp, one hand flying to her mouth, eyes wide with shock. Ethan peers through the gap and also pauses, his body tensing. His face holds no expression.

"What?" Lukri asks innocently, trying to see past the two.

Ethan turns to him and shakes his head. "I don't think you

183

want to-"

Anger rises inside Lukri. "I want to see!" He pushes Ethan out of the way, and the wizard stumbles aside in surprise.

Maybe he shouldn't have done that.

His eyes widen at the sight. The main hall - it's the same at the other palace, where one is led directly to the throne room - is dark, yet he can see what the other two probably already saw.

A body. Its skin is withered, tail shrunk to just barely a sliver, gray and rotting scales littering the floor around it, mouth agape in a silent scream. Its eyes are lifeless black sockets. It wears chain armor, much like what the guards he knows wears. Its hands are outstretched, as if it were trying to crawl away. And a silver spear pierces its torso, sticking upwards like a sort of marker.

"What...?" he breathes aloud. Without thinking, his legs take him inside the main hall. More guard bodies litter the ground, leading up to the throne. It's made of gold, or what he assumes to be gold, as it shines in what little light there is. All are impaled with either a spear or a longsword.

The king is even still sitting on his throne, a spear through where his heart once was. The circlet atop his skeletal head tells Lukri as much. It's silver, with a large faded blue water pellet inlaid in its center, between two open snake mouths. Tattered green cloth lay on the corpse's shoulders, quite possibly a magnificent robe at some point.

He ignores the other bodies around him, maybe fifteen in total, and walks right up to the throne. The king's empty eyes stare back at him. The circlet glimmers before him. The *king's* circlet.

"Serperas," he speaks aloud, his voice echoing around the empty hall, addressing the wizards whom he knows have already stepped inside after him, "are ruled by queens. We have one crown. I..." he hesitates. He shouldn't out himself. It could put him in danger, even if he's in the presence of those he considers to be his friends. They're wizards for ancestor's sake! They can turn on him whenever they want! And yet…

"I am only heir to our throne. But mom will have me marry. Wife… Wife will be crowned. She supposed to know everything. But that is me. I know everything. And I won't even rule. I was… never told…" he shakes his head, his voice catching. Slowly, he reaches for the king's circlet and plucks it off the corpse's head. He holds it in his hands delicately, as if it were to break at any moment from any applied force.

I was lied to.

All his life, he had been told that kings had never ruled. That the king is considered weak and selfish. That the king was only meant as a figurehead, a half to make a whole. A queen cannot sit alone, but a king cannot direct the people. And yet he was taught how to be a "queen". He hated every moment. It's why he sneaks out and sandboards. To give himself a small sense of freedom and carelessness. That his life isn't all palace walls and an impending marriage ceremony. He doesn't even know what his people think of him. They hardly see him, just as he hardly sees them.

How much of their known history has been made up? How much has he been lied to?

He doesn't even know what happened here. A battle, sure, that's clear enough. But why, and who did it, and when? Is this why the king stopped ruling? Was it something… *he* did, whoever this dead king was?

First it was wizards. Now it's kings.

Tears sting his eyes, still staring at the circlet. It's a relieving, confusing, and sickening sight, reminding him of his mother's golden circlet she always wears, a circlet he was never going to get. He still can't believe it. He thought this was going to be a fun morning, exploring the old palace and getting to know the wizards more. And yet there wasn't really a way to prepare for all this. He didn't even know it was *here*.

185

Two hands are placed, one on each of his shoulders. One for each wizard. Lukri sniffs and looks at the two, Amber on his left and Ethan on his right.

"Sorry..." he whimpers.

"It's only natural," Ethan replies calmly. Amber just smiles, appearing to be feeling the same sadness as Lukri, though probably for different reasons.

Ethan turns to look at the rest of the body-littered hall and says, "These poor souls. We should put them to rest."

Amber nods and appears to swallow hard. "But how?"

"Well, first we need to remove those weapons. Not completely; I'm sure some are so old that they'll break right off. Just as much as we can."

"Why?" Lukri asks quietly.

"Well..." Ethan hums, "it's more out of respect. Do you not honor your dead?"

"W-We do..." Lukri stammers. Indeed, they have ceremonies for those who are passing, have passed, and will pass, as well as for the ancestors of old. "Sorry..."

To free up his hands, he puts the cold circlet on his head as he makes his way back down the steps that lead up to the throne; the circlet remains perfectly balanced as he looks down to watch his feet as he descends. He passes Amber on the way, who is yanking a spear from the nearest body. The shaft breaks, leaving the tip still impaled in the body. With a sigh, she casts the shaft away, and it clatters on the floor loudly.

Lukri approaches a guard with a sword stuck in their chest. *Ancestors honor you for your sacrifice,* he says, though there's no Serperas around to read it. He grabs the hilt and tugs. There's a very audible *snap*, and the blade comes free. Well, most of it. There's a clean diagonal cut across the middle of the blade. Clearly there's still some sword inside the corpse, but-

The smell of the corpse hits his nose, an aged and putrid rot only released by the disturbance of the broken sword, and he

186

resists the overwhelming urge to vomit. He does step backwards a good distance before doubling over, a hand over his mouth and other over his nose.

He doesn't look forward to the next corpse he has to tend to. And yet a king's got to do what a king's got to do.

He collects himself and puffs out his chest to encourage confidence, approaching the next dead Serperas. This one has a spear. He grabs the shaft and pulls with all his might. After one or two good attempts, he lets out a few huffs and shakes his head. This one is in deep!

Readjusting his grip and *carefully* placing a sandal on the corpse's back, he tries again, leaning into the pull with all his might. He feels the weapon begin to slide free. Once again, he pulls with his entire body. There's more of a jolt this time, the spear almost popping right out. He straightens himself and gives it a fifth try.

"Ah!" he exclaims in surprise as the spear suddenly flies free. The tip is still on and everything! He backs away from the corpse before the smell has a change to reach his nose and inspects the weapon.

Shockingly, it's in relatively good condition. The tip is a little chipped and there's a slight fracture in the shaft, but otherwise it seems to not be as time-touched as some of the other weapons appear. Nothing a little love and attention couldn't fix.

"This one is good," he says, mainly showing the spear to Amber. She drops the half of a sword she holds as she stares at the weapon he presents to her.

"That's surprising," she replies, gesturing to a trail of discarded weaponry left in her wake. "Everything I've pulled out so far is shattered beyond repair."

"I'm *lucky*," Lukri boasts simply. He twirls the spear in his hands and jabs at the air a couple times. Not only is it light like sand, but it moves through the air with ease. Yes, it's a good

187

weapon alright. Whoever made it knew their craft very well. Maybe he'll keep it, just as a keepsake.

He carries the spear around with him as he pulls out more half-broken weapons from bodies. He gives some of them prayer, like the first one he went to, but not all. He doesn't want to make himself sick of saying it. At least he's kind of doing what Ethan said. Respecting *some* of the dead, at least.

"Rest in peace," Amber mutters, retrieving the last broken spear from the final body. The two stand together and stare at the amount of weaponry they had removed.

"That's a lot," she comments.

Lukri nods. "Yes. Maybe can be used again."

"I think you'll be asked where you got all *this* from," she replies, gesturing around the hall.

"Ah, true." He doesn't even know what he'll say if he were asked. "Maybe leave, then. For now."

"I agree."

The two approach Ethan, who observes from the dias the throne sits on.

"You didn't even help," Amber pouts.

Ethan smiles back at her. "Don't worry. I had some preparation to do of my own." Amber makes a small *tsk* noise and folds her arms.

Ethan rolls his eyes, then turns to Lukri. "I wanted to do this one with you." He waves to the king. Lukri nods in agreement. He would like to pay his respects to his ancestor, whoever he may be.

"You can wait outside if you'd like, Amber."

Amber nods. "I'll give you two space. Lukri, I can hold that for you."

Lukri passes her his new spear. "Thank you."

The two boys watch her walk among the dead and eventually exit through the big front door, her pink hair waving at them before completely disappearing from view.

188

Ethan lets out a deep sigh and turns to the body. "The weapon first."

"Right."

Lukri steps forward and grips the spear shaft. He takes a breath, mustering his strength, and gives the weapon a yank. It comes clean out, tip and everything, though the damage is clear. The shaft around the spear tip is already cracked through and splintering, and the tip itself is flat, having been smashed into solid metal.

"No good," he mutters, mostly to himself, as he casts the spear carelessly aside. It bounces down the steps, the tip separating from the shaft along the cracks as it goes.

It takes a good long moment for the spear's metallic ringing to fade away.

"Press your palms together, like this," Ethan presses his palms together, holding his hands at chest level. Wordlessly, Lukri does the same. The two turn their attention to the dead royal before them.

"Try and repeat after me. It's okay if you get some of the words wrong,"

O spirit, though Death was not yours to choose, we release you.
To reunite with your loved ones in the White Beyond,
and to have your story be told to generations to come.
To never be forgotten, and to live on eternally.
Rest peacefully.

Lukri closes his eyes and does his best to repeat, but some of the words come out a little slurred. However, he pushes through to the end. When he opens his eyes, he sees the royal's body erupt into rich purple sparkles, fading away. It's not long before the throne sits empty.

Lukri drops his hands to his sides and lets out a heavy sigh. Ethan places a hand on his shoulder.

"A lot to take in?" he asks.

Lukri nods. "Many questions."

The wizard pats his shoulder, then turns to stare out at the rest of the hall again.

"This will take a while," he says. "Why don't you wait outside with Amber? Get some fresh air."

Lukri nods slowly. He'll come back in anyway. There's still more to explore, after all.

He steps down from the dias and trudges to the door, keeping his head high so as not to look at the dead around him. The circlet on his head grows cold, reminding him of its presence. How long has such an item been sitting here for? And, more importantly, *why*?

Chapter 17

Amber and Lukri are drawing in the sand when Ethan finally emerges from the main hall.

"It's done," he says, causing the two to look up from what they were doing. Lukri is bent over a collection of small pictures, one finger outstretched, with Amber standing over a half-finished face, using the spear Lukri had recovered earlier as some sort of oversized quill. He can see an eye, nose, and mouth. The second eye and hair are still missing, however.

"That took a long time," Amber says.

Ethan nods. "It was a lot to do," he turns to Lukri and asks, "Have you heard of such a battle taking place?"

Lukri shakes his head. "No. Why?"

"Well, those bodies didn't seem very old," he folds his arms and scowls at the ground. "It was hard to judge their age, seeing as they were preserved fairly well, but they shouldn't be more than a couple hundred years old at the very least."

"*Only?*" the prince gasps.

Ethan shrugs. "It's just a guess. I could be wrong."

The three fall silent.

"Well," he speaks again, rubbing his hands together, "we can go back inside now, if you want. Or do we need to go back?"

He glances up at the sky, where the sun is just starting to make its way across the bright blue above, the stars shining very faintly in the background.

Lukri also looks upwards, though only for a moment.

"No," he replies slowly, "we can explore."

"Are you sure? Won't your mother-"

"I want to stay," Lukri snaps back angrily. "Stay longer. All day if we can."

"But Lukri," Amber exclaims, "your people will get worried!"

"Let them," he growls. He storms back through the palace doors without another word, keeping his eyes down at the ground. Ethan simply stares after him.

"Think he'll be okay?" Amber asks quietly, appearing at his side.

"It sounds like he's got some damage to sort out," Ethan replies, readjusting his hat. "Maybe he will, maybe he won't." Amber nods, though still appears worried. Ethan is, too. Who knows what panic is stirring back in town.

He nods to the door. "We don't have anywhere else to go, so we may as well keep an eye on him."

"Sure."

Amber goes in first, Ethan only a step or two behind her. The throne room is empty now, the faint smell of rot still lingering in the air. At least the dead have finally been laid to rest.

"Where's Lukri?" Amber asks aloud, looking around. The young prince is nowhere to be seen.

Ethan bites his bottom lip. If they somehow *lost* the heir to Mirage and are caught by the other Serperas… "He couldn't have gone far. You can take a look down here. I'll scout upstairs." Amber nods with his suggestion.

The two split up. Amber enters a small doorway on the left side of the throne room as Ethan makes his way to the stairs. There's two sets of stairs, one on either side of the throne, but both lead to the same place. The second floor.

Some of the steps are full of chips and cracks. Most are relatively intact. Some sort of red paint runs down the center of the stairs, almost like a fake carpet. It's been mostly chipped away, however.

Yes, a lot of materials the palace is made from seem to not have come from Mirage. This place was clearly built back when there was still some sort of trade between the Serperas and the other islands. The walls are made of white stone. The building's exterior seemed to be made of some sort of red clay. The torn fabrics woven in a distant land. Metals and rich wood. Even the weapons didn't seem like something the Serperas would even make anymore due to their isolation.

The second floor consists of a long hallway that stretches to a corner and turns, making a sort of "U" shape out of the building. Doors line the hallway, all of them closed except for one. Ethan approached the cracked door, which is positioned directly between the two staircases, just behind the throne down below.

"Lukri?" he asks, pushing the door open.

He finds himself standing in a sort of study, with a worn wooden desk and chair, and large bookshelves lining the side walls. A window takes up most of the back wall, opening up to a small balcony. Lukri stands there, leaning on the railing, staring out at the scenery behind the palace.

Slowly, Ethan makes his way to the balcony, running his hand over the rugged surface of the desk as he goes. Once outside, he sees a large depression lined with gray pebbles, and surrounding it a mass of dead trees. Rotted wood, snapped trunks, yellow-orange remains of leaves. Some bushes remain as well, though they are no more than a mere collection of fragile twigs. Somewhere in the chaos, he thinks he sees a small wooden shack, its roof caved in and one of the walls starting to peel away from the rest of the structure. Needless to say, it's a

193

mess.

"Once a spring," Lukri says, still staring out at the decaying nature. "Dry now."

"Maybe it just ran out of water," Ethan suggests. Lukri tilts his head, his expression troubled.

"I think it's more," he says. "I have a feeling."

"Maybe it's a royal instinct?" Ethan chuckles. Lukri just rolls his eyes.

"Why?" he mutters. He turns to Ethan and repeats, "Why did she lie to me?"

"Who?"

"Mom."

Ethan just shrugs. "She may have many reasons. Safety. Protection."

"Fear. Be-little-ment," the prince growls quietly.

"I don't think she'd mean any harm-"

"You don't know."

Ethan folds his arms with a scowl and turns away from the Serperas. "You're right, I don't know."

"…But," the prince mumbles, "would be nice to live here."

"The place sure is big."

"Imagine before. What it would be like."

"It was probably very lively."

"Palace would be open. Big celebrations in the hall. Feasts…" Lukri trails off, smiling wistfully at whatever fantasy is playing out in his own head.

"Does that not happen?"

The prince's smile fades as he shakes his head. "I don't leave palace much. Just me, mom, guards and gardeners. And… it is too far to host celebrations."

"You never spend time in town?"

"Can't. Always busy with *duties*. And sandboarding… very lonely."

"Well, you have me and Amber now. And speaking of

194

whom, we should go check on her," he says with a slight elbow nudge against Lukri's arm. "She's looking around downstairs for you."

Lukri lets out a reluctant sigh and turns away from the dead nature. "Might as well."

The two make their way back downstairs, and Ethan leads the way to the hole in the wall where Amber last disappeared through. Beyond it is a long room with a stone table down the center, and stone chairs carved with all sorts of fancy symbols. A couple he notices include symbols Lukri has been drawing outside moments before.

"Some sort of language?" he asks, pointing to the chairs.

Lukri nods. "Old written language. Not used much but often than spoken," he points to one of the chairs. "Where prince would sit. Then queen," the next chair up, and then the head of the table, "and king."

In fact, he stops at the king's chair and stares at it. It's decorated with many small pictures of Serperas - Ethan can see the tails - wearing silver circlets and holding scepters. Each one is slightly different, but he figures that they all mean the same thing. King.

"Oh, there you are!" he hears Amber exclaim, and Ethan turns his head to face her. Lukri does as well, though it's clear he really had to peel his eyes away to look at her. Amber smiles at the two as she exits from a second doorway not too far from where they stand.

"Kitchen," she says, gesturing at the doorway. "Very spacious but pretty empty, too. And there's a hallway at the other end, for the servants I guess, but it's kind of dark so I didn't go in."

"Maybe for the best," Ethan hums. Who knows what might spring from the shadows? He doesn't, that's for sure. Amber nods, her smile thinning ever so slightly.

Lukri looks around the dining hall. "Big place."

195

"It is," Amber nods in agreement.

"We can spend all cycle exploring the place if we so wish and still not see everything," Ethan hums, "yet I think we should go back now. Your mother might be worried, Lukri."

Lukri shakes his head. "I... want to stay longer."

"If you stay then your people will come looking for you here-"

"Don't care. Stay. All day."

"Lukri-"

The prince turns to Ethan in an instant, fire in his eyes. "Answers here! History! Things mom lied about. Like kings. I want to know *more*!"

"We can come back," Ethan replies firmly. "This doesn't have to be a one-time thing. Your people should be more important right now."

Lukri's anger seems to subside quite a bit at the mention of his people. Though he still appears irritated as he shakes his head.

Amber steps forwards with a supportive, though weak, smile. "It's for the best, Lukri."

"Late," the prince mutters simply. "Should be back sooner."

The wizards fall silent for a moment.

"Duties start now," Lukri adds with a bitter voice. "Not there, panic. Might as well stay."

"They'll come looking," Ethan points out.

The Serperas lets out a sigh. "Close the gate. Then... we can look more."

Ethan simply scowls. Lukri might as well just go home and get caught rather than staying in this ruin all cycle with two wizards and have his mother come looking for him in a rage. She'd not be in the mood for explanations. She would just want her son back.

A chill runs down the back of his neck as Riona's young

196

voice hisses in his ears, *I wasn't* asking*, Ethan.*

He folds his arms uncomfortably. It's been a while since he's heard it, though he's been pretty preoccupied as of late for it to manifest. Although… she's not a true queen.

He abruptly turns to leave. "As you wish."

"Ethan?" Amber breathes.

"Who am I to argue with royalty?" Ethan says over his shoulder. "If he's willing to bear responsibility, then we can stay a little longer."

Amber is quiet after that.

Cape flowing behind him, Ethan makes his way back into the main throne room and then makes his way to the large front doors of the palace. The presence of death presses against his skin. Spirits still linger here, he senses, though he is unaware if they mean good or ill.

He reaches the door and steps outside, the warm desert air a good refresher from the stuffy interior of the palace. The gate is still propped open with the ice he made earlier, the white-blue pillars sparkling in the sunlight. There's no easy way to let the gate down gently. Might as well go for the next best thing.

He rubs his hands together. "Spirit of Fire." Almost instantly, flames curl around his arms with all their might. He extends his arms towards the ice pillars and parts his legs, bracing himself as the magic collects in the palms of his hands. And then he lets the two fireballs fly.

They shoot through the air so fast he hardly sees them before they strike the ice. The pillars burst, sending glittering shards up into the air, creating a bright sparkling rain of crystals. The gate, free at last, crashes down with a loud *thump*, kicking up a large cloud of dust and sand in the process and it buries itself deep into the soft ground below it. His cape flutters behind him and hits the back of his legs as the fire dies and the spirit leaves him once more. He lets out a heavy breath as his limbs sag heavily. What's done is done.

Amber curled up on the floor of the throne room to rest for a bit. Ethan loaned her his cape to use to cushion her head. He said that rest is good for her memories. Then he went up to the study and has been reading those dusty books one by one ever since.

Like a child, Lukri ran through the entire palace *twice* at this point, the time now just past midday. Everything is twice as big as the palace he grew up in, especially the bedrooms. The beds - many left to rot, covered in sand and, when he tried to sit on one of them, extremely uncomfortable and easy to break - are, by far, much nicer than the one he sleeps on currently, which is nothing more than a small wooden frame covered with the best leaves from the garden, changed regularly. These beds here were made of actual *fabric*, and not the scratchy cotton kind of fabric from the palace garden. Though the nice clothes he wears are crafted from a small plant called *ingaris* that makes soft yet thin threads up to a certain length a day. One of his shirts takes at least a full *year* to make from that stuff, with there being few *ingaris* plants grown due to their high demand of attention and care, and his mother absolutely *refuses* to give him anything made from cotton.

Now he stands in the dark doorway at the other end of the stone kitchen, staring into the darkness of the small hallway Amber had mentioned earlier. It's completely unlit, and there's nothing around he could use as a torch to light his way. At least, nothing he's found. The palace is mostly empty, with many of the items left within it sanded over and falling apart. Still, he's unsure if it's any worth exploring the hallway to begin with.

He holds his arm out to his side, palm open. What sand there is around him swirls and gathers, until he curls his fingers around the cold shaft of a jade wand. It's nothing fancy, just a simple jade stick with a flat disk fixed to one end, his focal point.

He stares at it long and hard. Is it worth spending his magic to create some light to explore this hallway? He's spent so much already. It's either make light himself or…

A sharp chill rushes through his body, making Lukri stand rigid in place. There's no *way* he's braving the dark.

Fine… he lets out a small sigh and holds his wand up in front of him. The disk flickers for a moment and he concentrates his energy, trying to mentally push it through his arm and up into the wand. Eventually, the flickering light steadies into a soft white glow, bright enough for him to see. With that, he steps into the hallway and goes right.

The hallway is just barely big enough to give himself room to comfortably walk with his arms at his sides. The ceiling is low, just barely managing to scrape the top of his head if he bounces upwards a little too much, clearly made to be navigated with a tail and not legs. An adult Serperas would have a very uncomfortable and difficult time navigating this hallway on legs for sure. There are little indents in the wall with black-ash-stained torches fixed in place, though they all appear to be split in some way, shape, or form, and rotting due to age and neglect.

Eventually, he steps into a small room with much more space to stand and walk about. It has no windows, yet light streams in from the outside through cracks in the wall, revealing the mostly empty room without the need for his wand. With a thankful sigh, Lukri allows the light of his wand to fizzle out.

The backlash is almost instantaneous. His legs become weak and shake violently, threatening to have him collapse. Blood rushes to his head. His vision blurs, spots dancing around and blocking his sight. He takes a step forward and half-falls, half-lowers himself to his hands and knees, breathing heavily. Still, he keeps his wand in hand.

Once his vision clears, he looks up to inspect the room a little more closely. The only thing left in it is a single low stone platform or legless table, and two small statuettes that sit in its center, one gold and one silver.

Not wanting to crawl, Lukri forces himself to his feet and staggers over to the statuettes, kneeling before them on his weak legs. The silver statuette appears male in figure, and the gold one female. Idols of the king and queen, no doubt. He almost can't help but smile at the cute little figures before him, his heart warmed. Only for a moment. Why were these things left here?

He places his wand on the ground next to him and picks up the statuettes. While appearing made of real metal, they're a lot lighter than he first thought as he weighs them in his hands. Maybe it's for the same reason the king's circlet got left behind. At the thought of the circlet, the band of silver on his head grows icy cold. Right, he's even still wearing it.

He puts the statuettes back onto the stone table, closes his eyes, and takes a long, deep breath, placing his hands on his knees. He lets his body dance with his question:

Ancestors of this place… what happened?

It's quiet in the room. Peaceful, even. If he truly felt like it, he could probably live here on his own. It'd be a hard life, but a simple one. The silence is nice. The only other time he gets to hear it is at night, at the end of a wild day of lessons and berating.

Then, a sudden cold blast of air batters his face, and a voice behind him shouts, "Hey!"

It startles Lukri, making him jump and his eyes snap open. The room now suddenly looks completely different from how he first found it. The place is lit with a soft orange glow, emanating from two small braziers on either side of the stone table. Small clusters of vibrant flowers lay around the two statuettes, which remain in the same place from when he set them down. He spins around and sees that the ground is carpeted with dark purple cushions for kneeling. The place is some sort of prayer room, he guesses.

Standing in the doorway is a Serperas dressed in guard armor, giving him a rather stern look as he points to the doorway with his silver spear. "Throne room, *now*."

Lukri pulls a horrified look as he looks down at himself. No longer does he don his shirt and sash of royalty. Instead, he now wears a plain white shirt full of holes and stained with sand dust, that of a simple servant. He also has his tail out, but it's not *his* tail. His is supposed to have vibrant green scales, but *this* tail he's staring at is a clayish red.

He looks back up at the guard, fear piercing his thoughts. From the look of the guard and the sound of his voice, Lukri shouldn't argue with him and just... *go*. Somewhere down the hall, screams echo eerily.

Slowly, he slithers through the doorway of the prayer room, followed closely behind by the guard, his spear poking Lukri's back to keep him moving. The torches he passed on his way to the prayer room are now all lit without any signs of age or rot on them. Ahead of him, he sees other servants being herded into the kitchen by similarly dressed guards, carrying an assortment of swords and spears.

What is this? he can't help but wonder as his stomach churns sickeningly. He doesn't want to see what may lie beyond the kitchen.

When he reaches the kitchen doorway, the guard behind him leans forward and angles his spear to direct Lukri *into* the kitchen. The prince takes a shaky breath, trying to muster courage as he turns. The kitchen is full with various cooking utensils and abandoned food, clearly in the midst of being prepared for some sort of meal. Many fruits are left half cut or sizzling in pans over open fires. The dining hall is empty, aside from some guards eyeing his every move to make sure he doesn't do anything stupid. Still, he is followed from behind by the guard that found him in the prayer room. The commotion, screams and gasps and horrified chatter, grow ever louder as he nears the throne room.

He joins a collection of other palace servants all held back by even more guards. Some are crying. Others hide their faces and turn their backs to the hall. Others stare on, entranced. Lukri quickly falls into the third category as he stares in shock at the scene that lay before him.

Through the wall of guards, he sees the bodies of the Serperas he, Amber, and Ethan laid to rest that very same morning, all laying on the floor of the throne room with swords and spears sticking from their bodies. Simply a display, nothing more.

Slowly, he turns his head to the dias where the thrones sit. Some Serperas in regular town clothes are carrying down one of the golden thrones as the king lays held in his own. They're removing the queen's throne, yet leaving the king's. Two Serperas hold the king's arms down, and a third, a guard, points a spear at the king's chest. He stares on with a look of horror, disgust, hurt, and betrayal. His green robes are all cut, and any exposed sun-tinted skin of his is covered in bleeding cuts. And he's staring solely at the queen, who grins back up at him triumphantly from the bottom of the dias.

"*Traitor*," the king growls.

"Now, now," the queen tisks, making her voice loud so that the entire room can hear her, "we all know that *you* and *only you* are the cause for our spring drying up!"

A roar of confirmation rises from the guards that keep the servants in check, along with any other armed Serperas from the town outside who are present. The ones with the queen's throne carry the seat out of the palace doors, keeping their heads low.

"You are many things," the queen continues, "but the one thing you are *not* is a king."

The king opens his mouth again to protest, but the guard with the spear shoves the tip into the king's chest just enough so that a cry of agony masks his words instead.

"The ancestors have given us a second chance already. A smaller spring many dunes away from here is where we'll rebuild. And we will thrive without the rule of any shadow-kissed king. May your glorious legacy be hereby forgotten."

The queen gives the guard a single wave and turns away from the dias. The guard, with what looks to be a wide, eager grin from where Lukri sits, rams the spear into the king's chest as hard as he could. The king's eyes bulge, mouth agape. His body squirms in the firm grip of his captors in one final attempt to escape before ultimately growing still and limp in the very chair he once oversaw rule of the Serperas.

Lukri feels like he should be sick. But the more he stares, he only grows *sad*. His heart sinks in his chest at the scene. Tears spring to his eyes as a lump in his throat begs to leap up out of his mouth.

This is why he has no throne, no circlet, and no true authority. The legacy of kings died long ago. Right here.

"*Lukri!*"

His name pierces his thoughts, and in a blink the scene shifts back to the semi-dark room with the small statuettes and cold stone ground. His cheeks are wet from tears. His heart is still heavy as stone. Though it had only been some sort of vision, it will forever remain imprinted inside of him.

"Lukri!" his name is called once again. It's Amber, her voice light like a chime. "Where are you?"

Without thinking, he grabs the statuettes and his wand as he stands. He walks through the darkness of the hallway that brought him to that cursed room, not caring for light in the slightest. He turns into the kitchen, passes through the dining hall, and only looks up from the floor when he reaches the throne room once again. No longer is the place bright and colorful. Death lingers in the air much heavier now, pressing his shoulders down with its weight.

"Here," he mutters quietly. Amber, who has wandered to the staircase, and Ethan, who stands at the top of the staircase, stare at him with looks of relief at first, then concern upon noticing his crestfallen expression.

"Lukri?" Ethan asks simply, descending the stairs. Amber is already rushing up to Lukri. The closer she gets, the more Lukri wants to simply let everything out of him. Pain, sadness, hopelessness. The statuettes grow heavy in his hands. The circlet on his head is as cold as Ethan's ice.

Amber reaches out and puts a comforting hand on his shoulder. "What happened?"

Something snaps inside him.

His face twists into that of grief, lips trembling. Where he stands, he shakes and hiccups as tears flow free from his eyes, making his cheeks burn. His grip on the statuettes only tightens, wanting to crush them with his might.

The wizard, without a word, gives him a hug.

Lukri can't help but feel embarrassed on top of everything else currently going through his mind. The great prince of Mirage, a crying mess. And in front of *wizards*, no less! Why did he bother fighting to stay? Why didn't he listen to Ethan's suggestion and simply go *home*? Mother probably would have not been as angry as she may be now if he reappears at the palace doorstep. Now they should be somewhere in the midafternoon, night fast approaching. None of his people know where he is. He's with two wizards who don't exactly carry upstanding reputations among the Serperas for simply being *wizards*. He doesn't want to go back and face his mother, not yet. He's got nowhere to go, with two beings he's barely gotten to know as his only friends and comfort.

All those thoughts simply make him feel even *more* miserable.

He doesn't know how long he stood there crying his eyes dry, nor how long Amber hugged him for, nor how long Ethan stood off to the side to give Lukri space. But, at some point, he grows tired of crying, and he finally begins to calm himself down. He wipes his face dry with the backs of his hands as Amber steps away from him. The wizards stand in front of him, both staring on with deep concern.

"Sorry..." Lukri says, his voice still somewhat choked.

"Don't be," Amber replies gently. She offers him a sympathetic grin. "Feel better now?"

Wordlessly, Lukri nods.

"Would you like to talk about where you were?" Ethan asks, gesturing to the wide open floor of the throne room. Again, the prince only nods. He trudges forward, dragging his feet, then stops in the middle of the room and sits down. He wills his legs into his dark green tail, which appears underneath him fairly quickly. He curls it up into a tight spiral and lays on the ground on his side, staring off at a random crumbling pillar that continues to hold up the ancient ceiling above them.

Ethan balls up his cape and offers it to Lukri. "For your head." The prince accepts the kind gesture and props his head up on the make-shift pillow. It's... a rather comfortable pillow, actually. The other two wizards sit in his field of view to make it easier for him to stare at them. His stomach churns as he rests on the dusty ground.

"There is a prayer room," he says slowly, wanting to say everything right. He holds out his hands and reveals the small statuettes. "Idols of the king and queen. Prayer to them meant to bring good fortune. And... the ancestors gave me a vision. What happened..." his voice chokes up once again, and he falls silent or else he'd start sobbing again.

"The spirits showed you what happened here?" Ethan breathes with interest.

"Let him calm down again," Amber advises quietly.

Lukri takes a couple deep breaths to get his emotions back under control, then nods the best he can while laying on his

205

side. "It was the queen."

The wizards simply stare at him in silence, both of their eyes wide.

"She… was not nice. Blamed the dry spring on the king. She turned the Serperas against the king and took power. Left everything here, to make sure the legacy of kings died with him."

"Oh…" Amber gasps. Ethan just folds his arms, appearing to enter a state of contemplation. Even a simple recounting of the vision he witnessed just makes Lukri feel even more sick to his core.

"I… don't want to go home," he adds in a whisper.

"You have to go back eventually," Ethan says simply.

"Not now."

The wizards look at each other for a moment, then back at him with looks of understanding.

"Can we stay the night?"

Ethan lets out a low hum and closes his eyes, appearing to be thinking.

"I see no issue with that," Amber agrees with him. "Ethan?"

"I don't have enough magic to make us comfortable," the wizard replies, almost sounding a little disappointed with himself. "Maybe pillows and blankets at-"

"Ethan," Amber interrupts with a small sigh, "stop it."

And so he stops talking and just stares at her.

"We can make it work," she adds with a small, hopeful grin.

Chapter 18

Ethan retires to the study once again, leaving Amber to care for an emotionally wrecked prince in the throne room. The book he had been reading before stepping out to check on the other two still lays open on the desk, its yellow pages surprisingly smooth and intact. None of the books turned to dust under his fingers, thankfully.

Most of what he's read so far were history books and records from the royal court, back when the palace was alive and full of Serperas. None of the records are dated very far back in history, at least nothing that he's read so far. The oldest he's been able to uncover is only two thousand years old. It had the visible aging for such a record book as well.

He sits down again on the old chair left standing behind the desk and sighs down at the open book. It stares back up at him, the little black ink words and pictures waiting to be read. The edges of the pages are lined with small Serperan pictures, a small handful of them he recognized as ones that Lukri had been drawing outside in the sand earlier in the cycle, but the bulk of the content is written plainly.

He's in no mood to read anything more. His thoughts stew within him. He feels like he should be able to provide more for the other two. Do more to help Amber. Do more to comfort Lukri.

If Shadow were here…

But Shadow *isn't* here right now. It's just Ethan, all alone.

The Mirage sun outside is slowly sinking, its light filling the study with its red glow. His backside warms from the light beaming onto him.

He wonders what Shadow is doing right now. Since fleeing Asandra, the link between the two of them has grown cold once again. But last time it happened it made him hesitate, and it led to his friends getting attacked. He doesn't exactly know what he'll do now. Things have changed. He can't afford to hesitate again, regardless of how much he knows or not. He's already put Amber in danger and through enough pain already. Luck is only on his side for her because she's a Healer. But Lukri…

He remembers the large black cloud lingering in the distance from Anasi's home, and how she said that "dark things" were happening at the palace. Lukri isn't safe on his own island, either.

Without warning, an old conversation surges forward…

"Riona, why are there clouds in the sky?"

"Tch. You and Shadow stargaze too much."

"I don't think it's been affecting our performance-"

"I don't need your attention divided between those little specks of light and me!"

"Please, Riona-"

"You don't need the stars, Ethan. Now go do your job and don't bother me."

"…As you wish."

With a heavy sigh, he closes the book, having not touched it for some time now, and stands. Oh, how naive he had been at the time.

The palace is silent as he stops to listen. The presence of spirits hasn't faded in the slightest, leaving behind cold drafts of air as they drift about, their ever-so-faint whispers swirling in his ears. He'd not be completely surprised if Serperan spirits operated differently from wizard spirits.

He makes his way back to the throne room, where Lukri still lays on his side on the ground, Amber fiddling with the spear he gave her to hold at the cycle's beginning. Though, as if sensing his presence, she looks up to face Ethan as he stands at the top of the stairs.

"Hey," her voice echoes across the room. She both sounds and appears rather bored. Lukri shifts on the ground, lifting his head momentarily to see who Amber just addressed, but puts it back down upon seeing Ethan as well. He lets out a quiet, tired huff.

Ethan makes his way down the ruined stairs and approaches the two slowly.

"How are you doing?" he asks Amber.

She gives him a weak smile and turns back to staring listlessly at the spear in her hands. "My head doesn't hurt as much anymore, so I think I have most of my memories back. But..." She pauses, a scowl flashing across her face. "It's strange."

"What's strange?" he presses, lowering himself to sit by her side.

"I think I have all my first term memories, but... nothing before that."

"Nothing about your parents or childhood?"

She shakes her head. "No."

"Maybe they'll come back soon."

"Maybe..." Amber doesn't sound so sure.

The three of them stare at one another in silence. While an old ruin may not be Ethan's ideal place to spend the night right now, at least he's not here alone.

209

"Fire," Lukri eventually speaks, his eyes on Ethan expectantly, "for night."

"Right," he nods. It'll certainly be cold in here by the time night falls. Ethan stands, taking the initiative to put himself to good use. "I'll bring in some brush for us to use."

"Will you need help?" Amber asks as he strides over to the palace's front door.

"No, I'll be fine," Ethan replies over his shoulder. He reaches the door and opens it, tugging the heavy wood towards him to make the opening wider so that he's not struggling to bring anything in when he comes back.

The sky is turning to the blackness of night, stars twinkling high above him. The ruined town beyond the palace gate is blissfully silent as the warm air around him begins to cool. They'll need at least a small fire going soon if they want to stay warm.

He treads across the desolate front garden and around the side of the palace to the sad memorial of the dead back garden. Plenty of decaying leaves lay about, easy to collect and good enough for kindling. He peels some dead bark off rotting trees as well, which will burn a little longer. He even piles on a couple sticks from the lifeless bushes. It doesn't take very long to collect enough to fuel a small fire for a little while. And with all this wood just laying around, they'll not need to worry about running out of things to burn for a couple cycles. The thought makes him let out a semi-amused huff. If they ever stayed for that long, which he suspects that they won't.

The wood and sticks snag on the sleeves of his robe as he carries his armful back around the side of the palace. It's not extremely heavy, but certainly annoying to carry around.

He looks up, careful not to tilt his head too far back for fear of his hat falling off. While it's not dark enough to see many of the stars, the few he can already make out wink back at him.

Can Shadow see them, too?

He reaches the corner of the palace and turns, striding

towards the front door. The pile of decaying nature in his arms is starting to grow heavy. He's not incredibly fit for a wizard. He never bothered to exercise anyway. He lets out a small sigh and continues on, his eyes fixed to the palace doors.

"Hey!"

The voice cuts through the silence like a sword. Ethan stops in his tracks and turns his head towards the front gate. A group of Serperas dressed in armor are gathered there. Some are bent over, hands hooked on one of the gate's horizontal bars, trying to lift it. One is standing just behind them, staring back at Ethan with a look of surprise and fury. It is this Serperas that then points at him.

"What are you doing here?" they demand. Ethan remains silent, unsure what to think or say. These Serperas are probably part of the royal guard. They're probably also here looking for Lukri. Why else would they be all the way out here at sunset?

He simply turns away from the gate and steps through the door. Amber is sitting upright on the floor next to Lukri, who remains in his low-energy state. She looks at the Husk wide, questioning eyes, and he can't help but be reminded of Riona back when she was still in ASM herself, who would give Shadow the same stare whenever it would appear in her dorm room.

He grits his teeth and turns his gaze down to the floor.

"Were you yelling?" Amber asks.

Ethan dumps the wood, sticks, and leaves next to the doorway carelessly, thankful to finally have them out of his arms. Some dead orange chips remain stuck to his sleeves and gauntlets, however.

He brushes himself off as he replies, "There's some guards at the gate. *They* were yelling."

Lukri sits upright in an instant, his eyes full of shock and anger.

"They're trying to get the gate open," Ethan adds with a small laugh.

211

"Will they be able to?" Amber asks, her brow furrowing into concern.

Ethan shakes his head. "Even if they did, I could probably pull it back down. But I don't think they've got enough strength to lift it in the first place."

Lukri storms past Ethan and out into the evening wordlessly. He didn't even notice the Serperas switch from his tail to his legs. Ethan stares after the prince, watching him approach the now-stunned guards down by the gate. The prince is yelling something to them as they are yelling back at him, but Ethan can't be bothered to decipher any of the echoey conversation.

"Oh…" Amber groans, now at Ethan's side and staring after Lukri from the doorway as well. She holds the spear in her hand loosely, tip pointed at the ground. Amber doesn't seem like the type of being to wield any sort of weapon, yet here she is.

The two watch the prince argue with the guards, waving his arms as if to shoo them off.

"*LUKRI!*"

The prince's name is cried with a loud, stern woman's voice, clearly with much practice with the call. The arguing at the gate dies out, and the wizards watch Lukri ball his hands into trembling fists. Over the young Serperas' shoulder, Ethan sees the guards part to reveal a woman storming up to the gate, her bright emerald eyes ablaze with fury. He can practically feel her anger from where he stands. Atop her sandy orange hair sits a gold circlet with a large water pellet, much like the silver one Lukri wears. Her chest is covered by loose green strands of fabric, and a long piece of silvery fabric embroidered with small water pellets and a long snake-like figure hangs over her white skirt.

"Looks like his mom is here," Ethan says.

"Are those *wizards*?!" the queen practically screams when she spots the two standing in the palace doorway.

212

"Does it matter?" Lukri bites back, just as loud.

"We should go back him," Ethan suggests.

"Uh…" Amber mutters quietly. Ethan doesn't wait for her, and starts to strut down the pathway towards the gate, hands in his pockets. He knew that they'd be found eventually. It was only a matter of time.

His gut churns as his thoughts immediately turn to Riona. It's only a matter of time before *she* finds him, too.

"…they're liars," the queen is saying, her face red with anger. "They use their magic to charm helpless beings such as yourself."

"*Helpless*?!" Lukri exclaims in rage. There's a long pause between the two as Lukri delved into his invisible communication.

"You are vulnerable to their tricks," the queen opens her mouth again, though her tone is significantly less angry and much more stern. "Magic is dangerous. How many times must I tell you this?"

Now, Ethan is standing almost next to Lukri, and yet the queen pays him no mind, despite the fact she apparently *hates* wizards with her heart and soul.

"You speak so fluently."

The queen pauses to glare at Ethan. He folds his arms and, keeping his expression neutral, simply stares back at her. Though, clearly, his statement has thrown her thoughts through a loop. She remains quiet, her eyes searching for something to reply with. Lukri's face melts into something of surprised worry, his gaze falling slightly to the ground.

"Is there something wrong here?" he continues.

"You… You…" the queen sputters back. "You stole my son! I demand you hand him back over at once!"

"We stole no being," Ethan asserts with confidence. "Lukri-"

"Ethan!" Lukri finally cries in a panic.

213

"-wanted to bring us here. And then he wanted to stay, so we stayed. After all, who argues with the prince?"

There's another moment of silence, though Lukri's eyes are drawn back to his mother. Whatever he seems to read makes him scowl again.

"I..." he says carefully, "do not want to go home."

"What?" the queen gasps.

Slowly, Lukri reaches up towards his head and takes off the circlet he's been wearing since the morning. His mother notices the circlet as soon as he lifts it into the air above him, and her eyes go wide. Most of the Serperas guards that are around and can also see the circlet gasp. The prince holds the king's circlet before him, showing his mother, with a gaze of anger, hurt, and betrayal.

"W-Where did you find that?" the queen asks.

"Inside," Lukri replies, his tone flat. "The king was killed and left here."

Silence.

"I will return when I want to."

"Lukri-" the queen starts, anger returning to her voice.

"Good night, mother," Lukri replies simply, turning away from her. He half-turns to Ethan and mutters quietly, "Seal the gate."

"As you wish, your Majesty."

Ice... crackles through his body as he gestures to the spikes of the gate that pierce the sand and hold the heavy metal bars closed. Ice shoots up from the sand, covering the bottom of the gate and keeping it rooted in place. The Serperas on the other side all back away with looks of horror.

"None of you will pass this gate unless the prince says otherwise," he says, though directs the statement towards the queen. He turns away from the gathering before any of the Serperas can reply and follows Lukri back to the palace. Amber lingers in the palace doorway quietly, her expression hard to read.

"Lukri!" the queen finally yells. "Come *back* here!"

Lukri inhales sharply, and he lowers his head. Ethan pats his shoulder encouragingly. "Don't listen to her."

The prince remains quiet, though he narrows his eyes all the same and replaces the circlet atop his head. Once they're back inside the palace, the queen yelling at them all the way, Amber closes the door, and the atmosphere of the hall overtakes them once again.

"So..." Amber speaks first, her voice filling the grand space, "what now?"

Ethan turns to the pile of decaying plant materials next to the palace doors. "We light a fire and rest, I guess."

***

Ethan points a finger at the small pile of wood and leaves, and blasts it with a burst of fire. The sun has completely gone down at this point, leaving the fire as their only source of light and heat for the night, until the fuel runs out at least.

Lukri sits the closest, letting his eyes absorb the orange-red flames. Ethan sits more towards the shadowy edge, his hat covering his face. Whatever happened at the gate...

Amber turns to the spear still in her hands. It's mostly warm because of how long she's been holding it. She doesn't like the air around her. It's... *uncomfortable.*

Should I say something?

She takes a deep breath, which already breaks the silence.

"Is... everything okay?" she ventures to ask.

Silence. The boys don't even react in the slightest. Her stomach erupts into butterflies, and she also looks down at her lap, face burning. The fire pops and crackles, thin gray smoke rising up to the ceiling of the hall.

She can't help but feel homesick. Well, as homesick as she can get. She wants to go back to Kimberly's ice cream shop and hang out with Jake. She wants to go back to ASM, surprisingly, and study in her dorm room. And what was her life *before* ASM like?

The void in her mind is deep and extensive. It's scary and intimidating to think about. And, not to mention-

Tch... She places a hand on her pounding forehead.

"Don't think too hard," Ethan finally comments, his hat lifting ever so slightly. "It won't do you much good."

Lukri turns to look at Amber, some curiosity shining through his flat expression. "Your memories...?"

Amber pulls a weak smile. "Yeah."

"What... were you like? Before Mirage."

"Oh, um... I went to school, worked a job, and..." she shrugs, "that's about it."

Lukri tilts his head. "S... k... ool?"

"It's where wizards work on their magic skills and learn about history."

"I just read and get ordered around," the prince sighs. He shakes his head and looks up at Ethan. "You were... calm."

Ethan nods once. "Yes, well, I've got some experience in dealing with upset royals."

"Are you talking about... Riona?" Amber inquires hesitantly.

Ethan shifts his sitting position and finally lifts his head, revealing his face. Oddly enough, he's smiling. About what, Amber can only guess.

"Don't get me started," he replies with a light chuckle.

"Who is... uh..." Lukri closes his eyes, seemingly trying to remember how Riona's name is pronounced.

"Riona," Ethan helps, his smile fading ever so slightly. "She's the whole reason why me and Amber are on Mirage.

"In the past, she was nice enough. She was shy and soft

216

spoken, and grew up in the time where wizards followed family tradition; her parents were Storm and Ice, so she was expected to study one of those branches of magic. But she ended up becoming a Death student instead, so her family refused to help her pay for tuition…" Ethan trails off for a moment, his gaze growing distant. Eventually, he lets out a shameful sigh. "My… *brother*, Shadow, offered to get a job to help her, and so she coaxed it to appear like… her crush."

Amber's stomach can't help but sink as Ethan outlines Riona's life. She, too, is shy around others, and while the "family tradition" aspect has long since changed, she's *also* struggling to make ends meet, which is how she ended up in this mess to begin with.

She can't help but think back to her first cycle at Kimberly's shop, when Ethan had suddenly exploded at Blaze for calling her "useless". Maybe this is why he did that. Maybe he sees a bit of Riona in her.

"She never talked to her crush," Ethan continues, "but it didn't stop her from imprinting him onto Shadow. And from there… things spiraled out of control.

"No being wanted to help her and Shadow was too immature to know what was wrong with her in the first place. The two ended up running away to Korodon together, where Shadow tried to teach her Shadow magic. But… well, it didn't work out the way Shadow hoped it would."

"What happened?" Lukri asks, leaning forward with a curious gaze.

Ethan's gaze falls to the fire, his dark eyes absorbing their light entirely, leaving behind only a reflection of their fiery colors. "She was incapable of learning Shadow magic. Or maybe she wasn't even trying to begin with. However, she *wanted* Shadow magic, to the point where Shadow generously let her 'borrow' some of its power. And that, I believe, marked the end to her sanity. Now…" He shifts his position and holds up an arm for the

217

two to see. Suddenly, a bright violet glow shines from where his gauntlet rests on his arm, revealing a ghostly shackle and chain. The chain links float in the air around them, segmented and fractured, disappearing through the ceiling of the palace. "…her desire to control her own life has gotten out of hand."

"Ethan…" Amber breathes, still staring at the broken floating chain, "what… *is* this?"

"A Binding Contract," he replies flatly, "though I've been able to suppress it through enchantments. Belle… was a big help."

"Who?" Lukri asks quietly, though Ethan doesn't seem too keen on clarifying her identity at the moment as he, too, is mesmerized by his own shackle.

"Shadow has it, too. It's what keeps us bound to her, unable to escape. It's an old form of magic that was once used to control slaves, but it didn't satisfy her need for complete control. And now, it seems, she's trying to expand her sphere of influence to other islands. Starting with Mirage."

A heavy silence descends on the three as Ethan lets his story sink in. Amber, feeling uneasy, looks to Lukri, whose gaze is dim and distant as he stares into the little fire between them.

"I've been meaning to ask," Ethan speaks once more, breaking the silence, "if you knew anything about those dark clouds, Lukri."

Lukri nods slightly. "Dark beings come at night. Every night. One… One got into my room once. And I…" he pauses, clenching his hands into tight fists, gaze glazing over as he relives the moment.

Ethan crawls closer to the fire. "What did the being look like?"

The prince licks his lips slowly and stares Ethan dead in his eyes. "Armored, with longsword."

A heavy silence descends on the three. Amber thinks she knows who Lukri is talking about. It's the only being that comes to mind that would be armored, and may possibly carry a weapon such as a sword.

Is it Shadow? she wants to ask, and yet it already appears that Ethan is thinking the same thing. His expression is hard to read, but his eyes sparkle with recognition. Just thinking about those glowing eyes behind its shadowy helmet makes her body tense up to the point of stillness, and shivers wash over her in a series of chilling waves.

"You fought it off?" Ethan finally asks.

Lukri nods. "I… make light. Tiring."

"And it left?"

Lukri simply nods again.

"Any reason why it'd be in your room? Why these Shadows are attacking in the first place?"

The prince shrugs. "They just attack palace. No reason, I think."

"And when did this happen?"

"Couple days ago. Why?"

Ethan turns to Amber, and the two share a silent moment. If Mirage started having Shadow problems recently, with Blaze, Kimberly, and Jake being targeted only a couple cycles ago as well, then…

Amber scowls. There's some sort of connection here, but she doesn't really know what it may be. Ethan doesn't appear to have many answers, either.

"I don't know what she's doing," Ethan finally says, hanging his head. "I imagine Riona wants something from the royal family. Probably your Shadows. But for what end, I-" he stops, thinking. "Oh…" Once again, he looks at Amber. "Maybe that's why she needs the other three. Because of the Serperas."

"W-What?" Lukri stammars, worry creeping into his voice.

Amber takes a breath. She wants to tell him so that Ethan doesn't end up confusing him. This is already a lot for him to take in in the first place.

"Riona can take… your Shadow," she explains carefully, placing a hand on her heart. "It's the thing that makes us move and use magic. She almost took mine. But, she did take the Shadows of some of my friends. They're… rather powerful wizards. I… don't think your people can stand up to them very well."

Lukri stares at her, his eyes dim and fearful. His mouth opens, but nothing comes out of it.

"We should be fine for tonight," Ethan assures him. "I don't think she'll know where we are right away. I don't even know how much of Mirage she is aware of, let alone these ruins. The island is pretty big, after all, and so far you've just been sleeping in that palace, so there has been no reason for her to focus her attention anywhere else until now. Speaking of, you should both get some rest."

"What about you?" Amber fires back.

Ethan gives her a weak smile. "I don't *really* need to sleep. Though it's a nice break from being… awake." He chuckles to himself.

Looking back at Luke, he's already curled up on the ground around his emerald tail, eyes closed and breathing even. Curious, she leans over and pokes at his tail. His scales are extremely smooth and glitter in the firelight. But the Serperas doesn't react to her touch in the slightest.

"Wow," she breathes in amazement at how fast he passed out. Then again, he *did* say that the cold helps Serperas to sleep.

"Amber."

Ethan sits up next to the fire now, staring down at the dying flames.

"What?" she asks.

The Husk fiddles with his cloth gauntlets, not bothering to look at her as he speaks, "I… would like your help."

"With what?"

"I… It'll… What I'm asking for, it's dangerous. But, I… would like you to help me stop Riona. And free us, me and Shadow."

"Me?" Amber can't help but breathe.

Ethan nods. "I've got no other being to turn to and nowhere to run. Going back to Asandra is too dangerous; no doubt Riona is watching to see if I ever return there. The other islands are useless in this case as well. And I can't go to Korodon alone."

Amber presses her lips together tightly. It's morbidly sweet that she's the only being he has left to ask for help from, but at the same time he's asking her to break the law of every island to battle a wizard she's never seen or heard of before and free a Fragment Shadow whom has only ever been hostile towards her and her closest friends. He's placing a *lot* of trust in her.

Ethan turns back to the fire, tilting his hat forward to hide his face. "You don't have to agree. I can probably hold out on my own for a little while, and I can send you back to Asandra where you'll be relatively safe for a short period of time, but I cannot guarantee that I'll succeed on my own, nor that Riona will simply leave you alone from now on. One way or another, you're *important*, Amber, for how much you know already, and…" He trails off, his words reducing themselves to incomprehensible muttering.

Amber shifts on the ground, folding her arms across her chest in an awkward hug. It's hard not to feel bad for him. He's been through a lot.

"Hey, Ethan," she speaks.

"What?" he asks.

"That's the name Riona gave you… isn't it?"

The Husk lets out a sigh, and he lifts his head ever so slightly to reveal a thin smile across his lips. "Well, it belonged to Shadow before me."

221

"Did you ever meet him? The real Ethan."

"Of course I did. He wasn't any being special. He didn't even know that Riona existed, so to speak," the Husk hums wistfully. "But we don't really talk anymore."

"He's still alive?"

"No, he Faded a long time ago. We continued to talk for a few more centuries thanks to my Mediumship. He's off enjoying his afterlife now. Although… being able to talk to him helped to open my eyes."

"To what?"

"To just how terrible Riona was. *Is*. Azna helped, too. That old Feni has a lot of advice." Ethan reaches for the edges of his cape and draws it close to his chest protectively, his expression turning to stone. "She's been part of my life for so long… I felt really stupid for not noticing everything sooner. But leaving her… it was never going to be as simple as walking away. I think about her. A lot. I-"

Amber shuffles closer to the Husk and places a hand on his knee, causing him to look up at her.

"At least she's not here right now, right?" she asks lightly. This makes Ethan grin again, though his eyes remain dull, reflecting only the fire before them.

After a moment, Amber turns her attention to the slumbering Lukri. "What are we going to do with him, though?"

"Lukri? I don't know," Ethan replies. "He's not safe here on Mirage, but he's not exactly safe with us, either. I think… we should bring him along. If he wants to come, of course."

"Bring him… to Riona?"

"Where else?"

"B-But he's the *prince*!"

"I know he is. The only reason why I'd want him with us is that he already possesses Light magic. It can help ward off the Shadows, for a time. Of course, we'd still need to be careful with him. If anything were to happen to him…"

A heavy silence befalls the two. If anything happened to the only heir to Mirage, surely there will be conflict across the islands. Maybe even war.

"We can't afford to allow Riona to get ahold of his Shadow in the first place," Ethan adds, sitting up to speak with new confidence. "With him in her possession, she can put pressure on the monarchy and take over Mirage in one fell swoop. No doubt that's why she's been attacking the other palace. It's also probably why she targeted the other three as well, to combat the Serperas."

"Why not take the queen's?" Amber asks.

"Lukri is young, still being prepared for the throne, so his Shadow can be manipulated much easier than his mother's, even with everything that surrounds their title of 'king'. Besides, his mother wouldn't want to hurt him, but the guards have no reason to usurp the queen if she begins to… *misbehave*."

So this is why the other three had their Shadows stolen. All for Riona to get her hands on Mirage.

"Poor Kim and Jake…" she can't help but mutter.

"Blaze doesn't deserve this, either," Ethan throws in.

"I guess so," Amber sighs reluctantly. Of course his insults hurt her, but at least he didn't cause her any harm beyond that.

"You should rest," Ethan suggests. "It'll be a long cycle."

"I'm not tired," Amber replies.

"Well, at least try. Would you like my cape?"

"No, thanks. I'll be fine."

"Are you sure?"

Amber shifts around on the ground, trying to find a comfortable position to sleep in. It's not very easy, as the ground is rather hard and makes her body ache. But dealing with temporary memory loss the past few cycles and releasing some dead Serperas to eternal rest, she doesn't really mind sleeping on stone for a night. If she could get to sleep in the first place, that is.

"Good night," she mumbles, closing her eyes. Ethan hums from where he sits, the fire still fizzling in her ear.

Chapter 19

"So you can look like… any being?"

The question rings in its ears as Shadow stares down at itself, wondering if it got the look right. The gauntlets, the cowl, the robe, even the shoes. It took a while for it to get a good look at Ethan's shoes.

Well? *it asks, looking up at Riona as it stands in the middle of her dorm room. She stares back from her desk chair, twirling her black hair between her fingers.* Do I look like him?

Her slightly-tilted head and flat face give nothing away as her onyx eyes study it, flicking her irises up and down. Something flutters in Shadow's chest, making it feel antsy, though it resists the urge to fidget.

Riona? *it speaks.*

"Hm," she hums finally, "it's close. His gauntlets are a little longer-"

Before she can even finish speaking, the gauntlets on Shadow's forearms lengthen.

"-and the robe doesn't reach your ankles-"

The fabric of its robe brushes the back of Shadow's ankles, making them tingle with a small itch.

"-and maybe your hair could be a little more… flat."

But his hair isn't-

"*You don't know him,*" *Riona growls in an instant, her mouth curving down into a scowl.*

The scene suddenly melts, leaving behind a foul air in its wake as the dripping colors swirl together into a corner cafe. It's bright, maybe midcycle. Shadow is cleaning one of the many outdoor tables with a bucket of water and a rag when there's a gasp. Instinctively, it looks up, only to find the real *Ethan standing across the street.*

Eyes wide, Shadow opens its mouth. Not to say anything, nor to make any other noise. Its jaw just drops in shock, the first time it's ever done that in its entire life.

The two just… stare at each other in silence. Not moving, not speaking. Water drips from Shadow's rag and plops onto the surface of the wooden table, the only noise audible in this otherwise empty space.

"*So,*" *Ethan finally speaks, the cafe twisting into yet another dorm room, where Ethan now stands in front of the closed door,* "*you're* not *some sort of illusion?*"

Shadow nods back. I'm just a Fragment Shadow. I can look like any being-

"*So then why do you look like me?*" *the boy demands, getting up in Shadow's face.*

Please, I-

"*I don't want to hear it!*" *Ethan instantly turns into a just-as-angry Riona.* "*You weren't supposed to meet him! I was supposed to meet him!*"

Riona, I didn't know he-

Riona steps away and lets out a frustrated sigh, shaking her head in what Shadow can only see as disappointment. It knows how much she's wanted to talk to him. So for it to speak to him first… it can't help but feel a little shameful.

I'm sorry.

The dorm expands, now a dance floor. Gray figures

226

dance around Shadow as it stands alone, hidden under a large hooded cloak. Riona is walking away from it, still upset, carving a path through the figures. While the air is festive, Shadow feels nothing but shame in itself.

The moment she's out of sight, a hand is placed on Shadow's shoulder, and suddenly Ethan is standing next to it, offering it a look of sympathy.

"I'm sure whatever it was, it wasn't your fault," he says calmly.

Shadow just shakes its hooded head. It *was* my fault. I-

"What happened?"

Shadow just blinks. It doesn't really remember, but whatever it did it made her upset.

It shrugs. Ethan lets out a hopeless sigh in response.

"Well… thank you for coming," he says. "I don't think my Fading Celebration would have been the same without you."

You have a lot of friends, Shadow remarks, staring at the gray figures around them. They laugh and drink together in small clusters as the dancers enjoy themselves swinging from one partner to the next. A part of Shadow wishes to join in the merriment, yet is reluctant to reveal itself to the massive crowd.

"Not really friends," Ethan corrects with a light chuckle. "But… I will say it's nice to see the beings I've helped before for one last time."

Shadow purses its lips. With Ethan satisfied with his life after only five centuries, how long will it take for Riona to Fade?

"You know, it's nice to see you taking agency," Ethan says. The statement catches Shadow off-guard, but that quickly fades when it turns to see the Spiritist's warm smile. The space around them falls to a flat black background, the two of them standing alone.

"I still check in from time to time," he chuckles. "I hate to call this entertainment, but after numerous centuries of drama? I can't help myself. Though, maybe once this is all over I can

227

finally rest easy.

"I'm sorry about Shadow. I know it's always been in a different position from you, and yet... I've thought about it. You were lucky she always sent you away. Stars only know what you would be doing now if you stayed close to her.

"I'm only here to offer some encouragement, though I doubt you need to hear anything from me anymore. You found some good beings this time around. Trust in yourself, Eth. They're relying on you."

Ethan wakes with a start, a surge of energy rushing through the hollow cavity that is his chest. He fell asleep and didn't even realize it. He still sits in his cross-legged position, arms folded before he woke.

The fire is dull, down to small orange embers that glow in the darkness, casting Amber and Lukri in dark shadow. The night is cold, though it hardly bothers him much. He's amazed that Amber managed to fall asleep in this sort of environment.

He can't help but let out a sigh of relief at the peaceful sight. They're still safe. He meant to keep watch, but...

He shakes his head at himself and stands, wishing to stretch his legs as his back aches from his prolonged hunched state.

He's surprised that his once-living counterpart decided to reach out. It's been... well, a *long* time since they last spoke.

Trust in yourself, Eth.

He looks back at the embers, at Amber and Lukri, full of doubt.

Even though he suspects that Riona is indeed trying to expand her territory to Mirage, he's confused as to the true reason behind her actions. She's never expressed an interest in taking her influence to another island before. She seemed pretty satisfied with Korodon for a good couple of decades, at least when she finished her campaign there.

228

And Shadow…

The violet. It's a sight he'll never forget. Its cold stare as it holds its blade high and-

Strike him.

A hand strays up to his scar, lightly touching it with his fingers. It stings ever so slightly under his fingertips, remembering the moment with him. With Ethan taking so many precautions against her magic, Riona has tightened her grip on Shadow. No doubt that's the reason behind their dead link. She'll only let him see what she wants him to see and when.

Trust in himself. He huffs hopelessly through his nose.

The palace is still, spirits swirling around him, their phantom breezes rushing past his body.

He holds out a hand out in front of him, and a cold grip squeezes it. He remains silent, enjoying the peaceful moment with whatever spirit is with him right now, as the others rush around him.

The spirit that holds his hand tightens its grip ever so slightly, a slight pressure against his lifeless skin. A sense of urgency permeates the empty space before him, where the spirit floats. It's a feeling he can hardly ignore.

Dread builds in his own chest, a hole that tugs at his hollow frame, threatening to make him collapse from the inside.

Darkness is coming, an old, whispery voice hisses in warning.

Panic flashes through his body. Did he hear the spirit right? He lowers his hand and spins around to survey the dark. All of a sudden, the shadows of the hall press against him heavily. His arms prickle and his muscles tense.

Yet… nothing happens.

He steps up to Amber and shakes her. "Amber, hey, wake up."

"*Mm*, what is it?" Amber moans sleepily.

"Here," Ethan grabs the spear Amber had been guarding

almost all of last cycle and presses it into her chilly hands. "Take it and get up quickly."

"Why?" she asks slowly, some sense of worry beginning to grow in her voice. Ethan doesn't bother to stop and explain, rather moving quickly to Lukri and shaking him, too.

"Lukri! *Lukri!*"

The prince sleeps on, undisturbed.

"Ethan, what's *happening*?" Amber demands.

"I…" he pauses, thinking of what to say. He doesn't know if they've truly been found yet or not. All he has is the word of a spirit he's never heard the voice of before. And yet… yet he feels like something terrible is about to happen nonetheless. So he sucks in a breath and says to her, "We need to go."

"We've been found?!" the Healer gasps in surprise.

"Yes!" Ethan exasperates. "Come on, Lukri, wake *up!*" Still, nothing happens. He doesn't even stir.

"I think it's still too cold for him," Amber suggests.

"Spirit of Fire."

Flames curl around Ethan's arms in a blaze, and he holds them over Lukri's slumbering body. Ever so slowly, slower than he likes, Lukri begins to shift and awaken. His eyes flutter open, and a low groan emanates from his throat.

"Lukri, come on, we need to go," Ethan says again.

Lukri sits up and rubs his eyes. "Hm? Why?"

"Shadows are here for us. We need to leave."

"But so tir-"

"You'll wake up more when you move. *Come on!*"

"Uh-" Amber squeaks. Not a moment after the noise escapes her mouth, a hard, metallic *clang* rings out, filling the dark hall. Metal striking stone.

Chest constricting, Ethan looks up, and Lukri turns around, his eyes now wide and awake.

"Shadow…" Ethan barely breathes. Shadow, black armor and all, stands by the front doors of the palace, its bright violet

230

eye cold and empty. It holds its sword a hair above the stone floor beneath it. Staring right as Ethan, it shows no signs of recognition. Even standing feet away from it, Ethan can't even sense it.

Shadow says nothing, instead raising its sword and pointing it at *him*. A challenge.

"You two run," Ethan says, standing and moving in front of Lukri to act as some sort of shield.

"*Where*?!" Amber exclaims wildly.

"Second floor study balcony. I'll join you soon."

"But-"

"I'll be fine," he assures her, raising his flaming hands in preparation for a fight. "Just protect Lukri."

He listens to the two moving behind him as he stares Shadow down, both waiting for one to move.

They will not get far, Shadow speaks, eyes narrowing. It slowly turns its sword.

Ice… replaces the burning inferno, and with a swift swipe of his hand he raises a dark blue wall of ice. Not a moment later, the tip of Shadow's blade appears, just barely piercing the magical barrier.

Behind him sounds a shrill shriek of surprise and fear, and a spike of adrenaline rushes through his body. *Amber!*

Storm… surges in, energizing his body. In one push, he dashes towards one of the staircases.

Graaa!

Ice shatters behind him as Shadow pulls its sword free. He steals a glance over his shoulder, watching Shadow rebalance the sword in its hand, glaring at Ethan with a look of hatred. Ethan can't help but grit his teeth in frustration. He can't fight Shadow if Amber and Lukri might need his help at the same time.

A second bounce sends him flying up the stairs. A third propels him towards the study, the doors already wide open.

There, he sees Amber and Lukri standing on the balcony. The desk is cut in two and cast aside, the sliced wood charred and smoking, and the chair lays on the floor in smoldering pieces.

Jake stands in the place of the desk and chair, sword raised, the blade surrounded in black flame. He still wears his armored boots, but is now dressed in shorts and wears some sort of t-shirt, with a hole where the left arm should be that stretches from his shoulder to the side of his stomach, an onyx band wrapped around his bicep instead.

Lukri is heroically staring the Shadow down with his own jade weapon, though there's a slight tremble in his form. Clearly, he's not been in an actual fight like this before. Behind him, Amber has her spear raised as the Shadow of Kimberly stands on a pillar of black ice on the other side of the balcony. While she's still in her usual shirt and skirt, her outfit is accented with sparkling black ice, which spiders down her legs and arms as some sort of light armor. Her hands, however, are completely white up to her wrists, glittering in the dim light of the rising sun. Snow.

Kimberly's glowing red eyes lock with Ethans' momentarily, and her face twitches ever so slightly. It's hard to tell if she's trying to identify him, or deciding whether or not she should change her target.

Ice... Ethan flicks his arm forward towards Jake, and a line of ice shoots from under his feet towards the Shadow. Hearing the crackling, Jake begins to turn to face him, but the ice reaches him first. Before Jake can even react, a large pillar of ice shoots upwards, pinning Jake against the ceiling. In his shock, Jake drops his sword the moment he's crushed against the ceiling, which clatters to the ground, rendering him useless.

Jake lets out a frustrated yell, trying to wriggle his way out of his tight spot, but the sparkling blue ice holds him firmly in place.

With this, the temperature of the room drops in an instant,

232

turning the cool air of first light into a deathly chill. White snow and black ice whirl around Kimberly, collecting together into these floating spikes of ice. With the simplest gesture of her hand, the spikes shoot forward, her snarl directed at Ethan.

Amber reaches up with her spear to help, managing to redirect one of the spikes into the side of the palace wall, but the others tear past her uncontested.

Fire... Ethan raises his hands, fire spinning in his palms. He blasts the spikes down to water, which splash onto his face.

Crack!

One just barely slips past his defense, running along his right wrist, leaving a thin black line in its wake as it tears through his skin, revealing his dark, hollow interior beneath it. It strikes the wall behind him and hisses as the air begins to eat away at it, turning the icy splash into dark water.

With a courageous yell, Amber surges forward and jabs her spear into Kimberly's leg. Kimberly shrieks, an ethereal cry in place of her voice. Amber stabs again at Kimberly's other leg, knocking her off balance this time. She falls from her pillar and lands on the ground below, her figure hidden by the balcony.

Ice... Ethan rushes towards Amber and Lukri, the prince swaying on his feet as he fights to keep his eyes open in the sudden cold air. Arm throbbing painfully, he throws his right arm out to his side, and a long platform of ice appears, leading directly to the top of the wall that rings the abandoned palace.

"Go!" he yells, pushing Lukri towards the platform first. The prince finds the strength in him to stumble towards the platform, hauling himself over the railing and slowly sliding himself towards the wall.

Behind him, the sound of fracturing ice rings out. He whirls around to find Shadow striding towards him and Amber, the pillar of ice holding Jake in place beginning to crumble. A single horizontal line runs through the pillar, probably created by Shadow running its sword through it with silent ease.

"Go," Ethan mutters to Amber next to him.

Out of the corner of his eye, he sees Amber shuffle behind him towards the ice bridge he made. Instantly, Shadow raises a hand towards her, but then narrows its eyes and lowers it just as quickly as Ethan hears her clamber onto the ice bridge with heavy breaths.

It was trying to command her Shadow, but... *couldn't?*

Sword raised high, Shadow rushes towards Ethan instead. His left hand immediately reaches for his cape, but he doesn't have enough time to use it as a shield before the blur that is Shadow towers over him, ready to strike. He raises his right arm to take the strike, the sword cutting through his gauntlet and deep into his arm. He grits his teeth, bearing the pain, and brings his cape around, flashing the symbol of Light at Shadow. Its eyes widen, knowing what's coming next.

"*Illuminae!*" Ethan cries, turning his head away from Shadow, unable to bear witness to its pain as it screams in pure agony.

Usually, whatever pain Shadow experiences Ethan also experiences, and vice versa. But without their link, Ethan feels nothing but shame for harming his very own Shadow.

The sword evaporates from Ethan's arm as Shadow reels away, its entire form disfigured and smoky, its eyes the only thing that defines anything about its body, marking where its head should be. A single rune isn't powerful enough to kill it if that were his goal, but it's enough to cripple it for a short time.

It's enough time for him to run.

Storm... He turns to the ice bridge, leaps over the balcony railing effortlessly, and reaches the wall in only a couple of strides.

He can't waste all his energy here. Not now.

He jumps down from the wall into the soft sand below him, the sand that lands on his right arm making his injuries sting. He grits his teeth harder and inhales sharply. Amber turns her head to look at him as she supports a weak-looking Lukri, her hands on his shoulders, with three sandboards waiting to be ridden. Magic deprivation combined with Kimberly's coldsnap, he looks closer to a spirit than his usual bronze Serperan skin.

"Can he ride?" Ethan asks.

"Yes," Lukri nods, struggling to push away from Amber. He sways and stumbles as he struggles, but the prince seems determined to stand on his own. Amber lets out a small sigh and releases him from her grip before hurriedly approaching one of the sandboards. Ethan jumps on a second, and Lukri balances precariously on the third.

"Where?" he asks simply.

"Archway," Ethan replies, pushing off.

"*What*? Why?"

Ethan ignores the questioning, too focused on getting as far away from the ruined palace as possible. With the rising sun, Riona's hold should weaken if the Shadows stay out too long. Shadow works better in the dark. Torn Shadows are simply better to handle in areas with minimal light.

He steals a glance over his shoulder, just to see…

Shadow stands on the ruin wall, staring at him as he, Lukri, and Amber ride away. Its form is still half disfigured, though its helmet and shoulders have already resolidified. On either side of it are Kimberly and Jake. The three Shadows don't move, appearing reluctant to follow them out into the open desert with the sun on the rise.

Lukri passes him, drawing his attention away. "This way."

Through the dunes the three of them glide, the sun appearing over the dunes and turning the sky a navy blue. The stars begin to fade away into the background, joining the hiding universe.

Something sickening stirs in his gut. He can't stare up at the stars for long, and yet he longs to get lost in them. To forget everything and just watch them dance above his head, always out of reach.

I'm sorry, Shadow, he can't help but think, turning away from the sky. *I'll free you soon.*

"Why Archway?" Lukri asks again.

"We're going to another island," Ethan says. "I suggest you come with us."

"Ethan!" Amber cries. "He's the *pri-*"

"Nowhere in Astria is safe for him right now!" Ethan bites back. "Now just *guide*!"

III

Korodon

Chapter 20

Sand digs under Amber's fingernails and fills her shoes, making her feel extremely uncomfortable. Ethan climbs just two steps above her, and Lukri two steps below. Slowly, they scale the tall dune of loose sand.

"Where was Blaze?" Amber can't help but ask.

"I don't know!" the Husk exasperates loudly. Amber presses her mouth tightly shut and fights the urge to try and shrink into herself, stomach churning in shame. *Maybe I shouldn't have said anything…*

They reach the crest of the dune and slide down towards the stone dias below, where the Archway stands sideways in the sand. It almost appears like it's sinking, just slow enough to where she can't even notice. Ethan starts to dig around in his pockets, searching for something.

Lukri turns to her. "What… is happening?"

"Oh, uh…" she pauses, thinking of how to break the news to him that they're dragging him along on a possibly dangerous mission. She doesn't know what Ethan wants to do with Riona when they get to her, but… "We're… going to… Mm, well… We're leaving Mirage."

Just as she says this, the Archway thrums to life, and a rip opens in its center. Cold air blasts the small group, sending a sharp chill down Amber's back. Beyond the rift is a dark land, the buildings gray and lifeless, and the land barren and dead. Twisting trees loom in the distance, their leafless branches stretching high into the air, trying to reach the sky. A sky which is inky black, a swirling mass of storm clouds.

Something heavy settles on Amber's chest, and she frees a hand to place over her heart. Lukri only gasps and shuffles closer to her for protection.

Ethan turns to face them, his black eyes mirroring the land beyond. He holds a smooth, dark gray stone in his hand daintily, almost as if it'll break if he holds it too tightly. He sucks a calm breath in and says, "We're going to Korodon."

Amber's heart skips a beat. Korodon, the abandoned island. This is the first time she's ever seen it.

"It's okay," Ethan tries to reassure the other two. "Despite the look, Ica is still safe… I think."

Ica… that's the capitol. Yes. It's been quite a while since she's had to think of anything related to Korodon. Ica is where the Korodon Archway is located. That's the place she can see through the rift, lifeless and still. And he's saying that it *might* be *safe*?

She turns to Lukri and finds his gaze fixed to the rift, its darkness reflecting in his emerald green eyes. It's stunned, horror, surprise, wonder, too many emotions rolled into one expression, one where his mouth hangs open, fangs flashing in the Mirage sunlight, and his eyebrows arch as high as they'll go on his forehead.

"Lukri?" she asks softly, reaching for his arm. The Serperas lets out a shaky breath when she touches him. He turns to look at her, his eyes wild.

"We're… leaving… Mirage?" he asks slowly. The way he speaks each word, the way his emotions clash in his voice, it's clear that it's a sentence he never thought he'd even consider saying. Amber offers him a sympathetic look.

"Do you want to stay?" she replies. He stares at her in silence, then down at the sand underneath his feet. The chill of Korodon blasts them again, a powerful gust wishing to be free from the dark land. It ruffles his hair for a moment.

"Do I…?" he mutters quietly.

Slowly, Amber lets him go again. She looks to Ethan, who stares quietly at the young prince. His eyes flick to her, and he just… shrugs. Lost for words just as she is.

She steps away, her footfalls quiet in the sand. She clutches the spear close to her chest, eyes to the ground.

"We shouldn't force him," she says to Ethan. He frowns. "I know why you want him along, but… he's never left Mirage."

"Right," he sighs. "We can't wait around long, anyway." He adjusts his hat and turns away from Lukri. "Keep that spear with you. We can always give it back later. You first." He waves to the rift before them. Amber takes a deep breath, mustering her courage to approach the Archway. Another cold blast streaks through her hair, pink strands whirling at the edges of her vision.

She steps up to the rift, one foot in front of the other, spear held tight till her knuckles are white as snow. She can practically reach out and touch the rift, even pass through it if she wants. Something in the back of her mind tells her to run away and hide. That danger and evil lurk beyond in the darkness of the island. The low one- and two-story mud brick buildings seem intimidating, as if a Shadow were to jump out at her and-

Come on, Amber, she encourages herself. *You've come this far already.*

She steps through the rift, passing through the thin barrier that separates the warm and inviting desert from the cold and unforgiving land of the ghost town beyond.

The chill of the air pierces the fabric of her dust-covered robe and shirt. She inhales sharply in surprise, suddenly wanting to turn around and run back through to Mirage and lay in the sand for the rest of the cycle just to chase the chill away.

The chill of suffering.

"Lukri?" Ethan calls behind her, his voice carrying through the rip crystal clear, almost amplified. She turns around to stare back at the desert island, and at the Serperas who stands with his feet dug into the sand and his head bowed.

He looks up, at the rift and back at Amber, his gaze lost. Not really knowing what to do, she gives him a little smile and wave. Whatever it means, it's up to him to interpret. She doesn't know if she's waving "goodbye" or giving him a little "hello".

He balls his hands into determined fists, however, as soon as she lowers her hand.

"I-I help!" he stammers, having mustered the strength to speak. He holds up a hand, and sand swirls and forms into his jade sword. With it by his side, the prince puffs out his chest and strides towards the rift with purpose and dignity. The circlet on his head shines and sparkles, almost as if it's approving his choice.

Amber holds out a hand through the rift, her palm getting one final taste of the Mirage sun. With a weak smile, he takes it, and she pulls him through to the other side. Ethan strides through not long after, and the rift closes.

One last gust of Mirage's building warm air billows at them, and Lukri squeezes Amber's hand tight.

"It's been too long," Ethan says aloud with a small, sad huff. He pockets the Keystone and starts to the edge of the dias they stand on.

Lukri holding her hand, the two slowly follow after him. The dias here is raised by a few steps, in the center of a rather large, circular square. Outdoor stalls, with tattered rugs that used to act as roofs, sitting spots, and old wooden stands ring the edge of the square itself. It kind of reminds her of the Serperas' town in a way, but with its own sort of character to it.

Ethan, at the bottom of the dias, raises his voice, calling,

244

"It's just me! I brought some friends!"

His voice echoes across the buildings and stretches into the distance. Then…

The windows of the thickly-shadowed buildings light up, little red pinpricks appearing in pairs, all of them aimed down at the square and, chillingly, at *them*. Ethan half-turns, though his gaze remains on the stary red darkness around them, a thin smile across his lips. And yet seeing him so at ease, Amber's heart leaps unevenly as she grips her spear like it's her lifeline.

All these Shadows… There's at least 30 of them. *Does Ethan know them?*

"Nightshade!" comes a cry, both cheerful and angry at the same time. A black form melts from the darkness, flanked by two guards. The three of them are Feni Shadows, though nothing like what Kimberly and Jake looked like. Whereas those two had their appearances almost completely changed and with outfits seemingly absorbing light as it shone on them, these Shadows are painted with a series of lighter grays, dressed in simple armor pieces overtop cloth clothing. The only thing these three have in common is a little white symbol on each of their right shoulders, the shapes of which Amber can't clearly make out.

The middle Feni, presumably the one who called out before, has long pointed ears and a bushy tail that sweeps side to side as she approaches Ethan, a sword hanging from a scabbard tied around her waist. She regards the Husk with shining crimson eyes and a strange glower.

"You took your time," the Feni scolds firmly as she folds her arms, her voice strong-willed. Every word is projected for all to hear, like she were to suddenly start giving an inspirational speech before charging into battle.

"I'm sorry, Tacha, really," Ethan replies. "The Council-"

"*Tch*," Tacha cuts him off forcefully, pulling a sneer. "Those aging elects… How long were they going to let us keep defending Ica?"

"In their eyes, Ica is gone. But before I could get them to take any action, I was forced to take my own." Ethan gestures to Amber and Lukri, and Amber shivers when Tacha's eyes lock onto hers. "This is Amber and Lukri."

"Can they fight?" Tacha asks as if she weren't even staring at them right now.

"Amber's a Healer and Lukri knows Light magic."

Tacha taps a finger on her arm impatiently. She studies Amber up and down, her cold gaze washing over her, before moving to Lukri, her frown frozen to her face. Lukri stiffens, sucking in a sharp breath as the Shadow's eyes flicker across his body. Then she turns back to Ethan.

"There's one you should see," she says finally.

Ethan tilts his head. "I thought there weren't any un-Twisted left."

Tacha just nods behind her, then begins walking away. Ethan turns to Amber and Lukri, motioning for them to follow, and starts after the Shadow and her entourage. Squeezing her hand, Lukri trails a step behind Amber as they, too, follow in silence, vividly aware of the red stares around them.

"What's going on?" Amber asks Ethan.

The Husk lets out a long sigh. "Tacha is the de facto leader of the Feni. The Shadows that live here in Ica now are the only ones left free from Riona's total control. Un-Twisted, meaning that they've kept their original forms."

"So... what's a Twisted, then?"

"You've seen a Twisted Shadow already. Two of them."

Amber frowns to herself. *We have?*

"Kimberly and Jake," Ethan clarifies simply. "They're larger, darker, stronger, and easier to control. They started as... experiments, to see if there was a better way to keep a Shadow subservient. She's tried other ways in the past. The Binding Contract was her earliest experiment." His hands stray to his gauntlets as he speaks. "The second experiment was through

246

enchantments, which is… why I know enchanting so well. You've seen my dorm room, Amber." Amber nods, recalling the mass of painted black runes adorning the walls of the odd dorm room she slept in that one time many cycles ago. Still, Ethan gestures to Tacha and the two Feni guards, particularly to the Feni's right shoulders, and continues, "She called it Branding. Though the most that could be done was simply imprinting a set of instructions onto the Shadow. And then her third and most successful experiment has been Twisted Shadows, altering the very essence of the Shadow itself to the point where its previous identity is forgotten, and it derives its purpose from the one that Twisted it."

"Oh…" Lukri mutters sadly.

Ethan nods slowly, his gaze dark. "It's not a process you want to experience, let alone know the details of. Tearing is not usually painful, but Twisting is agony. In any case, Ica is the last place on Korodon where Shadows live in… relative freedom, I guess you can say, though they can't leave the island."

They reach the end of the uneven cobble street, red eyes following them their entire journey, and step onto the start of a dirt road. The road itself is marked with white dust, the ground either side of it a dark brown, almost black, color.

"There," Tacha waves to the right, at a large fenced area of ground. Amber gasps in surprise, just as the ground begins to vibrate strongly. Large vines begin to weave themselves through the ground, waving up and down, pushing the dirt around. And standing at the other end of the vines, green light surrounding him, is the Shadow of Blaze.

Something stirs deep within Amber's gut. A sickening feeling as she lays her eyes upon the wizard who threatened her freedom and insulted her, all because of her being in the "wrong place" at the "wrong time".

"Amber…?" Lukri asks, drawing her attention. As she turns to look at him, she becomes aware of her deep and frantic

247

breathing almost instantly. Her heart pounds in her chest. He stares back at her with a look of concern. "You okay?"

"I…" Amber breathes, pausing to let herself calm down. "Yes."

"Tilling?" Ethan asks.

Tacha nods. "We should keep the land fresh for when we wake, no?"

"And when did he show up?"

"If I must guess, he's been here only a couple of cycles. Though we've been putting him and his magic to good use." She waves at the patch of land to prove her point.

"Hey! Ethan!" It's Blaze's voice, one that makes Amber's shoulders rise with swirling unease. It's cheerful. She doesn't believe that he's *cheerful*. The Shadow gives them a wave from across the field, vines sinking below the dark surface of dirt once more, tremors ceasing. He strides over the tilled dirt with a beaming grin. His smile can't help but make her hate him even more.

Blaze leans over the fence, balancing on his hand and tiptoes. "The tilling's done, Tacha."

"Thank you," Tacha nods.

"So, Eth…" Blaze begins to hum, though his cheery mood falters immediately as horror lights in his red eyes. "Eth… what happened to your arm?"

Ethan blinks once, stunned at his question as he raises his right arm to inspect it.

"Oh…"

His voice is quiet. Surprised, even. From his wrist to his elbow, a single long line of black stains his pale skin, with a second cutting down the middle of his forearm. The gauntlet is most definitely torn, with small strings of frayed fabric sticking up in the air, beginning to slowly unravel on its own accord.

Slowly, his hollow expression morphs into horror as pain glows in his wide eyes.

Instinctively, Amber reaches out to him and wraps her hand around just the very edge of his cut. Ethan, in response, grits his teeth and keeps back a yell, morphing it into an extremely restrained grunt. Gold glitter sparks from Amber's fingers as her magic surges forward. The glow of the glitter rushes along his injury, even spreading to the vertical cut as well. And now in place of the black, sparkling amber light takes its place.

She lifts her hand hesitantly and steps away from him. Tacha, Blaze, and Lukri stare at her, stunned, unsure what to make of what just happened.

"Um... sorry..." she mutters, her first reaction to the staring. But she's not sorry in the slightest. "Is it better?"

Wordlessly, Ethan runs his fingers across his glowing arm, the pain he had been feeling mere moments before now completely gone. He nods slowly, replying to her question, and her chest flutters with relief.

"What happened?" Tacha asks firmly, breaking the silence.

"A-An attack," Amber replies.

Lukri nods. "Bad Shadows showed up."

The Feni glowers at the two, her gaze distant.

"Riona got the other two, didn't she?" Blaze asks.

Ethan nods, dropping his arm. "She did."

The ground trembles beneath their feet as Blaze balls his hands into tight fists. Like Tacha, his anger doesn't appear direct at any being present, but at the wizard in the distant castle.

"I should have-" Ethan starts.

"Eth," Blaze interrupts him firmly, "don't start with that. It wasn't your fault."

Ethan clenches his jaw in silent protest, his eyes falling to the ground. The Shadow shakes his head and turns back to Amber, though his expression is softer this time. "Hey." Amber's entire face twitches, locked in a confused fight to portray anger

249

or hurt back at him.

"Didn't think I'd see you here," she manages to mutter.

Blaze rubs the back of his neck and musters a weak grin. "Me neither. And who's that?" He nods towards Lukri standing next to her.

Lukri grins at his question. "I am Lukri! From Mirage."

"He doesn't speak very well," Amber adds. "And this is Blaze, one of Ethan's other friends."

Tacha clears her throat, drawing every being's attention. "No doubt you have returned to finally take care of the Lady?"

Ethan nods. "I have."

"Do you have a plan?"

"No. But Blaze has one."

Blaze can't help but let out an amused huff. "I do?"

"Is there a place we can stay a spell?" Ethan asks.

"Of course," Tacha gestures back towards the buildings. "Let me show you."

***

Ethan can't exactly say he's happy to be back on Korodon. On one hand, it's nice to be with Tacha and the other Shadows of Ica again. Plus, it's a place he's pretty much lived all his life. On the other, he's not missed the heavy atmosphere, the dark clouds above that block out the stars, and the dreadful chill that permeates the air. And not only did he come back injured, but with a ruined gauntlet as well.

Faces peer at them from the darkness of the buildings, glowing red eyes silent and ever-watching, making his skin crawl. The sharp noise of his shoes hitting the stones beneath his feet ring out up and down the street, along with Amber's and Lukri's. The place fills him with a deep sadness that makes his chest constrict.

Tacha leads them into one of the homes close to the

Archway, gesturing to the dark gray space. "Make yourselves at home."

There are dusty stone chairs around a single aged table, the cracks of time very apparent. Two young Shadows stand in the darkest corner of the single room, staring at them with wide eyes, hesitant and curious at the same time. Their tails curl around each other protectively, and their ears hang low.

Ethan drifts over to them slowly and kneels to meet their eyes. "Are you two here alone?" he asks them gently. One of them nods furiously back at him. The other attaches themselves to their sibling tightly. He can only smile apologetically. "I'm sorry. Is it okay if we stay here for a spell?" The Shadows say nothing and remain still as statues, simply staring back at him with their wide eyes. Sadness and anger only well up inside him the longer he stares back. These young Feni don't deserve to be stuck as Shadows for as long as they have been. "We won't be long."

"Sure," one of them finally whispers.

"Go play outside for a bit," he suggests. The two siblings nod and dash into the darkness, disappearing from view. When he turns to face the rest of the room, he finds Amber and Lukri already sitting quietly, with Blaze leaning against the wall a few steps away from them. Tacha lingers in the doorway as well, but her entourage has left. All four of them stare at him expectantly, because he knows their enemy better than any other being currently present.

And suddenly he finds this massive weight resting on his shoulders, pressing him down to the ground. His body feels as hollow as it always has, lifeless and emotionless.

He looks down at his injured arm, and the glowing glitter that fills it. The edges are beginning to draw together, closing the rift Kimberly and Shadow created. But his gauntlet is starting to fall apart, just barely keeping itself together with the few intact threads it has. He doesn't have much time left before it completely falls apart.

He clamps his other hand around the unraveling gauntlet and lets out a heavy sigh. "Well, Blaze. Can you run us all through the plan?"

"Of course," Blaze nods, stepping forward to take his place next to Ethan. When he turns to face Amber, Luke, and Tacha, his expression is firm and assertive.

"I've learned quite a fair bit since arriving here in Ica, so the initial plan has changed slightly," Blaze continues confidently. "Korodon has a path that rings the island and a center path that leads directly from Ica to the castle. Originally, I wanted to use the ring path to reach the castle, as I figured that the center path would be well guarded just because of how short and direct it is from the Archway."

"However, Shadows are more likely to gather in towns all the same as when they were once alive," Tacha steps in. "Simply put, going around the outside of the island is rather foolish."

"Riona won't leave the center route unguarded, though," Ethan adds. "She'll probably put her strongest Shadows there just to make sure it's secure. At least, that's what I'd advise her to do."

"Actually, Pravon was completely empty," Blaze replies.

Ethan frowns at him. Pravon is the nexus town at the heart of Korodon, which leads to every other town on the island. Usually he'd assign a couple of Shadows to Pravon, just in case any beings were to wander down the road. Why would Riona recall them and leave the town abandoned?

"What?" he breathes.

Blaze nods. "When I escaped the castle, I passed through Pravon. No being was there to stop me."

Ethan's scowl deepens. It's either a very smart or very stupid move. Maybe Riona just has her Shadows spread thin with what is essentially her war effort in Mirage, leaving Pravon unguarded as a result. Maybe she's betting on an invasion at

252

any given time, and assumes that a strike force wouldn't go down the center pathway due to the very same logic he used, so she's leaving Pravon open so she can use those Shadows for other things.

Or maybe she's inviting them to come to the castle.

"Going through Pravon is our best bet right now. It's the fastest route and most likely still safe up until Eros."

"Eros is definitely well guarded," Ethan states.

"We'll deal with Eros when we get there," Blaze replies nonchalantly.

"Just don't wander into the empty fields," Tacha advises. "You'll be begging for a fight that way." The other four nod.

"When are we going, then?" Amber asks softly.

"As soon as we can," Blaze replies, straightening himself and rolling his shoulders. "The cycle has just started. It'd be best to get to the castle before nightfall, right?"

Ethan nods. "Though the clouds do provide the Shadows a slight edge during light, they'll become extremely dangerous once night falls."

"I wish you all luck," Tacha speaks, looking around the room at the rag tag team. "I must stay here with the other Shadows to make sure no *surprises* befall us." Her eyes eventually land on Ethan, and a slight smile tugs at the corners of her lips. "It's nice to finally see you take some action."

"It's been a long time coming," Ethan nods back at her.

Lukri rests his jade sword on his shoulders, puffing out his chest confidently. Amber holds her spear as firmly as she can, trying to appear ready for the journey ahead of them, though her eyes betray her anxiety. Blaze simply smiles, and Ethan can't help but smile back.

At least he's not alone.

Chapter 21

With the castle looming high in the sky, the four set off on the path forward. Ethan steals a glance behind him to see the Shadows of Ica gathered in the windows, atop buildings, and standing in the street, all watching them go.

Blaze pats his shoulder. "They all want us to succeed."

Ethan forces a light chuckle, trying to get his nerves out. He knows that already. They've been waiting on him for far too long. He doesn't wish to entertain the thought of failing them at this stage. This *has* to go well, or else he'll never be able to live with himself.

The dead environment around them is eerily silent. All the fields and orchids they pass are completely bare; no grass, no leaves, and not even any remains of rotten fruits and vegetables. The bark of the trees is ashen and hard. The sky only adds to the dreary atmosphere, with black lightning crackling through the clouds that spiral out from the very tip of the castle's tallest point.

Ethan twists his gauntlets uncomfortably, though stops once he feels the splitting fabric on his right wrist. His skin begins to prick with phantom gazes. Distant whispers begin to tickle his ears, the past trying to push its way forward, and he grits his teeth to keep the voices at bay.

The silence is starting to get to him.

They continue on, their footsteps the only noise that fills the emptiness of the island around them. It's always a sad sight for him, walking through the results of his own doing. Not that he *wanted* to turn Korodon into a lifeless land. It's just all so… *surreal*. Every single time.

Amber twirls her spear slowly, careful not to hit Lukri next to her. The prince laughs as he watches her, amused.

"No," he states, and Amber stops her spear spinning. He reaches for the weapon, saying, "Better way to do it." She relinquishes the spear to the prince with a sigh. Lukri holds the spear with both hands for a moment, staring down at it, as if marveling at its craftsmanship once again. Then, without warning, he holds it out in front of him and spins it so fast that the silver shaft becomes a circular blur.

"Wow…" Amber breathes as Lukri brings the spear to a stop once more.

"Practice," Lukri smiles. "Look." While Ethan can't exactly see what Lukri is doing with his hands, Amber watches intensely as Lukri slowly rotates the weapon once more. When the tip is once again facing the sky, he hands it back to her. "Try it."

Ethan watches quietly, and for a moment he's able to forget about the dead land that surrounds them. Laughter fills the air as the two play around. Something inside him flutters, his chest filling with warmth. He can practically smell the grass of the fields, freshly trimmed and covered with dew, as the light of the new cycle beams down on them from somewhere high above. Children scream with delight as the farmers tend to their crops and livestock. Kava stumble around on their stubby legs, leathery skin practically gleaming in the light of the cycle as they dip their heads down to eat. And the road is lined with flowering trees as they prepare themselves to bear fruit.

Amber and Lukri turn into Riona and Shadow.

I've never been to Korodon before, Riona breathes,

255

looking around in awe.

It's been a while since I've been back, Shadow laughs alongside her.

Well, now that we're here, when are you going to start teaching me Shadow magic?

Shadow shakes its head. *We're not there yet.*

"What are you thinking about, Eth?" Blaze asks, his voice cutting through the scene. The memory fades back to the emptiness of Korodon, with Amber and Lukri passing the spear between each other.

"The past," Ethan only replies.

***

Blaze hasn't gotten used to being a Shadow at all, living on an island where everything is in shades of gray and black and dead. Korodon only makes him feel sad.

There are so many things he has to wrap his head around. Amber not liking him. Lukri not knowing him. And Ethan... He doesn't know how to describe it, but just being around Ethan makes him feel more... complete? Like he's suddenly been given some sense of direction and purpose on this drab island.

"So, Blaze," Ethan says, "how did you manage to escape Riona?"

Blaze rolls his shoulders back to puff out his chest, his pride swelling. "The floor was cracked and it was easy for my vines to break through when she was trying to Twist me. She wasn't prepared for my attack and I was able to escape in the chaos."

Ethan lets out a snort of amusement, and a smile creeps across his mouth. A strong wave of euphoria washes over Blaze at his friend's happiness.

"You haven't been Branded yet, have you?" Ethan then

asks.

"No."

His friend hums, his smile disappearing in an instant. "When we reach Pravon, that will change."

Blaze frowns, unsure how to feel about it, yet reluctant to voice resistance. He doesn't think he needs Branding in the first place, at least not the kind that the other Shadows of Ica have. Their magical abilities are limited, which means they couldn't Brand Blaze themselves, and they can't leave through the Archway without explicit permission.

It's not like Blaze could leave, either. He tried to use a Keystone, taken from a Feni body, but nothing happened. He wouldn't be surprised if Shadows can't use the Archway, or if the runes on the Archway have been altered to explicitly prevent Shadows from using it. No matter what, he was stuck on Korodon.

Blaze looks up at the pathway in front of the small group, and sees the road begin to tilt downwards. It's a rather gentle slope, though steep enough to be noticeable. Up ahead, however, there *is* a rather steep decline, almost as if they're approaching a cliff. Beyond the decline is a rather large hole, with other roads leading to it from five more directions.

"Pravon is just up ahead," Ethan announces, sounding neither happy nor upset about it.

"What happened to the land…?" Amber breathes in wonder and worry.

Ethan smiles weakly and chuckles to himself. "It's a cannon crater dating all the way back to the Great War. Pravon has always been a rest stop between Ica and every other town on Korodon, before and after it was rebuilt."

They approach the edge of the crater with caution, huddling closely together. As one, they reach the crater edge and stare down into the depression. Sure enough, the crater is just big enough to hold a few dark and dusty buildings, with the

257

six roads that lead down to meet in the small town's center, where it appears a little market once was, with torn rugs and tattered tarps lining the outer edges of the square.

"Is it safe?" Amber asks.

"It looks safe enough," Blaze hums, folding his arms. "Let's see if we can take a small break here. Rest our legs and get ready for the last stretch of our journey." Ethan nods, though he continues to wear an agitated frown.

Slowly, the group descend into the crater town of Pravon, silence swirling around them. Blaze first, in case any trouble arises. Amber and Lukri next, the Healer helping the prince navigate the slope. Ethan quietly brings up the rear.

"Pick a place?" Blaze asks over his shoulder.

"Any building will do," Ethan replies flatly.

"That one!" Lukri points to a nearby house towards the edge of the town. No other suggestions are voiced, so they all drift over to the one that the prince chose.

Nearing the dark home, Blaze's legs begin to grow heavier by the step as he slowly realizes that he's far more tired from the walk than he thought he was. Shadows don't have all the stamina in the universe, apparently.

The house is a single open room, with a stone table and small stools pushed up against one of the side walls, an ash-filled fire pit in the center, and two cots standing against the back wall. Very minimalist.

Amber trudges over to the firepit and, with a relieved sigh, drops right to her knees. Lukri somewhat does the same thing, though his legs fuse into a bright green tail instead, and he puffs a little to catch his breath. No doubt he's not used to all that walking they just did.

Ethan pats Blaze's arm and nods towards the table. His arm buzzes pleasantly, and he does nothing to fight the sensation.

"A moment," Ethan says.

"Sure," Blaze nods. He drifts behind Ethan and plops down on one of the small stone stools. His legs throb happily, thanking him for the relief. Ethan brings one of the other stools around and places it to Blaze's right. Judging from his determined expression, his mind is on something besides having some sore legs.

"This'll sting," Ethan announces, reaching for Blaze's shoulder.

That's enough to snap him out of his trance-like state. Panic surges through his body, and he leans away from his friend's outstretched hands, his shoulder jolting back behind his body.

"What do you mean, 'this'll *sting*'?!" he exclaims.

"Ethan, what are you doing?" Amber asks, though she doesn't sound all that interested in Blaze's panic.

Ethan lets out a frustrated sigh. "I'm just going to Brand him, that's all. So he'll be less inclined to listen to Riona, or Shadow, or… or *me*."

"I don't need a Brand," Blaze states firmly through gritted teeth.

The flash of Ethan's cold scowl sends a chill down Blaze's back instantly as his friend shifts on his stool. In an instant it seems like he's become a completely different being.

"You trust me, don't you?" he asks. Unsure as to where Ethan's going with this, Blaze can only bring himself to nod along. The Spiritist raises a hand, pointing a single finger at the Shadow's chest. "Pain."

And with that one word, a sharp stabbing pain erupts in Blaze's chest, right where Ethan points. He lets out a strained grunt as he hunches over, his hands clawing at his chest hopelessly. His mouth opens, but an airy squeal is the only thing he can produce.

"If even I can cause you pain in my weakened state, imagine what Riona could do in the heat of battle."

The pain subsides, turning into a cold throb, and Blaze is allowed to catch his breath.

"With the wave of her hand," his friend continues coolly, "you could be rendered completely immoble and magicless. Or worse, she could force you to go against us, and you'll be unable to stop yourself."

"And a Brand will help?" Blaze asks skeptically, slowly sitting up straight again. Out of the corner of his eye, he can still see Ethan's empty, emotionless stare.

"It's an unending instruction. If you're constantly being told to do something specific, then you're less inclined to follow another unrelated instruction."

Still, Blaze frowns in protest. "What are you going to Brand me with, then?"

Ethan's expression softens at the question, some semblance of emotion returning to his being. "A protector's Brand, I'm thinking."

"For who?"

Ethan simply nods in the direction of Amber and Lukri, who stare at them in silence. "Better them than no being in particular," his friend replies, mustering a small smile. He lifts a hand, a finger already poised in the air and at the ready. "Roll up your sleeve." Reluctantly, Blaze complies, rolling his sleeve as high as it can go on his shoulder. Ethan leans forward and presses his fingertip against his shadowy skin. In an instant, a flair of burning pain springs from his touch, and Blaze grits his teeth and sucks in a sharp breath.

He can practically *track* where Ethan's finger is against his skin, though he has no idea what symbol he may be ultimately drawing. All he knows is that it just hurts.

After a moment, Ethan taps his arm, where it's colder. "I'm done."

Blaze blinks and looks at him, his shoulder still on fire. It still feels like his friend has his finger on him as his new Brand throbs. Ethan is sitting back on his stool, hands in his lap. Slowly, Blaze reaches for his shoulder and light touches the Brand. A spike of sore pain shoots through his body, making him wince.

"You probably shouldn't touch it for a little while," Ethan suggests.

"*Thanks*," Blaze only grumbles back. He tries to roll his shoulder to work off the pain, but only ends up causing even more of it to spread.

He looks up at Amber and Lukri. The two still sit around the ashen fire pit, passing the spear back and forth between each other and chatting. A strong warmth fills his chest the longer he stares, a sensation he can only liken to an older sibling watching their younger siblings play.

Ethan stands and fiddles with his clothes. Brushing his robe for no reason, fixing his hat, and fiddling with the clasp of his cape to make sure it's still there. His hand eventually strays to his ruined gauntlet, and he begins to pick at the edges of the frayed fabric. From his dark expression, he appears anxious.

"We should get moving soon," he says. "I don't want to still be on Korodon while it's like this when night falls."

Blaze nods in agreement. While it'd probably help him and his magic, the others would be at a disadvantage. And yet…

"Hey, are you two ready to walk again?"

Amber and Lukri turn around.

"Maybe," the Serperas mutters.

"I think so," Amber adds unsurely.

"Hey!" Blaze speaks up in annoyance. "Can I have a spell for my shoulder to heal a bit more?"

Ethan twists his gauntlets, expression conflicted. His hands appear to be shaking, his gaze lost in another reality. Blaze doesn't know what may be causing it, but Ethan is certainly in some sort of nervous stupor.

"You're not looking too great yourself," Blaze points out gently. "Maybe you should go take a quick breather, Eth."

Ethan lets out a shaky sigh. "Yes, maybe... But-"

"I think it'd do you some good to clear your head a little bit before we get going," he suggests, "so that you can think straighter."

Another quivering breath, but this time Ethan nods. "Sure..."

"We'll be here," Blaze assures him with a small, encouraging smile.

***

With a swish of his cape, Ethan steps outside into the empty town, leaving the other three behind in the dark house.

Amber's stomach churns. He *did* seem rather nervous. She hopes he's doing alright...

Blaze sucks in a breath as he shifts on his stool, his free hand gripping his upper arm hard and his face twisting into uncomfortable pain. Amber tries to not pay him much mind, but his gaze is fixed on his new Brand on his shoulder rather than on her and Lukri. Still, she can't help but take note of his condition.

Even if she dislikes him, she hates seeing another being in pain more. She doesn't know where this thought stems from, though. Maybe it's because she's a Healer. Maybe it's something to do with her missing memories. Or maybe it's a little bit of both.

Lukri shifts next to her, drawing her attention. The tip of his tail waves at her lazily as he curls up on the floor, hugging himself to keep warm. His eyes hang half closed, fighting to remain open. His sword rests on the ground next to him.

"Do you need to go on a walk, too?" Amber asks, forcing a light chuckle.

Lukri smiles weakly as he lowers himself to the ground. "Just rest..." Amber just pats his shoulder awkwardly. And now it's just her and that Shadow in the back still sitting around, wide awake with nothing to do.

Amber turns to her spear and fiddles with it quietly.

Spears stab, runs through her mind, a little something Lukri told her. They're not meant for waving around like a sword. They stab, and they can also be thrown. That's about the gist of it.

"He doing okay?" Blaze asks.

"The cold makes him tired," Amber replies.

The Shadow chuckles. "Guess Mirage is rather hot, then?"

She nods back. "They have a sun that follows the cycle. It's warm when it's up but cold when it disappears."

"Does the sky still brighten and darken?"

"Well, yeah," Amber bites in mild frustration. "Why wouldn't it?"

"I've never been to Mirage," Blaze replies calmly.

She turns to him and states firmly, "It's still a part of Astria." The Shadow regards her small outburst with a vacant gaze.

"Hey…" he sighs. "I… I know you don't necessarily like me much-"

"I don't," Amber curtly cuts him off, turning away from him. Anger swirls within her, only growing the more she engages with him.

"Right," the Shadow mumbles. "I just… want to apologize."

Tch, Amber breathes.

"I shouldn't have said all of that," Blaze continues calmly. "It was wrong to drag you into my plan in the first place, anyway, threats and insults aside."

Amber remains silent, still somewhat fuming. After all, she won't just let go of what he did because he's a Shadow now. It's still *Blaze* she's talking to. Yet, at the same time, he's got a point. He's not been rude or snarky with her at all since their meeting at Ica. He was even helping with the Feni's tilling. That's not something the Blaze of Asandra would have done.

"You don't have to accept it," the Shadow carries on. "I can't promise I'll be this way when I return to my body again, either. But… just know that, until then, I'll look out for you and Lukri as best I can."

Amber just nods. She doesn't have anything more to say to the Shadow. It's nice to know he'll be watching over her and Lukri, and yet she can't help but feel skeptical if all he is saying is true or not.

***

Ethan finds a dark alley between two homes and takes a seat on the ground, inspecting his arm once again. He can't quell the sickness in his gut as he stares hopelessly at his ruined gauntlet.

This isn't something he can simply try to stitch back together. The runes inside are damaged, and the magic of the enchantments are weakening. Even if the gauntlet stays together until the very end, its effects, the entire reason why he wears it in the first place, will be gone.

And he can already start to feel it. A pull, deep down inside of him, dragging him to the castle, even though he's already on his way there. But the longer he sits, the stronger the urge becomes to start moving again.

Riona is calling him back.

He clenches his hands into tight fists of frustration. What is he going to do if his other gauntlet gets damaged? What is he going to do if he lets his attention slip ever so slightly?

His thoughts stray to Amber and Lukri. The last thing he wants to do is hurt them with his own two hands. He doesn't want to bring everything he cares about crashing down. The determination will keep him sane a little longer, but it's not going to last forever.

He takes his gauntlet off. His arm prickles as it comes into contact with the cold air around him as he shoves his gauntlet into his robe's pocket with a reluctant sigh. He doesn't want it to fall off unexpectedly and lose it. When he returns to Asandra he'll get it repaired.

That's if you ever return, Riona's mocking voice hisses in the back of his head.

This makes him stand in a rage. He *will* return to Asandra, and he'll return with Shadow this time around.

He looks down at his bare wrist once more with a scowl. He's not used to seeing it without his gauntlet on. The others will note it as well if he were to return like this. He waves his other hand over his wrist, and in a puff of black smoke a replacement appears. It has the same cuts and tears in the fabric, but without the enchantments as the real one.

The others don't need to know it's missing.

Chapter 22

The group happens upon a low hill, and Ethan stops. Amber pauses mid-step to avoid running into him, almost tripping over herself. Her legs ache once again and long for some rest, but she also knows she has no time to sit down now. She'll just have to deal with the aching for now.

"Eros should be just over this hill," Ethan announces, gesturing to the rise in the land.

"Can I sit?" Lukri asks tiredly.

"No. You wouldn't be sitting for very long, anyway," Ethan replies, sounding rather irritated. He's probably just stressed, being so close to his end goal. Amber would probably be the same way if she were him.

"There are quite a number of Shadows waiting around," Blaze says. "The place is surrounded by old farmland, so simply walking around it won't be an option if we want to get past without a fight."

"I do not wish to fight through them, either," Ethan says. "Not only would we lose most of our strength early on, but it gives Riona some time to watch us fight and prepare, or crush us before we can even reach the castle. She knows we're here, but she doesn't know *where*, I believe..." He raises a hand to his forehead and closes his eyes. "Our link hasn't come back, at any rate."

"We still have to get past Eros to get to the castle, though," Amber points out quite literally as she gestures with her spear.

The group falls silent once again. Ethan's gaze is lost in thought, leaving Amber, Lukri, and Blaze standing around aimless.

Blaze lets out a confident hum, causing the other two to turn and look at him. "Whatever happens, you two are in good hands." The Shadow smiles at Amber, though he quickly turns to Lukri to include him in the moment. "I'll make sure you two get back to Ica if anything comes up." Amber only nods in reply, unsure what else to say or do.

"Thank you," Lukri smiles back at the Shadow weakly. He holds his sword a little firmer in his hand.

"I think I have a plan," Ethan suddenly announces. The other three turn back to the Husk, waiting for him to relay his idea. He fiddles with his gauntlets for a moment and takes a slow, deep breath to calm himself.

When he's ready, he looks up and stares at the three with a suddenly cold gaze. "Amber, Lukri… you're going to need to be tied up."

In an instant, panic stabs at Amber's heart, and she inhales sharply, hugging her spear tight. Her heartbeat pounds in her ears as it leaps up into her throat. Be tied up? *Why*?

"Ethan!" Lukri exclaims in fury.

"Please," Ethan motions for him to settle down with a simple hand gesture, "I know, I know, this isn't what you want to hear. But there's no other way we can get past Eros unharmed. It won't be for very long. At least until we get to the castle."

"What *specifically* is your plan?" Blaze asks coldly, folding his arms. Ethan's mouth opens soundlessly, his eyes partly widening as whatever spell came over him wears away, leaving him stunned.

"You're just going to have to trust me," he says eventually. He places a hand on his chest and composes himself the best he can. "I want to make the Shadows think that I want to return to Riona. It's already clear that Lukri is a target for her, but including Amber as well will make sure that both of you can get through."

Amber and Lukri look at one another. His emerald eyes are dark and fearful, seeming as if he's going to start crying at any moment. His chest puffs in and out rapidly. Amber doesn't feel much better herself. Her heart sinks low as her chest continues to constrict with panic and unease. Is this really such a good idea? She's been with Ethan quite a lot the last couple of cycles, but she doesn't know what goes on in his head.

"And how do we know you're not just going to hand them over?" Blaze steps forward, standing in front of the two protectively. The ground begins to shake under her feet, or, at least, she *thinks* she can feel vibrations below her. They're so faint she isn't completely sure.

"Come on, Blaze, you know me-"

"I *thought* I knew you," the Shadow replies harshly. It's the same tone he once used towards Amber, a tone that makes her heart ache. "Now? I don't know what to think."

"Do *you* have a better plan?" Ethan asks, his anxiousness quickly switching to defensive anger. The question appears to knock Blaze silent for a spell.

"No," he finally admits. "I'm asking how we can trust you not to turn on us?"

"Of *course* I don't want to go crawling back to her!" Ethan exasperates. "I've made too many promises to too many beings to-"

Amber steps forward, causing Ethan's voice to catch.

"Then can you make another one?" she asks lightly. Ethan tilts his head ever so slightly in confusion. "That... you won't ever return to her."

Ethan's shoulders sink as he sighs. "After everything she's done, of course I can promise that."

Amber nods. It doesn't make her feel much better, but at least he seems like he means it.

"Then what do we do?"

The Husk gives her a weak smile, if only for a short moment, and waves to Blaze. "We can use your vines as bindings, at least around their mouths and chests. They'll still need to walk, of course."

Blaze scowls unhappily, and yet two dark vines rise from the dirt without protest. Lukri's anxious gaze darts between the vine and Amber, looking for some sense of comfort. So she sucks in a sharp breath and stands a little taller. She's also worried, but she doesn't want Lukri to see it. He's already out of his depth as it is.

Gently, the two vines approach and begin to wrap around their waists, snaking up their torsos and arms. Amber holds her spear close to her side to make sure it's not poking her or stuck to her awkwardly. She looks over at Lukri, who has his eyes closed and appears to be holding his breath as the vine wraps around his chest, pinning his arms and sword to his sides.

And then the vine reaches her mouth, a single layer of shadowy plant matter that smells of dry earth. It presses against her lips so hard it keeps them pressed shut. Not like she'd want to open her mouth in the first place, or she'd taste the vine and probably not be very pleased.

Ethan is back to messing with his gauntlets, pacing back and forth across the width of the pathway.

"Ethan?" Blaze speaks up, irritation in his voice. Ethan looks up at the three, stares for a long moment with a gaze full of thoughts and emotion, and nods in satisfaction.

"Just walk behind them and stay silent," Ethan instructs Blaze. "And... look intimidating."

269

"Can we just go already?"

"Yes, yes…" the Husk nods furiously. He runs a hand through his hair and looks to the hill, remaining unmoving. Amber remains standing, the vine hugging her body just tight enough to where it's not uncomfortable, but she can't shift around much, either. She can't protest or comfort the Husk. Part of her wants to tell him to get on with it, or to reassure him that the plan will work, or to even ask if they can just turn around and go back to Ica. But she's in the vine now.

Ethan puts a foot forward, rolling his shoulders and fixing his hat, one last fidget. There's a push from the vine, an urge for Amber to walk, and she, too, puts her foot forward. She's marched over the crest of the hill, and there she sees Eros ahead of them, along with the base of the castle beyond the buildings full of Shadows. Even from the hill, she can see that they're all large, much taller than her, and shaded in various blacks and dark grays.

Her heart leaps and squeezes again, much harder this time. But all she can do now is walk forward to the very town that could possibly overwhelm them in an instant.

***

Ethan's gut twists into nervous knots as he leads the march towards Eros. Despite his anxiousness, he keeps his expression cold. If he fails, he may as well have thrown them all over the side of the island.

The Twisted Shadows wander the street ahead of him, aimless. It's sad to see such good Shadows in such a state, and not even given a task to do. It's just meaningless suffering.

His nervousness grows the closer they get. The hollow cavity of his chest is swirling with it. Sometimes he wonders how other beings experience emotion, or if they feel just like he does.

A Shadow finally turns its head. Its red eyes lock with

270

Ethan's. Quiet and still, it just stares for what feels like centuries. And then it opens its mouth and lets out a screech. It's an otherworldly screech, echoing and raspy, something a regular Shadow wouldn't even be able to produce. And it's not something he's used to hearing.

All the other Twisted Shadows stop and turn, cluttering the street. If this were any other time, they'd stand aside and bow as he passed them. After all, he was, for a long time, Riona's advisor. But the screech, the staring, the lack of movement… he feels deep down inside himself that something isn't right.

He holds his head high as a Twisted Shadow pushes its way to the front of the pack and stands at the entrance to the town. It towers over Ethan, causing him to crane his neck to meet its gaze.

He knows this Twisted Shadow all too well, even before it became Twisted. This is the old leader of the town, before Riona came and took over. He was strict but fair to the Feni who lived here; once becoming a Shadow, he was still allowed to care for the town. And now, as if in insult, the Twisted Shadow before him wears a lavish garb fit for a town leader, yet is left without a town to lead.

"Hello, Kaza," Ethan says flatly, focusing his energy into keeping his voice even and calm. He just has to uphold the act and, with any luck, they'll be allowed through without issue.

"*You have nerve, Husk,*" Kaza hisses back, cold and uncaring. "*Are you looking for death?*"

"No," Ethan replies carefully. "Although, if that were to happen, would you be prepared to face the wrath of the Lady's right hand?"

Kaza's face briefly contorts into that of alarm at the insinuation of facing off against Shadow, but he remains silent with his jaw tightly clenched.

Ethan raises a hand to gesture to the company behind

271

him, yet does nothing to acknowledge their presence beyond that. "I merely bring gifts for the Lady."

Something dark and hateful stirs within him as he says this. He can hardly believe he used to talk and act this way regularly. In a way, he doesn't even need to fake anything.

"*There is rumor that you had forsaken the Lady,*" the Twisted Shadow informs him, narrowing its eyes skeptically.

"There are some things she cannot get through her army," Ethan chuckles. "I didn't intend for it to appear that I was working against her. I was merely taking a different approach. Does she not want the prince of Mirage?"

Kaza lets out an airy huff of annoyance. "*She does...*"

"And the Shadow she let slip through her fingers. Does she not want him, either?"

Blaze draws breath, but Ethan raises a hand to calm him. Kaza just stares at him quietly.

"Consider this my peace offering to her, and a symbol of my dedication," Ethan adds with a slight smile. "Why should I suddenly turn on the Lady after the centuries we've spent together?"

Kaza points over his shoulder. "*Who is the girl?*"

"A being close to the Council of Asandra," he replies smoothly. Amber really isn't *that* close to Azna, but he certainly cares for his Healers regardless. "I figure she can be used as leverage against the wizards."

"*And the Shadow?*"

"He's under control, don't worry."

Again, Blaze inhales, but a little less sharply this time.

"*And all are for the Lady?*"

"If she is willing to take them."

Silence. Kaza remains staring, but says nothing. The other Twisted Shadows are quiet and still as well, like statues. Amber, Lukri, and Blaze make no noise, either, which makes Ethan want to turn and check to see if they're still standing behind him.

"*Go*," Kaza orders. The Twisted Shadow turns and waves at the crowd in a fashion that reminds Ethan of the old Kaza, a grand yet respectful gesture for the beings in his care to act. The crowd parts, a sight so familiar yet so foreign at the same time, revealing a path straight through Eros. Kaza also stands to the side, though continues to stare at Ethan intensely.

Unphased by their gazes, Ethan puffs out his chest and begins to walk down the corridor of Twisted Shadows, creating walls of black to his left and right, red eyes following him as he passes. Their gaze is only on him, the Shadows completely disinterested in his entourage. These eyes are full of skepticism and impatience, maybe even hate. Has this always been here and he never noticed? Or could it just be their temperaments from cycles of having nothing to do?

A dark thought begins to grow in the back of his mind as he strides deeper into Eros. He has Lukri and Amber at his complete mercy, and while Blaze is somewhat still a free-thinker, he can still be tricked and controlled to a certain extent.

What's stopping him from simply returning to Riona?
What's the point in fighting?

He looks over his shoulder with his dead gaze. Amber and Lukri stare at him, their eyes just barely visible over the dark vines that are wrapped around the two. Blaze's gaze is distant and blank, almost like he's bored. And Kaza, to mild surprise, soundlessly trails them. He casts Kaza an awkward glare and turns back around to face forward once again.

Eventually, he leads the four of them out of Eros, now on the path that leads straight to the castle that stands before them, its presence foreboding. The central spire towers in the sky, able to oversee the entire island and out into the Void. It's also arguably the best spot to stargaze on any given night, though the clouds certainly don't help with improving the sky's visibility.

"*Ethan*," Kaza speaks, causing Ethan to stop and spin

around. The Twisted Shadow shoves past Blaze, who casts daggers at the back of its head, and between Amber and Lukri, who stare at it uneasily. Kaza's expression, however, has gone from cold to troubled. "*Have you heard from the Lady at all?*"

Ethan folds his arms. "No… I've not."

"*She's not communicated with Eros for some years now,*" Kaza explains. "*The Shadows have nothing to do and nowhere to go. There is the Mirage campaign, but she's been more obsessed with her new* playthings." The Twisted Shadow spits the last word at the ground in distaste. Hearing a Twisted Shadow speak ill of Riona is new, but he can also see it happening with just enough resentment. Not even Twisted Shadows are perfect creations.

Ethan just stares at Kaza, his thoughts swirling. Eros has the highest concentration of not only Twisted Shadows, but also Shadows that have magic. So then why not use them for the Mirage campaign?

"That makes no sense," he can't help but mutter aloud.

"*It makes no sense to me as well,*" Kaza nods. "*The others grow restless. If you truly are returning…*" He trails off with a hopeful note in his voice.

"Kaza," Ethan sighs heavily, feeling just a little sorry for the Shadow. "I'll… I'll see what I can do."

This makes Kaza smile. It's a light one, relieved. Once again, something that shines through from the Kaza of old.

The Twisted Shadow does a short bow, then turns and hurries back to Eros, back to the gathering of the other townsfolk. Ethan turns away from the town and looks at Blaze for a moment. The Shadow stares back, along with Amber and Lukri, waiting for him to make his move.

"Come on," he says, waving to Blaze. "Until the door of the castle."

***

Amber lets out a deep sigh of relief as Blaze is finally allowed to untie her and Lukri.

"I hope it wasn't too uncomfortable for you," Ethan says with a slight smile.

Amber stretches her arms and grips her spear firmly. "Not very much." Next to her, Lukri also lets out a long stretch himself.

They stand huddled up against the main entrance to the castle. She can see Eros below, at the bottom of the rather tall hill the castle perches on, where the Shadows mill about once again.

"You knew that Shadow?" she asks.

Ethan nods with a solemn expression. "Kaza was the leader of Eros. Or, still is by the looks of things."

"Is he not supposed to be?"

"Ever since he became a Twisted one, a lot of his authority was stripped away. Though..." Ethan's eyes flash with something troubled, "apparently communication between Eros and Riona has been nonexistent for quite a while now, so he seems to be keeping some sort of peace between the Shadows."

"Any reason why?"

"I don't know." He folds his arms and hums at the ground beneath him, his hat hiding his face. "It's not only Eros that troubles me. Blaze, Kimberly, and Jake already seemed odd. The Mirage campaign is even stranger. Riona has been in contact with no being other than me and Shadow, and the only being alive in Astria she'd possibly be upset with is me..."

He trails off uneasily, and something in Amber's stomach drops. If the only being in Astria Riona would have an ax to grind with is the same being who she has been spending the last couple of cycles with...

"I thought she was being rational," Ethan speaks once more, looking up once again. His expression is dark, coming to a realization that he probably never wanted to come to. "I *hoped* she was being rational. But... I've always been her main target. Taking away my friends. Taking away places I can hide. And then bringing me back here... to either be forced into submission, or to be annihilated. Or both."

A heavy silence descends on the group. Amber holds her spear close to her chest, giving the Husk a sympathetic look. All this effort to ruin one being? And she used to be concerned about rumors only a handful of cycles ago. And speaking of rumors...

She takes a deep breath.

"Ethan."

Ethan looks at her with a dead gaze.

"I..." she forces a small smile, "I'm glad we met."

The Husk nods back at her, hope sparkling in his eyes. "I'm glad we met, too."

They stare at each other for a spell, not saying anything. She really is glad that they met. Ethan didn't need to step up and watch over her, yet he did so anyway. And she didn't need to stay with him when he wanted to come to Korodon, yet here she is.

Eventually, he turns away from her, looking up at the door that stands before them.

"This door leads to a main entrance hall," he says, "which will take us to the throne room. If the three of you can deal with the other Shadows, I can handle Riona. Well, hopefully."

"Okay," Lukri nods. He sucks in a breath as if collecting his courage, holding his sword with a firm grip. Amber weighs her spear in her hands for a moment, her stomach fluttering nervously. She's a Healer, not a fighter. So long as she stays out of harm's way, she can put herself to use if Lukri or Ethan get injured. Still...

Ethan pushes the great doors open with minimal effort. The hinges creak and the wood groans as they are put in motion after probably a couple of years without much use or care.

"Funny," Ethan mutters as the dark entrance hall is illuminated by the dim light from the outside world, "I used to oil these doors."

"What else did you do?" Amber can't help but ask as the group take their first steps inside the castle. A cold breeze rushes through the hall, blowing back her hair and sending chills up and down her spine. Lukri inhales sharply at the sudden chill and huddles close to Amber for warmth. She stretches an arm over his shoulders to give him a little more comfort.

"Many things, just to ensure that most of the castle wouldn't fall into disrepair," the Husk chuckles weakly, voice echoing up and down the derelict hall. They pass unlit torches mounted to the walls, their wood rotting from centuries of not being replaced. Small stone doorways hang open, leading into side halls that wind their way deep into the castle, bathed in dark shadow. "Though I couldn't do everything by myself. Not even the Shadows from Eros were allowed to enter and care for the place, and I didn't want the *entire* castle to crumble away due to neglect. After all, it was my home, too, for a time."

"So big..." Lukri comments quietly.

"Even I still get lost from time to time," Ethan reassures him, glancing over his shoulder just long enough to flash a strained grin.

And then, inevitably, they reach the end of the hallway. A single small door stands in their way, simple wood planks bound with metal bands and bolts. It's not the sort of entrance she was expecting to see for a throne room. Then again, the castle *is* rather old, so maybe the original door was replaced at some point. Or maybe this is what it has always been like.

They've already passed the point of no return long ago, but this really does feel like a last chance to turn around and run.

Then again, there's a large part of Amber that *does* want to see the being that has forced Ethan into slavery for his entire life. At least once. All he's ever done is talk about Riona, but he never really did describe her.

Ethan takes a breath and reaches for the door, flames beginning to swirl around his arms. Amber lets Lukri go and takes hold of her spear, feeling far from ready for a fight. Whatever happens, she'll just have to make-do and hope it works out.

The moment his fingers touch the door, it explodes from its hinges and flies deep into the throne room.

The time has come.

Chapter 23

The space is large. *Very* large. Ethan remembers Shadow telling tales that it had been told, of grandiose celebrations that would take place in this very throne room, full of beings of all backgrounds and races. How they'd mingle with one another without caring for who or what they were, allowed to simply be themselves and enjoy some complimentary food and drink from dusk to dawn.

Of course, he never witnessed any of those moments himself, nor did Shadow. They all passed long before Shadow ever met Riona. And now the throne room sits empty and lifeless, with tall marble pillars tinged a purple-blue, crumbling from age, and the flameless hanging braziers above them swing in the castle's cold draft. It's a dim and foreboding room, one where many decrees have been given that he had once carried out personally. Riona existed almost exclusively in this quiet hall, only retiring to her chambers when she felt truly exhausted.

The door sails through the air and is only stopped by a second blast of black flame, which reduces the wood and metal to cinder and scrap. The twisted metal binds clatter to the floor and skids to a halt at the foot of the raised dais that held up the throne of Riona. Some of the stones that make up the flooring of the room are cracked and partly uneven, clearly having been upheaved and replaced in the not-so-distant past.

He can't help but take note of the three Shadows that stand at the foot of the dias as well. Jake on the right, Kimberly on the left, their stares empty and lifeless. Shadow stands front and center, sword out at the ready by its side. Its cold gaze lands on Ethan, violet eyes pulsing from its helmet.

Then he looks up at the throne itself and almost does a double take.

He wasn't prepared for who his eyes lay upon. Riona, of course, sits atop it as a queen would, a long black staff in her hand. The staff is adorned with a large glowing amethyst, from which emanates two long spectral chains that hang in the air quietly, fading away the farther the links are from the gemstone. One is partially shattered, the links floating freeform in some sort of jagged line. That is Ethan's chain. The other chain, Shadow's, shines brightly, with the links twisting through one another, interlocking in a way to show that they are determined to never break. It winds down the shaft of the staff, with the other freeform chain hovering high in the air above the amethyst, almost like the shattered links are trying to float away and escape.

But Riona herself looks drastically different from the being he fondly remembers. Her black hair, once dark as night and light as a feather, hangs heavy over her shoulders and down her back with a greasy sheen to it. Her long black dress is faded, wrinkled and torn, and the purple fabric that hangs from her dull copper belt is horribly stained. Her sharp-edged collar is bent when it's supposed to stand straight, and the padded shoulders the collar is attached to seem to be trying to fall off her bony shoulders.

The sight of her only makes Ethan even more angry, as the dress she wears is one that he had bought for her with his own coin centuries ago, and he took good care of it for her, too. Her glossy black heels seem to be the only thing that has been left in an ageless condition, minus a small spot of white dust on the right toe, and they've certainly lost most of their shine. Her emerald eyes have sunk into her skull, and her body is much thinner from when he left. She used to perpetually look the young age of 37. Now it's almost as if she aged three centuries within the last three years he's been away.

"*Riona*?" he can't help but breathe in shock and awe. A part of him doesn't want to believe that *this* is Riona, but he knows that the wizard on that throne can only be her.

"Hello, *Ethan*," she says, spitting as she says his name aloud. Even her voice sounds scratchy and dry, a far cry from her eloquent shouts and sweet-sounding "compliments". "So nice of you to finally show up. Do you know how *long* I've been waiting for you to return?"

"Riona..." he takes a step forward, brow furrowed. He can't help but display his mild concern for her well-being. "What... What *happened* to you?"

"None of your concern!" she snaps back, jerking forward in her seat. The cheap copper-and-jade crown atop her head slides forward with her sharp movement, threatening to fall off completely. Her eyes flash with something dangerous and unhinged, a look he's seen more than once before. He quietly sucks in a breath and holds it, trying to ready himself for whatever she says next. A smile creeps onto her face, her lips jerking upwards as she does so. "You've probably come to beg to be at my side again, haven't you?" She sits back on the throne, appearing pleased with herself. "Well, I'm *done* listening to you, *Ethan*. I've grown tired of your constant whining. Though I must thank you for bringing the prince of Mirage right to my throne, but it's no way to win me over!" She lets out a cackle, sharp and shrill rather than smooth and rich. "I have no further need of your services. Take the Shadow and prince alive. Do what you will with the girl, but kill the Husk."

Ethan stands frozen in place, dumbfounded. Shadow's

figure instantly goes rigid. Even Kimberly and Jake eye the Fragment Shadow with unease, clearly feeling that *something* is amiss.

Kill… its hollow voice echoes, eyes widening, *Ethan…?*

The chain that wraps around Riona's staff wavers ever so slightly. Something faint tingles in the back of Ethan's head. A presence he's not felt in quite some time. He can just barely feel Shadow's mind, slow with thought yet alarmed all the same.

A tinge of red begins to return to Shadow's gaze as it stares back at him. Recognition. He knows it's beginning to feel recognition. It's a storm of relief, horror, longing, and confusion, all that makes his gut churn with the same sense of wanting to reach out and embrace it.

It recognizes Ethan standing on the other end of the throne room.

"Shadow?" Ethan asks quietly, though his voice still carries across the room with ease.

Eth-?

"Enough of that," Riona hisses from above. With a slight tilt of her staff, Shadow freezes, its weaponless arm half raised in the air, outstretched. The little red glimmer in its eyes dies, swallowed by bright violet, and the presence of hope fades once more.

What's the point in fighting? The intrusive question stabs at Ethan's thoughts once again.

Shadow narrows its eyes and steps forward, raising its weapon with clear intentions. A flurry of black ice and snow swirls around Kimberly's hands, and Jake hefts a blazing sword of ebony.

"Ready!" Ethan speaks up, his hands reaching back to grip the edges of his cape. Lukri steps forward on his left, squaring up with Jake with his jade sword raised high. Amber appears on his left, staring at Kimberly with a nervous expression, holding her spear out in front of her at the ready regardless. Beneath Ethan's feet, he can feel the tremor of vines shifting under the foundation of the castle.

Riona, once again, laughs. "Oh, you pathetic Husk. I don't want *all* of you destroying my throne room now."

She slams the butt of her staff down on the ground, and in an instant the shadows jerk to life. The darkness casted from the pillars stretch and curve, rushing towards the four. Ethan grabs his cape instinctively, but he's not fast enough. The shadows rise and wrap around Amber and Lukri in an instant. Amber opens her mouth, but her head disappears before any sound escapes it.

Just like that, the two are gone, leaving Ethan and Blaze behind.

Wordlessly, Kimberly and Jake step into the nearest shadow themselves, off to carry out Riona's orders.

What's the point in fighting, Ethan?

Ethan grits his teeth, anger raging in his chest. He's so close to the end. He just has to keep going a little longer.

"They'll be fine," Blaze mutters to him, referring to Amber and Lukri.

Ethan nods back, flames beginning to curl around his arms. "Then let's finish our plan."

***

The darkness subsides, and Amber's shriek dies in her throat as she lays eyes upon a bedroom. It reminds her of the study from the ruined palace on Mirage, with a door leading to the hallway on one side of the room and a balcony overlooking Korodon on the other. There's a bed on her left, rotting and unused, the faded fabric that once was sheets in tatters with age. On her right is a small desk, or what's left of it, anyway. The wood is gnarled, the structure sideways as two of the legs have separated from the top, laying crushed underneath.

283

It's dim as what little light manages to beam down through Riona's clouds streams in from the balcony doorway. And quiet.

Spear clutched in fear-gripped fingers, she takes a step towards the closed door, determined to return to the throne room to help Ethan as best she can. And if she runs into Lukri along the way, even better.

And then, before her very eyes, she watches the door freeze over in an instant, black ice coating the aging wood. The darkness warps once more, rising to form Kimberly's Twisted Shadow, ice and snow swirling behind her at her beck and call.

Amber's stomach sinks as her friend regards her with emotionless eyes. She now points her spear at a Blessed Cryomancer, a wizard she can't even begin to contend with.

"*I wonder if I should spare you,*" Kimberly hums, tilting her head ever so slightly, "*or kill you.*"

Amber's eyes begin to burn with tears. "Kim, please, I don't want to do this-"

"*This is not your choice.*"

The temperature of the room plummets as Kimberly raises her hand, and the ice and snow behind her rushes to form a floating black-white spike hovering just over her shoulder.

It releases, and Amber swipes at it. Using the spear, she forces the projectile into the ground, where the ice hisses as it comes into contact with the stone. When she turns her attention back to the Shadow, more spikes are now hovering around Kimberly's head, ready to be fired.

"*Maybe I will just freeze you instead,*" she says with an eerie grin. "*That is, if you keep up.*"

Amber drops to her knees as the spikes release at once, swiping away those that she can that may still hit her. Swirling snow stings her cheeks as it swirls around the room, collecting for another barrage.

Amber manages to scramble to her feet and bats away two more spikes, stumbling backwards as she struggles to find

284

her footing against the speed and force of the spikes being thrown at her. Keeping the spikes away from her is all she can really do, putting all of her concentration and energy into simply staying alive. She doesn't have combat experience. She doesn't have magic she can use to fight back. She's just a Healer with a spear!

It doesn't take long for her to wind up standing on the balcony, sending the ice spikes out into the ether of the clouds above or the ground far, far below.

Her heel hits one of the stone pillars that holds up the baloney railing. This is as far as she goes.

The spikes only get faster and faster, and the cold isn't helping her reflexes. As she heaves between swipes, she can see the air turn to mist in front of her. Her lungs begin to burn from the biting frost that radiates from Kimberly's figure.

"Stop!" Amber manages to cry.

The barrage stops, to her surprise, but at the cost of Kimberly smiling back at her menacingly. "*You wish to plead for your life?*"

Amber lets out a dry cough and tries to catch her breath in the biting cold. "Kim, I-"

"*If I were to spare you, then you would concede and join our ranks,*" she interrupts, slowly stepping closer and closer to Amber, ice spreading out from under her feet as they land. Ice spikes float around her head at the ready, bobbing up and down with her graceful movements. "*And if I were to not, then the Lady will have a new sculpture.*"

Amber doesn't reply, collapsing to her hands and knees with exhaustion as the cold sets in to her muscles at full force. Her saliva dries on her tongue, turning thick and sticky in her mouth. The cloud of her breath seems to crystalize into small ice particles, or it could simply be her vision swimming.

Just then, a scream echoes through the hallway beyond the iced-over door, ethereal yet raw all the same. It's pain, rage, and regret, all rolled into one. Amber musters the energy to lift her head to see Kimberly paused in the balcony doorway, frowning towards the hall door.

"*Jake...?*"

***

A gust of cold wind rolls over Lukri's arms and legs, but the darkness remains. His chest begins to constrict itself as he whirls around on the spot, trying to find any source of light he can seek solace in. To his left and right are walls, painted a cold blue that chills the air around him.

He tightens his grip on his sword. He has his magic, but if he uses it too much he'll pass out for sure. And since that wizard on the throne wants his Shadow and Amber is nowhere nearby as far as he can tell, he can't afford to pass out.

A small glow suddenly appears, but not a glow of comfort. It's distant as well, flickering against a dark stone wall. Black fire with faint white tips, engulfing a long blade that is held by the side of a leg.

His eyes dart upwards in an instant, and lock with the Shadow's red irises.

The Shadow raises his hand, flames burning in his palm. A flare of panic ignites within Lukri. They're in a small hallway, and he has no escape. He can't see any nearby doors, the Shadow is in front of him and endless, tight darkness is behind him.

The fire in the Shadow's hand expands without warning, filling the hallway with its dark flames. Lukri releases his sword from his hand and lifts his arms up in front of him, sucking in a breath and gritting his teeth to concentrate, even as his heart pounds in his chest with fear. His sword dissolves into sand before it hits the stone floor, and the orange grains fill the hallway to meet the flames. The roar of the fire fills his ears as it blasts his sand wall, trying to reach him. He can feel its scorching heat on his front, turning his back icy cold.

The blast ends after what feels like an eternity. Most of the sand that made his sword is now solid glass, leaving him with few grains left over, enough to make a single arrow. Converting the glass back into sand will take more effort than he currently has to spare.

Through the glass, as the final black embers die out, he notices that the Shadow is gone. His stomach drops as his feet spin him around, just to find the Shadow looming over him, his sword in the air and ready to strike.

Lukri twists out of the way, and the hot blade streaks past him and clangs against the stone floor. With a yell, he dives at the Shadow with all his might, sending the two to the ground.

Lukri reaches for the Shadow's sword, determined to get his hands on a proper weapon again, as the Shadow does his best to keep it from the Serperas. A fist rises and hits the side of Lukri's face, knocking him aside. His back slams into the side of the hallway, head spinning.

"*You*," the Shadow growls, pointing his sword at Lukri's head, "*are too troublesome.*"

Lukri doesn't reply, his mind racing as his senses slowly return. The Shadow is standing over him again, glaring down with mild anger. His attention is on Lukri's head and arms, and so is his weapon.

The Shadow bends down and wraps his burning hand around Lukri's left arm. "*Stand u-*"

Lukri wraps his tail around the Shadow's nearest leg and pulls with all his might. Surprised, the Shadow stumbles as his leg is pulled out from underneath him, and he falls on top of Lukri's body, his sword flying from his hand. It skids across the floor, the flames that surround it sputtering out, and plunging the hallway into complete darkness once more.

Lukri thrashes against the Shadow, his heat sense just

barely lighting the cooling hilt as he fights to free himself. The Shadow plants his knee on Lukri's back in response, lunging for the sword hilt as well. Lukri, with his outstretched hand, wills the little sand he has left at his command forward. The grains swarm the Shadow's face, attacking his eyes ferociously.

"*GHAAA!*" the Shadow cries, trying to bat away the sand. He rolls off of Lukri's back and scoots around on the floor frantically in a pointless attempt to escape the small sandcloud.

Lukri springs forward and finally obtains the Shadow's sword, long and slender, its hilt cold to the touch. He lifts himself up from the floor with his tail, then stands fully on his legs, turning to face the fading red figure of the Shadow.

He strides up to the Shadow's side and drives the sword into his chest without a second thought. The blade sinks through the Shadow's body with ease, almost as if he were made of air. And yet the Shadow roars in pain anyway, thrashing against the blade that now pins him to the floor.

Lukri attempts to channel his Light into the sword, but ends up making his fingers spark against the hilt instead. The harder he pushes, the harder the sword rejects his magic. It could be because the sword itself is made of Shadow, something that doesn't mix well with Light. While it's a good weapon for the time being, he can't use it as a conduit.

He holds up a hand and summons the sand still at his disposal, creating a knife with a blade as long as his index finger. He bends down close to the Shadow, places the tip of the knife next to the sword, and channels his magic once more. A large white flash fills his vision, and the Shadow screams even louder, his voice devolving into a single note of noise.

As the flash dies and his vision returns, he finds the Shadow's entire left side of his body turned to mist. His mouth is open, face full of agony, and yet his shout is suddenly silent. Lukri stands, his body feeling tired from a lack of energy. How much more magic would he have to use to kill a Twisted Shadow outright?

"*Jake?*" comes a distant call, muffled by the wall of glass. The other Shadow isn't far. Maybe they're with Amber as well.

Lukri steps up to the glass and places his free hand on its smooth surface. Even though he knows it's cold just from the blue hue he sees it as in the dark; the chill he feels is almost similar to the ice that Ethan made back on Mirage.

Slowly, the glass begins to crumble away into sand, starting from where his hand touches its surface. As the hole widens, icy air begins to blast at his arm and chest. The cold combined with his draining magic makes his eyes begin to droop. Training for battle is one thing, but using everything he has at his disposal in a proper fight is another. He didn't think he'd use his magic so much, nor wind up in an environment that he has to constantly fight off the urge to sleep. He doesn't have a torch to keep himself warm, like the guards do back on Mirage. He doesn't have Amber to keep his magic replenished. His willpower won't last him much longer if he remains in this low-energy state.

The glass completely disappears, replaced by a shifting mass of Mirage sand. He walks through the mass, willing it to reform as his trusty jade sword as he makes his way down the cold hallway. The blue wall of stone he follows slowly fades into white the farther he wanders, passing iced-over doors on his way.

"*Jake!*" the Shadow calls again, sounding much closer this time. A strong blast of cold air batters his face, sending chills down his back. "*Do not tell me you need help with that little pest.*"

Lukri bares his fangs, readjusting his grip on his sword's hilt. He wants to at least take a swipe at this other Shadow before his energy depletes.

Small wet pricks begin to batter his face, landing on his cheeks and nose. The smell of the air turns crisp, almost sweet in a weird way. He doesn't know if he's still getting closer to the

Shadow or if it has returned to whatever it had been doing to Amber before the interruption.

Lukri creates a small, brief burst of light to illuminate the hallway before him. The glow of his magic strikes against something black and glossy that sticks to the wall to his right. Ahead of him is an iced-over doorway, and standing in front of said doorway is the second Shadow.

The Shadow turns her head to stare in the direction of his light, and upon laying her eyes on Lukri her face contorts into surprise. Cones of black ice hang in the air around her, their sharp points protruding from some sort of glittering gray cushion.

Lukri grits his teeth and charges at the Shadow with all the energy he can muster. The movement shakes the Shadow out of her spell, and with fury in her eyes she extends an arm at him, an ethereal shriek leaving her lips.

With his arms weighed down with ever-growing exhaustion, he grips his sword with both hands and swings at the flying ice, using the flat of the blade to bat them away from him.

He plants his right foot down in front of him and begins to spin to the left. He slashes downward at the Shadow's extended arm, the blade passing through her like cutting through air. From her hand up to her elbow, her form bursts into black mist. With the momentum of the slash, Lukri swings his left leg around, bringing the blade up to chest height, and, with the tip of his sword scraping the wall of the hallway, he brings his blade to her neck. A flair of Light bursts from his sword, blinding him, as his own yell roars in his ears.

Once more, the flair dies, leaving his vision full of black spots. His mind is swirling, the cold stabbing his skin. As he tries to steady himself, his foot catches against his other leg, and he finds himself on the ground, sharp sores opening on his forearms.

The spots aren't leaving his vision, and his body refuses to move. The pain on his arms fades, numbness taking over. His breath is shaky, as breathing is all he can do now, as he lays on his front, sword still clasped in his feeble fingers. He doesn't know if he killed the other Shadow or not. He doesn't know if the first Shadow is still where he lay.

All he knows now, as he falls into unconsciousness, is that he's completely out of energy.

Chapter 24

The black ice recedes from the walls and, more importantly, the dilapidated bedroom's door, though its strong chill still hangs in the air. Amber forces herself to stand, pushing past her internal pain. Even though she's not experienced with physical injuries, with any luck she'll be feeling better very soon. Until then, the icy knives she breathes in will continue to stab at her chest.

She stumbles to the door and yanks it open, the joints of the hinges scraping against each other and creating a high-pitched metallic scream. Beyond, she is met with a cold stone hallway, quiet and still.

Cautiously, spear point first, she steps into the hallway and looks around. To her right is inky darkness. To her left, she can just barely make out Lukri's figure laying on the floor, the weak crystal cloud of his breath rising from his head indicating life. Kimberly's body fills the center of the hallway next to him, part of her right arm and her head turned to dark mist.

Amber hurries over to Lukri, golden sparkles shimmering from her fingers in preparation. With it being so dark, she can't see if he has any injuries. Though if he has been using his magic, which she figures he has, he'll need that energy injection.

She crouches down and touches the young Serperas' cold arm. His skin under her fingers glow with warm golden light as her magic flows into him, a fresh spring running into a dry pond. As she crouches there, waiting for Lukri to recover, her gaze strays to her friend's Shadow next to her. Kimberly's arm is slowly starting to reform, the mist banding together once more in long wispy ribbons. How much longer do they have until Kimberly fully heals herself? What about Jake, assuming that Lukri has injured him in the same way?

A small groan emanates from Lukri's throat, and his body begins to slowly shift. Amber drops her spear so that she can help the Serperas to sit up, careful not to break her connection.

His eyes flutter open, his tired gaze inspecting Amber's hand and tracking her arm up to her face.

"A-Amber?" he whispers.

"Feeling better?" she asks. The prince nods back at her, rolling his head and blinking furiously to try and wake himself up.

"What... about Shadow?" he asks, pointing to Kimberly's figure.

"I don't know," Amber replies. "What happened to Jake?" Lukri furrows his brow, confused. "The other Shadow," she corrects.

"Knocked out."

Amber's stomach sinks. She could hardly stand up to a single Twisted Shadow, and Lukri can't kill them, if they can even be killed to begin with. They're going to come after them again the moment they heal, and stars only know how Ethan and Blaze are faring back in the throne room, wherever that may be now.

"I can try," Lukri speaks, "to kill."

"Do you think you can?" Amber asks him.

The Serperas smiles at her in the dim light of the hallway. "You are here now. We can try."

Before Amber can respond, Lukri stands, stumbling a bit before steadying himself with her help. Sword in hand, he plants his feet firmly by the side of Kimberly's chest, and he plunges his blade into the center of her chest. A burst of dark mist erupts around the blade as the fresh injury dissolves into formless air.

He takes a deep breath, closing his eyes to focus. Amber's chest flutters as she turns away from her friend's body, anticipating the coming flair, placing her hands on Lukri's shoulders. Her magic swirls inside her, rushing into Lukri as he channels as much of his power into the Twisted Shadow as he possibly can. Amber's eyelids turn from dark to an intense bright orange. Aside from the bright color, the hallway remains eerily silent, cold drafts continuing to roll over them.

Eventually, the light dies out, and Amber cautiously opens her eyes again. The entirety of Kimberly's body is now a formless cloud of darkness. It moves slowly, wrapping around their ankles with its cold embrace as it spreads to cover the ground around them.

"Did I... do it?" Lukri asks breathlessly.

"I don't know," Amber replies. Her hands slip from his shoulders and picks her spear up off the floor. "Let's do it with Jake and get back to the throne room. At least they won't be able to heal in time."

***

Ethan and Shadow dance around each other in the center of the throne room. Shadow's long blade leaves scratches in the stone floor as Ethan tries his best not to burn Blaze's vines that surround them. Overhead, his friend's vines tremble as they collide with a blanket of darkness that stems from Riona's throne, her staff glowing with bright violet energy as the two engage in a battle of willpower.

The battle is infuriatingly unproductive. Every step Ethan manages to take towards the throne, Shadow pushes him back just as far. Every time Shadow tries to strike him, Ethan simply

294

ducks out of the way and blasts it back with his fire.

What's the point in fighting? the little voice in his head asks again as he sidesteps Shadow's swinging blade. *Amber may as well be dead and Lukri only has so much energy to spend. They're not coming.*

Ethan waves an arm at Shadow, and an arc of flames burst before him. The fire comes into contact with Shadow's armor and sputters out, leaving behind a small wisp of smoke and a shallow dent that repairs almost instantly.

Ice… Ethan stomps the ground, and a wall of ice springs up before him. A mere moment later, the tip of Shadow's sword appears just a hair away from his face.

He can't help but let his gaze stray to Riona, overseeing their little brawl with a toothy grin of morbid enjoyment.

You don't have to die, you know, her voice chimes inside of him. *Just give up and beg.*

Shadow frees its sword, retracting it back through the ice while leaving behind a large hole in the wall in its wake, and Ethan draws his attention back to the battle at hand. He takes a step away from the wall as the blade strikes again, this time appearing right where his nose was if he hadn't moved.

Storm… surges through his limbs, and as Shadow begins to wiggle its sword out of the ice wall once more, Ethan seizes the opportunity and makes a dash towards the throne.

"Careful!" Blaze calls from the back. The darkness above him trembles, bending downwards towards him as he runs. The ground rumbles beneath his feet, and he hears the roar of moving soil as the vines shift into position.

Gray vines rush forward ahead of him, keeping a ceiling high enough for him to run under. But the lowering ceiling is the least of his worries.

Behind him, he hears the ice wall shatter with a loud shimmering chime, and Shadow screeches after him. And above, long black spikes begin to pierce through the vines,

295

striking the ground around him, just barely missing his hat and cape. With each new spike, a somewhat stifled grunt of pain emanates from Blaze.

The vines, at some point, stop following overhead, and the shadows take the opportunity to begin to close in on Ethan as he leaps and weaves through the dim, perilous corridor. The spikes are just barely managing to keep pace with him, raining down on all sides as he runs, the stone floor cracking as they miss their target.

His cape is suddenly snagged, yanking Ethan to a halt by his neck. His legs fly forwards, still moving, and thus he lands on the ground on his back, his hat flying off his head as the clasp of his cape presses against his neck. Of the few things he needs to continue to live, breathing is sadly one of those requirements.

He kicks his legs, attempting to push himself backwards across the floor as he shoves his thumbs under the clasp of his cape to relieve himself of its pressure, unwilling to remove it as it tries to choke him.

Shadow then appears over him, the tip of its sword pointed directly into Ethan's open mouth. Ethan stares up at its unnatural violet eyes, his frantic breaths reflecting off of its blade and back into his own face. He can't yell like this. The word wouldn't come out clear enough to trigger the enchantment on his cape.

This is the consequence of your defiance, the voice in his head mocks, a mix of Riona's voice and his own, *death by the hands of your creator.*

And yet Shadow just stands there, staring downwards wordlessly, the sword slowly starting to tremble in its grasp.

"*KILL HIM!*" Riona roars in anger, her voice filling the massive throne room. The tremble of Shadow's sword increases, the flat of its blade rattling against Ethan's teeth. Its eyes narrow into small violet slits as it struggles against itself to try and fulfill her wish. Somewhere in there, Shadow continues to fight.

I- it strains, *I-*

"*Illuminae!*" comes a sudden cry. Never in his life has he felt so relieved to hear that word as his cape flares once more. Shadow lets out a screech of pain as it staggers back, its frontside turned to mist.

Ethan sits up in an instant and looks in the direction the shout came from. Standing just outside of a small, shadow-hidden doorway, Amber and Lukri stand side by side, not a scratch on either of them to be seen. Amber lowers her free hand that was half-cupped near her mouth, the one who shouted, a smile lighting up her face.

His hope fades instantly as he sees Lukri raise his sword, sand swirling to create the head of his wand, a white glow at its tip aimed directly at Shadow. Panic stings his chest. His cape may only be able to harm Shadow temporarily, but pure Light magic can certainly kill it.

Words caught in his damaged throat, Ethan lunges at Shadow's legs, tackling it to the ground. No sooner does his other half land on its back, a beam of Light streaks over them, piercing Riona's magic.

"Not Shadow!" Ethan finally yells. "*Her!*"

Lukri's attention snaps to Riona in an instant, and Amber steps forward to place her hand on his shoulder, giving him a magic boost. Still, with Amber by his side, Lukri appears to be wilting, his shoulders hanging low as his chest puffs with each of his labored breaths. He might have one or two more bursts of energy left in him before he passes out for good.

The ground quakes beneath the castle's stone flooring, and Blaze's vines surge forward once more, reaching over Ethan and Shadow and branching towards Amber and Lukri as Riona releases a second wave of shadow tendrils. What a gross misuse of his own magic, only using a single spell she obtained thousands of years ago.

As the vines come down to shield the two beings, just for

a moment there is silence. Ethan can't help but let out a heavy sigh, slowly rising to rest next to Shadow on his knees.

His whole body aches in a way he's not experienced before, his entire frontside charred somehow. Each breath he takes is slow and laborious, the air passing through his injured throat. Cautiously, he rubs where the clasp of his cape struck him. On the floor next to him, Shadow coughs coarsely and also rubs at its neck, violet still shining through half-closed eyes.

Ethan...? it rasps, its gaze landing on the Spiritist. *You...*

Ethan pats Shadow's hand that still lays by its side. "I wasn't going to leave you here."

Your scar... Shame begins to well inside Ethan's chest.

"Don't," he replies, standing. He raises his hands to his cape's clasp and unlocks it, letting the old piece of fabric fall from his shoulders. "It wasn't your fault."

Storm... Lightning sparks off his robe. Black spikes begin to poke through the vines around them, and somewhere behind him Blaze cries out in pain as the damage to the vines recoils back onto him. Slowly, the vines begin to curl upwards as they begin to die.

With a burst of new energy, Ethan dashes under the vines, his focus on the throne only a few feet away from him. Out of the corner of his eye, he can see Amber waving her spear around awkwardly, her other hand fixed to one of Lukri's shoulders. Any sort of darkness that gets too close to the two, she swipes at it, keeping it at bay the best she can manage. What remains of Blaze's vines circle the two as well, protecting them from as many black spikes as they can hold back. Lukri stands as strong as he can amidst the chaos, channeling another burst of Light into his wand to fire at Riona.

Ethan might not be able to take Riona down himself, but at least he can try and draw her attention away from Lukri.

Once more, the spikes rain down around Ethan as he runs, though this time they have little to latch onto to keep him back as he dances between them.

For a brief moment, his gaze locks with Riona's, and her sneer twists into a hateful, rage-filled scowl. Whatever few good times he remembers sharing with her, her face says it all: she never truly cared about him or Shadow.

She points her staff at him and screeches at the top of her lungs, "*STOP!*"

No sooner is the word spoken, the deep chill of paralysis begins to sink into his body.

Ice… In a desperate move, Ethan leaps, a pillar of ice appearing beneath his foot, giving him as much height as he can manage. As he rises into the air, all feeling in his legs disappears.

Fire… He brings his arms up as fast as he can just as his fingers go numb, freezing over with the command, and yet the fire swirls around them regardless, the unbridled power of the spirit already coursing through his empty shell.

He wills a burst of fire to leave his palms, aimed directly at Riona as his ascent finally slows, his body no longer responding to his commands for it to move. The fire streaks through the air, hurtling towards the crazed wizard. She raises a hand, and a wall of darkness cloaks her figure. Predictably, the flames lick at her barrier hopelessly.

And yet…

A second beam of Light fires, piercing through Riona's barrier. A single, shrill note of surprise escapes the darkness, echoing throughout the castle before falling silent. The moment the shriek dies once and for all, Ethan feels the rush of air against his skin as he falls, Riona's command losing all hold on his being.

Ice… A pillar rises to greet him, breaking his fall.

All around him, the darkness Riona summoned to protect her begins to fade away, turning to mist and dissipating in an invisible wind. He sees Amber supporting a weak Lukri, keeping

299

him from collapsing to the ground as he grips his wand with the last of his strength. Turning around, Blaze is curled up on the ground, his arms wrapped around his chest as he rocks back and forth, a soft green light escaping his fingers as he nurses his own wounds.

The throne finally reveals itself. All there's left of Riona is a collection of violet sparkles, an air of anger left in her wake as her spirit lingers. Her staff lays at its foot, masterless, its gemstone pulsing softly with magic. *Ethan's* magic.

He jumps down from his ice pillar and steps up to the throne as the last of the violet sparkles that once made up Riona's figure blow away with her darkness.

She's gone. He never thought he would see the cycle. So why does he feel so... *hollow*?

To his left, he sees Shadow appear at his side, also staring at the empty throne with a tired gaze, the violet finally gone from its eyes. They pulse a bright red, as they should, its form nearly healed once more.

I'm sorry, it says.

Ethan wraps an arm around Shadow's shoulders, pulling it close. "So am I."

Shadow twists and gives Ethan a hug, a wave of emotion washing over him. Hope, happiness, shame, anger, relief. They all clash together, swirling, trying to make sense of themselves in a storm that threatens to crush his empty figure. The only thing he can do is hug it back.

I missed you, Shadow whispers, its voice choked, clutching Ethan as hard as it can.

"I missed you more," Ethan replies, his forced chuckle coming out as a strained whimper instead. He doesn't mind. He has Shadow back, and that's all he cares about right now.

Finally, the two release, and Ethan finds himself staring at his double, a mirror of himself in blacks and grays, cape and hat aside. Shadow smiles, its mouth a bright white gap between its lips.

We're free now... right? it asks.

Ethan nods. "We are."

He bends down and picks up Riona's staff. The shaft is cold in his hands, and he can feel the heavy pressure of ethereal power radiating from it. He holds it out to Shadow.

"It's yours, after all."

Wordlessly, Shadow accepts the staff and weighs it in its hands, mesmerized by the chains that wrap around it, both of them now fractured to pieces.

Can we be rid of it? it inquires.

Ethan shakes his head. "Riona was the only one who could remove it forever."

Shadow just sighs tiredly, shifting its weight. He understands its disappointment. He doesn't want to be stuck with his phantom shackles, either, but sadly that's not how the spell worked.

I will... have our magic returned, it hums at last. *I don't know how long it'll take...*

Ethan nods, turning away from Shadow. "We'll leave when you're done."

He makes his way down from the dais and approaches Amber and Lukri, who now sits on the ground with his eyes closed.

"How is he doing?" he asks as he nears.

Amber looks up from Lukri and, without warning, leaps forward and wraps her arms around his neck. With a smile, he reciprocates her kind gesture.

"Thank you," he adds as they separate. "I didn't mean to get you this involved, and yet... here we are."

"I know," Amber replies with a small nod. She gestures to Lukri and continues, "He's spent. The magic injections finally took their toll on him."

"I see..." Ethan approaches the young prince and kneels

before him, causing the Serperas to lift his head. Ethan gives him a thankful grin. "You did well, Lukri."

Lukri smiles back at him. "Happy… Happy to help."

"Do you think you can stand?"

Lukri shakes his head. "No…" As his one-note moan fades, his stomach growls quite loudly, a small clap of thunder. The prince lifts his free hand to his stomach.

"I'm hungry, too," Amber comments with a light laugh.

"Well," Ethan hums, peering over his shoulder. Shadow stands at the throne with Riona's staff still, its eyes closed, focused, "when Shadow is done, we'll go to Asandra."

"Asandra?" Lukri echoes.

"I agree," Amber says, patting the prince's shoulder. "A senior Healer should make sure you didn't harm yourself with all your magic use." Lukri lets out a tired moan which rumbles in his throat, but he doesn't retort beyond that. Ethan won't be surprised if he's secretly looking forward to seeing another island of Astria that isn't Mirage.

Suddenly, a deep rumble shakes the castle, causing the stones to grate and dust to fall. Ethan whirls around as Amber and Lukri raise their heads.

In the great emptiness of the throne room's center, a large ball of dense shadow gathers, growing by the moment. It absorbs what little light there is still, as the cycle outside the castle fades fast into the darkness of night, appearing as a flat disk when it is, in actuality, a sphere.

Eventually, the rumbling ceases as the sphere of magic hovers in the air, its presence a great weight that presses down on his shoulders, trying to crush him with its sheer might. Amber shifts into a sort of brace position, clutching her spear close to her chest.

Shadow, staff in hand, steps up to the sphere, its expression unreadable. With its free hand, it reaches up, a single finger extended, and presses it against the condensed magic before it.

Soundlessly, as soon as Shadow touches it, the sphere trembles and shifts, slowly being drawn into Shadow's figure. It elongates and shrinks as it's absorbed, returning to its rightful owner.

At the same time, Ethan can feel it, this rush of magic filling the hollow cavity of his chest, like water filling in a bucket. It's a sharp, clear, refreshing chill as it courses through his body. The air that flows through his nose as he inhales has a different smell to it, sweet and clear. With the slightest twitch of his body, he can sense the shadows around him bend and mold to mimic his every gesture.

He exhales through his mouth, the buzz of magic brushing past his lips. The sensation of magic subsides, settling into the familiar rhythm of its pulse, filling his body with its essence.

He smiles, the smooth curve naturally forming across his face, as he watches the staff in Shadow's hand turn to dust, the last remnant of Riona disappearing forever.

Chapter 25

Ethan's dark double floats - yes, *floats* - over to Amber, Ethan, and Lukri, and holds its hand out to her. She can't help but flick her eyes from its hand to its feet, which are raised a good couple inches off the ground.

Shadow, it says with a gleaming white smile, its lips not once parting as it speaks.

"Amber," she replies cautiously, shaking its hand. Its dark gray skin is cold to the touch, and she lets go quickly as the chill begins to burn her hand. She musters an apologetic smile as Shadow stares at her with a mildly hurt expression. "You're just... so *cold*."

"Lukri," the prince pipes up from the ground, reaching up to Shadow to shake its hand as well.

I'm sorry, it says as it finishes shaking Lukri's hand. *I didn't mean to cause so much trouble.*

Amber nods. "I understand."

Are you from Asandra?

"I... am, yes."

Curiosity sparkles in Shadow's crimson gaze, and it leans in closer to her. *What's it like? Has it changed much?*

"Ah..." her gaze strays to Ethan, who stands off to the

side as he tries to cover his own wide smile with one of his fists. "I... don't know what to say."

"She's not as old as us," Ethan finally speaks up, a light chuckle in his voice. "The culture has changed, but the buildings haven't."

With that, Shadow backs away from Amber once more, its curiosity dulling ever so slightly. *I see...*

Amber looks down at Shadow's lack of contact with the ground once more. Wizards aren't supposed to be able to fly, so seeing a floating being is... odd, to say the very least. Does this mean Ethan can float, too?

"If you're finished, then we can get going to Ica now," Ethan adds, placing a hand on Shadow's shoulder. "The sooner we leave, the sooner we can get to Asandra's many cafes."

That seems to perk Shadow up, and it rises in the air with its white grin widening with eagerness.

"You can carry the prince," Ethan gestures to Lukri. Then the Husk turns to Amber. "Mind going with me?"

Amber can only grin back at him awkwardly. "Not really?"

Shadow scoops Lukri up off the ground and hovers above the two wizards below. Lukri peers down at the ground with wide eyes, both filled with awe and fear. Ethan, on the other hand, begins to stride over to where his hat and cap lay in the middle of the throne room. Amber, not having anything better to do, trots after him.

"You can fly?" Amber asks.

"Well, *I* wouldn't call it flying," Ethan chuckles. "I can't reach the stars, sadly."

"Could you always fly?"

Ethan picks up his cape and fiddles with the clasp. "I could, but then Riona took that away. She took a lot from us but never really did anything with them herself." He plucks his hat from the ground and adjusts it on his head. "Maybe she couldn't even use them. Or maybe she didn't even care to try."

The four make their way to the throne room's entrance, Shadow and Lukri floating overhead as Amber walks behind Ethan and his cape. A large hole now pierces the middle of the stitched rune of Light as the thin-threaded diamond shimmers back at her.

As they pass through the small entranceway, Amber can't help but look back at the empty throne room that they're leaving behind. Some being seems to be missing…

"Where'd Blaze go?" she asks.

"Released," Ethan replies, "back to his body."

"Oh…"

"You sound disappointed."

Amber presses her lips together. She *is* disappointed… somewhat. He had been so nice, and a part of her wanted to thank him for that before he left. Though that's too late now.

"I was just wondering," she replies quietly.

Finally, they step out of the castle to a much different Korodon than when they first arrived. The clouds in the sky are gone, revealing the stars with all their majesty glittering high above them, nightfall setting in quickly.

And where the land was dead and barren, the planes and tree-lined paths are full of greenery and life. Empty dirt fields are surrounded with grass and wildflowers. The trees are now dressed with vibrant leaves that sway in some magical breeze they can't feel. A couple are decorated with small pink spots which Amber can only assume are blooming fruit flowers. It's green as far as she can see, all signs of Riona's dark influence completely gone.

Off to the left rises a bright golden wall that glitters with the same beauty as the stars in the sky. It's so large that it fills her entire vision, her mind trying to process all of the glittering beauty that seems to stretch on endlessly in every direction. Behind the silver-gold shimmering is a plane of bright blue that bobs up and down playfully, like waves.

"Wow…" Lukri gasps in awe.

"It's beautiful, isn't it?" Ethan asks, also taking in the sight, his black eyes seeming to steal the glow of the wall as they reflect its bright color.

"Yeah…" Amber breathes back. She never knew that Korodon used to look like *this*!

"What… is that?" Lukri asks slowly.

"That," Ethan points to the wall, "is the Border Barrier."

"I figured," Amber can't help but comment. "We learned a bit about it, but…" Her voice fades, her words quickly leaving her mind. Seeing the real thing before her is different from reading about it in a textbook.

"It appeared when the Great War ended," Ethan continues, talking to Lukri. "It created the Void and kept us safe for all these millennia. Korodon is the only island you can see it from. But Riona didn't like looking at it as much as she didn't like us stargazing, so she hid it with clouds and darkness."

"Oh…" Lukri mutters downheartedly.

With that, Ethan turns to Amber and holds his hand out to her. "Ready to go home?"

Amber's heart flutters. Going home. Back to ASM and her studies, seeing Kimberly and Jake, working until she can afford her second term. With the massive gap in her memory still, it feels like her school life thus far is the life she's only ever known.

Her stomach cuts through her thoughts with a loud rumble, and an aching soreness begins to take hold of her limbs. No matter how long it's been since she left Asandra, she'll be happy to sleep in a proper bed again and stuff herself full of sandwiches.

Slowly, she takes his hand. He grips her tight, to the point where it feels like he's going to crush her bones if he presses any harder, and effortlessly lifts the both of them into the air. Her feet kick at the air below her in surprise. Next to her, Shadow appears in the air, Lukri still in its arms.

"We won't be up here very long," Ethan reassures Amber.

She watches Korodon streak by below her as Ethan and Shadow float side by side, her hair whipping around behind her as they go.

"I've got a lot of places to take you, Shadow," Ethan says.

Will I be able to eat cake? Shadow asks hopefully.

"Yes, you'll be able to eat as much cake as you want," Ethan laughs back. "But I've got a few affairs to get in order first before we can do anything else."

Shadow lets out an airy huff. *Riona's finally gone and you still have work to do?*

"It's expressing gratitude more than work. I don't expect it to take very long. *Then* we can go and get cake."

The two begin to slow and lower themselves to the ground as they come upon the Archway of Ica. The small city is quiet and empty as they land, no Feni waiting to greet them, Shadows or otherwise.

"Where did all the Feni go?" Amber asks as she regains her footing on the ground.

"They're probably still getting used to being in their bodies again," Ethan replies, digging around in his pockets. "It's been, what, two decades for some of them? Longer for others." He pulls out a small white stone and holds it up to the Archway, which hums and glows in its presence. The rip that opens reveals a quiet Asandra School of Magic campus. "It'll take a while for Korodon to get back on its feet anyway. Crops don't grow in a cycle, you know, even with magic. After you." He gestures towards the Archway with his free hand.

Amber nods and steps through, now staring at the dorm rooms and the ring of Halls before her. It feels so strange to suddenly be back on campus after everything she's been through.

"The other three should still be in the infirmary," Ethan says, appearing next to her, Shadow standing next to him. "You should probably go tell Azna that you're okay."

Amber blinks in surprise, the statement catching her off guard. "I should?"

"Well, you *did* disappear rather suddenly."

She purses her lips. He does have a point.

Wordlessly, Ethan leads the way through campus, with Amber and Shadow drifting behind him.

This place hasn't changed much, Shadow says.

"Have you been here before?" Amber can't help but ask.

It was a long time ago, Shadow replies, its face scrunching up uncomfortably. *But I mostly saw through Ethan's eyes.*

"Shadow wasn't allowed to leave Korodon," Ethan throws over his shoulder. "It's not been back to Asandra for a couple thousand years at this point."

"Oh…" Amber mutters quietly. "I'm sorry…"

Shadow halfheartedly smiles back at her but doesn't say anything more, its attention quickly being drawn back to the buildings around it.

They leave campus and walk down the pathway towards the infirmary, nighttime quickly setting in around them. The stars sharpen, glowing down upon them with their full fury, guiding them to the doorway.

"Ethan?!" comes a cry of surprise the moment Ethan opens the door. Then Amber steps in, and she sees Clare shoot up from her seat at the reception desk, her eyes wide with surprise. "Amber!"

The Enchanter steps away from her desk and rushes up to Amber, throwing her arms around Amber's neck and hugging her tight.

"Oh, thank the stars you're okay!" Clare says, her entire body shaking. When she pulls away from Amber, her eyes are wet with tears. "When you went missing, I thought… I thought…"

Amber offers Clare a small smile. "Well, I came back in

one piece, didn't I?" Her eyes dart over to Shadow, who still holds Lukri in its arms. The prince musters a smile and a small, weak wave. "But he's suffered a lot of magic deficit. I want to make sure he's not injured himself too badly." She points to the Serperas.

Clare's head snaps to Lukri, then jumps back when she finally notices Shadow.

"Ah…" escapes her mouth as she processes Ethan's dark twin. Shadow just smiles back at Clare somewhat weakly.

"Clare?" Amber asks the receptionist. The wizard blinks once and shakes her head free of her spell, straightening her posture to regain her composure.

"Right, uh," she starts, turning to Ethan, "if you want to see Azna, he's with your friends. They woke up not that long ago and the entire infirmary got sent into a bit of an uproar. Amber, we can take… uh, those two to a room. There should be some vacant ones nearby."

Amber nods. "Thanks, Clare."

Clare only smiles back at her weakly, her eyes still scanning the rag tag group before her.

"I'll see you later," Amber says to Ethan as she passes him, Shadow floating by her side.

He tips his hat back at her. "Come stop by when you can."

"I'll try."

"This way," Clare directs, the three entering the long white halls of the infirmary. Healers are rushing around frantically as they attempt to navigate to an empty room. Eventually, Clare manages to open a door, and the two girls and one Fragment Shadow duck inside with Lukri quietly observing from Shadow's arms.

The room is quiet compared to the hallway outside, with a bed and chair already set up against the back wall.

"I'll go find a senior Healer," Clare announces, quickly ducking out into the fray of the hallway before Amber can say anything back to her.

"You can place him on the bed," Amber tells Shadow, waving to the bed. It nods, setting the Serperas down as gently as it can.

Lukri lets out a yawn the moment he's out of Shadow's arms. "It's cold…"

Amber nods. "Yes, Asandra is often chilly-"

Lukri doesn't seem to be listening to her, instead shifting on the bed to lay on his side, his legs turning into his tail with ease. He curls into a small circle around his tail and lets out a heavy huff, falling asleep in an instant.

Uh… Shadow mutters, its eyes wide. A tinge of distress begins to fill the air around it.

"It's fine," she assures it, "Lukri sleeps when he gets too cold."

Ah… Shadow sighs thankfully.

***

"Ethan Nightshade! What in *Astria* is happening?"

Ethan musters a small smile. "Hello to you, too, Blaze."

Blaze is the only one out of bed, but Kimberly is awake as well. Jake, however, is missing from the room entirely.

"I've been stuck in here for almost eight whole cycles now!" Blaze cries. "*Eight*! And where have *you* been all that time?"

"Before you go tearing the infirmary down," Kimberly says from her bed, propping herself up against the backboard, "how about you give Ethan some space to explain?"

"*Euhg…*" Blaze sighs, placing one hand on his forehead and the other on his hip. Clearly he's not very pleased and has lots of questions. He just doesn't want to be patient about getting the answers he quite certainly deserves.

Ethan laughs back at him. "I'll tell you everything I know in

311

a moment, Blaze. But first… where's Jake?"

"He started coughing up blood as soon as he woke up, so they moved him to another room," Kimberly explains, gripping her bed sheets nervously. Her brow furrows, fear filling her tired eyes. "Azna said he's just got some magic sickness and needs some time to collect himself, but…" She trails off, her mind wandering.

Ethan nods slowly. Jake having magic sickness that violently is worrying indeed. "His magic will return. As for his health after that, I can't really say. He's quite resilient, though. He'll tough it out."

A small smile of comfort briefly flickers across Kimberly's lips, and she relaxes her hold on her sheets.

"Okay, Eth, now tell us what happened to *us*," Blaze steps in forcefully, folding his arms.

Ethan scowls back at his friend in confusion. "You don't remember?"

Blaze lets out a snort and deadpans, "Should I?"

"Well… yes?"

There's a slight buzz in the back of his head as he feels Shadow's attention turn to him. Its presence is usually not so… *uncomfortable*.

{*Riona didn't do anything with his Shadow as far as I'm aware,*} Shadow says, its voice ringing in his head. {*He ran before she could.*}

"What about you, Kim?" Ethan asks.

Kimberly looks Ethan in the eye quietly, her expression unreadable. Her eyes say it all; she remembers things she doesn't want to know about. The castle, the Twisting, and stars only know what else.

"There was a fight," she says, her gaze drifting to Blaze. "You were there."

"I was?" he asks, puzzled.

"Your Shadow was," Ethan replies. "Your body was here

312

in the infirmary."

"All 'hollowed out', right?"

"Excuse me?"

"Did you think I was *asleep* the entire time?" Blaze scoffs. "You and Azna and that girl were all talking in here at some point about us being 'hollowed out'. Am I right or wrong?"

Ethan glowers back at Blaze, releasing a cold blast of magic. "*That girl* has a name, you know."

"*So?*" Blaze retorts.

"Ethan, just answer his question," Kimberly sighs hopelessly.

"Yes, you heard correctly," Ethan answers through gritted teeth. "*Somehow.*"

Before anything else can happen, the door to the room opens once more. Ethan turns to the newcomer, half expecting it to be Azna. After all, he has yet to speak with the Feni. But he still smiles when Amber steps in, her eyes dreary. Behind her, the dark shadow she casts shifts ever so slightly, Shadow hiding in plain sight.

"Lukri is being cared for," she tells him.

Ethan lets out a thankful breath. "That's good to hear. I'll take him home when he's feeling better."

Amber then turns to Kimberly and waves. "Hi, Kim-Star."

"You look terrible, Amber," Kimberly chuckles back.

"It's just events catching up with me," the Healer replies with a sluggish shoulder shrug. "I'll be happier when I get some sleep in a proper bed." Her gaze strays over to Blaze, and she pulls a strained smile.

The other Life wizard just scowls back at her, appearing to be picking his words carefully. "I've got nothing to say to the likes of *you.*"

"I thought so," Amber hums sadly. "Where's Jake?"

"Not feeling too well," Kimberly replies flatly.

"I see…"

"He'll be fine," Ethan assures Kimberly once more.

Amber shifts her weight and looks around the room. "It looks like there's not much else for me to do here. Which is surprising, since the hall is still in chaos."

"I think they're all looking for excuses to stay late," Ethan replies with a grin.

"Well, I'm certainly not looking for any right now. I think I'm going to go and get some rest. Have a good night, you three."

Ethan pats her shoulder on her way out. "You did well, Amber."

"You should probably worry about yourself," she replies with a small chuckle. And with that, she is gone.

"I would like to go get some rest myself," Ethan says, turning to his friends. Though not specifically tired, he certainly needs a bit of time to let his mind process and for him and Shadow to spend some well-needed quality time together. "When do you think you three will be out?"

"Probably as soon as they come back," Blaze huffs, still slightly irritated.

"At first light?" Kimberly predicts. "And Jake probably next evening."

"I'll drop by at first light to check on you, then," Ethan nods. "Rest well. You'll need it."

Epilogue

Ethan specifically picked a window seat to stare out of as he waits. Through one eye he watches beings wander up and down the Straightway, first terms chatting happily as second terms trudge off to class. Through the other eye he watches Shadow zoom between patches of darkness, inspecting the beings with a great curiosity. It doesn't stay still for long, always moving after a spell to get a new angle on the view. Once again, he should be used to this, but instead he finds it disorientingly familiar. He remembers doing this all the time in the past, but now it's been so long since he's been able to that he's forgotten what it felt like.

A flash of pink grabs Ethan's attention, making him sit up in his seat and bringing all his attention to the small cafe, Shadow's view fading away.

Amber is smiling, dragging along a wide-eyed Lukri behind her. Ethan raises a hand in the window, drawing the first term's attention. She waves back, acknowledging his presence, then turns to Lukri to direct him to the cafe.

[*They're here,*] he says to Shadow. No sooner does he finish his thought, Shadow melts out of the darkness with a wide grin of its own as it takes one of the three empty seats at Ethan's table.

"Had fun?" he asks.

Shadow nods back. *So much has changed.*

"It sure has," Ethan agrees quietly.

"Here's a chair for you," he hears Amber speak as she and Lukri approach. Amber pulls out one of the other two chairs just enough to where Lukri can sit down, then helps him do so. Even though the young prince appears to be fine on the surface, his tired gaze tells a different story.

"How's he doing?" Ethan asks as Amber takes her own seat.

"He's alright, but he's been told to take it easy," Amber replies with a sad sigh. "Azna said that his magic needs a bit of time to settle in again on its own. He's allowed to roam, so long as he sits down occasionally and travels with a Healer."

"Wizards make miracles," Lukri chuckles weakly.

Amber nods to him. "That's our job."

"Well," Ethan speaks up, "I thought I'd take the time to celebrate while we still can. And with Shadow begging to have some cake, I thought this was the perfect place."

"Cake?" Lukri asks, adding yet another word to his growing vocabulary.

Shadow can't help but gasp with childish delight, eager to have found another being as out-of-their-depth as it. *You've not had cake, either?*

Lukri shakes his head. "I don't think so."

Ethan reaches for a menu from the stack that lay in the center of the table and slides one to Lukri. "Why don't you take a look at what they have to offer?" Amber quietly takes a menu of her own, with Shadow making no move to take the fourth.

Ethan doesn't really need to look at the menu, as he already knows what he wants. He's doing it for Shadow.

"Lazy," he mutters behind the menu, shooting Shadow a small glare. Shadow just smiles back at him playfully.

316

Many cafes offer cake as a small treat, but this one in particular serves the best in Ethan's opinion. After eating up and down the Straightway for just over a thousand years, he feels like he knows what he's talking about, though his opinion only stems from one cake in particular: rose cake. If they serve bad rose cake, then it's a bad place to have cake.

"...and that one is just a simple vanilla cake," Amber says, helping Lukri navigate the somewhat lengthy menu.

"We have vanilla!" Lukri announces proudly, finally finding something he recognizes. Amber can't help but let out a light laugh in reply.

A wizard dressed in purple and white approaches the table, smiling down at the customers while cautiously eyeing Shadow. "Are you four ready to order?"

"I'll take a slice of rose cake," Ethan starts, looking to Shadow.

Whatever he's having, Shadow says with a playful smile. The wizard nods once, his smile straining as he writes on a small pad of paper. Shadow's presence must unnerve the waiter, especially with Ethan sitting right next to it.

"I'd like an orabo-lime slice, please," Amber says, her gaze darting from the waiter to Lukri. Lukri stares back at her, appearing mildly confused. "Tell him what you want."

"Oh..." he mutters, his head bowing to hide in his menu. "Vanilla."

"Cake," Amber adds quickly for clarification.

The waiter just chuckles to himself as he finishes scribbling down the group's requests. "Your order will be ready shortly." He holds out a hand, waiting for the menus to be returned. Ethan passes his over, along with the unused one in the middle of the table. Amber hands hers over after, then slowly plucks Lukri's from his hands. Cafe property in hand, the waiter turns and strides over to the front counter, where all the cakes sit in a little iceglass display.

"What are you going to do now, Eth?" Amber asks.

Ethan folds his arms and leans back in his chair. There's a lot he needs to do, it's just a matter of which order he does it. "Well, I know what I'm *not* going to do."

"What?"

"Go back to ASM."

Amber presses her lips together, her brow furrowing into concern. "Why?"

Ethan half-smiles back at the first term. "I only needed the School for housing this time. The curriculum has hardly changed over the centuries, so I've known everything for a long time. Frankly, the School has been... *boring*, if anything.

"Even so, I won't have any time to focus on schoolwork now anyway. I need to speak with Tacha, Kaza, Belle, Azna, and maybe even the Council. Riona left behind a mess bigger than you may think and... I need to help clean it up."

Amber nods slowly. "Don't put too much pressure on yourself, Eth."

"I'll still visit," Ethan assures her.

"That's..." the Healer pauses, considering her words, then caps her decision off with a small sigh, "...okay. That's okay."

"It's just going to be a lot of talking, Amber. I don't think it'll be too much physical work." Ethan looks down at the table, pressing his thumbs together anxiously. He hopes he'll be able to do some physical work. From the lessons he's learned, one of them is that words only go so far, and he's never been one for the political game.

Just then, the waiter returns with their cakes, the four plates all crammed together on one black tray, fighting for space. One by one, he places the cake slices on the table before each being, smiling all the while.

"Thank you," Amber says to them with a warm smile.

"Enjoy your food," the waiter only replies, quickly rushing away to care for another table.

318

Her orabo-lime cake consists of a light green-colored sponge and a bright orange layer of frosting. Lukri's vanilla cake is a bright white, complete with a small chocolate topper of a white diamond and black circle, the symbols of Light and Shadow in their most basic forms. It's the little details that make Ethan feel warm inside.

And speaking of detail, there's a reason why he loves rose cake so much. It's a cake made of shades of red and sculpted in the shape of a flower petal. Not only does it taste good, but it looks *amazing* when made right. This is why rose cake is his trusty benchmark.

Wow... Shadow breathes, inspecting its own piece of rose cake with wide eyes. *It's... beautiful.*

"It's all about presentation," Ethan replies with a smirk. He picks up his fork and takes the first bite.

The flavor is a melt-in-your-mouth chocolate taste, mixing with the light top cream of dyed vanilla. It's both rich and subtle at the same time, and lingers in one's mouth for an age afterwards.

Amber also gets to eating her own treat as Lukri cautiously plays with his plate, as if expecting the cake to spring up and attack. And Shadow...

"You're... done?" he asks in surprise, noticing Shadow's plate is now suddenly empty and impeccably spotless.

I see why you enjoy it so much, Shadow grins back, patting its stomach. *Very delicious.*

"I thought you'd savor it a little more than *that*," Ethan replies with a huff. Shadow just rolls its eyes back at him.

"Are you going to eat that?" Amber asks, waving her fork towards Lukri's cake. The prince perks up for a moment, quiet as he looks at her with wide eyes, then *slowly* slides his plate closer to himself.

"Mine," he states. He finally digs his fork into the tip of the cake and shoves the tiny bite into his mouth as if to prove a point. His face goes from firm, to confused, and finally to delight as the flavor slowly takes hold of him.

Ethan leans back in his chair, looking at the table, and he can't help but feel at ease. For once, he's able to relax and indulge in something he likes with friends he enjoys being around. He has Shadow back, he finally has his freedom and magic back, and he's found beings he can fully open up to. It feels... *magical*.

Shadow can't help but let out a small snicker next to him, which he ignores through frowning and shooting it a sideways glare.

Yes, life has only gotten better.